"VIVID"
People

"SUSPENSEFUL"
Washington Post Book World

"TANTALIZING"
San Francisco Chronicle

"SMART"
Nelson DeMille

"CREEPY"
Arizona Republic

JONATHAN
SANTLOFER

THE
DEATH
ARTIST

HarperTorch
An Imprint of HarperCollins Publishers

This is a work of fiction. Names, characters, places, and incidents are products of the author's imagination or are used fictitiously and are not to be construed as real. Any resemblance to actual events, locales, organizations, or persons, living or dead, is entirely coincidental.

HARPERTORCH
An Imprint of HarperCollins*Publishers*
10 East 53rd Street
New York, New York 10022-5299

Copyright © 2002 by Jonathan Santlofer
ISBN: 0-06-000442-8

First HarperTorch paperback printing: September 2003
First William Morrow hardcover printing: September 2002

HarperCollins®, HarperTorch™, and ◆ ™ are trademarks of HarperCollins Publishers Inc.

Printed in the United States of America

Visit HarperTorch on the World Wide Web at www.harpercollins.com

10 9 8 7 6 5 4 3 2 1

FOR JOY

THE
DEATH
ARTIST

PROLOGUE

Even before it all went bad she had the feeling it was going to be a rotten day. She blamed it on the headache, the one she'd woken up with. But even later, as the headache eased, the feeling, almost a sense of foreboding, remained. Still, she'd made it through the day. Maybe, she thought, the night would be better.

She was wrong.

"How about something to drink, maybe some coffee?" He smiles.

"I should be getting home."

He looks at his watch. "It's only eight-thirty. Come on. I'll buy you a cup of the best cappuccino in town."

Maybe she says yes because the headache is finally gone, or because the day has turned out much better than she expected, or because she doesn't feel like being alone, not right now.

"Let's walk a bit."

The night air is cool, a little damp. She shivers in her thin cotton jacket.

"Cold?" He puts his arm around her shoulders. She's not sure she wants him to, turns the thought over in her mind, sighs audibly.

"What?"

She smiles weakly. "Nothing you'd understand."

Her comment annoys him. *Why wouldn't I understand?* He drops his arm from her shoulders—she wonders, why?— and they continue along another block, lined with restaurants and midsize brownstones, in silence, until she says, "Maybe it's simpler if I just catch a cab home."

He takes her arm, gently stops her. "Come on. It's just coffee."

"I think I should go."

"Okay. But I'll see you home."

"Don't be ridiculous. I can get home by myself."

"No. I insist. We'll take a cab, grab a cappuccino in your neighborhood. How's that?"

She sighs, doesn't have the energy to argue.

In the cab, neither speaks; he looks out the window, she stares at her hands.

The Starbucks on her corner is locked; the kid inside, mopping up, waves them off through the glass.

"Damn. I really wanted some coffee." He looks at her, sad, like a little boy, then offers up his best smile.

"Oh, okay. You win." She smiles, too. "I'll make us some."

At the front door to her building she fumbles with her keys, gets one in the lock, but the door eases open before she even turns the key.

"Everything's falling apart around here. They're doing construction, keep breaking everything. I'd complain to the super, but he's worthless."

On the second floor they have to step around stacks of wood and electrical supplies.

"I think they're making two apartments into one. Hoping for a big rent, I guess. It's been going on for weeks, driving me crazy with the noise."

On the third floor, she unlocks a dead bolt, then a police lock.

He walks past her into the apartment, immediately removes his coat, drops it on a chair, is making himself way too comfortable, she thinks. He sits down on her sofa—a layer of thick foam covered with a bold cotton print with pillows she'd bought on Fourteenth Street, one with a stenciled portrait of Elvis, the other of Marilyn. He runs his finger over Marilyn's garish red mouth, back and forth, back and forth.

She realizes she still has her coat on, removes it, hangs it on a hook behind the front door, turns the dead bolt, then slides the police lock into place. "Habit. You know." She smiles, nervously, turns into the kitchenette, a rectangular alcove attached to the living room, no bigger than a closet. She pulls a chain, and a lightbulb illuminates the half-sized refrigerator, two-burner stove, tiny sink, a shelf with a toaster oven and a drip coffee machine. She removes the top half of the coffeemaker, takes out a soggy brown filter, tosses it into a small plastic trash can.

"Can I help?"

"It's way too small in here. I'm okay."

She can feel him watching her in the tiny kitchen as she gets the coffee going; becomes self-conscious about the way she moves, the swaying of her hair. Maybe this wasn't such a good idea after all.

When she comes back into the living room, she chooses the hard-backed chair at her computer table across from the couch. "Coffee'll be ready in a minute." He looks up at her, smiles, says nothing. She plays with a loose thread at the cuff of her blouse, tries to think of a way to fill the silence. "How about some music?" She stands up, takes the few necessary steps to the CD player in the corner on the floor. "My one luxury."

He crosses the room, kneels beside her, plucks a disc from the neat stack. "Play this."

"Billie Holiday," she says, taking the CD from his hand. "She kills me."

Kills me kills me kills me kills me kills me kills me . . . The words echo in his brain.

A clarinet pipes out through two small speakers, followed by Billie's inimitable, soulful whine. The first lines of "God Bless the Child" fill the room with an unspeakable sadness.

He watches her kneeling beside him, humming along, head tilted, hair spilling over the side of her face. He's been watching her all night, thinking about this, planning. But now he's not sure. Start it all again? It's been so long. He's been so good. But when he reaches out and touches her hair, he knows it is already too late.

She jerks her head back, immediately stands up.

"Sorry. I didn't mean to startle you," he says, careful to keep his voice calm as he watches her, enjoying the way she moves, like a cat, jumpy, skittish. But when he sees her standing above him, looking down at him as though he were some kind of inferior being, there is no longer anything remotely kittenish about her. A flash of anger spreads through his body, and he's ready.

"I'll get the coffee." She turns away, but he grabs hold of her arm. "Hey," she says. "Cut it out."

He lets go, puts his hands up in a sign of truce, tries the smile on her again.

She folds her arms across her chest. "I think you should go."

But he settles back onto her couch, locks his hands behind his head, a grin on his lips. "Let's not make this into a big deal, okay?"

"Some things are. But I don't want to discuss it right now and . . . I doubt you'd understand."

"No? Why is that? Ohhh . . . wait, I think I'm getting it."

"Just go." She holds her defiant pose.

"I know," he says. "I'm the bad guy, right, and you're the innocent, put-upon woman. Oh, sure. Real innocent." He stands. "Well, let me tell *you* something . . ."

"Hey. Relax," she says, trying to regain control of the situation. "It's cool."

"Cool?" He repeats the word as if it had no meaning for him.

Do it!

"Just a minute!" he shouts.

"What?" she asks, but can see he is not really speaking to her, his eyelids fluttering as though he were going into some kind of trance.

He takes a step forward, hands clenched.

She drops her stance, makes a dash for the door. She's scrambling with the police lock when he lunges. She tries to scream, but he's got his hand pressed—hard—across her mouth.

Then he is all over her, pulling at her arms, shouting, mumbling, his voice harsh, unrecognizable. He stretches her arms above her head. She is surprised at his strength, but manages to wrench a hand free, smacks him in the mouth. A thin line of blood trickles over his lip. He doesn't seem to notice, knocks her to the floor, pins both her arms under his knees, all his weight holding them down, freeing up his arms to tear at her blouse, to grope at her breasts. She tries to kick but can't connect, her legs just thrash in the air.

Then he grabs her chin, leans down, presses his mouth against hers. She tastes his blood. She wrenches her head back, spits in his face, hears herself scream: *"I'll kill you!"*

He hits her hard in the face, then moves off her, stands beside the couch looking down. "How shall we do this?" he asks. "Nice or . . . not so nice?"

She is seeing double, unable to right herself, feeling close to being sick.

Then he is on top of her again, rubbing himself against her, cursing. She bites into the Marilyn pillow, concentrates on Billie Holiday.

But now his movements have become frantic, his cursing louder, and she is aware of the fact that there has been no penetration, and feels a sense of relief.

He rolls off her, says, "You just didn't get me hot," and pulls his pants up. It was a mistake.

Of course it's a mistake. Stick to the plan.

She pushes her skirt down.

"The new woman . . . so tough," he says, fumbling for words, anything to soothe his damaged ego. "So tough she can't satisfy a man."

She tries to think straight, just wants him out. "Yes," she says. "You're right, I—I'm sorry. It wasn't you, I—"

He grabs her face, turns her toward him. *"What?* What did you say?" She tries to push his hand off, but can't. "You patronizing me? *Me!* You fucking little slut!" He lets go of her face and then the slap comes so fast that for a moment she is stunned, then she screams.

"Get out! Get the fuck outta here!" She lunges for the phone. But he's too fast for her. He wrenches it off the end table. The cord jumps in the air as it's torn from the socket. Then he's got her by the hair and around the waist, practically dragging her into the kitchen; the scorching glass of the coffeemaker is scalding her naked back. He slams her against the wall. The coffeemaker falls; boiling coffee splashes against her ankles. She tries to scratch his face, misses, and he punches her hard.

An image of herself as a young girl in a white confirmation dress floods her mind; and then the white turns gray, and then everything is black.

He hardly remembers his hand finding the knife in the shallow sink, but the girl is quiet now. She's on the floor, one leg twisted under her, one straight out in front, and there is blood everywhere—splattered on the stove, cabinets, floor. He can't even remember the color of her blouse, it's all stained a deep, gorgeous red. Pinkish saliva bubbles from the corners of her mouth. Her eyes are wide open, staring at him in surprise. He returns her vacant stare.

How long has it been? Has anyone heard them? He listens for sirens, televisions, radios, signs of life from other apartments, but hears nothing. He feels lucky. *Yes, I've always been lucky.*

He rasps, "What a mess," his throat gone dry. He finds a pair of Playtex gloves beside the sink, squeezes his bloodied hands into them, washes the knife thoroughly and drops it into a drawer; then removes his shoes so he won't track bloody footprints, and places them on the shelf beside the toaster oven. He tears a few paper towels off a roll, balls them up, squirts them with liquid detergent, and works his way around the apartment cleaning off everything he can remember touching. He even takes the Billie Holiday disc off the player, puts it back in its sleeve, slips it into the middle of a stack of CDs.

He checks the couch for anything he might have dropped, anything torn off, buttons, even hairs. He sees a few hairs that he thinks are the girl's, but just to be safe he takes the Dustbuster from the wall in the kitchenette and goes over the couch several times, then towels it off, replaces it.

Unconsciously, he touches his lip, feels the soreness, remembers the kiss.

Back in the kitchenette, he takes a sponge from the sink, squirts it with more detergent, washes blood off the dead girl's lips, then shoves the sponge in and out of her mouth.

He lifts her lifeless hand. *Nail polish?* No, blood. *Mine or hers?* But here the sponge refuses to do the job, traces of red cling stubbornly beneath her nails. He jams the sponge into his pant pocket, right on top of the damp wad of paper toweling—the moisture oozes through the fabric and onto his thigh. Then he removes a small leather-bound manicure set from his inner pocket—one he always carries with him—and sets to work with his fine metal tools. Ten minutes later the girl's nails are not only spotless, but finely shaped. He takes a moment to admire his handiwork. Then, using his cuticle scissors, he carefully snips a lock of the girl's hair and presses it into his shirt pocket, just above his heart.

He moves in closer, touches her cheek. His gloved finger comes away bright scarlet. *That's it!*

Now, starting at the temple, his cherry fingertip creeps down her cheek, slowly, precisely, stopping once for a quick dip into the pool of blood on the girl's chest, then continuing just beside her ear, looping a bit before coming to rest at the sharp edge of the dead girl's jaw.

Perfect.

Now he needs something useful.

In the tiny bedroom, he takes a moment to consider a painting above the bed. Too big. Perhaps the large black crucifix on a heavy silver chain? He slides it from one gloved hand to another like a child's Slinky toy, before dropping it back into the dresser drawer.

But it's the small plastic photo album, which, after a glimpse at its contents, he decides is just the thing.

Back at the door he undoes the police lock and dead bolt, puts on his shoes, then his long raincoat.

In the hall, just outside the apartment, he hesitates. On the first floor, the drone of television dialogue, "Laura, honey, I'm home . . ." and canned laughter. He moves stealthily down the hall and out the front door. It closes behind him with a dull thud.

On the street, with gloved hands thrust deep in his pockets, he concentrates on walking at a casual pace, keeping his head down. Six or seven blocks from the dead girl's apartment he manages to work one of the gloves off his hand while it's still in his pocket; once it's free, he hails a cab.

He tells the driver where he's going, surprised at the calm of his voice.

Did it really happen? Was it some kind of hallucination? He's never quite sure. Maybe it was all a dream. But then he feels the wetness against his thigh, and the plastic glove still on one hand—and they're real enough.

The muscles in his neck and jaw clench; for a moment his entire body shudders.

Is this what he wanted? He can hardly remember.

Too late now. It's done. Finished.

He catches his reflection in the taxicab's streaky window.

No, he thinks, it's just the beginning.

1

Kate McKinnon Rothstein, "Stretch" to the girls at St. Anne's, having hit six feet by age twelve, strode across the pickled-ash floor of her penthouse living room, her mules click-clacking to the beat of Lauryn Hill's hip-hop soul, which echoed through the twelve-room apartment. The music bounced off modern and contemporary paintings, African masks, the occasional medieval artifact, and details that only the best designer in New York City could deliver: antique crystal doorknobs, brass bathroom fixtures sniffed out at Paris flea markets, embroidered pillows from Moroccan street vendors, a couple of near-to-priceless Ming dynasty vases beside pricey Fulper pottery.

In her nearly all-white bedroom, Kate kicked off her shoes, was tempted to stretch out on the king-size bed—an island of marshmallow fluff with its pure-down comforter and a dozen white and off-white lacy pillows—but she had exactly thirty minutes before meeting her old friend Liz Jacobs.

Still, after so many years, the splendor of the room, of her life, could stop her, and a picture—as clear as any painting on her wall—coalesced in her mind: the cramped, narrow bedroom where she had spent her first seventeen years—single bed, thin mattress, chest of drawers covered with faux-wood contact paper, wallpaper older than she was, peeling. Kate caught her reflection in the full-length mirror on her closet door. Lucky, she thought, damn lucky.

She stripped off her stylish business suit, exchanged it for a pair of charcoal slacks and a cashmere turtleneck, pulled back her thick dark hair—which only recently had begun to sprout a few silver streaks, exchanged for gold ones, thank you very much, Louis Licari, colorist to the rich or beautiful—fastened it with a couple of tortoiseshell combs, and dabbed the back of her ears with her favorite perfume, Bal à Versailles.

A Proustian moment: her mother in a party dress, tall and regal like Kate, despite the JCPenney label, tucking her in, kissing her good night. *Don't let the bedbugs bite, pussycat.* If her mother were alive today, thought Kate, she would buy her gallons of expensive perfume, fill her closets with designer dresses, get her out of that row house in Queens. A flush of embarrassment. Who *cared* about perfume and designer dresses? If only her mother could have stayed around long enough for Kate to have given her *anything*. She sighed.

In the bathroom, she ran a nearly colorless gloss over her lips, studied herself in the mirror, the face of this woman she had become; not really so different from the one she had left behind ten years ago—just take away a few lines, add a uniform, a gun, and an attitude that scared half the men in the 103rd Precinct. But that was a long time ago, another lifetime, one she would prefer to forget.

She'd never meant to be a cop, though it was in her blood— her father, her uncle, her cousins, all cops. Kate chose college, to study art history, but after four years of sitting in dark rooms staring at slides of famous paintings, a legion of papers dissecting works of art, *deconstructing* them, as they say, memorizing dates and terms—flying buttresses, pentimento, fresco, scumbling—after all that, not one single job for the Fordham-trained, full-scholarship art history major. Six months of temp work, typing and filing anonymous letters,

and she thought, why fight it? Cop work had always in-
trigued her. And the NYPD training proved to be a lot easier
than deciphering the symbolism in a Flemish painting.

With her background, Kate never had to walk a beat, and
naturally, the art-related cases landed on her desk, but it
wasn't until she was assigned runaways and missing kids—
an area the men happily handed over to her—that she actually gave the work her heart. A mistake. A decade of kids she
could not find or could not save and her heart was ready for
a transplant. Thank God for Richard Rothstein and a second
chance—graduate school, a Ph.D., time to write that art history thesis, and then her surprise bestseller, *Artists' Lives*.

Nowadays, Kate was saving kids *before* they got lost, and
that's the way she liked it. More than one troubled kid had
spent the night at the Rothsteins', sometimes nights spreading into weeks, with plenty of hand-holding and bowls of
chicken soup, even if it was the maid, and not Kate, who
bought the Perdue parts and steamed the parsnips.

Who, least of all Kate, would have imagined that one day
this motherless girl from Astoria would host a PBS series
based on her book, or throw parties for gubernatorial candi-
dates, CEOs, and movie stars, in her San Remo apartment.
Her life, all she had, continued to surprise her, sometimes
embarrass her, too; and she worked hard at giving back to
assuage some of the guilt that came with good fortune.

Mules exchanged for pumps, a lightweight jacket thrown
over her shoulders, and that was it; she was ready.

Heads practically did the *Exorcist* swivel when Kate
marched into the bar of the Four Seasons Hotel and spotted,
across the room, her friend Liz, half hidden by this month's
issue of *Town and Country* magazine, the one that featured
Kate's very own face backed by a cool abstract painting with
the caption "Our Lady of the Arts and Humanities."

"Put that rag down. *Please*," said Kate, in her deep,
throaty voice. "If they had taken the time to say one thing
about my sad and pathetic youth, I might not have come off

sounding like some stuck-up socialite born with a silver spoon up her ass!"

"Ah, the demure cover girl." Liz looked up, blue eyes peering over the air-brushed facsimile at the real thing.

Kate leaned down, pecked her friend on both cheeks, then, with her natural grace, folded herself into a high-backed caned chair. She took in her friend's freckled cheeks, the lack of makeup, no airs about her at all, smiled warmly, then ordered a martini from the tuxedo-clad waiter, who deposited a ginger ale in front of Liz.

"Still not drinking, I see." Kate pulled out a pack of Marlboros.

"Still smoking, I see."

"Still trying to quit is more like it. I wish I had your willpower." Kate lit a cigarette, dropped the pack back into her bag, took in the long mahogany bar, the cathedral ceiling, the elegantly dressed couples talking in whispers, laughing, enjoying their good life. She exhaled a long plume of smoke, watched it break up and disappear. Sometimes her entire life seemed as illusory as that smoke—discussing *Artists' Lives* with Charlie Rose one night, holding a teen's hand at an AIDS clinic the next. "I swear, Liz, I don't know what prepared me for this life."

"Saint Anne's School for—what was it? Wayward Girls?"

"Right." Kate laughed, raised her glass. "Here's to my dearest, oldest chum." They clinked glasses. "So what's brought my workaholic pal out from behind her Quantico desk?"

"A monthlong intensive training course in sophisticated computer skills right here in New York City."

"No." Kate slammed her hands onto the mahogany table. "Do not tease me, Liz Jacobs. No way Quantico would let you off an entire month to be here, with me, in New York."

"I tease you not. But honey, the FBI did not, sorry to say, send me here to hang out with you, though, naturally, you're the icing on the cake. I'm here to master the computer so I can at least understand how to access the very stuff that is changing my business faster than my butt is sagging. It's all out there if you know how to get at it—profiles, case studies, tracking every sort of criminal." She tapped a finger to her chin. "All of your missing children—if we'd had access to some of the stuff they've got on databases nowadays, you would never have lost that last kid—you remember her name?"

Oh yes, Kate remembered.

Ruby Pringle, aka Judy Pringle. Twelve years old. Last seen alive with three pairs of Calvin Klein jeans—two denim, one black, all size 5—flung over the shoulder of her Forest Hills cheerleading jacket as she headed into the dressing room of the junior department of the Queens Plaza Jeans Store . . . Kate attempted to blink the memory away, but failed. *A naked battered angel, eyes open wide, glazed with a thin film, a kind of inner eyelid, like a half-asleep cat, floating on a cushiony sea of wavy black plastic. Ruby Pringle stares up at Kate. Arms and legs stretched out, white nail polish, chipped, skin the color of newsprint. A telephone cord wrapped so tightly around her neck that it disappears in the flesh. Size 5 jeans bunched at her ankles. The smell of Ruby Pringle's death is undistinguishable, commingled with molding pizza crusts, coffee grinds, vegetable scrapings, soured milk.*

Homicide detective Kate McKinnon knows better than to disturb a crime scene, but cannot help herself. She yanks the jeans up to Ruby Pringle's waist, stumbles from the Dumpster, squints at the hazy midday sun, attempting to burn the image of the dead girl from her retinas.

"You ever miss it?" asked Liz.

"What? Oh." Kate came back to the moment. "Are you kidding? Between the book, the TV series—which, thank God, is over—and my work for the foundation"—Kate expelled a short breath—"I don't have time to pee."

"You know, I watched every minute of your PBS show just waiting for you to forget you were on camera and start cursing. But you were such a lady." Liz grinned. "How'd you ever pull *that* off?"

Kate rolled her eyes. "You didn't see the outtakes."

"I'll bet you get fan mail."

"Oh, sure. Bundles of it. Richard's given up his law practice to stay home and sort it out."

Liz laughed. "How is that sexy husband of yours?"

"Not sexy enough," said Kate with a wry smile. "The man works too hard. There's his usual over-the-top caseload, plus the pro bono work—which, I have to admit, I encourage—his work for the foundation, and now he's even taken on a few pertinent city cases. The nights Richard makes it home before midnight, he's like a dead dog."

"One of those long-legged, pedigreed types."

"Pedigreed? *My* Richard? You know very well, Liz Jacobs, that Richard and I shared the same SPCA upbringing—pure mutts, the two of us." She smiled. "Of course, when Richard *is* sexy, well . . . never mind." She smiled again. "So what about you? How are the kids?"

"They're great. Both of them in college. Amazing, isn't it? Damn good thing their lousy father's investments paid off."

"And that the little geniuses both got scholarships. You should be proud of them."

"I am," said Liz, unable to stifle that look all proud mothers get—the shy smile meant to disguise the burst of pride. "Oh, I shouldn't say that—"

"What? That you're proud?"

"No. That Frank's a lousy father. He was only a lousy husband."

"He gave you two beautiful kids." Kate knocked back her martini, imagined that it could actually leak through the tiny crack that had just opened in her heart. *Damn.* This is not what she needed right now, sitting next to her best friend, whom she loved, absolutely loved, but whom, in an instant, she suddenly wanted to trump with all the perks of that good life she had been putting down for the past quarter hour, because in that most innocent of exchanges—*How are the kids?*—followed by Liz's look of maternal self-satisfaction,

Kate felt as though her glittering, perfectly constructed world would surely crumble. *Damn. Damn. Damn.*

Liz caught Kate's faraway look. "You okay?"

"Oh. Sure."

Liz eyed her friend closely. "Really?"

"Truly." Kate painted on a broad smile. "Hey, when did you cut your hair? I like it."

"Just. I got too old for long hair."

"Uh-oh—" Kate fluffed the dark hair shot through with reddish-gold streaks from her shoulders. "What does that make me?"

"On you it works."

"Just tell me when I start to look like *What Ever Happened to Baby Jane?*"

"I'd say you've got about a year." Liz laughed.

"Very funny." Kate narrowed her eyes at her friend, but added a playful grin. "Do you realize I just turned forty-one? *Forty-one.* It's such a shock." Kate pictured herself that very first year on the force. She could still feel the ill-fitting uniform, pants bunched at the waist, blue shirt designed for a man tight across her chest. Liz had kidded her that it was probably the first and last blouse that would ever make Kate look busty. The memory made Kate smile, then she sighed. "I always imagined I'd be twenty-eight, thirty, max."

"Hey, I'm forty-*five.* You think you're gonna get any sympathy out of me? Forget it." She shook her head. "So what's on the agenda tonight?"

Kate's face lit up. "Richard and I are meeting up with our two favorite kids. Going to a downtown performance—something cool and oh-so-avant-garde, I'm sure." Kate rolled her eyes. "Hey, why don't you join us?"

"No can do. Tonight's devoted to computer manuals. Do I know how to live, or what?" Liz mimed a broad yawn. "But thanks. And, let me guess—you're talking about Willie and Elena."

"Natch." Kate smiled.

"They've become famous since your book."

"Oh, they'd have done it without me." Kate waved a dismissive hand. "Willie's got a group of paintings in the Venice Biennale next month. A *very* big deal in the art world. Then his own show right here, in New York, at the Contemporary Museum."

"Wow."

"Definitely wow. And Elena will be touring Europe this summer," Kate continued, her voice rising with enthusiasm. "Oh, I wish you could have been at her performance the other night. It was really something."

For the moment, the Four Seasons bar was exchanged for the intimate amphitheater of the Museum of Contemporary Art, Elena onstage, a solitary spotlit figure backed by an ever-changing series of pulsating, orgiastic abstractions—the translation of her vocal gymnastics fed through a computer.

"Elena could easily have a career as a mainstream singer," said Kate. "But she's chosen this incredibly difficult, though amazing, route. I mean, she had that crowd of swells and swelled heads riveted." Kate remembered the museum's director, Amy Schwartz, a fidgety type by nature, rapt, raving over Elena's multi-octave voice. And the senior curator, Schuyler Mills, proclaiming Elena brilliant; here, clearly, was a man of taste and culture. Even that pompous old bore, the Contemporary's recent chairman of the board, Bill Pruitt, managed to stay awake—no mean feat for a man who normally snored his way through the Contemporary's poetry readings and artist talks. As for the young curator, Raphael Perez, the guy could not take his eyes off Elena. But who could blame him? The girl was beautiful.

"I'm sorry I missed it—Elena's performance, that is. You've done a great job with those kids, Kate."

Now it was Kate's turn to try on that little smile that belied a bursting pride. Yes, it was true, she had more than a little to do with the way those kids turned out. Willie and Elena. Her two prized graduates from the very first class she and Richard had adopted through Let There Be a Future, the educational foundation for underprivileged inner-city kids, nearly ten years ago. Okay, so they were not her biological children. Not even adopted children. But could she possibly love any kids more than she loved those two? She didn't see how. Perhaps they were even closer because she had *not* borne them; because there was none of that parental angst that comes with blood, that pits children and parents against one another. No, there had been none of that with Elena or Willie. Oh, sure they'd had their moments, but nothing they could not eventually laugh at, or cry through to the other side. Willie and Elena. *Her kids*. And, yes, they would do. She smiled warmly. "God, I adore those little brats."

"Oh, Kate." Liz folded her hands into a praying position. "Please, please, *please* adopt me. I'll be good—keep my room clean, brush my teeth—I *swear*."

Kate laughed, dug into her bag, came up with her pack of Marlboros; a crumpled nicotine patch was adhered to its side. "Jeez, no wonder this thing isn't working." Then she lifted a folded photograph from the table. "Where'd this come from?"

"It fell off your nicotine patch. Maybe the thing gave birth."

But Kate had stopped laughing. She held the photo beside the small lamp in the center of the table. The picture was slightly blurry, the colors somewhat faded. "It's from graduation."

"I can see that," said Liz, plucking it from Kate's hand. "Nice."

"Except that I have no idea how it got here."

"You know, it's okay for even tough Kate McKinnon to admit she carries sentimental photos around."

"I would admit it, but the only photo I ever have in my bag is on my driver's license, and I'd get rid of that one if I could."

"Well, I guess someone else put it in there to surprise you."

For a moment, Kate felt something she had not felt in

years; something Kate the homicide detective used to feel when she knew she was onto something, or when she knew, though tried to deny, that it was hopeless, that it was over— that the kid she'd been looking for was dead. But she tried to shrug it off. "I guess Richard could have done it," she said. Though she couldn't imagine why. Or her housekeeper, Lucille, possibly. But why not leave it on her desk or the kitchen counter or a dozen other places that would make more sense? Kate dropped the photo back into her handbag—and with it any more thoughts on the subject. "Hey," she said, brightening. "Why not stay with me this month? I mean it. We've got rooms we never even go into. You'd be doing me a favor."

"Quantico's already booked me into a midtown efficiency, near the library."

"Oh, stop trying to impress me."

"It's okay, really." Liz popped a couple of peanuts into her mouth. "Anyway, Kate, I don't exactly fit into your world."

"Oh, brother. After all these years must I remind you that although I may shop, lunch, and party with the upper classes, I am merely trespassing among them? At heart, kiddo, we're two of a kind."

Liz gazed intently at Kate. "My dear friend. Look at *me,* look at *you*—then look around. I'm the only woman in this room wearing a color, for Christ's sake! And this orange blouse is one hundred percent poly." She got her fingers on the edge of Kate's sleeve. "Cashmere, right? Ralph Lauren or Calvin what's-his-face? And don't lie—I've been through your closet. Me? I can't even remember the last time I ate in a restaurant where you don't pick up your food on a *tray*."

"Lizzie, if you won't stay with me, you have to promise to spend at least half your time with me, two or three dinners a week—just the two of us." Kate riffled around in her buttery leather bag. "Here. Keys to my humble flat. My extra set. All yours. Come and go as you please. Cadge food from my fridge. Wear my Calvin what's-his-faces."

"You know, I've always wanted a twenty-room penthouse overlooking Central Park as my own little pied-à-terre."

"Twelve rooms. *Please.* Not twenty."

"Twelve lousy rooms." Liz dropped the keys. "Forget it."

"Okay. I'll throw Richard in. Wear my clothes. Sleep with my sexy husband."

Liz's fingers curled around the keys. "Now you're talkin'."

2

T he computer's screen-saver, blinking dollar signs—a
humorous gift from a client—scattered iridescent green
light onto the stacks of legal briefs, affidavits, and letters
that loomed over Richard Rothstein's sleek Knoll desk like
scale models of a high-rise apartment complex. Behind the
piles of work—past, present, and future—were framed photos, advertisements for the good life: a man and woman on
the porch of an obviously high-maintenance summer home;
the same couple in formal dress, dancing, faces pressed
cheek-to-cheek; the woman, alone, a studio portrait, perfectly lit, dark hair sweeping just below a slightly too-strong
jaw on an otherwise striking, intelligent face. Beautiful? He
thought so.

Just the other day seeing Kate in action at the Museum of
Modern Art, lecturing on Minimal and Conceptual art, of all
things, he could not stop thinking: She's mine—this brilliant, gorgeous creature—all mine. I'm the lucky guy who
gets to go home with her.

He couldn't help but smile.

Richard and Kate. Kate and Richard. On top of the world.

And who'd have believed it? Richard, the Brooklyn boy,
son of Sol, apple of Edie's eye, first in his class at CCNY. Ten
years ago he'd been a successful lawyer making plenty of

money. Then came the professor of African American studies, Columbia University, accused of reverse discrimination for his vociferous lectures, particularly the ones with that nasty anti-Semitic bias. Naturally, no one wanted to touch the case. Even the ACLU had hesitated. Richard Rothstein had not. The case was national news for six months: "Jewish Lawyer Defends Black Prof's Right to Free Speech." In the end, Richard had prevailed, as had his client, reinstated to his lectern, fueling the fires of hate.

That was his most famous case. His most lucrative? Keeping the CEO and senior partners of a very well known Wall Street brokerage firm out of jail, proving, against all odds, that it was not insider trading that had made the men their personal millions, but simply "coincidence." For that bit of brilliant legal maneuvering Richard received his usual fee plus a seven-figure bonus, which he and his legal partner, the one who specialized in real estate, plunked down on an assortment of then-depressed New York City properties. Only a few years later, with the economy booming, they sold the land to a hungry real estate developer, and Richard's seven-figure investment quadrupled. Then a keen money manager took the profits and made Richard Rothstein richer than most men ever dreamed possible.

It was soon after that that Richard took on the small case that came with a different sort of bonus: the chance to interrogate a young policewoman, Detective Kate McKinnon. He'd never forget her strutting down the courtroom aisle, all legs and attitude, tossing the long hair out of her eyes as she answered his questions.

The affair did not actually start until two months after the trial—Richard had to work up his nerve. His *nerve*? Richard Rothstein? "One of Manhattan's Ten Most Eligible Bachelors," cover story, *New York* magazine, fall 1988. But Officer McKinnon was something new for the handsome attorney.

Richard had tried to woo her with a series of expensive dinners—Lutèce, the Four Seasons, La Côte Basque—but it was a free opera in Central Park, *Tosca,* and the champagne and caviar and fancy French pastries that he'd brought for their picnic dinner that finally did the trick for Kate. For Richard it was watching Kate eat just about everything—so unlike the anorexic model types he was used to dating. That, and the easy way they talked, and the fact that they couldn't keep their hands off each other. By the fifth date—a pizzeria in Queens, which Kate had chosen as an antidote to all those upscale eateries—Richard asked her to marry him and she said yes in between bites of pepperoni pizza.

And Kate had been good for him, had surprised him, too, the way she had taken to their new life, earning her Ph.D. in art history while completely reinventing herself, becoming a fixture on the New York social scene without losing her social conscience or her chutzpah—as his mom would say—along the way.

Yes, they were a good team, he and Kate. Though lately she'd begun to balk at one too many client dinners. Still, she knew how to put on a good show—even if she'd rather be out there hustling for Let There Be a Future, or figuring out ways to help artists pay the rent.

Richard tapped the sleep button on his computer; the dollar signs disappeared faster than profits on junk bonds in a bear market. He scrolled down a computer page of numbers for what seemed like the umpteenth time that day. Once again, the numbers did not make sense.

He pushed back from the desk, leaned into his plush office chair, massaged the back of his neck, but could not relax. He flipped a switch. Hidden quadraphonic speakers filled the office with his own private Billie Holiday concert.

"Good morning heartache . . ."

No, not what he had in mind. Another button. This time it was Bonnie Raitt, giving them "Something to Talk About." Better.

Still, those numbers on his computer screen that refused to make sense nagged at him. Was it too late to call Arlen? The old man usually worked later than he did. He checked his watch. Already past seven.

Dinner. Damn.

He'd completely forgotten. Even if he left now, he'd be late.

A quick call to Bowery Bar. A message—he'd meet Kate later, at the performance—though he realized, as soon as he hung up, that he did not have the theater's address.

He turned back to the computer, hit print.

Maybe he should pay Bill Pruitt a visit. But that idea struck him as even worse than sitting in a dank downtown theater watching some deranged performance artist nail his penis to a table—no way he could sit through anything like that. Again. Still, for Kate he'd do it.

Pruitt. How the hell had that guy insinuated himself into the Contemporary Museum? He'd actually had the nerve, the audacity to be condescending about Richard's art collection, which, damn it, anyone who knew anything knew was one of the best contemporary collections in New York, maybe the country. Today, at the museum's board meeting, it was all Richard could do not to leap out of his seat, reach across the table, grab the guy by his double chin, and squeeze the life out of him.

Just thinking about Pruitt made Richard's neck muscles practically go into spasms.

He yanked the page of numbers out of his printer so fast the last few columns smudged.

Willie nodded in time to De la Soul's beat while he slipped into his new black leather jacket. William Luther King Handley Jr., Willie to his contemporaries, "Li'l Will" to the few remaining old school chums (a nickname tagged on in the eighth grade when he'd reached his full height of five feet six), and recently, "WLK Hand," the signature he used on his funky mixed-media canvases, could not decide if wearing his pricey new jacket was pushing it a bit too far for some East Village art performance. *Fuck it.* He could dress any way he damn pleased. Anyway, he'd combined it with his usual black jeans, the frayed cuffs of which grazed his clunky black Doc Martens. The other high-priced item—the Yohji Yamamoto white shirt, which showed off his clear amber skin (from his mother's side of the family) and green eyes (a genetic hand-me-down from his long-lost ancestor, John Handley, the white plantation owner from Winston-Salem)—was a gift from Kate, who would be happy to see him wear it. Kate, who was worse than his own mother when it came to how he dressed, if he was eating right, sleeping enough. Kate, who'd written about him in *Artists' Lives,* made sure he was part of the PBS series, who'd gotten the first curators and collectors into his studio; and Richard, who'd actually bought the first painting, giving it, and Willie, the necessary stamp of approval. Mentors. Collectors. Surrogate parents. Kate and Richard were all that. And more.

But Willie's other genetic gifts—the full lips and perfectly straight white teeth—were distinctly his real father's, or so it would appear from the man's only known photo: a smiling, handsome African American in U.S. Army fatigues, taken somewhere in Asia, or was it Africa? Either way, the man had never returned.

The fact that Willie's parents hadn't actually married made no difference to Willie's mother, Iris. The photo, in a gilded Woolworth frame, had maintained a place of honor next to Iris's bed in the crowded South Bronx tenement shared by Willie, his brother, baby sister, and grandmother, as long as Willie could remember. Six months ago, Willie had moved the three women into a garden apartment— which he paid for—in a middle-class Queens neighborhood, and the framed photo had been resurrected in Iris's new bedroom.

Willie's success came as a surprise to Iris. Not from any lack of faith in her son, but because she didn't know that kind of thing was possible. Willie knew she was proud of his making good, selling his pictures for big money. But Willie kept the exact prices (which had recently hit six figures) to himself, because Iris might see that as prideful and not quite

Christian, though he couldn't explain it to you unless you'd grown up in his family.

Then there was Henry. Willie's big brother. His "lost" brother. That's what Iris called him: *lost*. Still, every few weeks he managed to find his way to Willie's place, needing money for a fix. But Willie didn't want to think about Henry. Not now.

"I want to be an artist."

The words fluttered in the narrow hallway of the Bronx railroad flat, forever after to be associated with the scent of his grandma's lavender powder and the Lysol Willie's mother seemed to spray or wipe on everything.

"A *what*?" his mother said.

"An artist."

"What does that mean? An *artist*?"

Willie couldn't come up with an answer, had no idea, just a feeling. But, man, what a feeling. To be drawing, making lines into something, seeing the images come together, giving them life, getting lost way inside his head. Maybe it was just a world he created on paper, but plenty far away from the lousy world of the Bronx tenement.

The memory faded, replaced with another, the argument he had had with Elena, just the other day.

"I'm sick and tired of being referred to as a black *artist. I'm an artist! Period."*

"Look, Willie. It's not a good thing to deny your blackness. Impossible. Hey, I'm a Latina. And a performance artist. And a woman. That's who I am. It defines me."

"Deny my blackness? Are you kidding? Look at my work. It's a classification, see? A category. One of the best black *artists. A goddamn qualification! Like my art is something less, like there are different rules or separate criteria for artists of color—like I can't compete with white artists in the white art world. Don't you get that?"*

He still believed he was right, but wanted to patch things up. After all, Elena was his best friend, more like a sister. He'd see her tonight, could fix the argument then.

Willie shut off the television and stood in the silence. He was gripped by a sudden unease, a nonspecific gloominess about the evening ahead. *What is it?* He rolled his shoulders inside the leather jacket, tried to toss it off. Whatever it was, he'd soon forget it. After all, dinner with his three favorite people—Kate, Richard, and Elena—no way he could be depressed or anxious around that trio.

But out on the street, as he headed toward the East Village, there it was, this time as if someone had spliced microseconds of a movie into his brain—

An arm slicing through space. A twisted, screaming mouth in close-up. Everything blood red. Then black.

Willie sagged against the street lamp, gripped the cool metal for support.

His mother, Iris, used to say he could feel things before they happened. But it had been years since he'd had one of these visions.

No. Too many days alone in the studio. That's all. He just needed to get out more.

3

Crosby Street was clogged with traffic. Horns blared; a cabbie shouted obscenities at workmen tossing bales of fabric remnants out the back end of a truck angled across the street like a train wreck.

But once Willie crossed Broadway, the scene shifted to boutiques and contemporary art galleries jostling for space, and inconceivably stylish, good-looking people taking themselves very seriously in their studied black costumes.

One of them, a youngish man, hair stripped Harlow-white, with an inch of black roots that matched the perfect two-day stubble on his thin cheeks, called out to Willie.

Oliver Pratt-Smythe, Willie's least favorite artist in New York—which was saying a lot. He and Willie had been a double bill in a London gallery a couple of years earlier. Pratt-Smythe, the more seasoned of the two, and the more savvy, had arrived two days before Willie and had covered the gallery's floor with horsehair. Planting himself in the center of the space at a large noisy sewing machine, he would spend every day running horsehair through the machine making—what? Willie never could figure it out. About the only thing Willie could plainly see was that it was virtually impossible for viewers to reach *his* work without plowing through foot-deep horsehair, clumps of which had adhered themselves to

the heavily encrusted surfaces of Willie's paintings. For
months afterward, Willie was plucking the stuff out with
tweezers.

Now he nodded without enthusiasm, taking in the careful
paint smudges on Pratt-Smythe's otherwise brand-new
black jeans. Odd: the guy was not a painter.

Without being asked, Pratt-Smythe started ticking off ac-
complishments. "Having a show in Düsseldorf," he said, a
look of world-weary ennui in his flat gray eyes. "Didn't you
get the announcement? No, well, gee, I'm sure I sent you
one, but you'll get one for my New York show, which is all
set for November—the best month—*and* I've got an installation I'm trying to get together for Venice—the Biennale,
you know."

"More horsehair?" asked Willie. "I saw a couple of nearly
bald ones the other day, thought of you."

"No," said Pratt-Smythe, without a trace of a smile. "I'm
into dust now. Been collecting it for months. I mix it with
my saliva and spread it into biomorphic patterns." He picked
at his dirty fingernails, looked bored, and asked, "And you?"

"I'll be there, too," said Willie. "In Venice. I'm bringing
an industrial-sized vacuum cleaner, setting it in the space,
leaving it on all day, seeing what it collects, displaying that
as my art. Hey, maybe it'll be your dust."

For a split second Pratt-Smythe looked alarmed, then he
allowed the tiniest grin to crack his tight lips. "Oh, I get it,
man. You're having me on. Good one, man."

"Yeah." Willie grinned back. *"Man."*

"So I guess, you're, uh, showing . . . what? *Paintings?*" Pratt-
Smythe said this as if he were discussing not only the lowest
form of art, but the lowest form of all human expression.

"Yeah," said Willie. "I'll be showing *paintings*—about
thirty of them—in my *one-man* show at the Museum of
Contemporary Art this summer."

Willie turned away, left the other artist on the corner of
Prince and Greene Streets, trolling for someone—anyone—
on whom to lay his current CV.

Willie slung his leather jacket over his shoulder as he jogged between the two-way traffic on Houston, past Great Jones Street, heading into the East Village. He turned onto East Sixth Street, where the dozen or more Indian restaurants dispersed the scent of curry and cumin into the warm evening air, then jogged a half block to Elena's three-story raggedy-ass tenement.

A note, scribbled on cardboard, was Scotch-taped to the front door:

INTACOM BROK

"Oh, great." Willie shook his head. Elena, he thought, has got to get out of here. The East Village renaissance is, like, over. He tried giving the old wooden door a shove. It groaned open.

Inside, the place smelled musty and just a bit off, as if maybe the super hadn't been dealing with the garbage—as usual. The front hall was lit with a dim yellow bulb.

At the second-floor landing the smell was stronger; at the top of the stairs it was downright pungent. At Elena's door, Willie knocked. "Elena? You in there?"

Kate locked the Club across her steering wheel. Richard would go nuts if he knew she parked the Mercedes right on the street, in the East Village, no less. But to Kate, a car was a car, and she'd only be a few minutes, pick up the kids, then hook up with Richard at Bowery Bar, put the car into a nice safe lot.

She started up the stairs at her usual determined pace, half her mind looking forward to the evening ahead, the other half still back at the Four Seasons with her pal Liz.

And then there was that smell . . .

Kate's mind was suddenly filled with a rush of images—images that had lain dormant for a decade:

A homeless man found under molding cartons.

A suicide that the young detective McKinnon discovered

hanging from an attic beam almost a full two weeks after the knotted sheet had stopped all air and blood to the brain and heart.

Prying up floor planks of that oh-so-innocent-looking young man's basement apartment to discover the two bodies in advanced states of decomposition.

Now Kate was taking the stairs two at time, stumbling over her heels, the stairwell a blur, that damn smell getting stronger, killing other senses: She heard nothing, did not feel the scrape to her hand when she tripped on the top step of the second landing, was blind to the blood surfacing on her palm, across her knuckles. But at the top of the third-story landing Willie came into sharp focus, slumped against the wall, his head forward on his chest.

Scraping her knees against dirty floorboards, Kate got a hand under his chin, lifted his head, listened—*Yes, he's breathing*—fumbled in her bag for a mentholated Chap Stick, got it under his nose.

He blinked.

"Jesus—Willie! Are you all right? What happened?"

There were tears in his startling green eyes.

Kate followed his line of vision to the open apartment door. She turned back, gazed into his eyes, and in that one terrible moment she knew.

She pulled herself up and took the necessary steps toward the open door, that smell coming at her.

The Marilyn Monroe pillow was poking out from under the couch. *Oh, God. Oh, Jesus. Please. Please. Please. Let me be wrong.* Kate covered her nose with her arm, leaned against a wall for support, and then she was turning, taking in the dark vertical streaks and splatters of blood on the opposite wall, and lifting her feet from something thick and sticky on the floor, trying to make sense of the twisted leg jutting out from the space between the sink and the refrigerator. And then there was Elena's face. Elena's beautiful face—or what was left of it.

Kate turned away fast, spinning, heart pounding, the

smell of death so thick it sucked the oxygen from her lungs. *No. No. No.* She squeezed her eyes shut. The bad scene hovered behind her. But no. She would not look, would not validate it. *Oh, God. This isn't happening. I'm saving children now, not losing them.*

She was glued against the wall, the ability to put one foot in front of the other impossible.

She was too late. Again.

Waves of impotence and despair rippled through her, explosions, like tiny firecrackers, jitterbugged all over her body—fingers, toes, arms, legs, torso. Her organs felt as though they were imploding and exploding all at once. For a moment Kate truly believed she would die. *Yes. Let me die.* Hail Marys, bits of the Lord's Prayer, fragments of Sunday-morning service in Latin that she didn't think she knew were buzzing in her head.

She swiped the tears from her cheeks, opened her eyes.

Just that one garish pillow out of place on a bare wood floor. The place was too damn neat, that was for sure. As if nothing had happened here. No blood on the living room floor or walls.

In the bedroom— How did she get there? She had no memory of moving. The patchwork quilt was folded neatly at the foot of the bed. Above it one of Willie's early works, a small assemblage where he'd taken a page of Elena's handwritten music, cut it up, rearranged the notes, glued and sealed them onto fragments of metal and wood, glazed over them so that you could just make them out. It was so damn beautiful, Kate was crying again, feeling as though her heart were being pulverized. She swallowed hard, looked away, noted that the gate on the tiny bedroom window was locked and secure.

At the doorway to the living room she hesitated, prayed. Maybe that fierce, punishing God, the one she was schooled on, would perform one of his miracles and it would not be Elena.

But no. Once again, he'd let her down. For even now,

with the body so bloated with gases, Elena's face was recognizable.

My God. How many stabs does it take to kill one girl?

Kate fought the sickness rising in her, tried to count them, but couldn't; Elena's torn clothes were so blood-soaked that it looked like one huge wound.

Her eyes followed the vertical streaks of blood on the wall down to the floor where Elena had slid and bled to death.

Just a body.

Just a body.

Just a body.

A mantra Kate repeated to forget this was Elena, her little girl. *Just a body. Just a body. Just a body.* Again and again, in her mind, and aloud: "Just a body . . ." as she backed out of the apartment, careful not to touch anything, almost not breathing.

Outside, Willie sat on the front stoop while Kate finished calling the police. That vision he'd had earlier—the slicing arm, a scream—was *this* what he'd been seeing? He shivered, rubbed at his eyes with the arm of his leather jacket, caught a whiff of something sour. He sniffed.

"Nothing gets rid of that smell," Kate said in a voice so flat that it surprised her. When did it happen—this switch into her old self, the cop, whom she'd never wanted to be again? She could see from the look on Willie's face that she was scaring him. But she'd already made her decision—or it was made for her. No turning back now. Not if she was going to do something about this. And no way this hideous act would go unpunished. No fucking way. "You *sure* you didn't touch anything?"

"I told you. I don't think so."

"Don't *think,* Willie. You have to *know.*"

"Well, I *don't,* okay? I wasn't in there long. I just don't know! Shit. Shit. *Shit!*" He beat his hand against the brick wall. There were tears on his cheeks.

Okay, Kate would risk being human. She put her arms

around Willie's shoulders, and—boom! That was it: her hands were shaking, her chin quivering; one more minute and she would be fucking Jell-O. She pulled away fast. "Damn!" She sucked air into her lungs, tried to think of what to do next. Anything to keep from shattering. "There must be someone who saw something. Stay put."

At the first-floor apartment she turned her diamond ring into her palm, rapped at the door with the back of her fist. No answer. Down the hall, behind the door of the back apartment, there were slow, shuffling footsteps, then a fraction of an elderly woman's face, eighty, maybe older, appeared in the two inches between the door and the chain lock.

"Vat? Vat is it?" A scratchy voice heavy with Eastern European traces.

There were sirens in the distance.

"There's been an . . . accident," said Kate. "I need to talk to you."

"You the police?"

"No, I—I'm a friend."

The sirens were right outside now. What to do? Try to get something out of the old woman or go outside and protect Willie? The old woman made the decision for her, slammed the door shut. Whatever it was she would or would not say would now belong to the police.

he landing outside Elena's apartment was littered with cops. The tech team had descended on the place like antic, oversize roaches, infesting every corner. Kate peered in through the door. A woman in a dark brown pantsuit pulled on a pair of latex gloves. The next minute she was reaching under Elena's blood-soaked blouse—the thin stained cotton undulating as if an alien creature were about to burst from Elena's torso. Kate attempted to give her statement without crying or screaming to a cop young enough to be her son. Down at the end of the hallway, illuminated under a single bulb hanging from a chain, a uniform was talking, leaning into a guy wearing a bow tie. A detective, Kate figured, and high up, from the attitude the guy seemed to radiate. Kate strained to hear what the uniform was saying. "The old lady in One B, in the back, says she saw a black man in here last time she saw the girl alive." Bow Tie caught Kate's eye, turned the uniform around, whispered as he wrote something into a little NYPD notepad.

The young cop taking Kate's statement asked, "And then?"

"What?" A bulb popped, flashed inside the apartment. "Oh. Right." Kate continued with facts: time she arrived on the scene, called the cops. Another flash. This time, Kate was blinded—and thankful for it. She'd been staring at the ME, who had her fingers deep in Elena's mouth just as the photographer took his shot.

Kate went numb as a detective passed by, and then a couple of uniforms slid Elena's corpse into a dark green body bag.

Willie stared past the crowd, his vision blurred by tears.

"Why do I do it? No one wants this shit! Who do I paint for?"

When was that? Two, no, three years ago. Just before it all started happening for him, when he was ready to give up, quit painting, get a nine-to-five. Willie close to tears. Elena, taking his hand, speaking in her soft but authoritative voice. "You paint for yourself. It's important what you do, Willie, your painting. And someday people will see that. It's real, Willie. It's who you are. Hold on to that." Elena looking at him, total belief, confidence in him, right there in her eyes, on her face. The beauty of that moment. He'd replayed it often, whenever he was frustrated, close to quitting.

For a moment Willie was still in the middle of that perfect moment with Elena, desperately trying to hold on to it.

Curiosity seekers had filled the block. A couple of uniforms kept them at bay. Lots of cop cars, double-parked, flashers going. More uniforms and suits with cameras, bags, cases, surged up the stairs past Willie, into the tenement.

Elena. Murdered. At once so real and totally unacceptable. He should have insisted Elena get the hell out of this lousy neighborhood. And he had. Lots of times. But Elena always did what she wanted. Willie banged his hand against the wall, felt no pain.

"Hey, *you*. Tell me this: Exactly what the fuck were you doing here?" This from that guy on the upper landing, with the little NYPD notepad, now staring into Willie's face. He was maybe thirty-five, with a flattop, in plain clothes—if you could call a maroon paisley bow tie plain clothes.

But suddenly Kate was there, too, laying her hand on the

guy's shoulder. "I *asked* him to meet me here. What's the problem?"

Bow Tie turned to face her. "And you are . . . ?"

"Name's Katherine McKinnon-Rothstein." She thought fast. "Friend of Chief of Police Tapell's."

She saw the name register in the guy's eyes, could feel him giving her the once-over—her clothes, Prada bag, even her uptown hair. The whole time he was making a sucking noise, as if he were trying to get his tongue unstuck from the roof of his mouth. "Randy Mead," he said, not offering his hand, "Chief of Homicide, Special Task Force. And you're here . . . *why?*" His eyes, which were already small, narrowed to horizontal slits.

"Because I know the girl," said Kate.

"Well, the kid here was the first on the scene. He's gotta give a statement. It's procedure."

"I know all about procedure."

Mead's bow tie did a little blip over his bony Adam's apple. "Oh, really?"

"I was ten years on the force, in Queens," said Kate. "Astoria. Homicide and missing persons my specialty."

"Assstorrrria." Mead rolled the word around derisively.

Willie was quiet, watching Kate, a look on his face as if he was either impressed or in shock. Had she ever told him she'd been a cop? She couldn't remember.

"*Very* impressive," said Mead.

"Some people thought so." She crushed out a Marlboro under her heel. Mead, at about five feet ten, was practically cowering under her.

"Listen, man," Willie interrupted. "You gotta do something about—"

Kate cut him off. "I'll take care of this. Go wait in my car, Willie. *Please.*"

She led Mead back to the front of Elena's building. He sucked his teeth like a pissed-off rattlesnake. "You might remember," he said, "that he who finds the body is often the perp."

"Don't give me that Cop 101 crap, okay? I *told* you. It was all arranged. He was meeting me here. And the girl . . ." Kate stumbled a moment. *No. Not just some girl.* She could feel her emotions lining up at the starting gate, kicking up their heels like anxious Thoroughbreds. She took a deep breath. "And Elena," she said calmly, "has been dead for some time. I'm sure you can see that."

"Friend of our esteemed Chief Tapell's, huh?" Mead offered up a low-rent smile.

"Look," she said softly, "I don't mean to step on your toes. I know you've got a job to do. I'm just trying to help, explain a few—"

"Well, that's *real* sweet of you . . . Mrs. Rothstein, was it? But I think I can handle it from here."

Oh, man. Kate had to hold back from lifting Mr. Chief of Homicide right off the ground by his stupid fucking bow tie, watch his face turn blue. For a minute, her hands were twitching by her sides. But she was cool. The truth was, all that anger, right there, ready to explode, scared the hell out of her.

She managed to occupy her hands with her cell phone, hit the auto dial for Richard's office, but only got the machine. No luck with his cell phone either. *Damn.*

Mead took the opportunity to split, confer with a couple of uniforms, then he turned back, spit out the words: "Hey! You! Missus, uh—ex-cop! And your friend. Hang around. We need statements from both of you."

Even with the windows open, the air inside Kate's car had gone sour. Willie could not hear what Mead and Kate were saying, but it did not look friendly—Mead pointing in his direction, then mumbling something to a couple of uniforms. Willie tried to signal Kate, but she'd already turned back into the building. More suits and uniforms followed her. What they did inside, Willie could only guess at. Dust for fingerprints? Photograph the scene?

Willie turned Kate's ignition and switched on the radio, searched for something to distract him.

Babyface, crooning a sappy R & B ballad about becoming a father.

It was enough to make Willie think about the father he never knew. What was he like? Could he draw? Willie never asked his mother—she couldn't draw at all—and it must've come from somewhere. Willie could feel the tears on his cheeks—for Elena, or the father he had never known?

Babyface slid into a high falsetto, but the words no longer made any sense.

The crackle of a police phone startled him. A cop in the patrol car beside him, calling in details: "Female, Hispanic, stab wounds . . ."

"Excuse me." The man flashes the large Latino woman beside him a murderous look. Every time she strains to get a better view of the scene, her enormous straw tote slams into his thigh.

"Is exciting, no?" she says, staring up at the tenement steps, all the cops and technicians coming and going, then nodding at the police cars and ambulance and Crime Scene RV that are crowding the street, their sirens providing a shrieking slasher-movie sound track to the already cinematic scene.

"A girl's death? A young woman's life *snuffed* out? You call that *exciting*?"

The Latino woman's dark eyes blink with shame. "Oh," she says softly. "I did not know it was a girl. A young girl." Then, suspicious, she asks, "How do *you* know this? You live in this building?" The woman squints at him, but he is no longer paying attention, because just then, when she asks her stupid question, his entire body stiffens, his eyes, ears, every muscle in his body shift, ever so slightly, but with absolute certainty, toward the brownstone stairs. For just now, Kate is stepping through the door, and quietly, almost imperceptibly, except to him, he gasps a breath.

Magnificent.

He stares, transfixed, as Kate fumbles to light a cigarette,

sucks all that tar and nicotine into her lungs, where, he believes, he can actually see it cloud her organs, impede her
pounding heart, still the adrenaline that is racing through her
arteries.

He takes a couple of steps backward, allows the thrill-
seeking crowd to offer up a shield.

Well, now, what do you make of it?

He tries to telegraph this question to Kate, concentrating
so hard that his head begins to ache.

Kate puffed on her Marlboro, her eyes on the crowd, but not
really looking. If only *she* would remember that Cop 101
crap—the part about how some psychos enjoy being part of
the scene, like to come oh-so-close, get all hot and bothered
watching others clean up their mess.

And then she did.

Like the simple flip of a switch, the cloud lifted from
Kate's eyes. She scanned the crowd. But too late.

He's already fallen back, swallowed by the throng. He can
no longer see her. But that's okay. He's got to get moving.
That feeling is coming over him again, even stronger this
time. And the man is waiting. If he only knew what was in
store for him.

"Damn it." Kate flipped the ignition key. "You're going to
run my battery down. *Jesus,* Willie."

Willie's mouth opened as if he was about to say something, but no sound came out. He looked as if he might cry.

"Oh, fuck. I'm sorry." Kate felt like a total shit. A part of
her wanted to hug him and hold him, and cry for the rest of
her goddamn life. But no way she could chance it. Not now,
not here, in front of Elena's building with a dozen cop cars
and three dozen cops. And not if she was going to hold it
together long enough to get some answers. "You're going to
have to give a statement," she said, jamming in the car
lighter, pulling a Marlboro from her pack.

"What were you and that asshole in the bow tie talking about, pointing at me?"

"About your statement, that's all." The lighter glowed like a hot coal. Kate inhaled, pulled more smoke into her lungs.

A couple of uniforms headed toward the car.

"It'll be okay," said Kate, leaning across Willie, popping his door open. "Just tell them the truth."

"You're not coming with me?"

"I've got something to take care of." A deep breath. "Something I've got to—need to do."

Willie flashed an incredulous you-are-a-rat-deserting-a-ship look, and Kate felt like one.

"Hey," she said softly, her eyes on his. "You'll be fine. I'll call Richard, have him meet you at the station."

Willie didn't even look at her as he dragged himself out of the car.

Kate turned the ignition key, revved the engine, then rolled down her window. "Willie. Wait." She offered up a couple of tissues. "Wipe the blood off your sneakers."

"Hey." Mead rapped on the windshield, a snarl tugging at his thin lips. "Where are you going?"

"There's someone I need to see," said Kate.

"Oh, really?" Mead's snarl mutated into a tight smile. "Well, see them later. Right now you're coming with me."

5

Crooked. *The goddamn painting is crooked.*

William Mason Pruitt snared the corner of the offending object between his meaty thumb and forefinger. If there was one thing he could not stand, it was anything off-balance—especially one of his prized paintings. He stood back, expelled a puff of forty-dollar-cigar-tainted breath, assessed the sun-drenched Monet landscape—one of the master's late paintings, from Giverny—which he'd purchased from the New York Metropolitan Museum of Art— when was it?—six, seven years ago. He'd sat on the board then, got himself a very special deal, what with the museum desperate to raise cash. So what if the deal was not exactly board-approved? God, you'd have thought he was caught planting dynamite under their precious museum. After that, it was easier to resign quietly from the board than have it turn into a public brouhaha.

Bunch of stuffed shirts.

Pruitt laughed; his jowls did a minihula. He laughed because he supposed most people thought *he* was a stuffed shirt.

If they only knew.

Another laugh, this one deep from a gut that sagged over camel-colored Burberry trousers.

Eclectic tastes, that's what he had. Like his special fond-ness—some might call it weakness—for classical art.

With his clumsy fingers, it took a couple of minutes to get the damn tape off; another minute for the bubble wrap. Pruitt's puffy eyes languished over the delicate incising in the gold-leaf background that surrounded the heads of Mary and Christ. This time it had been a small rectory in Tuscany in need of cash. Too bad those spoilsport Italian authorities no longer sanctioned the selling off of their country's antiq-uities. Well, that was *their* problem.

Pruitt eased himself into a soft leather swivel chair, puffed on his hand-rolled Cuban cigar, sent short gray clouds of smoke toward the ornate plaster ceiling of this, his favorite room, the library; a man's room, all dark leather and ma-hogany. What was it that girl who thought she was so high and mighty had said about his library, about his whole Park Avenue apartment? *Straight out of central casting*—some-thing derogatory like that. At first, he'd liked her toughness. But not for long. She practically begged for some rough stuff, then didn't like it. Too bad.

Pruitt lifted the small altarpiece toward the amber light of an antique brass lamp, studied the brushwork and deli-cate color. So much care, attention to detail. Something Pruitt appreciated. Nobody had any standards anymore. Not his museum, the Contemporary, nor its curators, that's for sure, or those annoying board members, especially Mr. Ten-thousand-dollar-Rolex Richard Rothstein. *When will those people stop showing off?* Not any time soon, Pruitt was certain.

With the bubble wrap back in place, Pruitt slid the small fifteenth-century altarpiece into the deep lower drawer of his seventeenth-century American desk. He hadn't quite de-cided what to do with it—keep it, or . . . Well, that remained to be seen. He pushed himself up from the desk, feeling the full weight of those two to three daily martinis, foie gras at least once a week, black truffles when they were in season, blini and caviar as often as possible. He gave his belly a pat beneath the pink-and-white pin-striped custom-made shirt. Was it time for a diet?

He had stripped down to white boxers and high, thin black socks, but the bathroom scale confirmed the bad news. *The blini will have to go. For a while*. Pruitt's frown was reflected in the marble-framed bathroom mirror. He leaned in to study the bluish-red veins that crisscrossed the tip of his bulbous nose. Should he have them lasered?

Maybe. He gave himself an extra splash of rosewater eau de toilette. After lingering over his altarpiece and ruminating over his weight gain, there wasn't time for a real bath. Well, he could bathe when he got home. Tonight was, after all, rough-trade night at the Dungeon. By invitation only. He could hardly wait.

While he selected a fresh shirt, pale blue with *WMP* embroidered on the breast pocket, Pruitt thought about the good news he'd received today—Amy Schwartz had finally given her notice. And it was about time—considering that Pruitt had made her life at the museum about as miserable as possible since he'd come on as board president. Now he could choose his own director, which would certainly not be Mr. Upstart-Latino Perez, or Schuyler Mills. Pruitt couldn't care less if Mills had put in ten, twenty, or two thousand years as a curator.

Of course Pruitt knew that some people wondered what he was doing at an institution like the Contemporary. But really, he'd become quite fond of his new power base, thought it went well with the more modern image he was constructing. Of course most of what passed for art in that place was pure crap. His good friend Senator Jesse Helms was certainly onto something. But that's not why Pruitt was there.

He pulled the final loop through the Windsor knot of his Yale tie. The smile reflected in the mirror of his antique walnut armoire was one of pure satisfaction. After all, here he was, president of the board of the hippest museum in the city, treasurer of the attention-getting educational foundation Let There Be a Future, and now acquiring the kind of work rarely seen outside of the most revered art institutions.

He shimmied his tie into place just below his double chin. Yes, life could be sweet.

In the gray, windowless Interrogation Room there was no sense of time.

Kate checked her watch. Almost 10:00 P.M. Could that be true? It could be days. Weeks. To Kate, it felt as if time had broken. That from this day forward her life would be divided: Before Elena's death. And after.

And yet, she managed to do what was required of her: Follow the cops down to the Sixth Precinct, repeat her statement, sign forms.

She stared at the mirror. For a split second her reflection startled her. Was she really here, in a police station, witness to a crime? She knew that cops most likely were on the other side of the mirror watching her. After all, for ten years that had been *her* role, the cop on the other side of the mirror, judging, considering every gesture, weighing someone's guilt or innocence.

Kate pushed her hair behind her ears, the gesture immediately feeling false. She felt dislocated, alienated, and yet, at the same time, oddly comfortable. She knew all about station-house life—the role-playing, the petty jockeying for power, the camaraderie of good guys versus bad. And yet, right now all of it, even the dull beige walls and the damn fluorescent lighting, was somehow . . . reassuring. It could have been her old Astoria station.

Another look in the mirror. It was all there, right in front of her, a carefully painted portrait, like pentimento, thought Kate, the underpainting bleeding through, visible—those rough early years just barely masked by the elegant glazing of the last decade. Kate gave herself a knowing look. Whom was she trying to kid? All she had to do was peel off a layer and it was there for all to see: the toughness, the cop, the girl from Queens.

Were they watching her? No way they could think she was a suspect. But still they had to make her wait, answer the same damn questions. She knew that. It was part of the routine. The way it was done. The way it was always done: Ask the question again and again, see if the witness breaks down, if a suspect changes his story. But she'd had enough. And where the hell was Richard?

The door swung open. Mead referred to his little NYPD notepad. "You said you last spoke to the girl on—"

"Look," said Kate, "I've already told the other cop. Several times. And I'm tired." She leveled a stare at Mead. "And where's Willie?"

"They're still going over the facts with Mr. Handley. You want us to get them right, don't you?"

"Indeed I do," said Kate. "But it's time for me and Willie to go home."

"Just a few more questions." Mead sucked his teeth. "You said that you arrived at the vic's apartment around—"

"That information is in my statement."

Mead skimmed the page. "And Handley arrived before you?"

"Detective. Let me be clear. I have already answered those questions. They are, as I said, in my statement. I would appreciate it if you saved us both some time and read it."

"But I'd rather hear it from you."

"Well, I'd rather go home." Kate flipped open her cell phone, punched in a number. "It's me, Kate Rothstein. Sorry to call so late, but . . . Oh. You've heard . . ." Her voice trailed off. "Yes, I'm here—at the Sixth Precinct—answering questions. But . . . What? Yes. He's right here." She handed the phone to Mead, said, "Chief of Police Tapell wants to speak to you."

"Yeah, Chief?" Mead's eyes flitted here, there, up to the ceiling, across the floor, anywhere not to meet Kate's. "Uh-huh. Yeah. Uh-huh." His body sagged against the wall as though his muscles had decided to go on strike. "Right." He hugged the cell phone to his ear. "Uh-huh. Uh-huh. Uh-huh." He sighed, clicked off. "Tapell says you should come right up."

"And what about Willie?"

"He can go home."

"I want a uniform to drive him."

Mead nodded, without looking at her.

One more time, Kate managed to go through the necessary motions: Maneuver her car up the West Side Highway, pull off the exit, stop at red lights, open her wallet, remove her New York State driver's license and show it to the uniformed guard posted outside Tapell's West Side brownstone.

Now she sat behind the wheel of her car, head back against the padded headrest, eyes closed, tears pulsing down her cheeks while a montage of images played in her mind: the face of a defensive twelve-year-old who'd won her heart; snippets of conversations over so many dinners; the two of them arguing like any mother and daughter about the practicality of a thin cotton coat right in the middle of Urban Outfitters; Elena's Juilliard graduation; and again, Elena's performance piece at the museum less than a week ago.

Kate choked on her tears, the pain like a hot skewer twisting into the delicate muscle of her heart. But once again, miraculously, she managed to survive, dabbed her red eyes with a tissue, fixed her lipstick, put one foot in front of the other.

Minutes later she was inside, waiting, staring at floor-to-ceiling bookshelves. Law reviews. Case studies. Every known book on criminology. Hundreds of them.

The library, to Kate's mind, suited Tapell perfectly. What was it she'd been hearing people call the chief lately—Unflappable Tapell?

Hell, what did they expect from a chief of police—some touchy-feely, soft-hearted mark? Even back in Astoria, when Tapell ran the precinct and Kate was one of the cops, Tapell was all work and no play. But the two had immediately hit it off. Maybe each sensed that the other was going places, that Astoria was just a launching pad. It wasn't long before Tapell was running the entire Queens NYPD; then, within a few years, Manhattan's Bureau of Operations. By then, Kate had left the force, was fast becoming a mover and shaker in New York's elite circle—one that included the mayor. When a cops-on-the-take scandal brought down the former chief of police and his staff, Kate recommended the straight-as-an-arrow Tapell to fill the vacancy.

The door to the chief's inner office opened. Two heavyset men in ill-fitting suits—detectives, Kate surmised—were practically glued to the chief's sides.

Kate took in Tapell's statuesque proportions as if it were their first meeting: almost as tall as herself; broad shoulders accentuated by the pads of the herringbone suit; sturdy, though not quite shapely legs in ultrasheer stockings. Her face was all angles: sharp cheekbones; jutting chin; a high forehead accentuated by hair spiked with gray, pulled tightly back and braided into a severe bun. Her skin tone, a dark burnt sienna, was clear and practically unlined for her fifty-one years. Other than the reddish-brown lipstick that accentuated her sculpted lips, it was hard to tell if she was wearing any makeup. Clare Tapell, New York's first female chief of police, and an African American, was not what you would call pretty, but she was certainly a striking figure.

Tapell clasped Kate's hand in hers. "Sorry," she said. She nodded at the detectives, who immediately took off. "Late-night meeting," she said. "A man in a phone booth was shot by a passing car—on upper Madison Avenue, no less." She stopped, still holding Kate's hand, looked directly in her eyes. "I'm so sorry, Kate. About . . . your Elena."

The library walls seemed to echo the words in Kate's ears: *your Elena your Elena your Elena . . .*

"And I'm also sorry if the police put you through anything. I'll have a word with Randy Mead."

Kate shrugged. "It's okay. He was just doing his job. I'd had enough of it, that's all."

Tapell nodded. "I'll have him put his best people on the case right away. Mead may come across as a bit of a clown, but he's smart enough to have gotten himself in charge of the city's special homicide at the age of thirty-six, which is not bad. He'll get the job done."

"I want to be a part of the investigation," said Kate.

Tapell was about to speak, but stopped, walked across the room, ran her hand along the top of the wainscoting. When she turned, there was a painful frown pinching her strong face. "I don't see how that's possible, Kate."

"Anything's possible, Clare. You, of all people, should know that." Kate locked eyes with the chief of police. "I was a cop, under your tutelage, remember? And a damn good one."

"I know that," said Tapell. "But that was a long time ago. Now you're Mrs. Kate Rothstein, well-known art expert, socialite, philanthropist—and one of this city's greatest attributes as far as I'm concerned. How can I justify putting you on this case?"

Kate let herself sink into the soft leather couch, her adrenaline starting to wane. She closed her eyes; Elena's bloodstained face winked behind her lids. "There was something there," she said. "Something . . . I know this sounds weird . . but something familiar in that scene."

"Like what?"

Kate closed her eyes, tried to see it again—the spare room, pillows on the floor, Elena's body—but this time it eluded her. "I don't know. I'm not seeing it now, but—"

"You're too emotionally involved, too close to the victim, Kate."

"Balls! I got close to half the runaway kids I found, and you know that."

"*After* you found them," said Tapell.

"My feelings—my emotions—helped me find them," said Kate. "And I've got a feeling about this, too."

Tapell took a seat across the room, locked her long fingers together. "Look, Kate, I'd like to help you out, but you've got to give me more than a feeling if you want to be advising on this case." She shook her head, stood. "Do yourself a favor, Kate. Go home to that wonderful husband of yours and tell him that the chief of police has promised to take care of this—and I will." She took Kate's hand in hers. Tapell's eyes were sympathetic, but her hands were perfectly cool. "Go home, Kate."

The ice in Richard Rothstein's second glass of Scotch had melted. He looked at his illuminated watch dial: twelve-twenty. He was tired, agitated.

He wondered if the restaurant had given Kate his message, and if she was annoyed. She had probably tried to call him on his cell phone, the one he was currently recharging, the batteries having gone dead hours ago.

He moved to the windows. Somewhere below, on Central Park West, a siren blared. Street lamps illuminated the trees that bordered the edge of the park, dappling light onto Strawberry Fields. Across the park, the ornate mansard roofs of Fifth Avenue hotels painted a haphazard geometry against a black sky.

But even if Kate was annoyed with him, he knew she would forgive him for not showing up. Kate, he thought, would forgive him just about anything.

Richard gulped down the watered-down Scotch, flipped the switch of a modernist zigzag lamp. It cast a yellowish light under one of his recent purchases, a mask from the Ivory Coast, for which he had outbid the Museum for African Art. The piece looked absolutely perfect beside the one-eyed Picasso, a sketchy self-portrait the artist had tossed off in 1901.

Just when he was wondering how an East Village performance could go on past midnight, he heard the front door. He called out—"Kate?"—then peered into the darkened hall to find his wife leaning heavily against the wall. "Darling? What's the matter?" The words were lost a bit as he hurried toward her.

"Oh, Richard—" For the first time in hours Kate could not find her voice. She let go and collapsed against her husband with deep, choking sobs.

Richard let her cry. In all the years he had been with Kate, he had rarely seen her in tears. Yes, after the miscarriages, and when it had become clear that they would not be having children of their own, then she cried. But even then, not like this. He stroked her hair, slowly moved her into the living room, onto the couch, where he held her to his chest and waited.

Finally she managed to tell him about Elena.

"Oh my God." Richard reared back as if he'd been hit, and Kate started sobbing all over again. It was another ten minutes before she pulled herself together enough to tell him about her meeting with Tapell.

"Be part of an investigation? Are you insane?"

"I know it sounds crazy, Richard, but . . . I have to do it."

Richard shot her an incredulous look as he moved toward the handcrafted mahogany bar, mixed gin and vermouth for Kate, refreshed his Scotch. He pinched the bridge of his nose; his frown lines deepened. "Wasn't there a reason you gave that all up, Kate? I thought you *wanted* out of police work."

"I did, but—" Kate tried to collect her thoughts, which was not easy with Richard's blue eyes—so sweet a minute ago—now focused on her with total disbelief. She reached for his hand. "I'm going to need your support on this."

For a moment he hesitated, then his fingers closed around hers. "Of course. You've got it."

They were quiet a minute in the dimly lit living room, then Kate remembered she'd been trying to reach him for hours. "Where were you?"

"When?"

"Tonight?"

He hesitated a moment. "At the office, and then out with clients. Plus, my cell phone died. God, I'm so sorry, honey. If I knew—"

"I needed you there with me—to throw your weight around. Get the cops off my back."

"They were rough on you?" Richard's blue eyes sparked with anger.

"No. Not really." She closed her eyes. Again, Elena's face—destroyed, bloated—flashed.

"You okay?"

"Yes." Kate shook her head, whispered, "No." She leaned against her husband, let him lead her toward the bedroom.

"Lie down, darling." Richard's hands gently pressed her shoulders onto the bed.

Her eyes sought his. "I love you, Richard."

"I love you, too." He took her hand, squeezed it.

Kate let her body sag into the big white bed, pressed her eyes closed. She pictured Mead in his stupid paisley bow tie. *The finder is often the perp.*

The man was way off with that one. *But who then? And why?*

6

Two miserable days in the Hamptons. How Richard had ever convinced Kate that it would do her good to get away, to walk along the close-to-perfect stretch of beach nestled below the dunes of their East Hampton home, Kate would never know. When she wasn't crying, her insides were raging. Another day out there and she'd have been shooting up the local farmers' market.

Two days. *Two days!* Damn it, she knew what time meant to a murder investigation. Even if Richard had insisted that little or nothing would get done over the weekend, Kate worried that little or nothing would ever get done—no matter what Tapell said. This wasn't the kind of case that got attention unless someone was pushing, and pushing hard.

At least now, back in Manhattan, she could be active.

After Richard left for the office—Kate having assured him she'd be fine—she'd been organizing her own small office, making neat stacks from the papers that had previously sprawled over most of the authentic Biedermeier wooden desktop. First, her art history research. Hard copies of every lecture she'd ever given, dozens of reproductions with handwritten notes, art journals, periodicals and magazines, literally hundreds of art postcards. Thank God for her filing cabinet. Not that she was going to organize any of that right now, but it was a place to store it.

But now what to do with a decade's worth of miscellaneous information? A folder on New York's finest restaurants with the names and personal telephone numbers of each maître d', a list of caterers for every possible occasion, information on the best florists in New York and every major American city, catalogs from South American hothouses specializing in mail-order orchids, articles and clippings on noted French and domestic vineyards.

All of it seemed totally absurd. She dumped the papers into the antique silver wastepaper basket, just one of the many gifts Richard had given her when she first set up this office. It had been after her second miscarriage, after the hand-stenciled balloons on the walls and puffy white painted clouds on the ceiling had been latexed over and the crib returned for good.

What was it that seemed familiar about Elena's crime scene? Kate closed her eyes, tried to reconstruct it, but it was no good.

She turned her attention to the two cartons of books that had been stacked in the corner for years, and chose from among them Hervey Cleckley, *The Mask of Sanity,* Sheilagh Hodgins, *Mental Disorder and Crime,* Robert D. Hare, *Without Conscience: The Disturbing World of the Psychopaths Among Us.* She blew dust off the cover of David Abrahamsen's *Crime and the Human Mind,* thumbed through it, noted her own faded yellow highlighted markings, scribbled margin notes. Certainly there had to be new findings, new studies. It had been ten years since she had even looked at them.

A call to Liz. If anyone would know, Liz would.

Of course, Liz was more interested in Kate's state of mind than in helping her focus on criminology. But five minutes on how she was doing was about all Kate could take. Another second and she knew she would break down. "Enough," she finally said. "Let's just pretend I'm fine, okay?" Then, quietly, she said, "I've got to feel like I'm doing something, Liz—whether I've got the legal clout or not."

"You think that's a good idea?"

"Probably not. But what can I do?"

"Let the police handle it?"

"I didn't ask to have this back in my life, but shit, it's crawled back in through the front door."

"Okay," said Liz, resigned. "What do you want me to do?"

"I've made a list. I figure with your FBI status you can pull the information a lot faster than I can."

"Like what?"

"Recent studies on sex murders, as well as updates on violent crime that might help me see this more clearly."

"Kate, are you aware of how much information on violent crime Quantico alone has produced in the last few years? Enough to stock the Library of Congress."

"That's why I called *you*. I made a bunch of notes this weekend about what I observed at Elena's scene." Kate spent the next five minutes filling Liz in. "Can you run any of this through VICAP, and NCIC, see what the computer spits out?"

"You say there wasn't any evidence of a break-in. Could be date rape rather than homicide."

"Even if it was, Liz, Elena is dead. It *is* a homicide." She took a breath.

"True. I'll see what I can get my staff to pull together."

Kate thanked her friend, hung up, reached into her bag for a smoke, came up with an empty pack. *Damn.* She turned her bag upside down: keys, gum, lipstick, comb, an atomizer filled with Bal à Versailles, tissues, and a dozen cigarettes, half of them broken, spilled onto her desktop, along with that color photograph.

This time, Kate regarded it more carefully. Elena in cap and gown, Kate beside her; high school graduation, five—no, six—years ago. A familiar photo. In fact, Kate thought she had one just like it.

In her library, she flipped through a dozen leather-bound albums until she found it. *Identical.*

She tried to remember that moment outside George Washington High School. A sunny day. Elena's camera. Richard took the photo. Elena sent her a dupe. Right. So this one in her hand would be the original. Elena's?

Kate bent the gooseneck on the high-intensity lamp closer to the snapshot. A thin film, something flesh-colored, had been meticulously painted over Elena's eyes so they appeared, on closer inspection, to be closed, blinded, dead—like some creepy Surrealist painting by Dalí.

Kate dropped the photo as if she'd received an electrical shock. But a moment later she got her magnifying glass. Yes, it was paint on those eyelids. Careful work, too. Something for a lab to go over, though by now any fingerprints would have been smudged, ruined. And what lab? Whom could she possibly bring it to? And what would she say: *Oh, this picture made its way into my bag, mysteriously, you see, and look, there's this odd paint on the girl's eyes, and oh yes, this girl is now dead.*

Emotion rippled through like a spider crawling along her arm. Or was it simply fear, knowing that someone had taken this photo from Elena and planted it on her?

Kate knew that some psychopaths had a need to participate—the ones who stood in the crowd as the police found the body, watched the TV news to see what was said about their crimes, had scrapbooks filled with newspaper clippings. Was he one of those?

Kate would have to show this to Tapell.

The phone was ringing in her hand.

"Oh, Blair." Kate couldn't hide the fact that she was in no mood to talk with her benefit co-chair.

"Kate, darling. I tossed and turned all weekend. Didn't sleep a wink. I've exhausted my supply of Valium. I look a wreck. Oh, it's so awful. Awful, awful, awful." She took a breath. "But how are *you* doing?"

Kate wanted to say: *It's not about you, Blair! Can you*

possibly understand that? But she said, flatly, "I guess you could say I'm coping."

"Kudos, darling. That's the Kate I know." Blair waited a beat. "Now. You know I hate to bother you at a time like this, but we need to tie up a few things. Let There Be a Future's benefit is practically upon us and there are still lots of little details to discuss."

Kate heard it all—seating arrangements, flowers, party bags—but none of it registered, let alone mattered. Sure, the benefit had to go on, and other kids needed their help, but *party bags*! Jesus. Blair was lucky Kate didn't take her head off. Sure, it was Blair who had first welcomed her into New York society, rough edges and all, who had given her a few select pointers along the way, and had signed on when Kate chose Let There Be a Future, giving it a lot more cachet than it would have had without her. But flower arrangements? At a time like this?

No way.

No matter how many times Kate had seen Arlen James, the founder of Let There Be a Future, he never failed to impress her. Even leaning on a cane the man was larger than life.

Six feet three, a full head of bone-white hair, clear blue eyes. His fine wool suit was English, his shoes Italian, but the back story—son of a poor tenant farmer who likes to build model planes grows up to create an airplane construction company and makes millions—was pure American corn. Yet Arlen James was no ordinary capitalist. The man had a conscience, and put it to work. Let There Be a Future was his payback, his dream-child: educational money for any poor kid who wanted it.

Ten years earlier, on a rainy Saturday night, only three months after becoming Mrs. Richard Rothstein, Kate had been introduced to Arlen James at a cocktail party. Monday morning she was in his office. On Friday, she was in the South Bronx, walking into that seventh-grade classroom, kneeling beside desks, asking each kid what they wanted to be when they grew up. The answers? Well, a few Michael Jordans, but for most of the kids Kate's question seemed merely to puzzle. Growing up was enough of a challenge. Of course, Willie had an answer. "An artist," he said, sketching so hard his pencil broke in two. And Elena did too. Kate waited, watched as the dark-eyed twelve-year-old rolled the idea around in her mind. "I'm not sure," she finally said, looking Kate directly in the eye. "But I like to sing and act things out, you know?"

By the end of that day, she had talked Richard into signing on to adopt the entire class, to support any and all of them through high school and hopefully college. A decision that had altered Kate's life forever.

Arlen James put an arm around her, and Kate actually felt, for the moment, safe. But that was about as much fathering as she could take. Memories of her own father crawled into the back of her mind, the tantrums, beatings. No way she wanted to think about that now. She pulled away, gently asked, "Are *you* okay?"

He nodded, though she worried that he didn't feel quite as good as he looked. Recent trips to the doctor and talk of a pacemaker had made her painfully aware of the man's age, and the inevitable fact that this man who she loved would not be running the foundation forever.

"Have you seen this?" His fist came down so hard on the *New York Post* article, his desk shook.

SCHOLARSHIP GIRL SLAUGHTERED!

James started to cough, the veins in his forehead standing in high relief against his reddening face.

"Please, Arlen. Take it easy."

"I will not!" He snatched up the *Post*. "Listen to this . . . 'The victim, Elena Solana, was a graduate of the educational foundation Let There Be a Future, brainchild of high-flying billionaire-philanthropist Arlen James.' " He shook his head. " '*High-flying?*' *Me?* And I'm not a billionaire, for Christ's sake. Where do they come off writing this?"

"It doesn't matter, Arlen. It's just some writer—"

"And here . . . 'Police have no motive for the crime as yet, but it looks as if it might be a case of bad luck. One of those *Looking for Mr. Goodbar* stories. Woman picks up man. The wrong man.' "

"*What?!*" It was Kate's turn to explode.

"Wait," he said. "There's more. 'The only suspect the police have is another foundation graduate, but his identity is being withheld. The suspect is no longer in police custody, the police claiming there is not enough evidence to detain him. It has been suggested, by an unnamed source at police headquarters, that the do-good foundation has stepped in to protect one of its own.' "

" 'The *do-good* foundation'? Let me see that." Kate snatched the article from Arlen's hands, picked up from where Arlen left off. " 'Or could it be that our new mayor has put a lid on the case, now that he's been funding the foundation as part of the city budget?' " Kate threw the paper on the desk. "Jesus."

Arlen James sighed. "And I hear this is nothing compared to the *News*."

PERFORMANCE ARTIST'S LAST GIG

No way. Her eyes must be playing tricks on her, thought Kate, staring at the *Daily News* clipped to the top edge of the kiosk. But no, it was real. Headlines, no less. Whoever said that a culture gets what it deserves was really onto something.

She knew she shouldn't buy it, but what the hell, her day was already ruined.

Below the banner: "Young Woman in East Village Stabbed to Death. Story on page 5."

Kate turned the flimsy sheets of newsprint.

Three grainy pictures, side by side: Elena's high school

graduation, Arlen James in a publicity shot, and one from the back of Kate's book. "Katherine McKinnon Rothstein," read the small print, "well-known art and philanthropic figure." Then a couple of lines copied off the dust jacket of *Artists' Lives,* a mention of her PBS series and the fact that it was Kate who discovered Elena's body. But the real surprise was that the reporter had done some homework, come up with Kate's past life as a cop, even her specialty, missing kids.

Oh, yes. Her day could get worse.

He drags a finger across the steel tabletop to create a path in the thick dust.

How thoughtful, considerate, really, that this should be left here, as though someone were watching over him, thinking about his needs. *A guardian angel.* He likes the sound of that, the image, too. He looks up—thin shafts of light stream through the cracked ceiling—pictures a naked winged angel riding the ray like a rodeo cowboy, smiles.

He spreads all three New York newspapers out on the long steel tabletop, opens them to the story of Elena Solana's murder, which, he would say, not one of them has gotten right. He flips from one paper to the other, looking to see if anyone has commented on his signature. He sits back, disappointed.

Fools!

But a moment later, he's got his X-Acto knife in hand, carefully cutting out the newspaper photo of Kate, turning the grainy image this way and that. Then, with his cheap disposable auto pencil, he begins to sketch a pair of crude wings onto Kate's back. After a moment's consideration, he adds a halo. He pins it to the wall with a steel pushpin, stops a moment to admire his work.

A guardian angel. Indeed.

He sets his books onto the table, thinks about the girl.

He'd been watching her. The way she moved. Her extraordinary voice. That's when it came to him. Not exactly a plan. More of an improvisation. But he was getting so good at it. The way he had to improvise with the man, too. Good? No. Great.

But has Kate understood his message?

He wonders, pictures her on those brownstone steps looking so bruised, destroying her lungs with all that tar and nicotine.

It's time he stopped improvising, began planning, taking himself seriously, as others surely would.

He empties the shopping bags onto the steel table, begins to organize his tools.

The place is damp. He shivers, stares into the cavernous space past beams and pitted walls, the light from the river beautiful, peaceful.

A rat scampers across the dank floorboards. A flick of the wrist. The X-Acto knife in flight, and—*Gotcha!*—the squealing rodent is pinned to the floor.

His reflexes have always been good.

He watches the rat's tiny claws twitching, tail sweeping up a mini dust storm. Always fascinating, the loss of life.

But enough. There's work to be done.

He wants to create another message, something bold, something to convince her that they are in this . . . together.

He props his latest souvenir, the small altarpiece, against a couple of books, loads the film.

With each pop of the flashbulb he's blinded, an image winking in the back of his mind—a knife through a woman's flesh, a man's dying gasp, a young girl's scream. They fade to the Polaroids laid out in front of him, a new set of images developing before his impatient eyes. The last picture's details are just filling in, but he's already cutting them into tiny fragments, rearranging them haphazardly, gluing them down so that the original image is unrecognizable.

He plucks the finished work up with gloved fingers.

Should he actually send it? The idea so seductive, it gives him a thrill to tease like this.

Of course he's sending it. No way he's going to stop now.

He slides the collage into an envelope, sits back, stares at the newspaper photo with wings and halo until the grainy gray dots that make up Kate's face blur.

Lucille swirled a paper towel over framed Mapplethorpe photographs that lined the taupe-colored hallway—flowers so seductive the maid avoided looking at them. "A very good evening," she said in her singsong island accent. "I made some lemon chicken for you and Mr. Rothstein. And some cold orzo salad. I wasn't sure if you were eating in tonight."

Kate thanked her housekeeper warmly, then noticed the large FedEx package from Liz, slipped it under her arm, and headed directly into her home office.

By the time Lucille poked her head in to say she was leaving, the sky outside Kate's office window had gone blue-black. Kate had already read two of the monographs Liz had sent over: Nicholas Groth's *Men Who Rape* and Robert R. Hazelwood's *The Behavioral-Oriented Interview of Rape Victims: The Key to Profiling*. She'd filled half a yellow legal pad with notes.

Hours later, the images continued to echo. Dinner was solemn as Kate attempted small talk with Richard.

She picked at her lemon chicken. "Is it all right if I bounce a few ideas off you?"

Richard refilled their glasses with a California cabernet. "Sure."

"I'm trying to piece together what happened that night. First, the intruder, the street person/junkie theory is no good. Elena had to have been killed by someone she knew."

"Why's that?"

"One: There were no signs of a break-in. Two: The front-door lock was not picked or broken. Three: The window was still locked. And four: She was making him coffee."

Richard peered at her over the rim of his wineglass. "How do you know that?"

"There was an open bag of Colombian coffee on the kitchen counter next to a box of filters and a broken glass percolator on the floor." Her eyes glowed. "So, Elena makes him coffee—but they never drink it. No dirty coffee cups anywhere—not even the sink."

"He cleaned up?"

"Maybe. Probably. But I also have a feeling it progressed to sex before they got to the coffee." Kate lifted her glass, but did not drink. "It may have started out consensual, but they never made it to the bedroom. The bed was still made." She took a breath, seemed to draw strength from it. "Obviously, something went very wrong." Kate drummed her fingers on the crystal glass. "I've got to figure a way to get my hands on the coroner's report to know if Elena was raped. Don't you know anyone in the coroner's office?"

"Not really." He frowned. "And then what? I mean, once you get the autopsy, what do you do?"

"I'm not sure yet. But it will certainly tell me more about what happened."

Richard frowned again. "It worries me, you acting the cop again. You're my wife now. And I love you."

"Then be patient, okay?"

Richard managed to smile.

Kate smiled, too. But at the same moment her mind was flooded with images: shards of glass around Elena's feet, the geometric pattern of the bedroom quilt, congealed blood on the kitchen floor. "Hold me, okay?"

Richard was up fast. He slid an arm over her shoulder, the other around her waist. For a moment, Kate could play the little girl, a role she had to give up too early in life. For a minute, she considered showing him that creepy graduation photo, but no, not now. She didn't want to ruin the moment.

Richard's fingers skipped lightly over the flesh of her arm.

"If I asked you to make love to me, would you think I was weird? I mean, is it too soon?"

He grabbed her ass playfully. "Never too soon."

"You're a classy guy, Rothstein." She hugged him closer. "I think I need to lose myself." Her words, soft in his ear, were little more than a breath.

"So let's get lost."

In the bedroom, Kate tapped the music control panel, selected a favorite fifties Motown singer, Barbara Lewis, and sang along with "Hello Stranger" as she tugged her sweater over her head.

Richard stood. Unhooked his belt. Unzipped, yanked at his pants, which jammed at his cordovan oxfords.

"I think it's shoes and socks first, *then* pants. Didn't your mother teach you anything?"

"Not about this." Richard laughed, unlaced his oxfords, tossed them to the floor.

Kate shimmied out of her slacks, lay back against the white cloud of pillows.

"You look beautiful," he said, standing above her in boxers and high brown socks.

"You would, too." She made a face. "Without the socks."

Socks off in a flash, he unhooked her bra even faster, kissed her breasts.

Barbara Lewis crooned about how long it had been.

"I agree with Barbara," said Kate. She gently tugged Richard's head up toward hers, gazed into his night blue eyes, kissed his lips.

His tongue moved gently in her mouth.

She closed her eyes: a blue screen, shimmering purple, then red. Richard's hand was on her breast, fingers teasing her nipple hard. Now the red went deep plum, congealed in the dark theater of her mind's eye into long vertical streaks. A flash of light—a photographer's strobe. Stark white. Kate's lids twitched open. Richard's face in close-up: foot-long eyelashes, pores like craters. But his lips lay warm on hers; his tongue still dancing.

Kate locked her eyelids shut. Blackness. Yes, that's it, what she wanted. The void. And touch. To feel alive. His hand stroked her thigh, fingers grazed the edge of lace panties, then slid under.

But now the black had brightened. First umber, then sienna, then to the gray-pink of sickly flesh, which morphed into an arm, a leg, one jutting straight out, another bent; around them, pools of blood as red as overripe tomatoes, spread as though the heart in that violated torso were still pumping. Kate strained to hear the music, but the whoosh of ventricles, aorta, drowned it out—or was that the sound of her own heart beating in her ears?

Richard was on top of her now, erect, wedged between her thighs, warm breath on her cheek.

Behind Kate's closed eyes, Elena's stagnant pupils reflected nothing.

Kate's eyes flipped open. Beyond her husband's naked shoulder, linen curtains, just barely discernible, undulated like ghosts. Her breath caught in her throat.

"You okay?"

"Yes," she lied, pulled him closer. "I'm fine."

Yes, it was okay. She was okay. She'd keep her eyes open, that's all. She picked out objects in the dark, stared at them until their shapes were tangible, clear: the antique brass handles of the armoire; a bottle of Bal à Versailles on her dresser; Willie's assemblage—shards of wood, curling wires, impasto paint. But beside the painting a dark-bronze abstract sculpture appeared to pulsate on its stand, then slid off like primordial goo and slumped toward the baseboard, where it coagulated into something vaguely humanoid. From nowhere, a woman in a brown pantsuit materialized, stabbed at the lumpish form with gloved fingers.

She gasped just as Richard entered her, his body moving against hers, his cock a gently determined piston.

Eyes opened. Shut. Opened. Shut. No difference. Now it was blood streaks, flashbulbs, body bags.

Kate cried out.

Richard stopped short. "What's the matter?"

"Nothing," said Kate, hugging him to her.

"You sure?"

"Fine." Kate stared at the freckles on Richard's shoulder, the hair curling behind his ears; inhaled the smell of his aftershave—anything to keep her in the moment; anything that would make her feel alive.

7

Willie stared at the return address, slowly opened the padded envelope. Inside, a sheet of white paper and a book. He noted the date: just days before Elena died.

> Dear Willie,
>
> I'm sorry we fought. You know I love you and support you. What I said to you comes from my own experience as a Latina woman, which is possibly very different from your experience, though I doubt it. (Uh-oh, there I go again. SORRY.) Still, the whole thing about artists of color is an issue that I want to keep talking about (just try to shut me up!). I thought you'd enjoy this book of Langston Hughes's poetry. Read "Theme for English B." It addresses the whole race/color issue in relation to art. Truthfully, I'm not sure if Langston Hughes makes a better case for my argument or yours, but that doesn't matter. We will already have kissed and made up before you read this.
>
> Love you. E.

Willie pinned the letter to his studio wall. He stared at the words until they were nothing more than a blur through his tears.

The paint was drying on Willie's large glass palette. He picked at a blob of hardening pigment with an aluminum palette knife. If there was one thing Willie knew to be true, it was this: art was—and always had been—his one salvation. It had kept his spirit alive all those years in the projects, and it would save him now. He also knew it was exactly what Elena would say if she were here with him now. He plucked a large white bristle brush from a Maxwell House coffee can, swiped it through some cadmium red paint.

Hours later—how many? Willie couldn't tell. He was lost in his painting. The central image of his newest piece, an over-sized man's head copied from the back of the Langston Hughes book of poetry, had been rendered with an intentionally crude hand—but the likeness was strong. Across the poet's face a few lines of "Theme for English B" were painted in shimmering aquamarine; surrounding them, and the head, tenement buildings were painted in heavy black and white strokes.

The doorbell's first buzz was lost under the Notorious B.I.G.'s heavy rapping. The second time, Willie decided it was just some jerk passing by, hitting all the buzzers—hardly anyone in Manhattan drops by without calling. But a minute later the damn buzzer was going again—one long bleat followed by four staccato hits. Willie slammed his paintbrushes onto the palette.

His brother's raspy voice through the intercom's static: "It's me."

Henry. Shit.

Henry had lost weight, his cheeks more sunken than usual, eyes haunted. He looked a lot older than he was—at least ten years older than Willie instead of three. No one would take them for brothers. Even as kids, they had looked totally different. Henry's face, much like their mother's, was long and thin; Willie's features were rounder, softer, closer to that soldier's—the one who never came home.

Henry shifted his weight from one foot to the other, nervous, jumpy. His shoes were split and worn; he wore no socks, and it was a cool, damp day, more like March than May. He folded his thin body into one of Willie's wooden kitchen chairs. "You got something to drink?"

"Coffee?"

"You got something stronger?"

"I've got a few beers, some bourbon, that's about it."

"Bourbon sounds good."

Willie set a pot of water on the stove, searched under the sink for the half bottle of bourbon that someone had left in his loft over a year ago. He watched his brother pour himself a shot, toss it down. "Can't wait for the coffee, huh?"

Henry looked up, that mean scowl on his face, the one Willie remembered from the last year Henry had lived at home with the family, when he'd gotten heavy into drugs and was always fighting with their mother, with Willie, with anyone who would bother to fight back. "You got a problem with that?"

Willie sighed. He didn't want to fight. "No, Henry. No problem."

Henry fiddled with the bowl of sugar packets, tore several open at once, poured the crystals into his mouth. Willie recognized the junkie's craving.

"It's real good to see you, little bro." That troubled look was back on Henry's face. "It's been a bad time for me— these last couple of weeks." He helped himself to another shot of bourbon. "Things ain't been as good to me as they been to you."

Willie dragged his palm back and forth across his forehead; a headache was beginning to take hold.

In the background, the CD was playing loud and Willie wished he'd thought to turn it off before he brought Henry up. Now he didn't want to make a move, so he had to sit there listening to the Notorious B.I.G. going on about "somebody's gotta die."

Henry grabbed Willie's wrist. "Nice watch, man. How much you pay for that?"

"It was a gift."

"Oh yeah? Nobody ever gave me a gift like that. You got yourself some fancy girl, that it? A white chick, right? What's it worth?"

"It was a gift. I have no idea," Willie lied. He had a very good idea. It was a birthday gift from Kate. He'd seen similar platinum watches in stores, knew what they cost, had been kind of shocked, and pleased, too, by the extravagance.

Henry nodded toward Willie's studio. "You got yourself a real good scam here." He cocked his thumb at the new Langston Hughes painting. "You sell that shit?"

"Yes," said Willie, the word hissed between clenched teeth.

"How much?"

"It depends," he said, not bothering to hide his annoyance. "I only get to keep half. My gallery splits everything fifty-fifty."

"That so? Sounds like they got a even better scam going than you." He poured more bourbon into his empty coffee cup. "So, like, how much is your half?"

"None of your business."

Henry squinted at him, his dark eyes cold. "I could've done that, been a fucking artist. You know that?"

That sad old could-have-been song. Here it comes. Willy nodded halfheartedly.

"I had talent, little brother. A lot of talent."

"Yes, Henry. I know." Willie sighed. "You were good."

"Damn good. Better than good. I had *real* talent." Another cock of his head toward Willie's studio. He downed a shot of bourbon. "Fuck, I could do *that* shit blindfolded."

The Notorious B.I.G. was stuck on repeat and that same damn rap song—"Somebody's Gotta Die"—kept playing over and over and over.

"You got all the breaks, little brother."

Willie stood, tired of waiting for Henry to ask for the money he knew he'd come for. Henry never came by unless he wanted something. "I don't have much money here," said Willie, impatient. "And I give a lot of what I make to Ma."

"Yeah. I know that." Melancholy erased the scowl from Henry's lips. "That's not why I come."

"No? Why then?"

Henry looked down at his hands, picked at a scab. "You think I only come for money?"

"Just tell me what's on your mind, okay, Henry?"

Bourbon spilled over the sides of Henry's cup, his hands had begun to shake. "You know I really like that little girl-friend of yours. You know that, don't you?"

"Who? You mean . . . Elena?"

Henry nodded, poured the last of the bourbon into his cup. *Jesus*. Henry interested in Elena? Of course Henry had known Elena for years, since they were kids back in the South Bronx. But romantically? Was he kidding? Willie took a long, hard look at his brother: his coffee-colored skin gone gray with a junkie's pallor, his bloodshot eyes, his cheekbones like two hard slashes in his too-thin face. But now there was that scared look under the street-battered defiance, and it tore at Willie's heart. "Yeah. She likes you, too, Henry." Speaking of Elena in the present hurt. He paused, took a breath. "Do you know what happened?"

"I like her a lot, man, and—"

"You already said that." Willie was losing patience again. "I asked if you *knew* what happened, to Elena. That she's . . . dead."

"Yeah." Henry's body shuddered. "I know that."

"How? How do you know?"

"I can read," said Henry.

Willie sighed. "So what about her? What about Elena?"

But Henry seemed to shrink into himself, his eyes glazed over as though he were listening to some inner voice.

"What *is* it, Henry?"

Henry stared into his empty coffee cup. "You got more bourbon?"

"No." Willie snatched the bottle from his brother's shak-

ing hand, flung it into a metal trash can. The sound of breaking glass was like atonal music.

Henry bolted up, slammed his angular body against
Willie's, the veins in his forehead pulsing, his sudden
strength fueled by anger.

"Relax, Henry. Be cool."

"Cool?" Henry's eyes were black granite.

Willie pulled out of his brother's grip. "Jesus, Henry.
What's with you?"

Henry stared at him, then sagged. "Sorry." He shook his
head, then his arms, legs, the anger falling off him like snow.
"I didn't mean it. It's just that—" There were tears in his eyes.

"Oh, shit, Henry. I'm sorry, too."

Henry waved him off, started shuffling toward the door.

"Hold on." Willie disappeared into his bedroom, returned
with his wallet. "All I've got is thirty-six dollars." He pushed
the bills into his brother's stained hands.

"They laid me off at the messenger place. But I'll get another gig, man, another messenger job, real soon. I'll pay
you back."

"Sure you will."

"I didn't do anything, Will."

"Who said you did?"

"But . . . they might."

Willie stared into his brother's eyes, the dilated pupils,
bloodshot whites. "What are you talking about?"

His brother swallowed hard. "Nothing." His hands had
begun to shake again.

"Shit, Henry. What's wrong?"

But Henry was shaking so bad now, he couldn't speak.
Willie hugged his brother to him. All the strength was gone;
Henry felt like a bunch of dried twigs about to crack. Willie
held on to him until the tremors subsided.

"I'm . . . okay," said Henry, pulling away.

"Hey, wait a minute." Willie dug into a dresser drawer,
came up with a pair of wool socks. "Put these on. It's damp
out today."

Henry pulled his shoes off, rolled the socks on gingerly, as though even the soft wool chafed. Willie stared at his brother's blotchy, swollen feet. He felt tears burning behind his eyes. "Don't you have a coat, a jacket?"

"Lost it," said Henry, looking away.

Willie yanked an old blue parka off a hanger, laid it over Henry's shoulders. "Hey. By next month it'll be warm," he said, trying to smile.

But once Henry was gone, it didn't matter what Willie tried to do in that new painting, or how many times he changed the goddamn music. Nothing worked.

8

Homicide Detective Floyd Brown Jr. was just sitting down to dinner—three hours late—when the phone rang. His wife, Vonette, took the call, whispered "Mead," her hand over the receiver.

Floyd dropped his fork. Mead must be calling for an update on the arrest of the Central Park Shooter, the cause for the three-hour delay of his dinner. Floyd suspected that Mead was worried they wouldn't get the charges to stick; the wacko had hit five people in the past six months, but no victim had lived long enough to make an ID. Still, Floyd wasn't worried. This afternoon he'd spent over three hours with the psycho. This one needed to confess, and Floyd had been ready to help the guy unburden his tortured soul. Now he'd get that vacation he'd earned after two months of working nights and weekends.

"Brown—" Mead was interrupted, someone shouting a question, lots of muffled voices in the background. "Sorry. Good work today. I hear you were even better than usual."

"Thank you." He waited. But there was nothing from Mead. "I'm sure about this one," he finally volunteered.

"Huh? Oh, yeah. Sorry. Slattery's shovin' something under my face."

Brown waited again. His shell steak and baked potato

were cooling. "Is there anything else you need on the shooter, sir?"

"The shooter? No. Look, I'm not calling about the shooter—of course I wanted to congratulate you—you did fine work, but you already know that." Mead sighed into the phone.

There were moments Brown almost felt sorry for Mead. He could tell that he made the chief of homicide nervous. Partly because Mead wasn't sure what kind of political clout a black cop like Brown might have these days, and partly because Brown was an old hand—a seasoned cop who couldn't quite cover up his doubts about the likes of his new superior. Brown hated to see men like Mead make it up the ladder so fast without putting in their time.

"I need you to get your ass over here. Park and Seventy-eighth. Number—shit—what's the number over here? Slattery! What's the fucking address here?"

"Right now?" asked Brown.

"Shit, yes. *Now.* I want you to see the scene before the tech boys destroy it. We got a stiff in a bathtub. Could be an accident, but the ME is gonna want to do his thing. So I need you here ASAP."

Floyd Brown stared at his reheated dinner, cooling down for the second time. He wondered if nuking your food too many times could give you cancer or something. He looked over at Vonette, holding her coffee cup against her cheek, staring at the wall, probably trying to figure out why she had stayed married to a cop for twenty-seven lonely years. Damn pretty woman, Floyd thought, and her fiftieth birthday only a month away.

Floyd wanted to stay in tonight, catch up on a little love and tenderness, but . . . He looked at his watch. "I guess I can be there in about a half hour."

Vonette glanced over, sighed, looked away.

Randy Mead hung up before Brown could say another word. He didn't need to take crap from his own men, not after months of heat with this goddamn psycho shooter driving everyone in New York nuts, and Chief of Police Tapell breathing down his neck. And now this guy, dead in his goddamn bathtub, and it didn't look like an accident. He moved out into the living room, barked at a tech man dusting for prints. Lots of art out here. Mead noticed a sunny landscape, decided that the Monet signature had to be real in a snazzy place like this. He jotted a note to have his detectives check with the victim's insurance carrier to make sure nothing valuable was missing. Could be an angle on the murder—if it was murder. And hardly anyone drowns in their goddamn tub. Nor was there any suicide note, nothing. And the floor around the tub was sopping, like the guy splashed around a lot.

Plus, the guy was some fat-cat socialite.

Jesus. Did he need this?

Mead knew there were people waiting in line for his job, and figured the chief of police probably wanted someone black. He made a mental note to be nicer to Floyd Brown, took a breath, hoped this rich guy's death was just some kind of freak accident.

"Hey, Mead. Get a load of this." One of the crime scene cops, heavyset, balding, moved slowly across the somberly decorated living room. Hanging from his plastic-gloved hands was a large piece of flaccid black leather: a hood, bondage variety, with crude stitching, cutouts for eyes, nose, mouth.

"Where'd you find that little number?"

"Bottom dresser drawer."

"Anything else?"

"Some porn mags, and we're still looking. Could be this guy picked up some rough trade, and it got a little rougher than he wanted."

The idea of this fat cat being some sort of S and M freak brought a smile to Mead's face. "McKnight!"

The heavyset, balding cop lumbered back over. Mead nodded at the bagged leather hood. "Keep this item under your hat, okay? Nothing to the press about it. No leaks. Got it?"

"Yeah. Sure, Chief." McKnight shrugged.

Mead lifted a black permanent marker out of McKnight's hand and printed the victim's name in large block letters on the top of the plastic bag: WILLIAM MASON PRUITT.

id she cry when her mother died? Why can't Kate remember? Everything else about that day was etched in acid: Sister Margaret coming to the classroom; the metal taps on Kate's shoes echoing off the gray-green corridor walls; the nun's frown—taps were forbidden—softened by pity on the old woman's face; the taxicab waiting to drive her home; her father standing in the doorway, dusky gray suit only a shade darker than his ashen face. And, naturally, Aunt Patty, cooking and cleaning, preparing for the onslaught of relatives to the McKinnons' home, the house already smelling of Pine-Sol cleanser and stewed cabbage, and her mother dead only a few hours.

But did she cry?

"Katie, are you there? I mean, after all, the girl was like a daughter to you. It's okay to be upset, to cry."

"Yes, of course, Aunt Patty, I know that," said Kate, coming back to the moment. She pictured her father's sister in her Forest Hills apartment, balancing on the arm of the plastic-covered sofa in her floral-wallpapered living room. But then, she looked up, saw that damn photo she'd pinned above the desk, Elena's eyelids painted over. She'd been planning to show it to Tapell, and she would, but the idea of Tapell telling her to go home and take her feelings with her for a second time just didn't appeal to her. She had to know more.

"Why don't you take a break, Katie. You know, come on out to Queens. I'll even whip up a batch of my chili that Richie likes so much."

"That's really sweet, Aunt Patty. And we will, soon," said Kate, but she was no longer listening. A small banner on the front page of the Metro Section had caught her eye: "Financier/Socialite Found Dead."

"Aunt Patty," she said, sliding the *Times* closer. "I've got to go. But I'll call you later. And thanks."

Kate skimmed the article on Bill Pruitt's death. It listed his association with Let There Be a Future, his various clubs—Yale, Century—the fact that he was president of the Contemporary Museum's board, and that he was discovered in his tub. *His tub? Did he have a heart attack?*

She immediately called Richard. Did he know? She tapped her fingernails along the counter, waiting, listening to the phone's ring. Richard was in court. The Wall Street firm that had been taking up too much of his time lately—the partners suing one another. Greed versus Greed, Richard had called it.

Kate went back to the article, was searching for details when the intercom sounded. Ryan, the young doorman. A package for her. He'd bring it up, he said, a bit too eagerly.

Ryan's eyes practically caressed Kate's shoulders. She pulled the sash of her terry robe tighter.

A standard manila envelope, messengered to her, no return address, simply her name typed in all capitals onto a self-adhesive sticker.

Inside, about the size of an ordinary postcard, was some kind of mosaic design, a hodgepodge of colored bits glued down. Some artist's exhibition invitation? Kate flipped it over. Nothing. If it was an invitation, it was surely an enigmatic one. She ran her finger over the surface, felt the cut edges. It was handmade. Especially for her?

Kate's nerve endings were tingling, that graduation photo

flashing in her mind. *Could there be a connection? Why had this been sent to her?* She dropped it, watched as it looped its way to the floor, then retrieved it, along with the magnifying glass she used to study those tiny details in the corners of Flemish paintings. It confirmed that it was a collage, the tiny pieces part of a photograph.

Ten minutes of straining her eyes through the magnifier, and Kate was fairly certain it was a painting—perhaps a Madonna, from the fragments of a cross, gold leaf, and a breast she had detected.

And she knew just the man to help her be absolutely certain.

All the way in the cab Kate's heart beat fast. Someone was sending these things to her—but why?

With the collage back in its envelope—she wished she hadn't gotten her hands all over it, but too late for that now—Kate stepped into the elegant brick town house just off Madison on Seventy-fifth Street. No need to read the small bronze plaque. She knew what was engraved on it: *The Delano-Sharfstein Gallery*—an oasis of quiet beauty, a world of blue-chip paintings and high-end objets d'art.

With its dark wood and Oriental rugs, Delano-Sharfstein looked like a small, very private museum. Except here everything was for sale. Talk about giving rich people what they want.

As a student, Kate had made it a habit to stop in on a regular basis. It was on her third, maybe fourth, visit that she was confronted—ever so politely—by a tiny, compact man with a beautifully chiseled face interrupted by a shocking beak of a nose. He stood beside her a moment, observing her, she determined, while she, in turn, pretended to study a sixteenth-century portrait.

"Exquisite, isn't it?"

"Indeed," she said, taking in the man's elegant three-piece suit.

"I couldn't help but notice you over the past few months."

His voice was cultured, but created, Kate determined—and she should know, having created one herself. He extended a small, perfect hand. "Merton Sharfstein."

"Oh," said Kate. "This is *your* gallery. A pleasure."

And it was. After Kate told him she was an art history student, she received a personal tour of not only the first floor, but the second floor's private viewing rooms—normally reserved for serious clients—where she was treated to a selection of fine art she didn't think existed outside of museums.

Kate became a gallery regular, and Mert's continued attention paid off. When Kate married Richard years later, she brought him to Delano-Sharfstein, and though Richard's main interest was contemporary art, Mert let Richard know that an art collection without "history" was not—how did he put it?—"important enough for a man of your taste, Mr. Rothstein." Oh, yes, Mert was good. Richard couldn't wait to plunk down a few hundred grand for a piece of "history."

"Joel. How are you?"

"Very well, thank you, Mrs. Rothstein." This spoken barely above a whisper by the pretty young man behind the discreet mahogany desk—no big white island counters here. "Mr. Sharfstein is expecting you on two."

Kate cut through the public exhibition space with its enormous marble fireplaces, inlaid floors, decorative plaster ceilings; everything about it whispering in your ear: *Money. Money. Money.*

The gallery's grand circular staircase was a set for that actress of yesteryear, the one Kate's mother liked so much, Loretta Young.

"A cup of coffee, tea?" offered another young man, even prettier than Joel, this one whispering as though a baby were asleep in the next room as Kate took a seat in one of the small viewing rooms outfitted with a suite of Goya etchings.

"Will Mert be long?"

"Just a few more minutes," he whispered. "He's with a client."

Kate perused a Goya. Up close, the print was impossible to read, nothing more than washes of black and gray ink, dark and mysterious.

The assistant urged her to back up. She did, and the image sprang to life: a matador slashing a bull.

"You were too close to see it," he said.

A good point.

Kate moved up again, studied those misty grays, then back, just as the door to Mert's office swung open and the art dealer emerged, trailed by a young man in skintight leather pants and silky lizard-print shirt open to the navel.

"Kate Rothstein. Mr. Strike."

"Strike, man. *Just* Strike." He raised his head of wild blue-black hair toward Kate.

"Oh, the musician. I just love 'Mosh Pit Stomper.' " Kate snapped her fingers, then let loose with her best Joan Jett: "Kick me, punch me, love me to death, oh, mosh pit stom-perrrrr . . ."

Mert stared at her, mouth open.

"Musician, that's the ticket, luv." Strike threw his multi-tattooed arm over Kate's shoulder, gave her a mascara-heavy wink. "To everyone else I'm just a bloody rock star."

"Mr. Strike, excuse me, *just* Strike, has a finely tuned aesthetic sense. He's just selected three old master drawings, a Rubens and two Dürers."

"Don't know about that, luv. But they fucking well set me back. That's for damn sure."

"Yes." Mert managed a smile, but after another minute he dispatched Strike with his usual grace, then let out a dramatic sigh.

"Honestly. The riffraff one must deal with these days."

"Strike just dropped what—maybe a mil, or two—and I'm supposed to feel sorry for you? 'Fraid not, *luv*." Kate kissed Mert's cheek. She laughed, then got serious. "Mert, I want to show you something." She slid the collage out of the envelope, her fingers trembling slightly. "Would you put on gloves. Please." It might be too late as far as her prints were concerned, but why contaminate it any further? Just looking at it again, Kate was unnerved.

Mert eased his delicate hands into white cotton art-handler gloves. Kate gave him her magnifier. He squinted through the glass, his eye enlarged to the size of a tennis ball. "Could be a figure, a child, or— Hold on. I have an idea."

Moments later, another of Mert's pretty boy assistants was scanning the collage into one of the gallery's computers—the image enlarged on the screen four times its original size. Mert tapped his lip, then pointed out one tiny fragmented image after another. "Blow them all up. And print them."

Fifteen minutes later, the assistant had not only enlarged over a dozen of the tiny fragments, but, under Kate's and Mert's direction, cut them out like puzzle pieces. Now, Kate shifted them around on Mert's desk, linking up ones that fit together to create about a third of the painting: a child's head, a breast and an arm, a good part of a royal-blue robe— a Madonna and Child.

"It's like a graduate-school art history test. Name the painting from the fragment." Kate pushed another piece into place. "From the way it's painted I'd say it's too sophisti-cated to be anything medieval, but . . . not quite Renaissance either. What do you think, Mert?"

He smiled. "Quite astute, my dear. I'd agree. About four-teenth century. Definitely Italian."

"Who in New York collects this sort of stuff?"

"Well, offhand, your husband comes to mind."

"Only one or two pieces—thanks to you. And not since it's gotten so expensive, he doesn't. Who else?"

Mert twisted up his mouth. "Your Contemporary presi-dent, Mr. William Mason Pruitt, expressed interest in a piece I had about six months ago, but he balked at the price."

"Bill Pruitt?"

"An absolute cheapskate—or was. Forgive me. I just heard the news. But he tried to get me to sell him a Rubens water-color for half the price—because he was *so* important. I told him to look elsewhere."

"Anyone else you can think of?"

"Several people, but I'd have to check my files. And there are a few other dealers in New York who trade in such works, several in Europe, naturally—not all of them reputable. As you well know, Kate, stolen paintings and artifacts are a thriving enterprise, and—" Mert stopped short, regarded the cut-up fragments. "Wait a minute." His canny eyes narrowed, his beak practically twitching as he hit the office intercom. "Joel. I need to see the most recent listing we have on stolen artwork. No, make that the last six months. Right away, please."

"Mert, what is it?" Kate caught some of his excitement.

"We get updates every month," said Mert, flipping pages and pages of stolen-art reports until he found what he was looking for. He slapped it onto the desk beside Kate's incomplete puzzle painting.

The report, one page, had a large color Xerox of a Madonna and Child at the top, a paragraph below:

Italian. 14th Century. Sienese.
Egg tempera on wood panel
This small altarpiece, part of a church predella from
    Asciano, Italy, disappeared on or about March 11.
The work is attributed to the School of Duccio, possibly
    even painted by the master himself.
Approximate worth: three to six million dollars.
Art dealers should look for the identifying crosshatch
    design in the gold-leaf background.

Kate looked from one image to the other, raised the magnifier to her eye, noted the identical crosshatching in both. "Mert, you're a genius!" She snatched the stolen-art report, slid it into the envelope along with the enlarged cutouts and the original collage. "I need these."

Mert's eagle eyes narrowed. "What's this all about, Kate?"

"When I find out," she said, "you'll be the first to know."

10

Dark suits. Black dresses. Everyone appropriately solemn. The minister, who obviously didn't know Bill Pruitt, mouthing empty declarations of praise for the man's "good works." No one volunteering when he asked, "Would anyone like to say a few words about the deceased?" Kate was almost tempted to say something—*But what?*—simply to break the uncomfortable silence.

She surveyed the crowd in the Upper East Side chapel: the staffs of the Contemporary Museum and Let There Be a Future, several recognizable Republican politicos, a handful of New York's ruling class, the soon-to-be-defunct director of the Contemporary Amy Schwartz, curators Schuyler Mills and Raphael Perez, on either side of her, stone-faced—though the red carnation in Mills's lapel seemed inappropriately celebratory. Across the aisle, Blair, Kate's friend and co-host of the foundation benefit, rolled her eyes with each tribute the minister managed to conjure.

A decent turnout, though people were checking watches, twitching with boredom, one man actually whispering into a cell phone.

Richard had refused to come, would not be a "hypocrite." Others had no such problem with hypocrisy.

Even Pruitt's mother, the venerable socialite, kept yawning into her lace handkerchief.

Twenty long minutes later, the group was turned out into the rarefied afternoon light of upper Madison Avenue. Blair leaned into Kate, whispered, "Darling, if I should suddenly drop dead, *please,* say something, *anything* about me other than my charitable works."

"How about Olympic shopper, or . . . fabulous luncher."

"Bitch," said Blair, laughing. Then: "Kate, have you checked all those things for the benefit?"

Kate ticked them off on her fingers. "Florist, caterer, PR people. Check."

"Fabulous." She air-kissed Kate's cheeks. "I'm off to Michael Kors. The final fitting for my gala dress. Who's doing you, darling?"

"Oh—" Kate hadn't even thought about it. "I guess Richard, though not often enough."

Blair's trilling laugh was cut short as the driver closed her into the airtight BMW.

Mrs. Pruitt laid a hand on Kate's arm. "How lovely of you to come for Bill, dear." Her frosted-helmet hair glittered with lacquer.

Kate felt a slight pang of guilt. She'd come purely out of obligation. "Well," she said, "Bill was always so . . ."

The older woman waited for Kate to come up with something.

" . . . neatly dressed," she finally said.

The older woman nodded, then sighed. "Care for a drink? I'm only around the corner."

Kate hardly felt she could refuse.

Winnie Armstrong-Pruitt-Eckstein arranged herself on an Empire couch upon which the Empress Josephine would have looked, and felt, perfectly at home.

The Park Avenue apartment had that Sister Parish look that the late great decorator to the staid old rich made famous: the English manor house in the middle of Manhattan, brocades and chintz, worn Persian rugs, a grand piano with an enormous bouquet of wildflowers, a wall of paintings—all of dogs.

The maid arranged the tray between them, poured each a martini from a deco shaker.

"Cheers." Winnie tipped her glass toward Kate, her eyes, under blue-shadowed lids, sparkled.

The toast and Winnie's demeanor were not quite appropriate to the circumstances. The woman had always reminded Kate of an old-time actress, any one of a dozen, but particularly the one who played Cary Grant's mother in Hitchcock's *North by Northwest*—one of Kate's favorite old movies—a sort of combination heiress/showgirl. How she ever produced a son like Bill was a total mystery.

"How is that marvelous husband of yours?" asked Winnie.

"Overworked. But fine."

Winnie's voice dropped to a conspiratorial whisper. "You know, my mother always said that Jewish men make the best husbands." She tossed Kate a wink. "I thought I would be married to Bill's father, Foster Pruitt, forever, but then, well, he was gone, and to be absolutely truthful"—she leaned toward Kate—"he did not leave me quite as well taken care of as I would have liked. Not that I married Mr. Eckstein for money. Heaven forbid!" Her hand fluttered to her bosom. "Larry Eckstein was the most fabulous man in the world!" She sighed, dramatically. "Oh—I miss the man terribly." Her eyes went moist. She raised a tiny bell from the nearby table, gave it a firm shake. "Another drink?"

Minutes later, the maid had refilled Winnie's martini and supplied Kate with a fresh one.

"My son was the only one who actively showed his disapproval when I married Larry."

"Some people find it difficult to accept change," said Kate diplomatically.

"Oh, bull! He was a snob. We had a terrible falling-out over my marriage." She shook her head. "Though, after Larry's death we had a bit of a rapprochement. I think, to his credit, William now feels a bit guilty." Mrs. Armstrong-Pruitt-Eckstein pursed her lips. "Oh, my, I'm talking as though he were still alive."

"Well, it is hard to believe he's gone. He'll be . . ." Kate found it difficult to say the word: "Missed."

Winnie raised a skeptical eyebrow.

Poor Bill. His own mother didn't like him. Kate searched for something to say, gestured at the wall of doggie portraiture. "Obviously, you shared your son's love of art."

"Oh, no. Our tastes were completely different, dear. Of course, I adore his Impressionist paintings. Who wouldn't? But those religious paintings, well . . . they're a bit too Catholic for me." She polished off her second martini. "I have one here. Bill left it with me."

"A medieval painting?" Even after two martinis, Kate's attention was piqued. "May I see it?"

Winnie rooted around in a closet of the wood-paneled library, came up with a crucifixion scene, painted on wood, no bigger than an average paperback novel. She handed it over to Kate as if it were nothing more than a copy of last week's *TV Guide.*

Kate was momentarily disappointed. But had she really expected Winnie to come up with the Madonna and Child in the collage?

"I believe it's quite old," said Winnie with a disinterested shrug.

Kate stared at the cracked paint, the remains of gold leaf around the borders. Richard, she thought, would kill for it—if it was authentic. She regarded it more closely.

"Do you think it has any real value?" asked Winnie.

"It's hard to say," said Kate. "It's not really my area of expertise. But very possibly. When did Bill give this to you?"

"Oh, a couple of months ago. It was a bit odd. He asked that I take care of it for him. Like it was a pet or something."

"Has he given you any others?"

"One or two of the wonderful canine portraits." Winnie beamed, then stopped, thought a moment. "You know . . .

there was a another religious painting I saw in Bill's apartment, just the day before he died. It was on the desk in his library, only half wrapped. I took a peek at it. A Madonna and Child." Winnie looked away a moment, puzzled. "Come to think of it . . ." She retrieved a few papers from her desk, ran her finger down a page. "Let me see . . . No. The Madonna and Child is not here. That's odd." She handed the paper over to Kate. "It's a list of the art in Bill's apartment. The police furnished it. Very annoying they were, too." She pursed her lips. "They expect *me* to check with his insurance carrier to see if anything's missing. I mean, really."

"You're absolutely sure you saw it—this Madonna and Child painting?"

"Kate, dear. I may be old, but I'm not senile."

"Oh, sorry. I didn't mean that." Kate scanned the list, then got the cut pieces of the Madonna and Child out of her bag, arranged them on Winnie's library desk. "Did it look anything like this?"

"Goodness." Winnie tilted her head one way, then the other. "I mean, I'm no expert, dear, but it certainly looks the same."

Kate thought a minute. "Could Bill have sold it?"

"I can't imagine that. It was just the day before he died that I saw it. There wasn't time."

Exquisite.

His eyes linger over the delicate crosshatching in the gold leaf, the tiny fissures in the egg tempera, the tender look in the Madonna's half-closed eyes. It's so beautiful, so terribly moving, he is almost afraid to look at all that emotion the artist has dared put into a painting meant for reverence and piety.

He was right to take it. The man did not deserve it.

He thinks back, tries to relive the moment when he held the man's spindly legs in the air, watched the old fool thrash about in the water. That was nice. Funny, too. But the best part? He raps his pencil along the steel table's edge. Oh, yes, finding that cleaning bill. The perfect prop.

Still, it felt a bit too much like work.

Now he wishes he'd taken something, a talisman, a souvenir. He peers across the vast space to what was once a window, now a lopsided, jagged-edged square framing a piece of river like an old photograph.

That's it. A camera. Next time, he'll take the Polaroid with him.

Now he tugs the heavy volume over, skims through the pages. This next one must be more fun.

How to make it both essential and pleasurable?

Such an odd pursuit, pleasure. Had he ever really known any?

As a child it was so elusive—the smell of a cat's burned fur, the parakeet's tiny heart pulsing in his hand. But they were incomplete pleasures. They had no *reason.*

But now his head has begun to ache. He rubs his hands across his forehead, fingers pushing, pulling until the flesh tingles, sits back, breathes in deeply. A moment's respite.

He slides the gloves on, turns the pages with care, stops at a possible prospect. But where would he get all those rifles? No, not viable. Not yet, anyway.

Here's something. Stark. Dramatic. Vivid. He likes that. Thinks the artist will like it, too. Maybe it's too vivid, too good. But does that really matter? After all, the guy's just a pawn, a bit player.

How easy it was to secure the date. Flattery. It never failed—especially with an artist. And the accent was a nice touch.

He pictures the artist in his isolated Hell's Kitchen studio, surrounded by those boring little paintings, slides back in his chair, runs his hand along the pitted wall, his fingers looping over bumps and snags, stopping at the newspaper photo of Kate, his little guardian angel with her graphite wings and halo.

Is he overwhelming her with all this information? He's already given her a lot to think about. How much has she figured out? How much does she understand?

Well, that part is her job. And this time he's not going to make it so easy for her.

He checks his watch. Feels the heat, the hunger stir inside him.

Soon.

"How do you do?" he says aloud, practicing his clipped German accent.

11

Ethan Stein rearranged the copies of his art reviews on the paint-stained table just beside the entrance to his Hell's Kitchen studio. He'd had them enlarged by ten percent—just enough to make them look bigger, more impressive, without the reader's knowing quite why. Too bad they were a few years out of date.

What was it exactly the collector had said over the phone? That he was a "longtime admirer" of Ethan's work? Something like that. Whatever. It was goddamn music to his ears. Mother's milk. And every other cliché Ethan could think of. Lately, he hadn't been hearing many compliments; the collectors and curators were not exactly beating down his doors.

Maybe that's why Ethan had neglected to get any particulars, just that the man saw a painting of Ethan's—where was it again? In another collector's home? Somewhere. What mattered was that the man was coming to the studio "with the intent to buy." That much Stein had heard loud and clear.

Ten years ago he was one of the young turks—a twenty-five-year-old mover and shaker in the world of Post-Minimal Conceptual art, and damn proud of it. But it had been six years since his last New York show. Six long years. Well, that would have to change, and soon. This was a good sign. An omen. And these new paintings were good. Not exactly revolutionary. But that didn't matter. His work had always been about the pure thing, about honesty.

He splashed some turpentine onto his large glass palette. He hadn't painted in a week, but wanted the studio to smell as if he had.

He tried to recall the collector's name while sorting through his CDs, looking for the perfect music, mellow jazz, he decided, that would complement his minimal abstract paintings.

Had the guy even given him a name? He really needed to start paying attention. Maybe it had been something foreign. The man had definitely had an accent.

The artist surveyed his studio just as the sun dropped behind the old McGraw-Hill Building, checked the bottle of Sancerre chilling in his half-sized fridge, quickly dumped Terra chips into a bowl, rearranged his art press for the umpteenth time. He hardly ever stayed late, felt just a bit uncomfortable in the totally deserted building, all the businesses having cleared out at exactly 5:00 P.M., and the street, at night, Eleventh Avenue, so far away from any life. But this was worth waiting for.

The buzzer sounded. Ethan checked his watch—8:00 P.M. The collector, right on time.

When he came back to the conscious world, Ethan Stein wished he had not. He couldn't move his arms or legs, every breath was an effort, his thoughts were muddled, his head ached as though his skull had been shrunk too tight for his brain.

What happened? All he remembered was answering the door.

Oh, right. The hand across his face, the chemical smell, the slightest struggle before the room went black.

Ethan blinked. The man's shoes passed in front of his eyes. He was lying on the floor, his cheek against cheap, paint-splattered linoleum, dust in his nose. The man was whistling.

For a second, the irony sloshed through Ethan's drugged mind—sure, he likes it rough when it's play, but this . . .

The panic rose so quickly, the smell of ether, or something like it, still so strong in his nostrils, that Ethan thought he would surely vomit. *Were those gagging noises coming from him?*

"Calm down."

A voice from above.

Ethan strained to see, but could not move his head.

The man bent down, his face an inch from Ethan's face, features a blur. "This is going to take a while. Relax."

Now the man was on a chair. Ethan could hear him unscrewing floodlights, half the room going dark.

"Patience," the man said.

Ethan's heart pulsated in his ears, sounding like a tennis match in the rain, the ball soggy, leaden. *Plop. Squish. Plop. Squish.* And were those tears on his cheeks? He'd never felt so helpless, so utterly terrified. He felt cold and, looking down at his chest, realized he was naked. His panic rose. There were noises emanating from somewhere deep in his throat, but he couldn't form words. His lips and tongue were thick, immovable.

Now the man was beside him, unfolding a paper, mumbling to himself. Ethan strained to turn his head. Impossible.

The man's hands came into view, the straight razor glinting.

Noooo! But Ethan couldn't scream. The words dribbled out of him, pathetic, just bubbles of spit on his lips.

"I'll start with the leg," the man said, grabbing Ethan by his ankles, hoisting his legs up, arranging it so that Ethan's naked heel was against the back wall wedged between two of his minimal white paintings.

Ethan was hanging upside down now, staring up at the man, but couldn't make him out. The lights' glare had turned the man into a dark silhouette. All he could see was the way the man referred to the paper in his hand just before he started slashing Ethan's calf with the straight razor.

It wasn't the pain that made Ethan faint. He only felt the slightest tug, a sort of pinch. No, it was seeing that the man was plying the razor under the skin, chopping away stubborn muscles and tendons, lifting flesh off bone as if he were skinning a chicken.

12

ARTIST FOUND DEAD IN MIDTOWN
The body of Ethan Stein, 36, was discovered late
last night in his Hell's Kitchen studio by main-
tenance man Joseph Santiago, at 427 West 39th
Street, when the man noticed blood pooling out
from under the artist's studio door.

The murder, which appears to have ritualistic
overtones, is so far baffling the NYPD. The
artist was . . .

Morning light poured through the tall penthouse
windows, dappling across the kitchen counter, Kate's
cup of black coffee, and the *New York Times*.
Ethan Stein. Kate hadn't heard much about him in the
past few years. One of those artists who seemed to fall
through the art world cracks after their style and moment
ceased to be fashionable. Richard had bought a painting
about five or six years ago. It used to hang in the Rothsteins'
living room, was later demoted to a guest room—a small,

minimal piece, layers of white and off-white paint built up with palette knife and brush, the faintest grid of gray. Nice. Not terribly exciting. Now it made Kate sad that they had never kept up with the artist, or that they moved his painting, or . . . she wasn't sure. A life cut short was always tragic. But ritualistic overtones? Blood under the door? *Jesus*.

Her head ached. Those ninety-proof martinis with Winnie Pruitt, topped off by a couple of glasses of cabernet with Richard's clients last night. Kate could barely make conversation. Not like her. And Richard noted it. More than once. It was not as if she didn't want to be sociable, but her mind was obsessed with that collage, and with the idea that Bill Pruitt could have been dealing in stolen art.

She slid the Metro Section aside, was about to look at the Dining In section when the photo slipped onto the counter.

A Polaroid, almost totally white, the faintest suggestion of an image, something gray and out of focus in the corner.

What's this? She studied it a moment. Could it possibly have gotten stuck, accidentally, inside her newspaper? A week ago she might have thought so. Not now.

Kate washed down two Excedrin, quickly got the cordless under her chin. A call to Richard.

"Sorry, Mrs. R. He's in a meeting." Richard's true-blue secretary.

"Just tell him I called, Anne-Marie."

"Sure thing. And thanks for the fudge. It was yummy."

"Hey, you deserve it—and don't you share one bit," said Kate, who intended to keep that woman working in Richard's office well past retirement age. She also intended to maintain Anne-Marie's plus-size figure. Handmade truffles for Valentine's Day. Candy canes and pound cake at Christmas. Even a five-pound chocolate turkey at Thanksgiving. "Tell him to call me, okay? Thanks."

But enough small talk. Her hands were shaking.

Kate lifted the Polaroid for a closer look, but there was nothing to see. It was mostly white with a hint of gray, a complete blur. She put it down, reached for her coffee, and stopped. The Polaroid, resting just beneath the banner of Ethan Stein's murder, was suddenly a juxtaposition so compelling, she was on her feet.

Jesus, was this from him? How had he gotten to her newspaper? The thought was almost too chilling to consider.

In the guest room, Kate held the Polaroid beside Ethan Stein's minimal painting. She couldn't be sure, but yes, a definite similarity—the whiteness, the hint of gray.

In her office, she rubbed sleep from her eyes, trained the magnifying glass on the photo. *Brush strokes.* It *was* a painting.

The graduation photo. That was first.

Then the Madonna and Child collage.

Now this.

True, there was no way actually to connect the Polaroid to Ethan Stein, but the similarity and coincidence—after two other missives—had her hands shaking.

Why were these things being sent to her? Was there a connection, or was her mind, so distressed by Elena's death, creating mysteries where there were none?

No. Kate was sure it was something. It was the kind of feeling the young Detective McKinnon used to get.

Time to see Tapell, but first some validation.

Kate threw on a pair of slacks, a silk blouse, ran a brush through her hair, and didn't bother with makeup.

Kate slid into the coffee-shop booth. "Thanks for meeting me, Liz."

"That's okay. Anything to get away from the twelve-year-old computer instructor who's been shouting at me for days like I'm some kind of idiot." Liz peered at her friend over the rim of her coffee cup. "So what's up, Kate? You didn't ask me to scoot out of FBI headquarters just to share a cup of joe and tell me how great I am."

"Well, I might have, but . . ." She pushed her hair behind her ears, got serious. "Remember the graduation photo—me and Elena?"

"Attached to your nicotine patch?"

"Exactly. Well, there've been others." Kate laid them on the table: a copy of the Madonna and Child collage, the Polaroid, which she thought was somehow related to Ethan Stein's paintings and possibly his murder. "These were sent to me. I think *meant* for me, Liz." Kate tried to control the slight tremor in her fingertips.

"What do you mean?" asked Liz.

"Well, the graduation photo is clearly Elena, and . . . she's dead. The collage is an altarpiece that may have belonged to Bill Pruitt, also dead. And the Polaroid looks suspiciously like an Ethan Stein painting, and he . . ." Kate took a breath.

"The artist who was killed. I just read about that." Liz looked from one image to the other, concern spreading across her face.

"It's all starting to scare the shit out of me." Kate massaged the tight muscles at the base of her skull.

"Well, it should scare you. I mean, if someone's trying to contact you . . ." Liz's eyes narrowed. "This is serious, Kate. You've got to tell someone about it—and I mean *now*."

"I'm going to see Clare Tapell." Kate stopped rubbing her neck, started playing with the fine gold chain at her throat.

"Chief of police. Good idea."

"But what if I'm totally overreacting—that it's just some crank?" Kate released the chain, started tapping her fingernails along the table's edge.

"Hey, do me a favor." Liz pointed a finger at Kate. "Just go. It could be a crank, but it could also be someone who wants to do you damage."

"Me?" Kate forced a laugh, but her fingers did not stop tapping. "I'm way too tough for anyone to mess with."

"Kate." Liz laid a hand over Kate's nervously tapping fingers. Her blue eyes had no humor in them at all. "I've been dealing with this kind of stuff for the past ten years. If there's a psycho out there, and he's targeted you—" She shook her head. "These guys are tenacious little bastards, real hunters—"

"Hunters?" Kate tried hard to maintain her cool, but there was a riot brewing in her gut.

"Most killers—the serial variety—come to hunting humans gradually, but hunt they do." Liz looked up, her blue eyes gone dark. "As young boys they have rather undirected anger, violence against small animals, occasionally other kids. But as their fantasy worlds grow and take shape, they start to focus on what really gets them off. That's when they start hunting—for *worthy* victims."

"Oh, I swear, Liz, I'm not worthy."

"I know you, Kate McKinnon. Trying to act all brave and sassy." Liz frowned again. "All I'm saying is that these guys look for someone to work out their violent fantasies on— they're sick fucks who love getting off on the game, and—"

"I can take care of myself." Kate laced her fingers together to keep them from tapping.

"Designer heels are not made for chasing felons, *Ex*-Detective McKinnon." Liz pinched the bridge of her nose. "Sorry, that was below the belt."

"*Way* below," said Kate. "I do not like any references to my size twelves—designer or otherwise."

"Personally, I'd prefer if you stuck to figuring out art."

"I never said I was giving up art—or the foundation—or anything else, for that matter. But I can't walk away from this, Liz. I won't. This all has something to do with me, and maybe even the art world. I don't know what yet, but *something*." Kate effected an unconvincing smile, patted her friend's hand. "Relax. I'll go see Tapell. Right now."

The red brick, slightly Mayan cube of a building brought back some memories: a couple of meetings after she had made detective, seminars with that criminal psychologist on the pathology of the runaway. Kate McKinnon, Astoria cop, did not spend all that much time at One Police Plaza, but she knew the place—the surrounding maze of walkways and plazas, the startling views of the Criminal Court buildings, City Hall, all framed through archways, cop cars, and vans ringing the complex like an irregular chrome necklace.

The lobby was something out of a poor man's Leni Riefenstahl propaganda film: flags, statues, banners, slogans—COURTESY, PROFESSIONALISM, RESPECT—and guards everywhere you looked.

Kate signed in, went through the metal detector, twice—her keys and a Zippo lighter setting it off—finally into the elevator, the whole time anxious to keep moving, explain to Tapell what she thought was going on.

Kate spread everything out on Tapell's desk: the graduation photo of Elena with her painted eyelids, the collage and enlargements made at Mert's gallery of the Madonna and Child, the Polaroid that she thought looked suspiciously like an Ethan Stein painting.

She tapped the graduation photo. "I got this just before Elena Solana was killed—no, after. I mean, I hadn't yet realized that Elena was dead when I got it."

"You got it—*how?*"

"I'm not sure. I think it was planted on me. It was in my bag, my purse."

Tapell arched an eyebrow.

"The collage was delivered to my apartment. The enlargements are made from it. It's a religious altarpiece, possibly stolen, and it may have belonged to Bill Pruitt."

The line between Tapell's eyebrows deepened. "William Pruitt? Stolen from him?"

"Yes. But he may have stolen it, too. Well, not exactly. I mean, he may have bought it knowing it was stolen."

"What are you talking about, Kate?"

Okay, slow down. "Was I a good cop, Clare?"

"Absolutely."

"Okay. Then bear with me a minute." Kate took a breath. "What I was trying to say is that Pruitt may have had the altarpiece in his possession, and now whoever killed him might have it." She shook a cigarette out of her bag.

"Smoke-free building," said Tapell.

Kate crumbled the cigarette into Tapell's trash can. "The Polaroid I just got, the morning after Ethan Stein was murdered—and it looks suspiciously like one of his paintings."

"How did you get it—the Polaroid, I mean?"

"It was inside my morning paper."

"Jesus." Tapell shook her head. "So what you're telling me, Kate, is that a killer—or possibly three different killers—are communicating with you?" Tapell's eyes widened with disbelief.

"No. That wouldn't make sense."

"Well, thank God. I was afraid you'd lost it."

"It would have to be *one* killer."

Tapell's mouth opened, then shut, her lips disappearing into a tight line. "Do you have any idea of what you're implying, Kate? I don't know every detail of these cases. But I can tell you the MO for each is totally different. So you're way off base here."

"Look, there's a possible connection between the victims—Elena Solana and Ethan Stein were both artists, and Bill Pruitt was chairman of a museum board. It *could* be one killer. That's all I'm saying—and it's a connection some reporter might make, too."

"Jesus, Kate." Tapell tugged at the flesh of her neck. "You're suggesting a serial killer. You realize that?"

Kate leveled a hard stare at Tapell. "I realize that there were three deaths and someone might be contacting me about them."

"If that's true, I want a guard on you twenty-four-seven, but—" Tapell paced the length of her spare office. She did not want to consider what Kate was saying, but history had proved Kate's feelings were often on target. "It could be a crank. You're a public person."

"Yes. I've considered that. What are your homicide people telling you about the murders?"

Tapell stopped pacing, leaned back against her desk,

sagged a bit. "Nothing much. But Pruitt's death could have been accidental."

"Maybe. Look, Clare, I'm not saying I have any answers here, just that . . . well, you wanted more than a feeling— and this psycho is providing one. I should be working with your homicide people, advising or—"

Tapell sagged into the chair behind her desk. "The idea of a serial killer . . ." She sighed deeply. "God. You'd better have a look at those case files."

13

A hundred bucks' worth of corkboard from Gracious Home was plastered over one entire wall of Kate's home office. Another hundred had gone to the delivery guy who had stuck the cork panels up for her. Sure, she could have done it herself, but her rationalization was good—spread the wealth.

It took only a few minutes for Kate to pin up her collection of images: the creepy graduation picture with the painted-over eyelids, the collage of the Madonna and Child, the enlargements she had made with Mert, one blurry Polaroid.

She was doing it just the way she used to do it back in Astoria—photographs, scraps of evidence, notes, all tacked up like an exhibition. She always needed to see everything. To look, and look again. She could still see her old wall of missing kids—those sweet young faces.

She moved from one image to the next. Nothing at all similar about them, and yet . . .

Kate opened the brown cardboard accordion file, removed three off-white folders stamped NYPD, laid them on her desk. Her fingertips played along the edge of the first folder. If only they'd indicated the cases on the outside. She'd rather not open Elena's first.

But she was starting to get that feeling, too, adrenaline pulsing into her bloodstream, nerve ends tingling, a mix of excitement and dread.

WILLIAM M. PRUITT

Good. She could handle this.

She noted the toxicology report, contents of Pruitt's stomach: a heady mix of drugs and alcohol. *Pruitt?* She wouldn't have suspected drugs. Was it enough for him to drown in his tub? Time of death was set between midnight and 4:00 A.M.

Along with the report, an envelope of startling color photos—the man dead in his tub from every angle. A few close-ups of his face—mouth stretched in agony, a purplish bruise on his chin. Kate pinned them all to the wall, stepped back, then forward, moved from one photo to the next. Something nagged at her— *What is it?*

And what was that in Pruitt's hand?

Kate laid her magnifying glass above the photo.

A dry-cleaning bill? Now that was bizarre.

She hadn't a clue what to make of it.

She moved to the next folder.

ETHAN STEIN

CAUSE OF DEATH: LOSS OF BLOOD. TRACES OF CHLOROFORM ON THE VICTIM'S NOSTRILS, LIPS.

FIBERS IN HIS NOSE

TOXICOLOGY—pending

A rag dipped in knockout drops held to the victim's face. Kate could picture it, though she was not quite prepared for the photos. The studio floor a sea of red, the artist naked, on his back, leg propped up, or what was left of it—it looked like a bloody stick—half of Stein's chest, too, maroon red, exposed muscle like steak in a butcher's shop. *And is that bone?*

Kate steadied herself, a hand on the edge of her desk for support. She scanned the report for the details: "Victim's right leg and left pectoral, skinned."

Skinned?

She forced herself to look at the pictures again. Ethan Stein's face was a mask of excruciating pain. *Jesus Christ. Skinned . . . alive?* The report didn't say, though the tremendous amount of blood loss—the heart still pumping at full speed—might indicate it.

Why such brutality?

Kate pinned Stein's gruesome crime scene photos beside the ones of Pruitt, noted the dramatic lighting: half of Stein's destroyed body bleached bright, the other half plunged into inky darkness.

Again, she stopped: There was definitely something oddly familiar about this scene, too. *But how could that be?*

Okay. Elena's file. Kate could not delay it any longer.

The particulars of Elena's death—temperature of the body, a few facial contusions, multiple stab wounds—added nothing to what Kate already knew. She dumped the envelope of photos onto her desk. They scattered like mini-sleds on ice, one skittering off the edge, corkscrewing to the floor. Did it have to be a close-up of Elena's face? Kate stared at the odd pattern of blood along the girl's cheek, then at a shot of the full body collapsed at the foot of the half-size refrigerator.

She arranged them all on the wall without really looking, then stood back, lit a Marlboro, glad for the veil of smoke which snaked in front of her eyes. She was reminded of those Goya prints in Mert's gallery. Was she too close to see what was going on here, too?

Kate fanned the smoke away, studied the grim gallery of photos. There was something here. She was sure of it. *But what?*

She got her magnifying glass, ran it over all the photos,

stopped at a tiny picture of a violin stuck to the surface of one of Ethan Stein's paintings. Odd. Was the artist branching out into imagery? It didn't really make sense.

For twenty minutes Kate went from one photo to the next, peering through the magnifying glass, but nothing clicked. All she was getting was eyestrain and a headache.

In her Carrara marble bathroom, Kate adjusted the antique brass bath taps, added a few capfuls of an aromatherapy gel to the oversized tub. She peeled off her clothes, tossed them onto her bed, grabbed the latest *New Yorker* off her night table. The soak would do her good.

The bathroom was already steamed up, the damp air permeated with the smell of hyacinth. Kate tested the water with a toe, stopped short.

The tub!

She threw on her terry robe, charged down the hallway.

In the library, she yanked books from shelves, tossed them onto the leather couch, a few tumbled to the floor. Finally, the one she was looking for, a venerable old tome. She tucked it under her arm, raced back to her office, started flipping pages so fast they tore.

Okay. Calm down. The index. *Right.* Kate could barely turn the pages now, her hands were trembling so. But there it was, the famous historical painting, one that Kate had studied in college, even wrote a goddamn paper about: Jacques-Louis David's *The Death of Marat.*

Bull's-eye.

Marat, the man in the painting, dead, his head cradled by a towel, leaning back against the rim of the tub. Kate's eyes ricocheted between the photos of Bill Pruitt pinned on her wall to the image in the book. Both heads—Pruitt's, Marat's—in the identical position; Pruitt's arm draped over the side of the tub exactly like Marat's. Kate's eyes were ping-ponging back and forth. Pruitt even had a piece of paper in his hand, just like Marat. *Jesus, how could I have missed it?* Kate tore the page right out of the book.

Now she eyed the grotesque photos of Ethan Stein. Yes,

this was familiar, too. But what, exactly? She flipped more pages, but nothing registered.

Down the hall again, in the library, she was momentarily stymied. So many books. *Think. Think.* Her eyes skimmed over row after row—books, journals, magazines, periodicals—but nothing came to her.

She dashed back to her office, plucked two of the Ethan Stein crime scene photos from the wall, snatched the report, too, reread it as she hurried back to the library. There was definitely something there. But what? *What?*

All those books were beginning to feel more intimidating than helpful.

Kate took a breath, sagged on the office's small leather couch. She needed to stop a minute, to think clearly. She stared at the photos in her hand—the artist on his back, naked, the skinned leg and torso. *Skinned. That's it!*

Barefoot, on the step stool, she wrestled the huge volume, *Renaissance Painting in Italy,* from an upper shelf, lugged it back to her office. Then she got all the Ethan Stein crime photos fanned out on the floor beside the book, riffling pages so fast the images were doing the jitterbug. There it was. Another goddamn bull's-eye. The great Renaissance painter Titian, *The Flaying of Marsyas.* A horrifying scene, the man being skinned alive—exactly like Ethan Stein. Kate noted the crime scene picture of Stein, then the painting, both figures naked, strung up, the skin of the leg half removed. And the violin. Of course. That clinched it. In Titian's painting, Apollo plays the violin while Marsyas is being flayed.

Jesus, this guy was a stickler for detail.

Shit. Kate sat back on her heels, took it all in. It *was* about art.

Now, if she was right about Pruitt and Stein, the same must be true of Elena. But here she was stumped. Elena's crime scene photos offered up nothing more than heartache.

Back in the library, Kate scanned the shelves—book after book about painting, art history, individual artists, the titles beginning to blur.

She needed another break, settled onto one of the living room couches, closed her eyes, tried to erase any thoughts, all images. *Okay. Breathe. That's it.* Eyes open, Kate's vision drifted slowly across one of Willie's assemblages, a couple of Richard's religious altarpieces, a large abstract painting, finally coming to rest on their prized Picasso, the one-eyed self-portrait.

Holy shit!

Kate bolted down the hall, snatched the close-up of Elena's butchered face, raced back, held the crime scene photo beside the Picasso with a shaky hand. A dead ringer. The Picasso profile replicated—forehead, nose, and chin— down the side of Elena's cheek in a wavy line of blood.

Kate froze. *My God, has he been here, in my house, seen the painting?*

She whisked the large *Picasso & Portraiture* catalog off the antique brass music stand just beside the portrait, riffled pages until she found the reproduction: *Self-portrait. 1901. Oil on canvas. Collection Mr. and Mrs. Richard Rothstein.*

Kate breathed a small sigh of relief. *Of course.* She and Richard would be identified as the owners of the portrait in any recent book on Picasso.

But then he chose the image knowing it was my painting. Why?

That she couldn't answer. Not yet. She felt as though she were on an adrenaline IV. She wanted to call Richard, tell him what she'd figured out. But she was speeding. She'd tell him later. She gathered everything up. Tapell had to see this.

A couple of minutes for Kate to line up the crime scene photos beside the paintings she'd selected. Ten minutes to spell out her theory.

Tapell took it all in. "You're absolutely sure?" she asked, knowing the answer, just not wanting to admit it.

Kate nodded. "As sure as I can be, Clare."

The two old colleagues locked eyes.

"All right." Tapell exhaled. "You'll have to explain it all

again to the Special Homicide Task Force." She surveyed the photos and pages Kate had torn from books one more time. "I'll make the call."

Kate only half listened while Tapell was on the phone, her adrenaline still pumping madly.

"It's set," said Tapell, replacing the phone. "You can work along with Mead's squad—*unofficially*. Naturally, the man's not thrilled with the idea, but I didn't give him a choice. You'll have to demonstrate to him what you can add to the investigation."

"Thanks, Clare. I—"

"You'll have to play by Mead's rules. And no heroics, okay?"

Kate nodded.

The chief of police gave her a solemn look. "I don't want the press to get wind of this. Not a word, Kate. We just got the goddamn Central Park Shooter out of the way. The last thing this city needs is talk of another serial killer."

entral Booking was too familiar. A lot bigger than
Kate's old Astoria station, but the story was the same,
even the same stale air—smoke, sweat, day-old
bologna sandwiches, bad coffee.

Kate paced. It was clearly Randy Mead's idea of how to
show her who was boss. She took in the greasy-haired guy
handcuffed to the leg of the nearby metal desk: the crude
blue-black tattoo on his forearm, a really lousy drawing of
an eagle, and, just below it, a lopsided heart with a name—
Rita?—barely legible inside. Across from him, a tired-look-
ing cop asked rote questions, typed with two fingers.

The place had that curious buzz—activity devoid of life.
Detectives and uniforms parading the usual perps—hookers,
druggies, small-time hoods—through rows of metal desks
into small cubicles, or past them into holding tanks; felons
screaming about their rights or so drugged the cops had to
drag them.

". . . motherfucker, cocksucker, asshole, faggot, junkie,
whore . . ."

The words floated on top of the stale air like funky
Muzak.

Two woman cops, detectives in plain clothes, looked Kate
over. She returned their stares until they looked away, then

shoved her hands deep into the pockets of the designer jacket she was sorry she had worn here.

She wished Tapell had come with her, made the introductions personally.

"McKinnon?" The uniform looked as if he'd just graduated from the Academy. Kate nodded. "The squad's ready for ya."

The conference room was gray and beige, someone's idea of sober, serious decor, but it was simply depressing. The overhead fluorescents bathed everything in a cold bluish light. The only "life" in the room snaked out of about thirty color crime scene photos pinned to a corkboard wall—ashen bodies enlivened with purple bruises and maroon wine blood. Among them Solana, Pruitt, Stein—three bodies Kate had become too familiar with. She sat back in a stiff metal chair, rapped her fingers on the folder she had brought with her, tried hard not to eyeball the other detectives whom Tapell had summed up in one-minute histories.

Floyd Brown: ace homicide cop, difficult by reputation, a lifer.

Maureen Slattery: formerly of vice, two years with the Special Homicide Squad, smart, tenacious.

Kate took in Detective Slattery's teased blond bob, bubble-gum-pink lipstick outlined in cherry red, asked, "How long you been in homicide?" even though she knew the answer. Something to break the ice.

"Two years," Slattery answered, not much emotion in her Brooklyn- or Queens-tainted speech. "I did a nickel in vice before this."

"Five years is a long time in hot pants and halter tops." Kate smiled.

Slattery rolled her eyes, something wary pulling at the corners of her mouth. "Tell me about it." The way Maureen Slattery saw it, homicide might not be all that different from vice, except that here the men wouldn't be looking at her ass. She took in Kate's expensive blazer, the grooming that went along with privilege, wondered why this obvious up-town gal was slumming.

Floyd Brown leaned against the far wall sipping coffee from a styrofoam cup, his eyes skirting the rim. When Kate was introduced, he nodded. Barely.

Randy Mead bolted into the room with a stack of manila file folders under his arm. "So, everybody get acquainted?" He swallowed, and his Adam's apple did a little dance just above his bow tie, this one with blue polka dots, which, Kate thought, made him look about twelve. He made that teeth-sucking noise she remembered too well from their first meeting. He threw Kate a sideways glance. "McKinnon, here, has got a little theory that Chief Tapell wants her to share with us."

Kate decided to ignore the condescension in Mead's tone. "First of all," she said, "I'm here unofficially—but on Clare Tapell's authority." She let that sink in, then: "For the record, I was a cop, in Astoria, for over a decade."

"Wait a minute." Brown shook his head, confused. "Aren't you the art lady from Channel Thirteen?"

Kate smiled. "I had a series about art, on PBS, yes."

Maureen stared at her blankly. She'd obviously never seen it.

"So you're here . . . why?" Brown asked.

"I think that will become obvious, Detective Brown." Kate opened her folder, placed a Pruitt crime scene photo beside the image torn from her book. "What you are looking at is *The Death of Marat,* a famous eighteenth-century painting by Jacques-Louis David. Note the similarities. Not just the tub, but how Pruitt's head is cradled by the towel, the way his arms are placed, just like Marat's. Pruitt even has a note in hand, as does Marat in the painting."

Brown leaned in.

"The fucking laundry list," said Slattery. "Like Pruitt was just sitting there, reading his goddamn laundry list, and had a heart attack—"

"But it's no heart attack," said Kate. "I'm sure of that. The laundry list is merely a prop."

"Staged," Brown mumbled, almost to himself.

Slattery asked, "Why's he in the bath, this Marat guy, in the painting?"

"A nasty skin condition," said Kate. "He had to stay immersed in his bath because of the pain."

Mead sucked his teeth again. "Any significance between Pruitt and the guy in the painting?"

Kate thought a moment. "Well . . . Marat was a political leader in the French Revolution, and Pruitt was a museum president. Maybe it's that the two guys were leaders." She thought again. "And one could say that the Contemporary Museum is somewhat revolutionary."

Mead appeared to take this in. Brown made a note.

Now Kate laid an Ethan Stein crime scene photo on the conference table beside the picture she'd torn from her book on Renaissance painting. "This one's by Titian. It's called *The Flaying of Marsyas.*"

"Damn." Brown eyed both sets of pictures.

"The crime scenes are very carefully staged," said Kate. She sat back, waited until all three sets of eyes were on her. "The guy is making art. Living tableaux—except that they're not living. They're re-creations."

"But *why?*" Mead pressed.

"When you catch him," said Kate, "ask."

"So," said Brown, looking at one picture, then another. "Our killer knows something about art."

"Yes. But anyone with art book or poster could stage the scenes." Kate tapped her lip. "I was just thinking . . . In the Titian painting, Marsyas gets flayed because of his vanity. Perhaps that's another message. You know, the vain artist."

"Poor bastard," said Maureen Slattery. "So what'd this guy, Marsyas, do?"

"He challenged the god Apollo to a music contest—and lost."

"Tough crowd," said Slattery.

Kate regarded the mask of horror on the dead artist's face.

"What tipped me off was the skinning, the flaying. Just like in the painting. Also the little picture of a violin stuck onto Stein's painting." Kate pointed it out in the photo. "You can see it clearly under a magnifier. I'm sure the killer put it there. Did anyone take it?"

"It's probably still there," said Brown. "We'll get it."

Kate looked back at Stein's file. "I'd also guess that when you get the toxicology report, there's going to be some kind of paralyzing drug in Stein's veins. No one could sit still for that." She turned to Mead. "Did your crime scene boys notice anything about the lights in Stein's studio?"

"What do you mean?"

"I think the killer was aping the painting right down to the chiaroscuro."

"The *who*?" Maureen frowned.

"The intense black-and-white side lighting. Rembrandt used it. So did Caravaggio. A lot of painters have. Titian uses it for dramatic effect." Kate placed another one of the crime scene photos of Stein's body on the table. "I think if you revisit the Stein scene, you'll find that half of the spotlights in the studio have been unscrewed or unplugged."

Maureen made a note. "We'll check it out."

"So, if you're right, then we're looking at the same unsub for Pruitt *and* Stein," said Brown.

Unsub? Oh, right. Unknown subject. "Yes," said Kate.

Brown said something to Slattery, the two of them whispering.

Mead put up a hand to silence them. "Look, no one is saying anything definite here. Let's not go jumping on any serial-killer bandwagons—not just yet." He offered Kate what she guessed was a look of sincerity. "I know Tapell thinks you're onto something, and hey, maybe you are, but we gotta substantiate everything—and I mean *everything*—before we go saying serial."

"I absolutely agree," said Kate.

"Good. Now what about Solana?"

"Also staged," said Kate. "Though you might say it's a bit

more subtle." She strained to sound matter-of-fact as she opened the *Picasso & Portraiture* book to the one-eyed self-portrait. She selected the crime scene photo close-up of Elena's face, laid it beside the Picasso self-portrait. "Notice that the Picasso portrait has two faces in one—a full face and a profile right down the middle. The killer has selected the profile, which he's painted along Elena Solana's cheek."

"In blood," said Brown. "Economical."

"Or maybe he wasn't quite prepared," said Kate.

"What's with the one eye?" asked Slattery. "Any significance?"

For a moment Kate realized it could have been worse— that the psycho could have gouged out Elena's eye if he'd wanted to replicate the entire portrait. *Thank God for small blessings.* "Picasso tended to paint fast," said Kate. "When he felt as though he'd painted enough, gotten his message across, he'd just stop, move on to another painting. He left studios, *houses,* filled with paintings in all states of what you might consider unfinished." She paused. "Maybe that's also true with the killer—that he felt he'd left us *enough* of a message." Kate paused again. "But the choice of this particular Picasso is significant because . . . it's *my* painting."

"What do you mean, *yours*?" Mead's small eyes narrowed.

"I mean, I own it. It's in my living room."

Brown looked alarmed. "You mean this guy's been in your house?"

Kate put up a hand. "I thought that too, but look at the book. It's right there, my name, the fact that I own it." Kate couldn't stop looking at the profile in blood on Elena's cheek. "I don't know why, but I think he chose it for that very reason—that it's mine."

Mead leaned toward her. "You got any enemies, McKinnon?"

"Half the art world, I imagine."

Slattery cocked her head toward Kate. "Why's that?"

"My art book was a bit unconventional—and way too

popular. Then the PBS series." Kate shrugged her shoulders. "Success. It breeds envy—and enemies. Maybe." Kate looked from one crime scene photo to the next— Elena, Bill Pruitt, Ethan Stein. "There are just too many connections here," she said. "Elena was a graduate of Let There Be a Future, and William Mason Pruitt was not only on the board of Let There Be a Future, but also served as its financial adviser. Plus, he was president of the board of the Museum of Contemporary Art, which was the last place Elena Solana was seen . . . alive." Kate faltered a moment. "I should add that I'm also on that board and that I knew the victim—Elena Solana—well." She paused. "But you already know I was one of the people to find the body."

For the next twenty minutes the squad reviewed the grizzly details of Elena Solana's murder: the seventeen stab wounds, the position of the body, the lack of fingerprints.

Kate surprised herself at how she could listen to it all, as though it were any ordinary case. Funny, she thought, how quickly the cop thing kicked in, the ability to detach.

"There's evidence here to suggest you're dealing with a very *organized* killer," she offered. "Not only does he take his time with the crime scenes, but he cleans up. And according to your tech boys, he left no prints. And I'd say that both the Pruitt and Stein murders took some serious planning, too."

"I agree." Brown tilted his head in her direction, narrowed his eyes. "But why do *you* say that?"

"You ever try to slip past a Park Avenue doorman, Detective Brown? Not easy. If someone wanted access to Bill Pruitt's building they would have to know when the doormen switched shifts, or waited, possibly for hours, for the doorman to leave his post, and then slip in. It would take planning or patience—or both. As for Stein, well . . . who's seen his place?"

Brown nodded. "Gates on the windows. Police lock on the front door. Neither tampered with or broken."

"So Stein let the killer in—which is what I'd guess about Solana."

"Unless Solana is a crime of passion," Slattery offered. "You said before that the unsub may not have been prepared."

"Or the girl could have been hooking," said Mead.

Elena? Hooking? Mead's words shot through Kate like amphetamine.

The other detectives turned toward her, waiting to see what she would say, do. She'd already told them she had been close to Elena, and now, she guessed, they wanted to see if she could take it.

Kate gripped the edge of the metal table. "Maureen, you searched the apartment. Did you find any sexy outfits?"

"Mostly flannel PJs."

"I see. How about a little black book with lots of initialed appointments? Anything like that?" Under the table, Kate's foot was tapping.

Maureen shook her head.

"And the contents of the medicine cabinet? Any condoms, poppers, amyl nitrite, ludes, ecstasy, that sort of thing?"

"No. Nothing."

"Very tame hooker." Kate locked her eyes on the young blond policewoman. "You said you worked vice for five years, so you would recognize a prostitute's apartment, yes?"

Mead cut in. "We get your point, McKinnon." He offered up a cheesy smile. "All I'm suggesting here is that your scholarship girl might not be so squeaky clean."

Brown displayed a sheet of paper from the Solana file. "Your statement here says you were with Solana earlier that evening, before she got killed."

"Not together per se." Kate felt the slightest crack in her armor. *The amphitheater, Elena onstage, alive.* "She gave a performance. At the Museum of Contemporary Art, which I attended."

"Says you left her around nine."

The quickest good-bye. A kiss good night. "Yes. Right after her performance. We had planned to go out for dinner, but Elena was tired and—" *Elena's broken body. A pool of congealed blood edging into cracked linoleum tiles.* Kate almost gasped, the image so vivid in her mind. She took a deep breath. "It was a few days later that I, we, that is, me and Willie Handley, found her body."

"So, let me get this straight," said Brown, scanning one file, then the other. "You knew both vics—Solana and Pruitt."

Kate blinked. "Yes. That's right."

"What about Stein?"

"I didn't know him, but I own one of his paintings."

"You seem to know everyone, McKinnon." Mead's tiny eyes narrowed even more.

"Not everyone. I don't think I ever met Ethan Stein, though I may have, in passing—because of my art-world connections." Kate took another breath. "There's more." She slid the graduation photo onto the table. "This was somehow planted on me. It's of me and Elena Solana. I got it before she was killed. That is, before I *knew* she was killed. Look closely. Her eyes—"

"Better get it to the lab," said Mead.

"I also have these." Kate laid out the blurry Polaroid, the collage, the enlarged fragments of the Madonna and Child, explained how they were sent to her, what she thought they meant.

"Why *you*?" asked Brown.

"That I don't know."

Mead's mouth had gotten even tighter. Is this why the chief of police had sent her to him—for baby-sitting? "You show these to Chief Tapell?"

"Of course."

"Well . . ." He sucked his teeth again. "We'd better get a tap on your phones—and a guard at your place." He scribbled a note.

"Tapell's already seen to that," said Kate.

"If McKinnon is right," said Brown, "we should be talking to everyone in the New York art world."

"I agree," said Kate. She offered up a *Gallery Guide*. "A list of every gallery and museum in the city, by area." She nodded at Mead. "I'd send uniforms around for statements from every one of them."

"Would you?" Mead gave her another lipless smile. "Well, thanks, McKinnon. But let's just pinpoint the obvious first. That okay with you?"

"I think we should do them all," said Brown, flipping through the *Gallery Guide*.

"Maybe you've got the time to question every little art world gofer." Mead tugged at his bow tie. "But I'm dealing with a dozen other cases and don't have the manpower."

"Look," said Kate. "I'm here to help, not hinder. But you've already got three bodies. You really want to go for four?" She glanced at Brown and Slattery. "I can start with the staff of the Contemporary Museum, because I know them."

"I already got statements from them," said Slattery. "Since that was Solana's last stop."

"Good work." Kate offered the young detective a smile. "But if you don't mind, I'd like to talk with them, too."

First one painting, then another fills the small screen, each somewhat fragmented, all intensely colored.

The camera pulls back, reveals the paintings on a museum wall, a woman walking slowly down a ramp, white silk blouse, black slacks, hair loose around her shoulders.

His breath catches in his throat.

"Les Fauves," says the striking woman on the screen, an earnest look, eyes on the camera, warm, inviting, intelligent. "That's French for wild beasts." She smiles.

He smiles, too. *Wild beasts*. He likes the sound of that.

"And it was not a complimentary term," she says, eyebrows arched. "It was attached to a group of artists—Matisse, Derain, Vlaminck, Marquet—simply because their work was different, uninhibited. So different that the paintings were put into a room all by themselves, isolated from the more conventional art at the Parisian Salon d'Automne in 1905. The paintings were so bold, so . . . powerful that they actually incited fury in others."

Different. Uninhibited. Isolated. Oh, God, how she understands him. "Yes," he whispers at the small screen. "I hear you."

" 'Color for color's sake,' said the painter André Derain." She gestures at one painting, then another. "You see, it's all about color—heightened, exaggerated, distorted. Gaudy purples, bright pinks, acid greens, blood reds."

Blood reds. It brings him back to Ethan Stein, the floor of the artist's studio. So beautiful.

"My name is Katherine McKinnon Rothstein. And this is . . . *Artists' Lives.*" The camera zooms in for a close-up.

He moves in, too, skin picking up electric static from the TV screen, so close he believes he can smell her perfume, feel her incredible warmth.

He freezes the frame.

Kate's smiling face hovers, a shimmering pixilated-dot screen of color, more Impressionist than Fauve.

He slides his cheek against hers.

15

Schuyler Mills, senior curator at the Museum of Contemporary Art, had a headache. Was it the fact that no one—absolutely no one—at the museum appreciated him? Or was he just light-headed from skipping one too many meals and overdoing it at the gym this week? He flexed his biceps, pleased. Wouldn't his high school chums be surprised! *Lardo,* they used to call him. Well, forget that. There wasn't an extra ounce of fat on Mills's six-foot frame.

Now he checked his reflection in the glass as he headed into the museum, straightened his blue-and-red-striped tie. He looked great. Distinguished, too, with his prematurely gray hair.

If only the museum would understand his worth. Not that anyone ever had. Even back in art school it was the other students, the ones who could dazzle with a quick splash of paint, that got the professors' attention. Probably why he switched to art history.

Schuyler passed through the reception area not bothering to say hello to that new girl they'd hired—the one with the pierced nose, lip, and God-knew-where-else. Whose decision had *that* been? And then, to make matters worse, he stepped into the elevator at precisely the same moment as his colleague, his *junior* colleague, Raphael Perez. He couldn't believe his poor timing.

The two men just barely nodded at each other.

Mills smoothed back his hair; Perez played with a set of keys in the pocket of his sleek Andrew Fezza blazer.

"New jacket?" Mills asked.

"Yes." Perez ran his long fingers along the double-breasted lapels. "If you must know. Brand-new."

"So that's where you were all day yesterday, *shopping*."

"I was busy," Perez hissed through tight lips, "with art business—*outside* of the museum walls. I do not subscribe to that curious old notion that a curator should spend his days locked in an ivory tower. There's a *fabulous* world out there: young artists, new things happening. But I don't imagine you know about that—or care to. You're too busy, what—*reading*?"

"You would if you could," said Mills. "No, I was *writing*. Comments for my talk at the Venice Biennale. I want to say something meaningful about American art today—not simply spout New Age rhetoric." He smiled, mean.

Perez stared at the floor-indicator panel, spied Mills's reflection in the polished steel doors. He felt like smashing the man right in his arrogant face, but wouldn't dare. He'd caught a glimpse of Mills in a polo shirt, the bulging muscles; and though Raphael Perez, at twenty-seven, might have almost twenty years on the man, Mills, he was pretty sure, was stronger. *Damn it*. He sneered a smile at his colleague.

The elevator doors opened. The two men hesitated.

"After you," said Perez.

Schuyler Mills sauntered ahead of him thinking that was exactly the way it was and always would be: Raphael Perez *after* him.

Kate pushed through the elegant smoked-glass doors at the Fifty-seventh Street entrance to the New York Museum of Contemporary Art—the last place she had seen Elena alive.

She wanted a thorough accounting of everyone's whereabouts for the past week. But how to get it? Sure, she could ask them outright—Where were you the night that so-and-so died?—but she'd learned from experience that it was better to get an answer without asking a question, to get someone talking while she figured out their weak spot, what they wanted and what they thought she could do for them.

The multipierced receptionist, hunched over a biography of Frida Kahlo, immediately sat up straighter as Kate entered. Kate offered her a smile, moved quickly past the bronze wall plaque, which listed, among other patrons, Mr. and Mrs. Richard Rothstein.

Now, in the hallway, twenty, maybe thirty feet, a bowling alley of pure heavenly white, all six feet of Kate had suddenly become diaphanous. Cool fluorescent tubing created the illusion—the work of an artist, not an architect. Some people hated it. Kate loved it. Here, she was Tinker Belle, floating.

The main exhibition space, with its vaulted ceiling and white-tiled floor, had the look of an ultramodern swimming pool, minus the water.

For a moment, Kate thought they must be in between shows. Then she spotted the practically invisible white papers, individual squares of toilet paper, pinned to the museum's enormous white walls.

On closer inspection, each had a word—love, hate, life, death, power, weakness—scribbled, in what appeared to be ballpoint pen, in the center of the squares.

Minimal? Conceptual? Disposable? All three, thought Kate, sniffing at the one-ply tissue. *And unscented.*

"Kate!" Senior curator Schuyler Mills strutted across the highly polished museum floor. The toilet paper flapped on the walls. "I'm so glad you've stopped by." He smiled broadly, then rearranged his features, frowned. "I tried to catch you at Bill Pruitt's memorial, but—" The curator leaned in, whispered, "Was he drunk, or what?"

"What do you mean, Schuyler?"

"Well, drowning in his bathtub? Come on." The curator bit his lip. "I guess I shouldn't say that. Forgive me." He went uncharacteristically solemn. "Oh. I hope you got my card. I am so sorry about Elena. She was such a talented girl. We had the nicest conversation just before her performance. Poor kid was a bit nervous. I gave her a glass of brandy— you know, the stuff I keep on hand to ply generous museum patrons, like yourself." Another smile.

"Did you speak to Elena after her performance?"

"No. I went directly up to my office for a little catalog editing." He paused. "I often work at night."

"It isn't lonely?" she asked, thinking, *Can anyone verify that?*

"I like the quiet."

Kate could easily picture the curator, all alone, in his office, his nose buried in a book. He didn't seem to have much social life outside of museum and art functions. She shifted gears. "Did you know Ethan Stein?"

"Horrible," said Mills, shaking his head. "But no, we never met."

"I wonder"—Kate tapped her lip, formed her question carefully—"if he was still doing minimal paintings?"

"I wouldn't know."

"You didn't follow his work?"

"I'm not particularly interested in Minimal art."

"No?"

"No. I like art with more life in it."

"But you have to admit Stein made a contribution to the movement."

"I suppose." Mills shrugged.

"And you never included his work in a show, never visited his studio?"

"I already told you, Kate. His work didn't interest me. No." The curator's lips twisted into a suspicious smile. "You're starting to sound like a cop. The role hardly suits you, Kate."

"Really?" Kate laughed. "You mean you don't see me as

the Angie Dickinson type—tough, beautiful, not a hair out of place?"

"Angie *who*?"

"Next you'll be telling me you never heard of *Cagney and Lacey*."

"Are they TV characters?" The senior curator sneered. "I never watch television. *Never*. Oh. Except for *your* wonderful series. Of course."

"Of course." Kate tilted her head, threw Mills a skewed look.

"No, really. I did. And it was wonderful." He smoothed back his hair. "Normally, I have neither the time nor the patience for most popular culture." He sniffed. "If you ask me, it's destroying the civilized world. A disease that won't go away. Like herpes!"

"A lovely analogy, Schuyler. Is that Proust or Molière?"

The curator did not smile. "I am simply trying to uphold a tiny fragment of taste and intelligence in this declining culture of ours."

Kate's eyes fell on one of the fluttering squares of toilet paper.

"I had nothing to do with *that!*" Schuyler's lips turned white, the words barely able to squeak through. "This exhibition came to us via an *independent* curator. I am not, I'm afraid, the museum director."

"Perhaps you will be now that Amy is leaving." Kate laid her hand on the arm of his blue blazer. "You know," she said, "I could speak to the museum board on your behalf."

"Would you?" Mills's stiffness melted.

"Sure. Give me your schedule for the past month. That way I can not only be up on what you do, but can let them know how hard you work—which I'm sure you do."

"You have no idea," he said. "The work is my life. I'd be happy to write something up for you."

"Oh, don't go to any trouble, Sky. Just Xerox your date book."

*   *   *

Raphael Perez plucked a four-by-five color transparency from the mess on his desk, held it to the light—a man licking the very obvious sweat from his own armpit—and placed it on one of several stacks of slides, transparencies, and photos. It was time he'd gotten this damn exhibition finished and on the museum walls—and if Bill Pruitt hadn't fought him it would have opened when it was supposed to—a full year ago. Now Perez worried that "Bodily Functions"—which he was absolutely sure would put his name on the art map—might just be a tad out-of-date when it finally opened in the fall. He prayed the art world's notoriously fickle fascination would hold. Of course, in the end, it would hardly matter. Curator at the Contemporary was just the beginning. *Now, Director* . . . He rolled the title around in his mind while offhandedly glancing at another possible contender for his show. In this one, an eight-by-ten color glossy, a young man was perched naked on the toilet, his face contorted with obvious effort. Perez tossed it to the floor. If he had the time or the energy, he'd have torn it to pieces and flushed it down the toilet, just for the irony.

"Sorry to disturb you," said Kate, leaning into Perez's office, taking in the young curator's straight nose, full lips, eyes fringed with dark lashes.

Perez jumped up like a jack-in-the-box, pulled out a chair, nodded for the important museum board member to sit—all so fast, he actually created a breeze in his windowless office.

"I was just walking through the exhibition," said Kate, very nonchalant, "thought I'd say hello."

"How wonderful," said Perez. "I hope you enjoyed the show. It's such a commentary, don't you think?"

"I'd say . . . more *sanitary* than commentary."

Perez laughed too loud, too long, too hard.

Kate collected the photo from the floor. "Is this someone applying to clean the rest rooms, or is he just trying to prove he knows how to use one?"

"Artists," said Perez, almost sneering. "So many out there,

and all of them looking to be famous. Perhaps you'd like to use him in your next book." He arched his dark eyebrows.

"I suppose I could devote a chapter to bathroom art, trace it back to Duchamp's famous *Urinal*. But I'd rather leave all that *heady* stuff to curators, like yourself." She smiled. "How's your exhibition going?"

"Delayed. I'm trying to get it on track."

"I'll bet that's a lot easier without Bill Pruitt breathing down your neck. Oh, God, I can't believe I said something so tasteless. Forgive me."

"No need to apologize to me." The young curator tried to suppress a smile.

"It's just that I know Bill had rather conservative tastes."

"I'll say."

"You know, Raphael, with Bill Pruitt gone, and Amy Schwartz stepping down, well, the museum is going to need a lot of new direction."

The curator sat up like an eager puppy.

"You should give me an account of everything you've worked on for the past month—and I mean everything, your entire schedule, day and night. The board should know who is working hard—and who isn't—if you know what I mean."

Perez nodded his head like a puppet.

"I know," said Kate. "You can Xerox your date book for me."

"I use a Palm Pilot and, unfortunately, delete the prior week. But I'll write it all out for you, everything I worked on."

"Make sure to account for your nights, too, any dinners with collectors or artists, any nights spent working here or at home, even if it was just thinking about museum work."

"The past month only?"

"I think that would do to give the board an idea, don't you?"

Perez nodded again, drew a hand through thick black hair set off by a shocking streak of white just to the side of his widow's peak.

"By the way, I hope you got to talk with Elena, meet her

the night she performed here. She is—" Kate took a breath, fought to keep her voice even. "—was an extraordinary person."

"I'm afraid I had to leave right away," said Perez. "A dinner engagement. A couple of artists I know. I went to their studios, then we ate in a little dive on East Tenth Street."

Four blocks from Elena's apartment, thought Kate. "There are so many wonderful little restaurants down there. Where did you eat?"

"Let me think . . ." He tilted his head one way, then the other, the white streak flipping back and forth like a cartoon question mark. "Oh, yes. It was called Spaghettini."

Kate made a mental note. The fact is, she knew the place, pictured the tiny garden in back, remembered drinking cheap red wine there with Elena, both of them digging into bowls of pasta. "You see, Raphael, that's a perfect example of the kind of information you should write up for me to take to the museum board. Dinner with artists. Totally work-related. So just jot it all down. The date, who you were with. Where you went. Like that."

"I'll have it for you right away."

"Good," said Kate.

The Contemporary Museum's auditorium was down a wide flight of stairs that an artist had currently transformed by coating every inch of it with gold-leaf paper. A comment on consumerism—making the ordinary—a staircase—extraordinary? Or just gilding the lily. Whatever, thought Kate, it was glorious.

Now Kate stood on the stage looking out at row after row of empty upholstered seats. It was here that Elena gave her last performance. She tried to reconstruct the last minutes of that night. Richard, back to his office to prepare a brief. Willie, home to paint. Elena, she remembered, wasn't in the mood to go out. A kiss good night, and that was it. The End.

It was enough to send her reeling. Then something stirred

near the back row of the auditorium, distracting her. Kate squinted into the grayness.

A young man slowly made his way down the aisle. He stopped by the first row, leaned on his long-handled broom. "Sorry. Didn't mean to startle you."

She took him in: late twenties, sideburns like General Custer's, a drooping mustache, sandy hair, handsome. "You work at the museum long?"

"About six months. I'm an artist. Just doin' this to pay the rent, you know, until the big show comes along."

"I'm sure it will." Kate returned his smile, couldn't help herself. His eyes were a cool sky blue. "What's your name?"

"David Wesley." He extended a hand. "Hey, I know you. You're the woman who did that series, *Artists' Lives*. Really cool. I've got your book, too." He got shy a moment, or pretended to. "I'd, uh, love to show you my paintings sometime."

"I'd be happy to do that. You should send me slides of your work."

The artist beamed.

"Do you happen to work here on Sundays?"

" 'Fraid I do." He sighed, brushing the sandy hair off his forehead. "Sunday through Thursday you can find me here pushin' a broom, polishing floors, like that. Exciting, huh?"

"So you're here for the Sunday events?"

He looked down at his heavy work boots. "I'm usually gone before they start. I finish at five."

"What about last Sunday? Elena Solana."

"I read about what happened. Bummer."

"So you were not here."

He scratched his ear. "Actually, I was."

"I thought you said you didn't normally stay for the events."

"Well, I happened to meet her when she came in, Elena Solana. She was a fox, you know. So I hung around."

"And you stayed through the performance?"

"Yeah. Thought I'd get lucky."

"And you did?"

"Not." He shook his head. "She blew me off. Said she was tired."

Kate waited a moment, but he offered nothing else. "You know, I'm thinking about a new art book, maybe even a new TV series. I *should* see your work."

"Anytime."

Kate pulled out a pad and pen, handed them over. "Write down your address and phone number."

The young artist was so excited he could barely write. Kate watched him grip the pen so tight his knuckles went white. He'd leave a perfect set of prints. But how to get it back from him without getting her own all over it? She plucked a tissue from her bag, dabbed at her nose.

"There." The guy offered up the pen, the pad, and a dazzling smile.

Kate scooped the pen into the tissue before he noticed. "Great," she said. "I'll be in touch."

16

Outside, the sun was glinting off the glass and steel of Fifty-seventh Street buildings, blue sky and puffy white clouds a reassuring sign that spring might actually make an appearance.

Kate zigzagged through a parade of women with shopping bags from Bendel's and Saks, past window displays of rare estate jewelry. Last week, it might have distracted her. But not today.

She should get that pen to the lab, and had to follow up on those date books from Mills and Perez. But right now she needed to clear her head. To think. And she knew just the place to do it.

Raphael, Rubens, Delacroix.
   Vermeer, Hals, Rembrandt.
   Room after room of great paintings.
   The Metropolitan Museum of Art.
   Kate nodded at a guard, smiled, moved into a room of Baroque painting, her attention drawn by Poussin's *The Rape of the Sabine Women*, the figures frozen in action like actors on a stage. Poussin, she knew, actually worked from modeled clay figures that he moved around a small stagelike setting of his own creation.

At the moment it was too reminiscent of another artist—
one who peopled his re-creations with the dead.

Damn it. Would she ever be able to view art without
thinking of his brutal and sadistic replicas?

In a side room, a small show of prints by Edvard Munch,
etchings of his most famous work, *The Scream,* a woodcut
called *Anxiety*—stark-white faces against a black ground—
and two lithographs Kate knew well: *Funeral March,* which
looked like a mass of dead bodies; and *Death Chamber*—a
group of mourners, all in black, standing or sitting, mute and
solemn.

She thought about that last year—her father fighting to
die, but somehow living past the stroke that had left half his
body paralyzed, his speech slurred. The father she had so
feared—and, yes, loved—replaced in those last months by
some frail, almost gentle stranger. Who would believe that
this sickly old man—the man she cooked and cleaned for
after her mother died—could be capable of such cruelty, of
the beatings he rained on his young daughter? And *why?* A
dozen or more years on a shrink's couch and Kate was still
not sure. Did he blame her for the loss of his wife? Didn't he
know that his wife was also her mother?

Still, there had been no question that she would be the one
to dispense the pills, keep his ever-deteriorating body clean,
empty the bedpans, rub ointment on his bedsores, and, eventually, inject the lethal dose of morphine into the vein of his
right arm.

The next room was all Titian and Veronese, large-scale
paintings, grand and ornate. Kate was immediately reminded of the master's late, great masterpiece, *The Flaying
of Marsyas,* and with that, the body of Ethan Stein.

Damn.

Kate turned, practically bumped into a young man—worn
leather jacket, shaggy hair, in need of a shave. He smiled.

"Sorry," she said.

She watched him a moment, wondered, Was this the sort
of guy Elena went for? Bohemian, not bad-looking if he

was cleaned up. It was funny, Kate couldn't remember ever meeting a serious boyfriend of Elena's, or even hearing about one. Sure, she knew some of her friends, mostly artists and poets, and there was mention of a filmmaker boyfriend once, but never again. Odd, thinking about it now, a girl like Elena, pretty, smart, not gay. At least not that Kate knew of—though that was something she might need to find out for sure. Could a woman have killed Elena? It hadn't occurred to her before this moment. The statistics, she knew, said nine out of ten violent crimes against women were committed by men. At least they used to be. She'd have to ask Liz if that had changed in the last ten years.

Kate cut through several rooms, stopped in front of Daumier's most famous painting, *Third-Class Carriage,* a dark, brooding piece, stripped of color—figures in a railway car thrown together by circumstance, emotionally distanced, each of them isolated, lonely; the central figure, a hooded old woman, staring out at Kate with blind eyes. The one-eyed Picasso winked in her mind, and then Elena's bloodied cheek, then the creepy graduation photo.

That's it. What she needed to do: Go through Elena's photo albums, see if that photo had been plucked out.

On St. Mark's Place it could be 1965. Kids in bell-bottoms—tattoos on their arms rather than painted flowers on their faces—hung out in groups, smoking, laughing, more than a few seriously stoned. Wasn't it a school day, Kate wondered—or were they past school age? To her, not one of them looked over fifteen.

She spotted the two uniforms as soon as she turned onto East Sixth Street—one on the corner, the other right at the doorway to Elena's brownstone. Kate showed him her temporary ID. He barely blinked.

Bessie Smith played quietly in the background. Elena twirled around the room in a long multicolored embroidered skirt. "I love it." She spun again. The skirt flared out above her knees.

"Oh, you should've seen me," Kate said. "Probably the worst bargainer ever. I swear this woman must've seen me coming. I was so busy trying to impress her with my Spanish that I think I ended up paying more than double what she originally asked. I'm sure by now they've got my picture up in every Mexican shop—with 'sucker' written across it."

Elena laughed. "Hey, try your Spanish on me—maybe I can get even more out of you."

The smell of death still lingered in the hallway. Kate glanced up toward the ceiling as if she could see right through the two floors. But the apartment, she knew, was empty now. No Elena twirling in a Mexican skirt.

She took the stairs slowly. Now that she was here, she was in no hurry to view the scene.

The police tape easily ceded its hold on the door, sliding to the floor, and lay there like a limp yellow snake.

Kate pulled on a pair of latex gloves and one more time went through Elena's apartment. Traces of gray fingerprint powder still clung to the window ledges. The bold cotton print fabric on the couch was rumpled, the block of foam exposed. Did the tech boys do that, or had it been like that? Kate couldn't remember.

In the tiny kitchenette, the utensil drawer was half open, the contents removed. On the walls, the bloodstains had turned brown; in the cracks between the floor tiles, almost black.

Elena's computer table was empty of everything but New York dust. Kate felt dizzy, realized she'd been holding her breath since she took that first step into the apartment.

She stared at the scene, tried to reenact what she saw that night: Elena's body slumped on the kitchen floor, all that blood . . . suddenly more real, more alive than any crime scene photo.

In the bedroom, she found what she had come for—three

small photo albums, two on a shelf beside a stack of poetry and art books, one on Elena's dresser. Two were filled with travel photos—one a trip to Puerto Rico, the other Italy. The third album was all childhood photos, nothing recent. There had to be another.

And if it was not here, the murderer must have taken it.

Kate forced herself to go through dresser drawers, the closet, but found no other photos, no original of that graduation photograph, only pieces of Elena—a blouse here, a printed T-shirt there—memories strong enough to rip her apart. And they would if she weren't focused on the fact that he had been here, too, moved through these same rooms, touched the same clothes.

Kate could almost feel him in the room with her now, watching, smirking, his presence palpable. She was suddenly aware of her breathing, the quiet, and then something moving, ever so slightly, behind her. She froze. Her skin prickled. But when she turned it was only a pigeon on the window ledge.

She let out a breath.

But a second later, there it was again, nothing specific this time, just a feeling, as if he had tapped her on the shoulder, said, Look here, and here.

Kate shivered.

In the living room she stopped a moment, picked up the Marilyn pillow. The faintest whiff of patchouli, Elena's perfume, sent her reeling. Another minute in this place and she would break into pieces.

She was thankful for the smell of stale cabbage that permeated the hallway—anything to extinguish that killing patchouli.

She'd like to get out of here, but not yet. She needed to talk to Elena's super. According to the uniform who took the man's statement, he wasn't around the night of the murder, but still he could have some useful information.

Kate sidestepped four rusting trash bins. Two without tops, overflowing with malodorous garbage, practically blocked all entry to the basement apartment. She squeezed through, but a good-sized swatch of the fine gray fabric of her blazer impaled itself on a jagged edge of the trash can.

"Damn." She leaned hard on the metal bell, thought it was either pitched for dogs' ears only or, more likely, dead.

She knocked. A few flakes of glittery blue-black enamel fluttered to the concrete like swooning drag-queen moths.

Nothing.

Another knock. The only response a few more flakes of falling paint.

There was a hole where the doorknob ought to be. Kate bent for a closer inspection, thought it looked like a mouth without dentures, pieces of the metal lock sticking out. She riffled through her bag—comb, cigarettes, lighter, perfume, Tic-Tacs—came up with a metal nail file, probed around in the hole until she heard a click, and the door popped open. Breaking and entering—something the young Detective McKinnon had always been good at.

"Hello?" Kate called into the semidarkness of a hallway littered with old newspapers, empty six-packs, a large bag of kitty litter, an open metal toolbox, a stack of skin mags, Roach Motels. She stepped over them, turned into what appeared to be a combination living room/bedroom with a lumpy pink-striped mattress on the floor, a couple of folding chairs around a fifties-style card table. Across the room, Jenny Jones baited her audience on the twenty-eight-inch Sony Trinitron.

When the black-and-white cat rubbed against her ankles, Kate leaped, almost screamed. "Oh, kitty, you scared the shit out of me." She took a breath, petted the cat, but as she straightened up, she caught the faintest glimpse of something massive and colorful just off to her right.

Then came the shove, and the gray-beige walls, Jenny Jones, the floor, all were coming at her fast. Kate got an arm out, grabbed on to something soft and fleshy, gripped hard, and pulled. The large, colorful thing—which smelled like weeks-old Campbell's chicken noodle soup—went down as

Kate found her balance. It—the thing—hit the faded linoleum floor with a loud clunk, sputtered like a dying diesel engine, and farted.

Kate stabbed her heel into the back of a neck like a Goodyear tire, yanked the hippo's flabby arm up and under his scapula—though she couldn't be sure there was any bone beneath the layers of fat.

Now she took him in: a good three-hundred-pounder in a parrot-patterned shirt.

He yelped like a pup. His breath, even from a few feet away, like aged farmer cheese, was giving his fart some stiff competition.

A couple of weeks earlier, Kate had been lunching with Philippe de Montebello in the private dining room of the Metropolitan Museum, discussing the finer points of Vermeer, had been having tea with the latest Mrs. Trump, securing that million-dollar check for Let There Be a Future. Now she was not only skipping tea and lunch, she was ramming her four-hundred-dollar heel into some fat guy's neck.

"Name?" Kate laid a little weight into that heel, watched it disappear into the folds of yeasty flesh.

He bellowed: "Johnson. I'm the fuckin' super here! Wally Johnson. You're breakin' my fuckin' arrrmmm."

"You always drop-kick your guests?"

"Y'broke into my place, f'Christ's sake!"

He had a point. "NYPD," she said, easing up on his arm a bit. She leaned closer, then pulled back. That breath. She managed to extract a promise from fat boy Wally that he would behave.

"Why didn't ya say so?" He rolled over, sat up, rubbed his arm, whined, "Jeesus."

"I knocked, called out. You didn't answer."

"I was takin' a dump, for Christ's sake." His eyes, tiny dark specks peeking through Venetian blinds of fat, assessed Kate skeptically. "You're a cop?"

"Working on the Solana case," she said, liking the sound of it. She was pretty pleased with herself, too, taking down fat boy Wally with one arm. Thank God for her personal trainer. Of course, Wally was in maybe the worst shape of any person she had ever seen—alive. "Look," she said, softening. "I'm not here to do you any harm—"

"Y'already broke my fuckin' arm." He pouted.

Kate resisted calling him a crybaby. "I read your statement. You weren't here the night Elena Solana was killed, correct?"

"I already told the other cops. I was at my sista's, on Staten Island. She cooked spaghetti wit' meatballs."

"Sounds delicious. But I'm looking for a little more than meatballs."

"Like what?"

"Like . . . did you ever see her friends, Elena Solana's—"

"Hey, I don't snoop."

"I didn't say you did." Kate softened her tone. "Look, Wally, you and I know that any good superintendent knows the comings and goings of his residents. It's part of the job, which I am sure you do *very* well."

He rubbed his arm, said, "She had a few nigger boyfriends."

For a second, Kate thought maybe she'd break his other arm, but that wouldn't get her any answers. "Tell me about them."

He shrugged. "What's t'tell? One was small. One skinny. One big."

"*How* big?"

"Like a bouncer, or a prizefighter, you know."

"What else?"

"The little one had that hair, y'know, like, uh—"

"Dreadlocks?"

"That's it. Dreadlocks. A young guy. He was here a lot." *Willie.* "And the skinny guy?"

"I only saw him couple a times. Looked like a junkie."

"And the prizefighter?"

"Hasn't been around awhile now. I guess, maybe they broke up. Boo-hoo, huh?" He grinned. Not a pretty picture: teeth the color of ripe bananas, a couple of black holes.

"Could you identify any of them?"

"The young one, the one with dreadlocks, for sure. Maybe the big guy. *Maybe*. I never got a real good look at him. But he was big, like I said. The other guy, the junkie, well . . . a junkie, you know."

Great. The only one of the three men Fat Wally could identify for sure was Willie, the one Kate already knew. It figured.

"Oh." Fat Wally leaned in a little too close. Kate took a step back from eau de halitosis. "There was this other guy, also kinda skinny, a white guy. Blond hair. Medium height. But slight, kinda feminine. Probably a fag, y'know."

"And you saw him . . . when?"

"I don't keep no stopwatch. A few times. In front, maybe, or ringin' Solana's buzzer. Maybe once or twice, the two of them goin' out together, arm 'n arm." He grinned. "Maybe he weren't no faggot after all."

Outside, in the cold afternoon light, Kate assessed her losses—one very good pair of pants and one even better blazer; then assessed what she'd learned—three men, excluding Willie, had called on Elena regularly. A large black man and a skinny one. Also, a pale white guy.

Who were they?

Back home, Kate headed for the guest-room closet, grabbed a chair on the way. She did not like the way she felt when Fat Wally came out of nowhere. Way too vulnerable. And the next guy might not be as out of shape. She had better be prepared.

She pushed aside a stash of silky scarves. There it was, the plain gray shoe box marked "Slippers, crushed velvet," in neatly printed Magic Marker. Exactly where she'd put it almost ten years ago. She tugged out the box, sat on the edge of the bed, pushed back layers of tissue paper as though peeling away time. Gently, she extricated her old Glock.

Kate turned it over in her hand, could still, remarkably, smell the slightly acrid odor of gun-metal cleaner. There was a full clip in the shoe box. Kate snapped it into place and felt the rush. The power she'd given up a long time ago, exchanged, you might say, for the power of money. Back in the old days, Kate hadn't known about money or what it could do. Her fingers tightened around the gun handle. Now she had a gun *and* a checkbook. And yes, she felt a lot stronger than she had only minutes earlier. Ask any fifteen-year-old who has had his hand around a gun and he'll tell you the power it offers, the sudden, stupid bravery. Who was the NRA trying to kid?

Kate exchanged her destroyed designer duds for Gap khakis and a plain blue cotton shirt. Much better. A lot less flashy than the way she dressed as a detective in the old days, when she favored miniskirts and V-necks. But those days were gone, no matter how many miles she logged on that damn treadmill.

Her reflection in the mirror told her she could use a solid week at a spa. She ran a brush through her hair, dabbed her wrists with Bal à Versailles.

Why was it she had always felt embarrassed, as though somehow it had been her fault that she didn't have a mother? It wasn't until the tenth grade, at St. Anne's, that she learned the truth: Mary Ellen Donaghue taunting her, "You think you're such hot stuff, McKinnon, well, at least my mother didn't kill herself," and Kate punching her, over and over, until finally one of the nuns pulled her off.

Why had they all lied to her? Did they think it was her fault?

Oh, man, the years spent on the shrink's couch over that one.

Kate tucked the Glock into her most sensible bag—a smallish black leather pouch with a long strap—looped the bag over her shoulder, then sorted through her closet for another lightweight jacket. The only nondesigner item was an old jean jacket with an appliquéd peace sign over the breast pocket left over from who-knew-when.

Outside, the trees bordering Central Park West had sprouted their spring greenery to spite the dreary weather. Kate patted the artillery in her bag. Insurance, that's all it was. It wasn't as if she were planning to shoot anyone.

17

Kate's heels echoed in the long dark hallway. Cata-combs, she thought. Peeling paint, damp cold. The basement of the Sixth Precinct. The Crime Lab.

Hernandez slid the graduation photo into the glass con-traption, lit the superglue.

The two women watched as vapors swirled around the collage, searching for prints.

"This is a mess," said Hernandez, removing the photo with tweezers. "Prints on top of prints."

"Sorry," said Kate. "I didn't know what it was when I got it. Had my hands all over it."

The technician gave her a sorry look, pulled gloves off her chubby hands, dropped them into the trash. She was maybe thirty-five, her ample figure straining against the snug lab coat.

Kate offered up the ballpoint pen wrapped in tissue. "This should be a lot neater. See if there are any prints that match what was found at the Solana scene."

Hernandez sighed.

Kate pulled out a Marlboro.

"In the hall," said Hernandez. "No, better yet, take a walk. Gimme a half hour to print the other ones. I'll see what I can get."

One coffee and three cigarettes later, Kate was getting the lowdown from Hernandez.

"The pen's got a few good prints, but they match nothing at Solana's or any other scene."

"It was a wild shot," said Kate. "What about the collage?"

"Not much. Mostly smudged. I got maybe one clean quarter-print."

"Could be mine, I must admit."

"They're called gloves, McKinnon."

"I don't wear gloves when I open my mail."

"Well, from now on you should." Hernandez handed Kate a couple pages of mechanical printouts—numbers, symbols, words. "Not much to tell you. The glue he used in the collage is acid-free but otherwise standard. The photo's a Kodacolor, four to five years old. The material over the eyes is some kind of tempera paint, water-based, for sure. The other one, the Polaroid—" She shook her head. "No prints. Unlike you, your unsub *is* wearin' gloves."

"Can you make copies of the collage and the photo for me?"

Hernandez nodded toward a Xerox machine in the corner. "You can do it yourself. The pictures are in plastic now. *Protected*." She offered a caustic smile.

A minute later, Kate was watching the Xeroxes spill out of the machine.

"Oh, McKinnon." Hernandez called her over. "Before you leave I wanna mess up your manicure. Gotta have your prints on file to check against anything else you decide to drag your hands across."

Floyd Brown squinted at the stat sheet.

NO SIGNS OF FORCED ENTRY

PROBABLE WEAPON: NINE-INCH SERRATED KITCHEN KNIFE FOUND AT THE SCENE (KITCHEN DRAWER) MATCHED 2 OTHER KNIVES IN DRAWER—NO PRINTS

He studied the photo. Seventeen stab wounds. Brutal, for sure.

Through a magnifying glass he searched for signs of pleasure. No bite marks, no nothing. And the usual trophies—nipples, earlobes—were intact. So what was the guy after?

UNDER NAILS: TRACES OF ALUMINUM

A manicure? Now that, even to Floyd Brown, who had seen it all, was odd. Some kind of ritual they hadn't yet figured out, or was the killer just smart enough to file away any traces of flesh that may have lodged under the dead girl's nails? Either way, Brown could see the guy took his time.

Three murders.

One killer?

Maybe.

Mead didn't want to believe it—hell, who wanted to think there was a serial killer out there? Brown pushed away from his desk, swiveled back and forth in his chair. Twenty-plus years of detective work told him this was no coincidence. McKinnon was probably right. Plus, he was impressed with what she'd already delivered—though he hated to admit it. Who was she anyway? Some uptown dame with all the answers.

Floyd pictured her pushing the thick streaked hair out of her eyes, the whiff of perfume he'd caught when he leaned in close to study those art pictures. Jesus, if there was one thing he didn't need, it was to think about McKinnon as a woman.

Still, he couldn't wait to tell Vonette that he was working with the art lady. She'd get a real kick out of that. Vonette, the art fan, who made him tape *Monday Night Football* so she could watch *Artists' Lives*. As if watching a tape of a game you already knew the outcome to was worth watching.

Small world, though, that was for sure. The woman who ruined his one good TV night working with him on a homicide—maybe a series of homicides.

A month ago, he and Vonette had discussed the possibility of his retiring. But not with the possibility of a serial killer out there. And he'd have to make nice. This wasn't just anyone advising. This was a friend of the chief of police.

The cubicle was just big enough for a desk and a chair, but it was something—Kate hadn't expected anything. Certainly not the NYPD temporary ID, clipped to her cashmere pullover. She lit up another Merit. Yesterday it was Marlboro. Last week she'd promised, absolutely sworn to Richard, she would quit. For the hundredth time. But not right now.

She opened to a clean page in her notebook, rapped her disposable, ecologically indestructible auto pencil against the page, started to list the obvious things she needed to check—Elena's friends, co-workers, mother, though she doubted Mrs. Solana would talk to her.

Kate thought back to Elena's senior year in high school, the teenager's tears as she confessed to Kate that Mendoza, her mother's boyfriend, had been coming on to her, heavy, for months, her mother turning a deaf ear. That's when Kate helped Elena get out of the house, find the East Sixth Street apartment, even paid the rent for the first couple of years. Now the thought of it stung: If Elena had stayed home, would she still be alive? She pushed the thought away, added Mendoza's name to the list, underlined it.

Kate pulled hard on the Merit—might as well be sucking on a Tampax. She had to get herself some real cigarettes; she was smoking twice as many of these.

She wondered if the other cops would play ball with her. She liked what she saw in Maureen Slattery, even recognized a bit of herself in the young woman cop—the slight chip on her shoulder, for sure, but no dummy. And she'd already been helpful, turned over Elena's phone records. Kate scanned them now, recognized her own number, Willie's, others she would have to check out later. They could be important.

But what about Brown? Maybe it was time for a visit.

"Your wife." Kate eyed the framed five-by-seven photo at the back of Floyd Brown's desk. "Pretty woman. She trying to kill you?"

"What?"

"There's enough starch in your collar to cut off your blood supply."

"She's particular." Brown fought a smile, pulled the Pruitt file over. "So, you knew this guy. Any enemies?"

"Probably a waiting list. The guy was a fucking ass-kisser, a phony, maybe even a crook."

"You sure you're from Park Avenue?"

"The West Side," said Kate, not specifying Central Park West.

"So what do you mean, *crook?*"

"There is the possibility of some stolen art."

"It's not in here," said Brown, fingering the edge of Pruitt's file.

"I just found out."

"You been workin' the cases, McKinnon? *Alone?*"

"I was curious." Kate smiled, then explained what Pruitt's mother had told her about the missing painting. "I'm venturing a guess that whoever killed Pruitt has the altarpiece."

"Find the painting, find the killer. That it?" Brown made a note, then tugged a page out of Pruitt's folder. "Did you see these statements?" He ran his finger down a list of names. "Richard Rothstein. Any relation?"

"Husband. He was at a museum board meeting with Pruitt, the morning of the day the man died."

Brown locked his dark eyes on her. "Your husband didn't kill him, did he?"

"Richard? Kill Bill Pruitt?" Kate snorted a laugh. "Well, you know, he didn't say. I guess I'll have to ask him."

"Do that," said Brown. He sat back in his chair. "I watched your show. Me and my wife."

"Thanks."

"I didn't say I liked it. Just that I watched it." He scrutinized her a moment, drummed his blunt-cut nails along the edge of the desk.

Kate waited. She knew to give the guy some space. It couldn't be easy for him. A crackerjack detective with over twenty years experience stuck with her, an ex-cop he knew nothing about except that she had connections in high places. If it were the other way around, she'd be pissed as hell.

"You haven't told anyone your theories, have you?"

"No one but Tapell."

Brown screwed up his mouth. "It'll be bad, real bad, if the press gets news of a serial killer—especially now, right after the Shooter."

"If people weren't so hungry to read about that sort of thing they wouldn't print it." Kate eyed the Pruitt file. "By the way, the contusion on Pruitt's jaw. Was it fresh?"

"I couldn't tell for sure."

"What about the coroner?"

"Way backed up. We'll have to wait awhile for the report."

"Maybe," said Kate. "And maybe not."

18

The coroner's office might be backed up. But a call from Chief of Police Tapell opened doors.

The plastic name tag—RAPPAPORT, SALLY—was pinned, slightly askew, to the chest pocket of the ME's lab coat, in between clusters of wine-colored stains, presumably dried blood, thought Kate, and not vintage pinot noir. Rappaport was anywhere from thirty to forty, medium height, thin. Skin that looked as if it hadn't seen daylight in two years.

"Sorry to keep you here so late."

"Are you kidding?" Rappaport shrugged. "I just started my shift."

"Graveyard?"

The ME frowned.

"Sorry," said Kate. She was desperate for any kind of humor. "Bad pun."

The corridor leading to the main autopsy room was that awful gray-green color from the floor to waist height, then off-white to the ceiling. Kate followed Sally Rappaport's thick-soled Adidas. They squeaked on the mint-colored ceramic tile floor.

An old Roman bathhouse. Multiple archways big enough for Liz Taylor's Cleopatra to make her triumphal entrance into Rome. Polished white tiles and stainless steel. So cold you could see your breath. The smell of formaldehyde twenty times worse than a tenth-grade biology class.

The Astoria morgue, the one Kate knew from the old days, was part of Queens Hospital—one room outfitted with three or four cheap gurneys. A dozen of them could have fit into this place, easy.

Rappaport led Kate past a couple of gurneys, bodies laid out under green plastic sheets, waxy-white, blue-veined feet protruding. She offered up a mask, tied one over her nose and mouth, patted her curly brown hair, which was held in place with two blue plastic barrettes in the shape of fish— the kind you'd buy in Woolworth's, if Woolworth's still existed. Kate wondered if Rappaport had saved them from when she was a girl or bought them from some tacky street vendor. But why did she care, here, of all places, in this frigid house of death where she was about to view the body of a girl who was the closest thing to a daughter she had ever had? Hell, she didn't need a therapist to explain that one. Plastic barrettes? Any distraction would do.

Rappaport plucked a pair of plastic gloves from a dispenser, nodded at Kate, who did the same. She moved to the bottom half of the east wall, all metal drawers, each with a large plastic handle and a slot holding an index card with numbers handwritten in black marker. An oversized library of the dead. The ME checked her clipboard, got a grip on drawer S-17886P, tugged. The drawer squeaked open.

Elena's body looked like so many bodies Kate had seen before—flesh the color of old piano keys, tracks left from the autopsy's thoracic Y cut, crude stitches where they'd literally reattached the top of Elena's skull—but this was not just any body. Behind the mask, Kate was just barely breathing. How could she do this? Was she mad? No, she wanted to do it. Must do it. A tune, that's what she needed. An old trick—plant some banal lyrics in the back of her mind—to make it possible to view the worst scenes.

"Baby Love."

A bad choice. But too late to stop it. Diana Ross and the Supremes—all bouffant hair, big skirts, finger poppin'—had already laid down the Motown track inside Kate's brain just as Rappaport began pointing to dark purple, almost black cuts in Elena's chest: ". . . two, three, four . . . ten in the upper thoracic. One, two, three—these three look as though they're one because they've run over one another, but it's three separate entries." She looked up at Kate, said "See?" then picked at them with a scalpel. "The original coroner's report said seventeen stab wounds. But it's really twenty-two."

The refrain from "Baby Love" was playing over and over.

Rappaport exchanged the scalpel for an X ray, flipped it up toward the harsh fluorescent light. "These two, here . . ." She pointed. "Pierced the lungs. These other two went directly into her heart. They're your killers."

"It's not the weapon that kills," Kate whispered.

"True," said Rappaport. She dropped the X ray onto Elena's gray-white thigh. "These other wounds, here, on the abdomen, basically superficial."

"Was she raped?" Kate managed to ask over the song, which continued to play in her brain.

"No semen, but some vaginal bruising."

"So, it's possible that there was an attempted rape—and that the assailant did not ejaculate?"

Rappaport was hovering about six inches over Elena's thighs, picking through dark pubic hair with a metal probe. "Possible. Yeah. Too bad there's no semen to DNA, though."

Kate gently lifted one of Elena's hands. It was stone-cold, rubbery. "Defensive wounds?"

The ME nodded.

"Anything under the nails?"

Rappaport regarded her clipboard, flipped a page. "Nothing. Surprisingly clean."

Kate stared at the lifeless hand in hers. What was it that seemed wrong? The nails. Right. She'd read the report.

"Do you think the assailant filed the nails postmortem?"

"Impossible to say." The ME's tired brown eyes look bored above her mask.

"Elena wore her nails long," said Kate. "He must have done it."

"Well, he did a good job, too. Nothing under them. No hair, flesh, nothing."

"Particles, hairs anywhere else?"

"Only the girl's hair so far. We've got prelims on stomach, liver, and kidneys in the report here. Tests will take about a week."

A week? Kate wanted to scream, but her voice remained cool. Maybe she'd call Tapell. "Can you get those to me when they're ready?"

"Test results will be sent over to Randy Mead's office." She squinted at Kate. "Tapell's aide said you're working with him, with Mead?" Her inflection turned it into a question.

Kate didn't bother to answer. She said, "I'll take those preliminaries now, see the rest later." She was about to reach for the file, realized she was still holding Elena's hand. For a moment, she did not want to give it up—as though holding on would keep them connected.

"The other body's waiting." Rappaport yawned. "We better get going."

Kate gently lowered Elena's hand to the gurney.

Rappaport gave the steel drawer a hard shove. It closed with a dull clunk.

Pruitt's flesh looked rubbery, waxen.

"What about that bruise on his chin?" asked Kate.

Rappaport leaned over the body, poked at Bill Pruitt's chin with her gloved finger. The flesh went from purple to white to slightly yellow, back to purple in about three seconds. "From the lividity, I'd say it probably happened during the murder, or certainly no later than the afternoon of his death."

So it was the perp, their artistic unsub, who slugged

Pruitt. Somehow that didn't make sense to Kate. "Why punch someone while you're holding them upside down under water? Seems like overkill."

Rappaport shrugged.

"What about Ethan Stein?"

"The autopsy's still in progress," said Rappaport. "Now *there's* a case of overkill." She shook her head. "I'll send those reports over once they're done."

Kate slid the preliminary reports on Pruitt into her bag along with the ones on Elena. She was more than ready to get out of here, and right now, she felt like firing a gun.

The smell of gunpowder hung in the low-ceilinged room like a cloud of acid rain. Kate squeezed the trigger, again, and again, and again. The gun jumped in her hand, sent tremors up her arm. She'd almost forgotten the thrill of shooting—all that force right in your hand. The target zipped forward. No bull's-eyes, but all of her shots would have inflicted serious damage. Not bad for years out of practice. She reloaded, emptied another round, concentrated on keeping her arm steady, her mind clear and focused. She couldn't help wondering what her friends, Blair and the girls, would think if they could see her now. That group? Every one of them would strap on a gun quicker than you could say "prenuptial agreement."

Kate was finishing up her forth round when she spied Maureen Slattery, just a few lanes over. Pumped up on cardboard killing, Kate strutted the three lanes over toward the young policewoman.

Slattery pulled her ear protectors off, dropped back to meet Kate at the screens.

"Nice shooting," said Kate, checking out Slattery's near-perfect round as the target zipped forward.

"Thanks. How about you?"

"Rusty."

"It doesn't take long to get it back. It's like swimming, you know."

"Or fucking."

Slattery gave her a look. "You got quite a mouth on you, McKinnon."

"I majored in Mouthing Off at Saint Anne's."

Maureen's face broke into a grin. "Saint Mary's. Bayonne, New Jersey."

Kate gave Maureen a conspiratorial look. "Uniform?"

"The usual plaid number."

"How short was *your* skirt?"

"Let's just say it prepared me for those hot pants in vice. You?"

"Exactly one inch below my panties." Kate made the sign of the cross. "Virtually impossible for me to bend over. If I dropped a pencil, that was it, lost forever."

The two women laughed like schoolgirls.

Maureen locked her gun into her holster as they headed toward the locker room.

"Anything new on the cases?" asked Kate.

"Checked out Perez. His dinner companions—couple of downtown artists—say they dropped him home right after dinner."

"But did he *stay* home?"

Slattery shrugged. "Don't know. But he also says he was out of town when Ethan Stein was murdered."

"I'm waiting for his calendar. Schuyler Mills's book, too. Then we'll see what they *say* they were doing on the pertinent dates and check it with others."

"Right."

"How about Mendoza?" asked Kate. "Did his alibi check out?"

"Mrs. Solana is sticking with her story that he was with her all night."

Kate nodded. She was grateful that Maureen had handled Mrs. Solana and Mendoza. She just wasn't up to dealing with Elena's mother. "Anything else?"

"Pruitt's effects are in the Evidence Room, on three. Check 'em out. Then I'll tell you the rest. Oh, and wear gloves, and I don't mean because you'll mess up the evidence. The room's a sty."

Floor-to-ceiling open metal files. Cardboard boxes. Some of them had been sitting there so long they had spiderwebs thick enough to wear as sweaters.

The Evidence Room. Kate was almost sorry she'd gotten the clerk to open it up.

"Over here," he said, sniffling. He was young, maybe twenty-two, a slight case of acne on his otherwise smooth cheeks. "All the new cases are in this corner, bottom shelf. I think Pruitt should be right over there." He pointed, then rubbed his nose. "Allergy. Dust, I think."

"Boy, do you have the wrong job." Kate offered him a sympathetic look.

"Mind if I get outta here?" His nose was twitching.

Kate took in the grim room, a black spider inching its way along the wall. More than a few minutes and she'd be itching and twitching, too.

The Pruitt carton was sad. A bar of soap in a small Ziploc bag; a washcloth, also bagged; a larger plastic pouch of toiletries—shaving cream, razor, a bottle of rosewater eau de toilette.

Within the large carton, there was a smaller one. Kate pulled on the required gloves.

Right on top, another Ziploc bag with WILLIAM MASON PRUITT printed on it in bold black marker. Kate popped it open, regarded the obvious S and M mask, the crude stitching around the holes for eyes, nose, mouth. *Could this possibly be Bill's?* If his name weren't written on the bag, she'd never believe it. She rooted around in the carton, came up with a stash of magazines, mainly porn. A few of teens, boys and girls, not young enough to qualify as kiddie porn, but cutting it pretty damn close. Kate was fairly disgusted, then somewhat stunned when she found the four or five devoted exclusively to young black transvestites, another group of sadomasochistic porn that made the flaccid mask look tame.

Under the skin magazines, over two dozen videos, XXX variety. The usual suck-and-fuck pictures on the covers, but these, particularly cheap-looking, lived up to the name of the company—Amateur Films—spelled out in bold black lettering. Maybe something worth watching—someday—if she had the stomach for it.

Kate leaned into Slattery's cubicle.

Maureen flashed a smile. "You saw the stash? The mask?"

"Yes. And it was a hell of a surprise, believe me. Bill Pruitt." Kate shook her head. "You never know."

"Get ready for more," said Slattery. "I did a little bar-hopping, the Branding Iron and the Dungeon, down by the piers." She made a face, mimed a shiver. "You ever been to those places?"

"Oh, sure. I put my husband in a dog collar every Saturday night, drag him over." Kate raised an eyebrow. "So?"

"The back room of the Dungeon—some guy in chains, suspended there for the customers. One's got a fist up his ass, another's gagging the guy with his dick."

"A regular Hallmark moment."

"You got it. Anyhow, our guy, Pruitt? I showed his picture around."

"And?"

"He was a regular. Oh, and you might find this interesting. A list of what they took out of Ethan Stein's studio. Some very tasty items."

1 TUBE CERULEAN BLUE OIL PAINT (on floor, beside body)

PALETTE KNIFE (as above)

POLAROID FILM—BACKING PAPER (no Polaroid camera found on premises)

VICTIM'S CLOTHING (removed before murder)

blue cotton work shirt, black Levi's jeans, Calvin Klein knit boxers, white socks

SWISS ARMY WRISTWATCH (found on chair)

CERAMIC BOWL—filled with chips (Terra brand)

DATE BOOK

2 SETS METAL HANDCUFFS

BLACK NYLON WHIP

NIPPLE CLAMPS

2 SILK MOUTH GAGS WITH BALL COCK

6 DILDOS—2 DOUBLE-HEADED

37 MAGAZINES (SADO/MAS)

Kate scanned the list. "Jesus. No dignity in death, is there?"

"Not when you're into this kind of stuff."

"Wait a minute—" Kate focused on the last group of items. There were artists she knew of who used that kind of dark subject matter in their artwork—but not Stein. This must have been strictly for personal use. "This is too weird. I mean, Stein and Pruitt, obviously dabbling in the same sexual arena."

"Uh-huh." Slattery handed Kate a one-page typed report. "And get this. A report from the uniforms I sent off with Ethan Stein's driver's license. They also showed Stein's picture around the Dungeon and Branding Iron." She threw Kate a look. "Pruitt was not the only regular."

"Jesus. You think Stein and Pruitt ever met there?"

"No one can actually put them together at either place, or they just don't remember."

Kate was trying to take it in. "Can it possibly be a coincidence that these two guys had the same predilection, hung out in the same bars, and are both now dead?" Kate shook her head. "When can I see Stein's personal effects?"

"Brown's got his date book and wallet. Ask him."

"I will."

Slattery shifted gears. "By the way, the old lady, on one, at Solana's building . . ."

Kate thought back to the night she found Elena, the glimpse of the old woman's face through the cracked open door. "Yes. I talked to her. For about ten seconds."

"Well, she says she was home, watching TV. Uniform took her statement that night. Says she saw a black man in the apartment building. But that was all he could get outta her. No details. No nothing. I tried, too. Nada."

"Let me take a crack at her."

19

A pit stop, that's all Kate was intending. But someone had left the *Post* on her desk, and there was no way she could ignore it.

THE DEATH ARTIST

The ritualistic murder of artist Ethan Stein may just be the third in a series of brutal murders. Though NYPD officials are vehemently denying any rumors of a serial killer, uniformed police have been canvassing galleries from Chelsea to SoHo to Fifty-seventh Street to Madison Avenue. Apparently, the killer arranges his victims into poses mocking famous paintings.

One artist interviewed put it succinctly, "The guy's a regular death artist." A gallery director, who wished to remain nameless, worried that New York's finest might have a disdain for people in the art community. This, after a cop, who was making inquiries into the Stein murder, made some disparaging comments about the dead artist's paintings.

It is rumored that the NYPD has called upon the services of former cop Katherine McKinnon

Rothstein, socialite, and best known for her recent PBS series *Artists' Lives*. No one at One Police Plaza would confirm or deny this information, and Ms. McKinnon Rothstein was not available for comment.

Jesus fucking Christ!

Kate dropped the paper back onto her desk. She never thought she'd be reading the *New York Post* so damn often.

The death artist?

He lays the newspaper carefully onto the table.

Was it Kate who figured it out? He focuses on the crack of light streaming through the old rotting beams. He hopes so. If not, it would be such a waste. Of course it was Kate. Who else had the information?

Still, he hadn't expected her to figure it out quite so soon. *She's smart. Smarter than you.*

He grabs his Walkman, rams the tiny headphones into his ears, but the voices are more powerful than any music. *Moronmoronmoronmoronmoronmoronmoronmoron . . .*

Hands clasped over his ears. *SHUT UP!*

Scattered over the tabletop, the copies he's had made, Kate with wings and halo, replicated a dozen times. It soothes him to look at them, even chases those voices away. For the moment.

Lately, he's been trying to make sense of his dreams, the nightmares, this other person inside him. A brother? A twin? This one who has been with him, it seems, forever—quietly at first, then stronger, until the demands just had to be met.

Cycles: Dormant. Active. Controlled. Fierce.

How clearly he can think about it. No way he's crazy.

Which one is he? Does he even know?

He wanted to send her those things. It made him feel so close to her. And now he'll send another. He lifts a red Magic Marker, uses it to create a border around the image, and then, just for fun, writes HELLO in large block letters.

But this is just a gift. Just to show her how important she is to him—just for being so smart that she figured out the first part so swiftly. Not that it was such a big deal to figure something out *after* the fact—and with his help.

But now he is gearing up for part two.

No more mementos. These will be warnings.

His fingers stroke the Walkman's smooth plastic body.

Will she get it?

Well, that's her problem.

Careful.

He turns the Walkman up against the voices.

Who needs to be careful when you're lucky and smarter than everyone else?

His mind is ticking away so fast, excited by the prospect of creating previews of coming attractions.

Let the games begin.

20

The lobby was claustrophobic. The air stagnant. Kate knocked at the back apartment. Someone was home for sure, the television turned up high, a lot of hooting, hollering, and clapping. Either a game show, or Sally Jessy. What's-her-face.

No response. Kate knocked harder.

"Vat is it?"

Kate maneuvered her temporary ID into the three inches of open space. "Mrs. Prawsinsky? Sorry to bother you. Police business."

The chain lock released, the door opened. Five feet tall, five-one tops. Kate towered over her. Penciled eyebrows, turquoise-shadowed lids, scarlet lips Lucille Ball–style. Strawlike yellow hair crimped with bobby pins against her scalp like anemic snails. "I already talked to the police," the woman said. "Lots of them. You want I should make something up new to tell you?"

"I just need to ask you a few more questions."

"So? Ask." The elderly woman folded her thin arms across the top of her flowered housedress.

"You said you saw a black man here, in the building."

The old woman nodded, but that was it.

"Can you describe the man?"

"Honey. Can *you* tell them apart?"

Kate stifled an urge to slap the woman. But no, she had a job to do, and it was not delivering a lecture on cultural diversity. This was a lonely woman; she had to work with that. "Mrs. Prawsinsky," she said warmly. "You're a woman living alone in a tough neighborhood. I can really appreciate that."

"Dahlink, you don't know the half of it—"

"Oh, I do know," Kate said patiently. "That's why I'm sure you have to be extra diligent." She offered the old woman a sobering look. "Now I sense you're a *very* observant woman. Is there anything—and I mean anything at all—you can remember about this strange man in your building? I mean, was he young, old, tall, short?"

The woman squeezed her eyes shut, pursed her thin lips. Crimson lipstick creeped into vertical whistle marks. "Medium. I'd say he was medium."

"See, you remember plenty. That's terrific." *Medium? That tells me absolutely nothing.* "What else?"

"I would say he was between thirty and forty. And . . . " She squinted again. "Skinny. Very skinny." She opened her eyes, smiled, proud of herself.

"That was *very* helpful, Mrs. Prawsinsky." Kate was relieved. The description eliminated Willie—he was young, short, solidly built.

"What else? Any distinguishing marks about him? You know, anything special?"

"What do you mean special, dahlink?"

"Scars? A limp? Like that."

She shook her old head. "No. Nothing. But . . . now I can see his face." She squinted again, getting into it.

"And?"

"Mmm . . . It was a couple of nights before they found her, the girl. It was night, late. I know it was late because I was watching that Nick at Nite station. You know, the oldies station. My favorite."

"Oh, right . . . " Kate took a deep breath. "Mine, too."

That did the trick. Minutes later Kate found herself in Mrs. Prawsinsky's cramped living room, an exact duplicate in layout of Elena's. But where Elena's desk would be—the focal point of Elena's spare apartment—was Mrs. Prawsinsky's twenty-two-inch color TV, its static glow casting overgrown rhododendrons and plastic slipcovers in shimmering electric tones. Kate perched on Mrs. Prawsinsky's plastic-slipcovered sofa, balancing a cup of weak Lipton tea on her knees.

"*Me*. I watch every night," Mrs. Prawsinsky said. "*I Love Lucy, I Dream of Jeannie, Bewitched*." She lifted a bowl with packets of Sweet'n Low. "Sugar, dahlink?" Kate shook her head no. "I love the mother, you know, Agnes Moorehead. My friend Bunny, God rest her soul, said I look like her, Agnes Moorehead, on *Bewitched*." She raised her chin, posed.

Kate affirmed Bunny's assessment. Mrs. Prawsinsky snorted a laugh, but it was obvious she was pleased. "Anyway, I wasn't watching *Bewitched*. It was *The Dick Van Dyke Show*. The old one with Mary Tyler Moore as his wife before she had her own show, the single-girl show. A very good show, too, but not as good as *Dick Van Dyke*."

"Frankly, Mrs. Prawsinsky, I *never* got over Rhoda's marriage. I never thought that guy Joe was right for her."

"Oy vey! Are you ever right. Vat a mistake. She should have gone right on living upstairs from Mary. Such good friends, those two. Adorable."

"So . . ." Kate took another breath. "You were watching *Dick Van Dyke* and you saw the man—"

"Yes." Now the whole face was squinting up—a prune, no a raisin, Kate thought. "Let me start at the beginning. It's coming back now. I thought I forgot, but . . . let me think . . ."

"Good. Get it right." Kate tried not to sigh out loud. "Just take your time, Mrs. Prawsinsky." She rapped her nails against the teacup.

"It was earlier. Definitely earlier. It must have been *Taxi*. I don't like that as much as *Bewitched* or *Dick Van Dyke* or even *Jeannie*, but that short guy, Louie, very funny."

"Oh, yes. A scream," Kate encouraged. "So, earlier? What do you mean earlier?"

"I heard a noise. Like a crash. From upstairs. Like maybe someone fell or they dropped something heavy."

"And you went to see?"

"No." She shook a bony finger at Kate. "Don't get ahead of me, dahlink. No. It was in the middle of *Taxi* I heard the noise. A thump. Had to be from the girl's apartment because no one's living on two. I didn't think too much of it. I went back to *Taxi*. A minute later, another thump. Then another. I go to the door, I peek out. Nothing. I figure maybe I'm imagining things."

"And then?"

"Then? Nothing. *Taxi* is over. But later, I'm watching *Dick Van Dyke*. It's the one where Laura buys the new dress but she's afraid to tell Rob because . . ." She was off and running. It took Kate a good ten minutes to get her back on track.

"I get up to turn off the light, just there." She pointed to the near-shredding Chinatown paper lampshade hanging over a bulb just inside the door. "I like to keep it on most of the time. Scare the robbers away. But it was bothering my eyes, making it hard to see the TV. So I get up to turn it off and I hear the outside door bang. Like someone's slammed it shut. But I had it backward." She stopped, a dramatic pause, arched a penciled eyebrow.

"What do mean backward?"

"He was coming *in,* dahlink, not going out. The front door, you see, it banged open. It hit the wall. *Bang.* So I open my door very, very quietlike and take a few steps into the hallway and there's this colored man—like I described to you, skinny—on the stairs. He's going up and—and look, come, dahlink, I'll show you."

Mrs. Prawsinsky tugged her into the hallway. "Now bend down so you're like my height, dahlink. There. Now take a peek."

Kate did as instructed; she was practically on her knees, and no more than three feet from the staircase.

"He was on the first, maybe second stair when I looked. I was eyeball to eyeball." She put a hand to her cheek, shook her head. "Oy vey. You shouldn't know from it. I thought I would die. A stranger! A colored man! On the stairs! In the middle of the night!"

"And what happened?"

"Happened? Nothing. He didn't even look at me. Like maybe he was *on* something, you know what I mean? Drugs," she whispered. "So, I scoot back to my apartment and close the door, quick."

"Did you hear any noise after that? More crashing-about upstairs? Fighting?"

"Nothing. The noise, the thumps, dahlink, that was *earlier,* remember?"

Kate thought she remembered more of the *Dick Van Dyke* episode, but she nodded.

"To tell you the truth, I figured it's none of my business. The young people today. Who am I to judge? Anyway . . ." She leaned close to Kate, who was still bending down, her back starting to ache. "The girl, she was Spanish, you know. So . . ."

Kate pulled herself erect. "Mrs. Prawsinsky, were there other men who visited Ms. Solana?"

"That night, dahlink?"

"In general?"

"Let me think." Again, the prune face. "Yes. There was her friend. Also colored."

"But he was not the one you saw that night."

"Oh, *no.* The friend is a very polite young man. He holds the door open for me, like I'm a queen." She beamed. "One time, he even helped me with groceries. A very nice boy—though I don't understand what he's doing with his hair." She made a face.

That made it definite. The guy on the stairs was not Willie. Kate was so relieved she could have kissed the old woman's racist prune face. "Mrs. Prawsinsky, I'd like you to do two things."

"So ask."

"One, sign a statement about the two men not being the same. And two, the other man—the one you saw on the staircase—do you think you could describe him, his face, to a police sketch artist?"

The old woman's eyes lit up. "You mean like on TV?"

"Just like *Perry Mason*."

"Oh, I love that Della Street."

"So, you think you can do it? Describe the man?"

"Dahlink, if I could paint, I'd do it myself."

Kate assisted Mrs. Prawsinsky up the long flight of stairs to the precinct's second floor.

The old woman stopped halfway, a hand on the railing, panting. "Oy. No elevator?"

"Are you okay?"

"Fine, honey, fine." She stopped again, caught her breath. *Oh, please don't die, Mrs. Prawsinsky. I need you.* "You sure you're okay?" Kate asked.

"Why? You gonna carry me?"

"You kidding? I think you could carry *me*."

Mrs. Prawsinsky cackled. "That's a good one, dahlink."

Four police sketch artists sat in front of computers listening to victims, making eyes smaller, adding and subtracting beards and wrinkles with the touch of a key. Kate hadn't had time to get used to the computer guys, though she figured she'd better. Soon they'd be the only ones left. Maybe it was her interest in art, the fact that she liked to see the charcoal going down, the constant erasing and redrawing, the rearrangement of features, the artist, police or otherwise, getting his fingers dirty. Today she was in luck. One of the dying breed was still in operation.

Balding, sallow-complexioned, maybe fifty-five, fingers stained with charcoal. His name tag read Calloway.

"You free?" asked Kate.

Calloway scowled. "I was just goin' home. It's almost six."

"Just one more? *Please.*" Kate gave him her best smile.

"I'm on the Special Squad. With Randy Mead. I'll put in a word for you."

"Big deal. I got two months till retirement."

"How about a hundred bucks then?"

He eyed her suspiciously. "You from IA, or something?"

"Internal Affairs? No. No way. Just desperate. What do you say?"

Calloway sat, resigned.

Kate planted Mrs. Prawsinsky opposite him. Calloway raised his charcoal, asked: "Oval, square, round faced?"

The old lady scrunched her face up. "I was watching *Dick Van Dyke* and—"

Kate handed Calloway her card. "Call me when it's ready."

Mrs. Prawsinsky squirmed in her seat, anxious to keep going, her squinty, turquoise-lidded eyes sparkling.

Kate asked Calloway to fax the sketch to her home office. She needed a break. Time to think quietly. She patted Mrs. Prawsinsky's wrist. "I've arranged for your ride home." She checked out Calloway. A scowl twisted his mouth. "Just take your time," she said. "Calloway here, I can tell, he's a very patient man."

The guy was about as subtle as Andy Warhol's wig, thought Kate, his backward baseball cap, manic pacing, darting eyes practically broadcasting *I-AM-A-COP*, here, in front of one of New York City's snazziest Central Park West addresses.

Kate nodded at the plainclothesman the department had stationed in front of the San Remo. He nodded back without looking up, kept pacing. The doorman gave him a get-lost-you're-bringin'-down-the-neighborhood look, but smiled at Kate.

Had her neighbors noticed him? He was pretty hard to miss. Just what she needed, something else to remind the co-op board that she was getting way too much attention.

Inside the safety of her apartment, Kate kicked off her shoes, dropped her jacket onto a chair, shuffled down the penthouse hallway not bothering to turn on the lights.

She stripped off her slacks and blouse, left them all on the bedroom floor, padded to the bathroom, avoiding the mirror—who needed proof that she looked a wreck?

In the shower, she kneaded a sponge of foaming bath gel over the black-and-blue forming on her right elbow, then over the scraped knuckles on both hands, the rainbow-hued bruise making an appearance on her knee. *Thank you, Fat Wally.*

She needed to pull herself together, meet Richard at that new restaurant everyone was talking about and couldn't get a reservation to.

She checked the fax machine. Nothing yet. Mrs. Prawsinsky must be driving Calloway mad.

Back in her bedroom, she started writing up her notes from the meeting—the black man on the staircase the night of Elena's murder. Was it the guy Fat Wally had seen with Elena? She yawned. Made a note. Yawned again. Maybe just a five-minute nap. She took the phone off the hook, tucked it under a pillow.

Marilyn Monroe, leering, not quite human, lips like appliquéd velvet. The Fourteenth Street pillow, on the floor of Elena's apartment, zooming into sharp focus, the room around it dark, airless. Elena's face still. Eyes flat. Blood on her cheek. Kate stares at the swirls of crimson. Then, from somewhere beyond the apartment walls, her name is being called. Softly at first, then louder.

"Kate. *Kate.*"

Richard's face replaced Elena's.

"Oh. Richard." Kate rubbed at her eyes. "What time is it?" Her body felt thick, heavy with sleep.

"Nearly eleven."

"Oh. I must have dozed off . . ." Kate touched his cheek. "I'm sorry."

"Well, it was really embarrassing."

"Why didn't you call me?"

"I've *been* calling. And calling."

"Oh . . . right." Kate retrieved the phone from beneath the pillow. "Sorry again."

"What about your cell?"

"In my bag, in the hall." Kate tried on a sheepish smile.

Richard pulled away, slipped out of his Hugo Boss jacket, arranged it onto a padded hanger in his walk-in closet. "I kept saying, oh, my wife will be here any minute—all the way through dessert—which was really good, by the way."

"Do you know how many dinners I've sat through waiting for *you* to never show?" Her voice went artificially light. "Oh, Richard? Yes, a tad late. I think it's his night to fuck the secretary. You understand."

"Okay. Okay." Richard sighed. "But I was worried, and these dinners are important, Kate—and I want you with me. We're a team, remember?"

Kate managed a smile. "Just give me a little time, all right?"

Richard sighed again, came to the edge of the bed, touched the bruise on her elbow, the scraped knuckles. "What'd you do to yourself?"

Kate shook her head. "It's nothing."

"Nothing? It looks like you got hit by a Mack truck."

Kate pulled herself up, ran her fingers through her hair, tugged the robe over her knees. No need to let him see all her bruises at once. "It looks worse than it is. I banged into something, that's all."

"Or something banged into *you*." Richard frowned. "Police work?"

"Sort of."

"I thought ten years ago you desperately wanted out of police work—that you couldn't wait to get married and give it up, get back to art history."

"That was then. And I will get back to it—and to our dinners, and social life, and everything else. But I need to see this through." Kate got quiet. "For Elena."

"I know you miss her." Richard's tone softened. "I do, too."

"Really?" Kate could not keep the challenge out of her voice. "Because you haven't mentioned her once since it happened." She folded her arms across her chest.

"I thought it would upset you," he said, laying a hand on her arm.

"To talk about how I felt?" Her eyes filled with tears.

Richard took her hand, folded it between his. "I'm sorry, honey. Really, I am."

Kate swiped away her tears. "Believe me, I'd like everything back the way it was, too. But it's not, Richard. It's just not." She pulled away, started to exchange her robe for a pair of silk pajamas.

"I'm sorry." Richard balled up his Egyptian cotton shirt, shoved it into the wicker hamper inside his closet.

Kate managed to shift gears. "Richard, do you think it's possible that Bill Pruitt could have been dealing in stolen art?"

Richard jerked out of his closet. *"What?"*

"Winnie Pruitt said her son had an Italian altarpiece that may have been stolen."

"Winnie said he *stole* it?"

"No. Just that he *had* it."

Richard pulled on a pair of striped cotton pajama bottoms, yanked at the drawstring waist so hard the elastic snapped. "Goddamn inferior fucking goods!"

"Take it easy." Kate slid under the puffy white comforter, wiggled her toes against the smooth cotton sheets. Richard seemed almost as tense as she was. She watched as he threw the torn cotton pants into the corner, huffed as he pulled on a pair of striped boxers. "So, what about Pruitt? Do you think it's possible?"

Richard yawned. "I'm tired. Can we talk about Bill Pruitt some other time?"

21

The art world's red-hot center used to be SoHo. Now it was Chelsea—a former swath of wasteland bordered by the Hudson River on one side and Tenth Avenue on the other, stretching up to Hell's Kitchen and down to Fourteenth Street's meat market. Here former warehouses, auto dealerships, and garages had ceded their land to overscaled art galleries, high-fashion boutiques, and the hippest of the hip new eateries. The transformation, still in progress, was spreading faster than fungus in the rain forest. Forget the total lack of public transportation (the art world habitués were partial to taxis and private drivers anyway), here you had wide streets and picture-postcard Hudson River views, though a few problems persisted. On off-hours, many of those streets in the West Twenties and Thirties were so desolate one felt as if one had entered the Twilight Zone. Then there was the odor. Eau de meat market: a particularly noxious bouquet that stuck in the back of the throat, making it hard to swallow without vomiting. But no matter. In a year or two those lonely streets would be overrun with clothing and shoe stores, home furnishing outlets, wine bars, more and more restaurants; and the wholesale butchers, unable to keep pace with the exorbitant rents that a big-time art gallery can pay, would haul their dead animal carcasses over to Long Island City or Secaucus. And then, in another decade, when the streets would become so clogged with shops and tourists that people stopped looking at the art, well, the art world would simply move on.

Willie did not feel like going to an art opening. But his art dealer, Amanda Lowe, had urged him to come, reminding him that with all the exhibitions he had coming up he was obligated to be "out there," promoting himself and his work.

Before Willie had become an artist he'd thought that was *her* job, that his was solely to make the work. How wrong he had been.

Still, the last couple of days his studio had begun to feel cramped, the smell of turpentine cloying.

The Amanda Lowe Gallery, a former auto dealership recently transformed into the epitome of postmillennial chic complete with green glass front, fifteen-foot white walls, and dull gray poured-concrete floors rough enough to skin your knees while you worship at the feet of the latest art gods, was located at the westerly end of Thirteenth Street. Less than a year before, this particular spot had been favored by African American transvestites, and though a few of these hardworking men in minis and wigs remained, their number had significantly dwindled now that the art mob had invaded the area.

Amanda Lowe's gallery, Willie's gallery, was *the* place for up-and-coming Young Turks. Here they rubbed shoulders with a few older art stars whose lights still burned, jostled for breathing space with the new ones just beginning to ignite, and watched their backs around the wanna-be sparklers.

From a block away, Willie spotted the crowd spilling out into the street. He had an urge to pivot on his Doc Martens, run all the way back to the safety of his studio. But no, he was a professional, or learning to be, and he could handle this even if his heart was not in it. He took a deep breath, squared his shoulders, said a few quick hellos, and then pushed past the outer herd.

Inside, the gallery was packed, humming, clusters of people exchanging bits of artspeak, always with an eye on the crowd, searching for someone more important.

As Willie made his way through the crowd, he picked up snatches of conversation, several people talking about the death artist.

"I tell you," said one thirtyish woman clad all in black leather with muscled arms tattooed from wrist to elbow as if she were wearing Pucci gloves. "It gives me the fucking creeps. The fucking creeps. I mean, I don't feel safe in my fucking studio."

"I know what you mean," said the fiftyish man with a bar through his nose and a shaved head. "I'm fucking scared, too. I had to take a handful of fucking quaaludes to sleep last night."

"Willie!" Schuyler Mills cut through the throng, got an arm around his shoulder. "Are we having fun yet?"

"If I remember it was you, Sky, who taught me this stuff was *work*, not fun."

The Contemporary Museum curator patted Willie on the back. "Good boy. See where my lessons have gotten you? You are, and always will be, my favorite pupil." He gave Willie's arm a paternal squeeze, then beamed an electric smile at someone over Willie's shoulder. "Ah! Queen of the night!"

Amanda Lowe brushed her cheek in Schuyler's vicinity while kissing air. A painfully thin woman in a high-fashion formfitting black Azzedine Alaïa dress, except there was little form to fit—her hip and shoulder bones threatened to tear the fabric. Unnatural eggplant-colored hair, blunt cut to her earlobes (one of which sported an earring so large it grazed her shoulder), formed a severe helmet around her stark white face. Her eyebrows were black commas, eyes lined with dusky kohl, her mouth a red gash. The total effect was somewhere between a Kabuki mask and a corpse.

She air-kissed Willie, then snagged him with one hand, Schuyler with the other, and led the artist and curator—the crowd parting before them like the Red Sea—for a closer inspection of the current exhibition.

"Death artist, death artist, death artist. It's all I'm hearing tonight. I'm sick to death of the death artist."

"Is that a pun?" Willie asked.

Schuyler laughed. "Well, you've got to admit this death artist *is* creative. And he'll certainly be remembered."

Amanda stared at him blankly, said, "Let's just forget him and concentrate on the art, shall we?" She offered Willie and Schuyler what might be a smile—the red gash opened and closed like a shark's mouth. "I think the NEA did Martina a great favor," she said, referring to the National Endowment for the Arts's very public revocation of several artists' grants for reasons of obscenity a few years back. "It set her free, forced her to simplify. Who needs expensive art supplies?" The art dealer gestured at the drawings. "Could these be any more basic?" she asked, indicating the artist's drawings created with her own menstrual blood on cheap rough newsprint paper.

Schuyler Mills said, "Oh . . . no cow heads, dead sharks, or Madonnas splattered in elephant dung? I'm disappointed."

Amanda Lowe signaled the artist over.

Martina, in heavy black boots, torn black jeans, and a black biker's jacket, stomped heavily toward them like a prizefighter entering the ring.

Mills's eyes flashed mischievously. "Tell me. Do you collect your menstrual blood in a bottle to use later, or"—he swiped at his crotch, then flipped his hand up and waved it like a paintbrush—"work directly from the source?"

"Direct," said Martina, playing with her nose ring. "It wouldn't make sense any other way. Look. If you start at one end of the gallery and follow the drawings around, you'll get it. The drawings replicate my flow. See? At the beginning the drawings are real rich and dense, then they start to fade. By the end they're almost not there."

"Ahhh . . ." said Mills. "The trickle-down effect."

Willie would have laughed except that his attention had been taken up by the appearance of Charlaine Kent, director of the Museum for Otherness, who poked her head between Martina and Schuyler. "What's absolutely great," she said as if she'd been part of the conversation all along, "is that the first drawings are so tough and visceral, while the last ones are ephemeral, almost . . . poignant. They walk the line between threat and seduction, don't you think?" She directed this question to Willie, her long black lashes shading her eyes, her fingers toying with an enormous crucifix resting in the cleavage above her pink tube top.

Willie smiled, taking in the dark fleshy curves of Charlaine's breasts, her tightly curled cropped hair bleached a striking platinum, the crimson lipstick that accentuated her sensuous lips.

"We've met before. Charlaine Kent. But everyone calls me Charlie." She extended her hand. "I am a great fan of your work."

The words every artist longs to hear. Willie took her hand, flashed his best smile.

Charlie ran her tongue over those crimson lips.

But the moment was interrupted as Raphael Perez managed to loop his arm over Willie's shoulder, edging both Schuyler Mills and Charlie Kent out of the way. Charlie looked as if she wanted to dig one of her stiletto heels right through Perez's delicate alligator loafers.

Willie, not wanting to offend any of these three art world movers, attempted to disengage from Perez as politely as possible, but, stepping back, stumbled into Amy Schwartz, director of the Contemporary.

Schuyler Mills swooped down on his boss, an arm around her plump shoulder, a kiss on her cheek.

Immediately, junior curator Raphael Perez insinuated himself between Schuyler Mills and Amy Schwartz. He whispered conspiratorially, "Amy. I really must speak to you about your resignation, about the possibility—"

"Please, guys. I'm off duty." Amy's eyes darted between

her two curators, Mills and Perez. "I'll just leave you two to chat." She forced a big smile, then regarded Martina's menstrual drawings, whispered to Willie, "Have you ever tried painting with semen?" She pushed her bushy hair away from her face with her pudgy, multiringed hand.

"I did," said Willie, "but after collecting it my hand was too tired to hold the paintbrush."

Amy hooted, took Willie's arm, led him away from the crowd. "Jesus, those guys, Mills and Perez, are gonna eat me alive. You'd think this damn director's job paid a million a year."

"Money's not the issue for Schuyler," Willie whispered. "Art is like the most important thing in the world to him. He's going to get it, isn't he?"

Amy whispered back, "Look, Willie, I know Sky has been a great supporter of yours, and yeah, he's a real dedicated guy. Sometimes too dedicated, if you ask me—it gives me the creeps. But I don't know who is going to get the job. Even if I did, I wouldn't tell you. It would put you in a terrible position. Just forget it, okay?" Amy looked up. Mills and Perez had moved in, peering at her. "Oh, brother," she said.

But Charlie Kent moved in, too, looped her arm around Willie's shoulders. "Are there any new paintings in your studio?" she asked.

"Yes," said Schuyler, before Willie could open his mouth. "But they are all on reserve for *my* show at the Contemporary."

"Well, not *all*," said Perez. "There's that large civil rights painting that neither of us cared for."

"Really?" said Charlie, eyeing the curators with derision. "Why is that?"

Perez ran his long fingers through his thick dark hair. "First of all, it's too big. Second, I found the subject matter a bit . . . dated."

"*Dated?*" Charlie Kent's eyes burned with indignation. "Might I remind you, Mr. Perez, that for African Americans like Willie and myself the civil rights movement has never ended, is *never* dated." She clutched Willie's arm, asked seductively, "Exactly how big is it, Willie?"

"Big," said Willie, smiling with his eyes. "A major piece. I've covered old newspaper images of civil rights marches with ash and wax, then nailed on a bunch of burned wooden crosses."

"Sounds amazing," said Charlie. She took Willie by the arm, turned him away from the two curators. "You know," she said, "if you've had enough of *this*"—she gestured at Perez and Mills, the crowd—"I'd love to see that painting—now, if possible."

Willie led Charlie Kent right out the door.

Some group on MTV were pretty worked up, their loud pattering faux black rap blasting from the television in what Willie considered his bedroom: a wooden platform and mattress bed, a metal coatrack on wheels instead of a closet. Books and periodicals were stacked up, scattered about—books on art and art history, specifically African art, black heritage, culture, and folk art, which created a sporadic trail across the fifteen-hundred-square-foot loft into the studio, where several more stacks stood like small off-kilter Mayan temples among the rolls of canvas, scraps of wood, metal, fabric, and found objects that Willie used to create his work.

Charlie Kent stepped gingerly over the bits of wood and boxes of overturned nails, around small anthills of sawdust and stacks of books. "Wow," she said, "I just love the way you use everything in your art. It's pure alchemy." She dropped her jacket onto a chair, revealed that pink tube top, the soft mound of her breasts, then arranged herself on a stool in front of his large civil rights painting, crossed her legs this way, then that. "God, the painting is even better than I imagined. Pure genius. I'm sure the board members of the Museum for Otherness will be absolutely thrilled to exhibit it—if that's all right with you."

"Oh. Absolutely." Willie's eyes took in Charlie's shapely

legs, firm thighs. "It's really cool you feel so strongly about the painting," he said. "Because, you know, this is one of my most important pieces." *At least it is at the moment.*

"Oh, yes. It *is* important. And not just to African Americans." She smiled, licked her lips.

An invitation? Willie returned the smile. *Am I reading the signals right?*

Charlie shifted her weight on the stool—a flash of lace panties.

Oh, yeah. Handwritten. He made his move. A hand on her thigh, a quick kiss on her full red mouth.

As Willie maneuvered her past the piles of books and rolls of canvas, finally into his bed, Charlie was still thinking about Willie's painting—how impressed the board would be with her finesse in getting it.

Willie pulled his sweatshirt over his head. For a split second everything went dark, then an image coalesced. *Charlie's pretty face, eyes wide open, her neck surrounded by a sea of deep, deep red.* "Oh."

"Something the matter?"

Willie blinked. Charlie's mouth, only a few inches from his, was smiling. "No. Nothing." He pushed her gently back onto the bed.

She wiggled out of her micromini, then the lace panties. "When can we pick it up?" she asked.

"What?"

"Your painting. For the museum."

"Oh, right." He rolled halfway off her, reached over for his Palm Pilot. "Let's see. It'll be photographed on Thursday, so anytime after that is fine."

"Excellent," she said, undoing the top button of his black jeans. "I'll have the museum's registrar call you to confirm the pickup."

Willie silenced her with his tongue in her mouth, then stopped. "Oh, one other thing. The piece has got to be in the front room of the museum—the main one, you know. I mean, because it's so important—to both of us." He tugged his jeans off. "And like, nothing else can be shown with it—unless you'd like to frame up some of the sketches for the piece. You know, like, sort of give the public an inside look at how the painting came into being." He rubbed a hand over her erect nipples.

"Sketches . . . Ohhh . . ." Charlie moaned.

"Feel good?"

"Oh, great, baby, great." Another low moan. "How many are there? Drawings, I mean." She arched her back, displaying her breasts to better advantage.

Willie licked one nipple, then the other. "About a dozen. You can choose whatever you like." He raised his head, smiled at her. "And, ah, choose one for yourself."

"A painting for my museum and a sketch just for little ol' me? Oh, Wil . . ." She took his face in her hands, kissed him hard on the mouth. Charlie was getting hotter and hotter. "Willie," she said, excited to finalize the deal. "Come with me to the Venice Biennale, and I'll get Otherness to foot the bill."

Venice! "Oh, baby!" Willie pushed her back on the bed, worked his cock between her thighs and into her more-than-willing flesh.

Charlie was picturing Willie's painting on the wall of her museum as she came. She wondered if it might not be a good time to hire a PR agent for the event.

By the time her physical tremors had quieted, she had decided yes.

He really shouldn't do this. Not here. What if someone came in?

But it's late. The door's locked. He leans back into the couch, his eyes trained on the video monitor.

How many times has he watched this? Thirty times? A hundred times? So many that the images are practically etched into his brain—and that's what he wants. Because this is the last time, and he wants to remember it—the image of her moving, alive—memorize it before he destroys it. Before he sacrifices it.

The girl's already undressed now, the camera licking at her nipples, the curve of her hip, in and out of the frame as she dances to some silent music—there's nothing on the sound track.

He breathes in, sharp, slides his hand inside his pants, strokes himself through his boxers.

Damn. Why can't they hold the goddamn camera steady? Amateur Films. They got that right. Still, it's why he's always sought them out, the reason for his collection of their films—the down-and-dirty production values, the nonactors they manage to employ. So real.

He just wishes the guy on the bed would disappear. It's her he wants to see. Vital. Sexy. None of the angry bitch here. Just pure lovely lust.

Her hand seems to echo his; her fingers flicking through pubic hair, touching herself, head thrown back, eyes closed.

Oh, damn. The guy again. Pulling her onto the bed, forcing her beautiful head down between his thighs. He always hates this part, doesn't want to see it. *Fuck.* Just when he was so close, too. He hits the fast forward. No good. They're screwing now. Reverse. That's better. There she is again, dancing, peeling off her clothes.

He watches another minute, transfixed, his hand working as the girl on the small screen dances.

Ahhh . . .

When it's all over, he slips on his gloves, pops the video out of the VCR, pulls a long loop of tape out of the cassette, and puts it in his pocket.

This will make the perfect gift. The perfect bait.

And she'll take it. He's certain of that.

22

The coffee would not take effect—and it was her third cup. A terrible night. Bad dreams. Plus, Richard tossing and turning beside her. Their bed could have registered on the Richter scale. Too bad they weren't having any fun.

Kate had the police artist's sketch on her desk—a black man, thin-faced, haunted eyes, the man Mrs. Prawsinsky said she had seen on the staircase the night Elena died. She'd already distributed the sketch to the squad. Uniforms were faxing it out to every precinct in the city.

Now to deal with her mail, three separate plastic bags full, rerouted by the post office from Kate's Central Park West apartment to the station house, bagged before anyone could get their mitts on it.

Kate tugged on a pair of plastic gloves.

The first batch, a Con Ed bill, AT&T, assorted catalogs. The second, more of the same. The third, a cable TV bill, *The New Yorker, Business Week,* more bills, a postcard from a friend in Belize, a confirmation from the hotel she and Richard had booked for the Venice Biennale. But it was the plain white envelope she now held that stopped her.

Inside was a copy of her author photo from the back of *Artists' Lives,* with wings and a halo drawn on, tied up with a black plastic ribbon. Kate's hands were shaking. Black ribbon. *A death symbol?* Maybe. A red border drawn around the picture, and a message—HELLO. What was it about the red marker, the printed letters that tugged at her memory?

Kate looped the black ribbon over her auto pencil, held it up to the light. It wasn't ribbon at all. It was a piece of video-tape.

"You don't have to wear the gloves *all* day, McKinnon." Hernandez set the copy into the case for fingerprints.

"Oh. Totally forgot I had them on," said Kate, watching the Krazy Glue do its magic.

"Sorry. No prints. Nothing. Whoever sent it wiped it down."

"What else can you do?"

Hernandez turned it over in her gloved hands. "Type the paper, see if there are any particles imbedded. I can't tell you where the copy was made, though. Too many copy shops in the city."

Hernandez handed back the piece of videotape, now inside a plastic bag. "Take this down to Jim Cross in Tech Services, Photo and Film Unit."

Jim Cross sat behind the video-splicing machine, half-glasses propped on the top of his head, pushing back what was left of his hair. The reels, tools, and tape cassettes that covered the nine feet of his running desk sprawled onto the two chairs and floor of the small office. He gestured for Kate to sit, but there was no place for her.

"Sorry." He swept a bunch of plastic reels off a chair. They hit the floor running, a few spiraled across the floor as if someone had sounded the gong for a race.

Kate held up the plastic-encased videotape. "Is there enough to see what's on this?"

Cross studied the tape through the bag. "I'd say you've got maybe twenty seconds of film here. I can splice it onto something else and put it on a cassette."

"How long will it take?"

"Just give me a few minutes." He turned away, cleared a path on his desktop. "You don't care what it's spliced onto, do you? I've got some old procedural footage here somewhere." He sorted through a dozen or more open cassettes until he found what he wanted, set it into the splicer, went to work. A few minutes later he turned to Kate. "Look through here."

Kate leaned toward a monitor that looked like a drive-in theater for ants.

Jim Cross hit a switch. The film started to play. The procedural footage, a diagram of some sort, maybe a floor plan—it was too small to be sure. Then an abrupt change—a figure? a woman?—breasts, yes, a woman, nude. Then it was the diagram again.

"It's too small," said Kate, straightening up.

Cross pulled the film out of the editing machine, snapped it into a cassette. "Here," he said. "Take it to one of the viewing rooms. Right next door."

Not quite the neighborhood Cineplex. A nine-by-ten-foot room. Peeling paint. Fluorescent light. Three televisions on stands. Six metal chairs for viewing.

Kate popped the cassette into a VCR, didn't bother to sit. There was a slight buzz in her head, muscles tense. She had to admit she was excited to see what he'd sent her. She hit play.

A minute or so of that old police footage—a diagram of a room, something out of an old manual. Then a sudden change. Poor color quality. Amateurish lighting. But it was a woman, all right, and definitely nude, touching herself. Then, for maybe three seconds, her face, in sharp focus.

Kate reeled back. *It can't be.*

Now it was that damn police diagram again.

It took a few seconds for Kate to lean forward, hit rewind, then play.

Elena.

Kate hit stop, let herself fall into one of the stiff metal chairs, stared at the blank screen.

What is this? And how did he get it to send to her? Had he been spying on Elena, secretly filming her?

She had to look at it again. This time in slow motion.

Excruciating. Twenty seconds stretched to a full minute.

Kate studied the details. It was not Elena's apartment. She was sure of that.

She played it again. And again.

Elena. The room. The bed. And just at the end, before that damn police diagram made an appearance, the shadow of a man entering the frame. Kate played it a dozen more times to see if she could identify him, but it was impossible.

She stared at the Xerox in her hand—the halo, wings, the red marker, HELLO. But nothing else would register. Those twenty seconds of film were seared into her brain.

Elena did not look as if she was under any pressure to perform. Nor was she alone.

What is it? Some kind of porno tape? Maybe a home movie, something Elena had made with a boyfriend? That was the most plausible excuse Kate could come up with. But then, how would he—whoever *he* is—get it to send to her?

The list of Ethan Stein's sexual paraphernalia flashed in the back of Kate's mind, then Pruitt's sadomasochistic leather mask and his porno tapes.

Kate didn't like making any connection between Elena and those two—conscious or otherwise. Until she knew exactly what it was, she was going to keep the knowledge of this tape to herself. She'd rather not read all about it in the *New York Post*.

She needed some answers.

Willie. She had to see Willie.

23

To Kate, Willie's studio was like a lab, a haphazard, slovenly one, but a lab nonetheless. A long table covered with dozens and dozens of half-squeezed-out paint tubes, brushes of every size, palette knives, bottles of oil, turpentine, varnish, and resins.

"You mind if I keep painting?" Willie dragged his palette on wheels—a converted tea cart covered with a thick slab of glass, half of which was encrusted with anthills of dry and semidry mounds of oil paint—toward the painting he was working on.

"Not if you don't mind me watching." Kate plucked a couple of oily paint rags off an old upholstered chair.

"Careful. There might be paint on that chair."

Kate shrugged. Her clothes were the last thing she cared about at the moment. She regarded his large, unpainted canvas, the rough indications of form sketched in charcoal. "Is this piece for a particular show?"

"If I finish it—for the Contemporary show this summer." Willie squeezed blobs of red and white paint onto his glass palette. "My two pieces for the Venice Biennale were shipped off the other day. You'll be there, won't you? In Venice, I mean."

"Yes. Sure."

"Great." Willie swirled a stiff white bristle brush through the creamy red paint and titanium white, the two colors momentarily married into a wavy motif of stripes before each ceded its ~~own~~ identity to form a lush pink. "I've been trying to make sense of it, of Elena's death," he said.

"I'm not sure that's possible."

"For me, the only way I can make sense of anything—and maybe this sounds wrong, or pretentious, I don't know—is through my work."

"Artists are always trying to fix their broken worlds with art," said Kate. "And you're lucky to have it, your art. Believe me."

Willie drew his loaded brush onto the canvas, gracefully at first, then scrubbing up and down, back and forth, working the paint into the canvas rather than onto it. A face began to take shape. "Maybe it's that I've been trying to make up for something, how I grew up, you know, like I could fix everything by being an artist." He laid his brush down, unscrewed a bottle cap, poured a thick unctuous liquid into a widemouthed bottle. Linseed oil. Kate recognized it from its golden color and particular smell, oily and sweet. Then he added damar varnish, pale yellow, like white wine; a drop of cobalt drier; then, finally, turpentine. With the wide-mouthed cap back on tight, he gently shook to create an emulsion.

It really is a lab, thought Kate. She'd seen him do this before, and other painters as well, this creation of an artist's painting medium; the particular blend they mixed up to add to their paint or dry pigments to help them create the effect they were after—slick or dry, fat or lean.

"Pretty idealistic, huh?" said Willie.

"Idealism is a good thing, Willie." Could Kate possibly hold on to her own?

Willie poured a bit of the newly mixed medium into a clean metal can, dipped his brush into it, and this time when he laid brush to canvas, the paint glided on, translucent, luminous. Then, with another brush, he outlined the pink form with jet black, stood back to study it a moment, then grabbed a rag and wiped it out, though traces of black remained in and around the pink oval—ghostlike features of what had been, instant pentimento.

Kate was fascinated by the process, always had been, by this magic known as painting. It was the first time in days that she'd felt anything other than pain or anxie~~~~ or suspicion.

"But there's no way I can fix what happened to Elena with my art. So, it's like, making art has no purpose anymore." He suddenly stopped working, dropped the brush onto his palette.

"Now you listen to me," said Kate. "You may not be able to change what happened, but I can tell you that if Elena were here she'd tell you to keep painting. She felt like you do, Willie. Look: Your job is to make the best possible paintings. Mine is to find out what happened to Elena."

"Will you?"

Kate sat back, was quiet a moment. "Yes," she finally said. "I think I will."

Willie reached for another brush, examined its bent bristles, tossed it toward a large metal garbage can, and missed. The brush skittered across the studio floor. "And can you keep the cops off my back?"

Kate reached into her bag, unfolded the police sketch she got from Calloway. "This should make you feel better. The man the police are looking for. He was seen entering Elena's apartment building. Does he look familiar to you?"

Willie eyed the sketch, then looked away. "I don't actually know every black person in the city."

Kate blinked as if she'd been slapped. "Did I imply that?"

"That sketch could be anyone, Kate." He frowned, reached for a new brush, stabbed it into a coffee can filled with turpentine.

Kate could see he was as touchy as she was these days. She let it go, opened her notepad, scanned Elena's phone records, the names and addresses that had now been matched to the numbers. "Maybe you can help me figure out who a few of these people are."

Willie left the brush to soak, leaned over Kate's shoulder. "J. Cook. That's Janine. You know, Janine Cook."

"Of course." A foundation dropout. A hard case even back in the seventh grade. A kid Kate never went to bat for. So why, even now, did she feel guilty? She couldn't save them all. "Do you still see her?"

"I did, but only with Elena. They were still friends."

Kate picked at a hardened piece of paint on the chair's arm. Okay, it was time. She couldn't delay it any longer. "Willie . . ." She sucked in a breath. "Was Elena involved in anything . . . well . . . prurient?"

"Prurient?"

"You know, sex."

"What are you getting at, Kate?"

"I saw a clip . . . well, maybe thirty seconds, of a film, of Elena, and it looked like it could have been a porno flick. I . . ." She pulled the paint off the chair, flicked it away. Her fingers were shaking. "It could have been a home movie. Probably was. But—"

"Whoa!" Willie expelled a breath, then thought a minute. "Home movie, you say? Maybe something she made with a boyfriend?"

"Yes. Exactly what I was thinking." *Hoping.*

"Well, there was this filmmaker guy. I met him a couple of times with Elena."

"You remember his name?"

"Damien . . . something."

Kate offered up Elena's phone records.

Willie wiped his hands on a clean paint rag, took hold of the paper. "Trip. Here it is. D. Trip. Damien. He's an NYU film student, I think—though a little old to be a student, if you know what I mean. Maybe a dropout."

"How long did they go out, he and Elena?"

"A few months, maybe. Elena got kinda weird about him. And I know she was thinking about breaking up, 'cause she said so."

"A film student?" Elena may have mentioned him one

time, but that was it. Kate stood. "C'mon. Let's drop in on them, Janine Cook and Damien Trip. If you tag along, it'll make it seem like it's just a casual visit."

"Cool. I'm like your cover, huh?" Willie's eyes sparked with excitement.

"This isn't an installment of *Law and Order*, Willie. Just take your lead from me. And don't say anything unless I ask you to."

Traffic was backed up on Second Avenue. Kate and Willie inched along through the East Village.

It gave Kate time to take in places she and Elena had known together. A half dozen Polish coffee shops with signs left over from the fifties—Veselka their favorite, where a cup of coffee served as a chaser to enormous servings of cheese-and-potato pirogies smothered in fried onions and gobs of sour cream; St. Mark's Café, a hangout for old beatniks and neo-ones with their sparse goatees and skinny tattooed arms. So many places, so many memories.

Finally, two blocks north of Elena's corner, Kate managed to hang a right on Eighth Street, and the traffic cleared. It was a quick shoot from there—just four blocks—but the scenery changed as if a film editor had spliced together two different worlds. Here Polish gave way to Spanish.

"You sure the address is right?" Willie asked. "We're gonna end up in the projects."

"According to the phone company. What did Trip say when you called?"

"That he'd wait for us. He bought your idea—about a memorial service for Elena."

Just past Tompkins Square Park, Kate caught a glimpse of a black awning with bold white letters spelling out SIDE-WALK, and a window so densely packed with neon signs—Red Dog, Guinness, Rolling Rock—that it dissolved into a shimmering mass of artificial light.

"I had lunch there with Elena," she said softly. "Couple of times."

They were deep into Alphabet City now—the affectionate or not so affectionate sobriquet that distinguished Avenues A, B, C, and D—as if these less-than-modest, crowded streets weren't worthy of actual names.

Avenue B was crowded—people ladened down with shopping bags, pushing laundry carts, scolding children. With the windows rolled down, bits of Spanish, Asian, and Arabic tongues zipped in and out of the car like a linguist with Tourette's.

"The Poet's Café is just a couple of blocks over. Remember when . . ." Willie's voice trailed off.

Of course Kate remembered. She and Willie going to the café to hear Elena perform one of her latest pieces—a friend's avant-garde poems set to electronic synthesizer music, Elena, singing, if you could call it that, an abstraction of vocal exercises so staggering the audience was held in thrall.

Kate lit a Marlboro, pulled the smoke deep into her lungs—no way she would be quitting anytime soon. At the traffic light she rolled her window down, blew smoke out, watched a Latino man and a black woman sweep sidewalks in front of a strip of three-story buildings, each painted a different pastel color—lime green, sky blue, cream. "You know, in its own way, it can be beautiful over here."

"Yeah, I hear they say that about Watts, too," said Willie.

Kate felt a rush of embarrassment. "I guess that's one for you in the I'm-cool-and-you're-just-a-naive-white-woman contest."

Willie licked his pointer finger, scored himself an air point, laughed.

But the charm Kate had just noted was coming up short. An empty lot with stripped cars abutted a crumbling wall with a mural that looked as though it had been painted by Diego Rivera on acid: a ten-foot-tall Jesus with bloody tears streaming through half-closed eyes. As they turned the corner, another mural. This one all colossal white and black skulls, crosses, and the words "In Memory of Those Who Have Died." An image at once striking and chilling.

Kate slowed the car to a crawl, tried to read the building numbers.

"Three-something," said Willie. "Keep going. Trip's place must be near the end."

And it was. The very end.

Kate parked right in front of the five-story gray brick building.

Willie squinted through the windshield across Avenue D to the sprawling conglomerate of slablike monoliths that could only be a housing project. "Looks like home to me."

The ground floor of Trip's building was taken up by the Arias Spanish Grocery and a weathered orange awning that wrapped around the corner, FUCK YOU spray-painted on it in bright red.

Above the door to the right of the grocery were about a half dozen buzzers. Their wires snaked up the front of the building like leafless ivy. A real do-it-yourself job, none of them identified. But no matter; the door was unlocked.

The first-floor vestibule had that stale-cabbage smell that seemed built into these old buildings. The narrow staircase was steep, the layout of apartments—one front, one back—the same on each floor. On the first two the domestic sounds of kids and TVs blasting and Game Boys. On the third floor the apartments were boarded up. But on the fourth, it was another world.

Here, there was only one door, and it was shiny structural steel plastered with enough stickers from alarm companies to give a third-story man serious pause. Someone had shoved a card—"Amateur Films"—into a tiny metal holder beside the bell.

Amateur Films? The name resonated. Kate thought a minute. The stash of porno films belonging to Bill Pruitt. Coincidence? Maybe, but that old cop instinct was telling her it wasn't.

Kate leaned on the bell.

The heavy metal door squeaked open.

Damien Trip was maybe thirty-five, with the face of an

angel: pale pale skin, silky blond hair, translucent blue eyes, and a Harrison Ford scar on his chin that added such a perfect combination of toughness and vulnerability, it could have been self-inflicted. A cigarette—which looked out of place on the cherubic face—dangled from his soft, full lips.

The blond guy Fat Wally had described.

Willie shook Trip's hand.

A second later Kate did the same. "Kate McKinnon Rothstein. Elena's friend."

"Kate . . . McKinnon . . . Rothstein. Well . . . I'll be . . . damned." Trip's words seemed to ooze out of him. "Elena talked about you . . . The perfect mom . . . is what she called . . . you."

Was that a slight sneer on his full lips? Kate could not be sure. But the words—*perfect mom*—were so bittersweet, Kate felt a stab of pleasurable pain.

Trip squinted at her through the smoke snaking into his baby blues. He held on to her hand a few seconds too long. "I've seen . . . your book," he said. "You're like the . . . art goddess to the . . . masses."

Yes, he was sneering. Kate was certain. But she smiled.

Then Trip smiled, too. A mistake. His teeth were the color of sand and dirt. The angel fell to earth. "Man, I . . . can't believe it. Elena . . . gone." He shook his head slowly, the smile fading. "I hadn't seen her in . . . months . . . six months, easy."

"How come?"

Trip ran a lazy finger across the scar on his chin. "We sort of . . . drifted apart."

"Why's that?" asked Kate.

Trip hesitated a moment, his eyes narrowed. Then he smiled that rotten-angel smile again. "Tell you the truth, all she ever talked about was this CD she was cutting, and . . . well, I got to feeling the damn CD was more important to her than me . . . you know? A real . . . career woman. Don't get me wrong, Kate. I mean . . . I was real happy for her, but a guy can only take so much . . . you know."

Willie glanced over at Kate, eyebrows arched.

Kate nodded at Trip, taking in what looked like a combination office and sixties crash pad: fuchsia walls; a beat-up imitation leather couch; a couple of old cabinets, one painted milk-of-magnesia pink, the other sky blue; a big wooden desk that looked like something out of a thirties gangster movie, covered with dozens of art cards, invitations to exhibitions, reproductions, invoices.

Another bell went off in Kate's brain. She looked over at the cards, then tried to read those invoices upside down. Whom was she kidding? And without her reading glasses? Forget it.

"You live here?"

Trip leaned past her, tamped his cigarette out in a large ceramic ashtray, which he shifted, ever so slightly, to obscure Kate's view of those invoices. "We work here . . . mostly," he said, in his slow-talking, dreamy way. "I mean, sometimes we . . . crash here. When it's . . . real . . . late, you know."

It was practically as if he was crashing now, or sleepwalking. That was it. Kate finally got it. The guy was *so* stoned. It didn't match with the angel face or his superpreppy outfit—pink button-down shirt and pristine khakis. If he kept his mouth closed, the guy could be a walking Gap ad. "We?" Kate asked.

"My friend . . . partners."

"Amateur Films." Kate smiled, tried to make it warm, sincere. "What kind of films do you make?"

"Mostly . . . experimental."

"Have you always made films?"

Trip eyed her suspiciously for a moment. "No . . . I went to art school. Thought I might be a . . . painter."

"I went to art school, too," said Willie.

"Yeah? Well, it didn't do it for me. I, like . . . needed a bigger palette, if you, uh . . . get my drift."

Filmmaker. Art student. Pornographer. "Where'd you go to art school?" Kate asked.

Trip's eyes narrowed again. "That's . . . real . . . old . . . news. I mean, who cares?"

Kate scanned his desk, the art cards. "But you obviously still like art," she said, reaching for a reproduction of a colorful abstract painting.

"Not real␣␣" said Trip. "I get . . . dozens of these things. I must be on . . . a hundred mailing lists."

Kate regarded the mass of cards, reached for another that had caught her eye. She flipped it over, saw the name in print: Ethan Stein, and the title, *White Light*. The card felt hot in her hand. "Ethan Stein? You know him?" she asked, trying to sound nonchalant.

"Who?" Trip shrugged, glanced at the card. "Looks boring to me."

Then how come he saved it? "You mind if I keep it?" Kate asked. "I like the work."

Trip exaggerated a yawn.

Kate couldn't decide if it was an act, or if it was the grass that was making him so zonked out.

Trip slid into a seat beside the big desk, propped his feet up, popped an unfiltered Gauloise into his mouth, lit it. "So, uh, what about this . . . memorial?"

"A few friends want to put something together," said Willie. "We thought you'd like to be included."

"Oh . . . sure," said Trip, picking a piece of tobacco out of his stained teeth. "Put me down, man . . . for anything. I'm, like . . . there."

Kate looked past Trip to a heavy steel door. "Is that where all the creative juices flow?"

"There's *nothing* going on at the moment," said Trip, suddenly coming to life.

Kate felt like bounding across the room, smashing right through that steel door as if she were Superman. But no. If Trip was her man, she had to play it cool. Knowledge was power, and right now she didn't feel like giving any of it away.

Trip pushed himself up from the desk. "It's getting late. I've really got to get going."

"So soon?" asked Kate.

"Appointment," said Trip, stabbing his cigarette out.

"We'll be in touch," she said, sliding the Ethan Stein card into her bag.

"What?" Trip's eyes darted from Kate to Willie, then back to Kate.

"About the memorial." Kate smiled.

"Oh. Right." Trip hustled them toward the door. It closed behind them, accompanied by the sound of sliding locks and dead bolts.

"Did you know Elena was making a CD?" Kate asked, as she and Willie headed toward the car.

"She mentioned it. But that was a while ago."

"Who was she making it with?"

"My friend Darton Washington."

Kate remembered the name now from the phone list. "Was it ever finished?"

"I don't think so. I'm sure, if it was, I would have heard it."

Why hadn't she heard about it? Kate would have to find out.

But first, Janine Cook.

The young woman looked almost comfortable on her velvet couch, in her almost penthouse apartment on almost Park Avenue.

She was good-looking—dark brown skin, chocolate eyes, straightened hair done up in a bouffant. Her black leather micromini covered the top six inches of her fishnet stockings, and her tight cream-colored sweater, which was making a display of her nipples, still could not mask the fact that there was something decidedly mannish about her—the deep voice, tough mannerisms—that reminded Kate of the actor Jaye Davidson, the one in *The Crying Game*.

It had been some time since Kate had seen her, but still, she was struck by how much older, harder, Janine looked.

What exactly could have been the basis for the friendship between Janine and Elena?

Willie settled into a shiny leather recliner.

Kate took stock of the apartment, the furnishings—the couch was top quality, the rug looked authentic Persian, the wineglasses stacked on the built-in bar appeared to be crystal. "Looks like you've done well for yourself," said Kate, smiling at the young woman.

Janine said, "Uh-huh."

Kate tried again. "Your place is beautiful. Did you furnish it yourself?"

"What's that supposed to mean?" Janine's purple-lidded eyes narrowed.

Kate took a breath. "Just that either you or your decorator has wonderful taste." Another smile. "Me, I have to depend on a decorator."

"Yeah. Well, my *decorator* fuckin' died. So I had to do it all by my lonesome. Sad, huh?" Janine leaned back on the couch, eyed Kate across the marble slab of coffee table.

"Look, Janine, we're all hurting," said Kate quietly.

Janine closed her eyes, her hard edges momentarily blurring.

Elena's hair in pigtails; Janine's in cornrows. The jump rope snagging on broken concrete. So little sunlight able to penetrate row upon row of ugly buildings that made up that damn housing project in—what'd they call it—the courtyard? What a laugh.

"Elena was a real good friend to me," said Janine.

"I'm sure she was," said Kate softly. "So help me out here, okay?"

Janine opened her eyes. There were tears in the corners.

"Can you tell me anything that might make sense of why this happened?"

Janine turned away, chewed the purple lipstick that matched the color of her eyelids. "What's to tell?"

"Come on, Janine," said Willie. "Elena told you stuff. Girlfriends, and all that. Is there anything?"

Janine's jaw went rigid. "You a cop now, Willie?"

Kate touched his arm to silence him. "Look, Janine, it's just that we all want to know what happened. Don't you?"

"And what—exactly—do you think I can tell you?"

"You lost a friend," Kate said, her voice cracking. "But I lost a daughter." Now there were tears in Kate's eyes.

That seemed to do it. Janine actually laid her hand on Kate's, cried, too.

"Janine," said Kate, patting a hand with purple-pink fingernails long enough to scare a bobcat. "Was Elena still involved with Damien Trip?"

Janine nodded, but seemed to toughen with the sound of his name. "I saw them together, yeah, about a week ago."

"A week ago?" said Kate. "Are you sure?"

"If they were still together," said Willie, "then Trip lied."

Janine eyed Willie, then Kate. "You *already* talked to Trip?" She drew a breath, her eyes suddenly fearful.

"It's okay, Janine." Kate threw Willie a look.

"Elena's *dead*," said Janine. "I don't want to talk about her anymore." She turned away, but Kate could see she was fighting some real emotion. She tried putting her arms around the girl, but it was no good. Janine shrugged her off. "I can't help you." She stood, tugged her mini over her thighs. "I don't know nothing about it."

"I *asked* you not to say anything." Kate smacked the elevator button. "Were you intentionally trying to screw things up?"

"Sorry." Willie looked down at his shoes.

"I'm taking you home."

Willie blinked. *A woman, struggling. A huge, dark room. Murky water oozing up between rotting floorboards.* He squeezed his eyes shut, but it was still there. *Shadows and moonlight. A man and a woman, fighting. The woman turning, her face pulling into focus. Kate.*

"Willie? *Willie.*" Kate shook him. "What's the matter?"

Willie had fallen back against the elevator wall.

"Jesus, Willie. Are you okay?"

Willie rubbed a hand over his face. "I had another flash."

"Well, you're under a strain," said Kate.

"You were in it, Kate."

"In what?"

"This last ⬛ This flash, or whatever it is. You were *there*."

A light rain dappled the car's windshield. Inside, Kate and Willie sat silent.

She lit another Marlboro, cracked the window, felt the wind and rain on her face. A memory—another rainy day— floated into the back of her mind.

"I have a story about visions," said Kate. One she had tried to forget, though lately it had been gnawing away at her all over again. "It was a long time ago. When I was on the Astoria force. My last case, though I didn't know it at the time. A runaway. It seemed routine." Kate stared through the windshield, the rain heavier now.

Now it was another rainy day, and a different set of windshield wipers dragged and squeaked.

Kate lit a Winston, checked the handwritten map beside her, picked up speed at the junction of Queens Boulevard and Twenty-first Street. Please make me wrong about this one, she thought, squeezing down on the accelerator. The monolithic apartment buildings slid by like a movie. The deserted oil tanks, her next landmark, then a turn onto the nearly deserted street that led to the Astoria dump.

I KNOW WHERE SHE IS BECAUSE I KNOW WHERE I PUT HER.

The words, just below the map, in a looping script and red Magic Marker, looked as if they'd been written in blood.

Young Detective McKinnon's palms were sweaty as she brought her car to a stop just beside the large rusting Dumpster. She drew her gun. Her boot heels crunched in the pitted gravel as she got a foothold on the side of the Dumpster, pulled herself up.

That naked battered angel on top of wavy black plastic, aluminum foil fanning out from behind her head.

What was it about that last case that kept nagging at her? Kate stared at the rain, the wet road, the blur of the traffic lights. "The department had brought in a psychic," she said to Willie. "I listened to her. We spent almost two weeks following dead-end leads based on dreams and flashes and ESP. Maybe it was just easier to let someone else do the work. I was busy. Too busy. By the time I got back to the case . . . it was too late."

"We all make mistakes," said Willie.

"But they don't cost a life." Kate tossed her cigarette out the window. "I nearly got him, too. There was a fingerprint on the girl's backpack that didn't match up with anyone's— not the girl's, her parents', none of her friends'. I was sure we'd get him with that. I even bragged about it to a reporter." Kate shook her head. "Damn vanity."

But Willie had stopped listening, scared now, running his fingers over the edges of that police-sketch portrait folded inside his jacket pocket.

24

He's got to concentrate.

But sometimes it seems like he becomes a totally different person, as though he were in a fugue state. He's conscious, knows what he's doing, and yet a whole piece of himself is missing.

He shakes his head, arms, legs, needs to be wide awake, working. What it's all about. The work.

The game. The new rules.

He just hopes she can keep up with him.

Of course she can!

"Shut up!"

Even with the Walkman's music pulsing through his ears, those damn voices have broken through.

Failure!

A word he'd heard so often growing up. And *father,* the word he associates with it.

Your father loves you.

That's what his mother always said.

His father, who convinced his young wife that their brand-new baby boy should be left to cry, not touched, never hugged. His mother said she would lie awake in bed and cry with him. One time his father came home early and his mother, she says, was coddling him, cooing and humming.

His father went nuts. Beat them both. As further punishment, locked his mother in the bedroom for three days, the baby, only months old, left alone in the crib, crying and shitting all over himself.

He swears that to this day he can remember the stink. The loneliness. The shame.

Odd, how inflicting pain stopped his own. And the pleasure that accompanied it. Now that was a nice surprise.

The envelope is just where he put it, the lock of hair intact.

With precision and care, he lays a strip of masking tape along the edge of the hair, another piece on top of that, to create a sandwich, more tape to make a sort of handle.

He's already chosen the next image. And the addition of the hair will make a nice transition—a connection to his past work and a link to the new.

He lays the clump of hair down onto the reproduction, tries it here, there, decides he will glue it right onto the woman's head.

This one's not going to be so easy. A real teaser for Kate. She'll have to work hard to figure it out.

He plucks the hair off the image, whisks it across his cheek, over his eyelids, under his nose, breathes in what is left of the girl's perfume, then ever so softly over his lips, into his mouth, sucking on it. Almost immediately he's hard. If only that stupid girl could see him now. Well, he made the most of her, not that she cared, not that she deserved so much attention.

Just one more dalliance before he sacrifices it.

He unzips his pants, strokes the clump of hair across his scrotum, feels it tighten. Up and down his cock, just the hair, not his hand, no pressure, nothing obscene. Softly. Slowly. Up and down. Faster now.

He pictures the girl dancing, nude, touching herself, as he comes.

A moment later, he straightens up, feels a twinge of shame, pictures himself in a dark room, naked and alone, covered in shit, and crying.

Enough.

It's time to work. He dips the clump of hair into alcohol. It must be clean, spotless.

Two Hundred Sixty-seven Washington Street was an old brick structure, maybe once a printing house or small factory, now steam-cleaned, renovated into luxury co-ops. The breeze from the nearby Hudson River cooled the wide peaceful street. "Washington on Washington Street. Cool, huh?" Darton had said when giving Kate the address.

Inside, the lobby was sleek, industrial high-tech; the elevator, huge, of polished steel, like a giant cage. Kate checked her reflection in the shiny metal, ran a hand through her hair.

How should she handle him? A week ago, Kate had trusted people—something she had worked on for years. Now, she was thinking the way she had when she was back in Astoria—that everyone was guilty of something.

The entire north wall of Darton Washington's loft was floor-to-ceiling windows. The pale Naples yellow sunset dappled across the oversized black leather couches, two enormous rubber plants, and a handcrafted wooden table as long as a bowling alley surrounded by a dozen thronelike chairs that would look right at home in the Hearst Castle. But the loft's most startling element was the enameled floor, bright red, and so shiny it cast scarlet shadows everywhere.

Darton Washington leaned against a chair, smiling, handsome. "You like the floor? I took the idea from African ceremonial rooms."

"It's amazing," said Kate, striding toward two WLK Hand assemblages on an opposite wall. "Willie's pieces look fabulous here."

"He's a genius," Washington said, playing with the pencil-thin mustache that outlined his sensuous upper lip.

Kate surveyed the adjacent wall, filled with a suite of Jacob Lawrence prints, a chronicle of the slaves' experience from Africa to the American South. "These are marvelous."

"Yes. Simple, but absolutely on the mark," said Washington, in a clipped, practically British accent.

"Do you mind if I ask where you're from?"

"Harlem. But I don't have to sound like it, do I?" Washington smiled again. "And you?"

"Astoria—but I don't sound like it either—I hope."
Washington laughed.

"Whose are these?" She indicated four somewhat primitive-looking oils of black men.

"Horace Pippin."

"Oh, yes. Of course." She moved on to a series of photographs with accompanying text, minimal and elegant—a black couple in a doorway, at a table, in bed. Kate read some of the text. "Carrie Mae Weems?"

"You got it," said Washington. "One of my favorite Conceptual artists."

"They're lovely. Moving, too." Kate was impressed by Washington's eye, but it was the small, almost white painting tucked into a corner beside that huge dining room table that caught her eye.

"Ethan Stein?"

"I'm surprised you recognized it. Not that many people know his work. He's one of the few white artists I collect. I like the purity of it."

"Yes, it's lovely." Kate studied the painting, the overlay of white brushstrokes, the faint hint of a gray grid below. It was very much like hers—and also like the one in the blurry Polaroid—though, in fact, all of Stein's paintings were similar. Still, it was enough to give her the creeps. "I have one quite like it."

"Do you?"

"I bought it a few years back. When did you get yours?"

Washington tugged at his shirt collar, which Kate would wager he had bought at one of those Big Man shops. He was six feet three, easy. And that shirt collar that was giving him trouble—Kate couldn't even guess at the size. "Oh, a few years ago," he said. "Sorry I didn't buy another."

"Why's that?"

"Well, as I said, I like it, and . . . I guess Stein's market is about to go up. Sorry, that's a bit tasteless," said Washington. "So, you and Willie go way back?"

"Yes," said Kate, who had not failed to notice the man's change of subject. She folded herself into one of the plush leather couches, took in the picture-window view—the Hudson River, New Jersey, lots of sky—tuned in, for a moment, to the spare, beautiful music being piped into the space with concertlike clarity.

"Philip Glass," said Washington, as though reading her mind. "One of the great modernist composers." He slipped onto the couch opposite. "You're surprised, huh? You figure a big ol' black dude like me, hell, he's gotta be listenin' to Stevie Wonder or Bob Marley or some heavy-duty rappers, right?"

"I hadn't given it much thought, Mr. Washington, but Willie did tell me you represent some rap groups."

"I do. For the money," said Washington. "Rather, I did. I'm on my own now. Left that autocratic music company, FirstRate, just a couple of weeks ago. Now I can pursue any kind of music I want to. Rap, pop, jazz, modern, classical. Anything." He smiled. "I studied music and art in college. Didn't think I had the necessary talent for art—at least my profs didn't think so." He smiled. "But I'm perfectly content pursuing music. Personally, I'm into Steve Reich, Glass, Meredith Monk, Stravinsky; Bach always."

"I'm a musical moron," said Kate. "My idea of great is Mary Wells, Martha and the Vandellas, Sarah Vaughan, Ella."

"Not so bad." He lifted a long cigarillo from a silver cup on the coffee table, placed it between his full lips. "You mind?"

Kate pulled out a Marlboro so fast, he laughed.

Darton slid a large cut-glass ashtray across the coffee table, offered Kate a light. She touched his hands—which were huge and beautiful—to steady the flame. "Thanks."

She exhaled. "I was wondering . . . about the CD you were cutting for Elena Solana—was it finished, or—"

Washington's smile faded fast. "No. It was never finished."

"What happened?"

He shrugged his halfback shoulders. "I guess she lost interest—which was a shame."

"It was good?"

"It was great." Washington's eyes drifted away a moment, filled with—Kate wasn't sure. "It would have made her famous."

"I don't understand. If it was great, why wouldn't Elena—"

Washington stabbed the cigarillo into the ashtray with such force, it looked as if the glass would shatter. Kate watched the man reel in his emotions as if he were hauling in a killer shark. "All I can say is . . . it was going well, and then Elena seemed to . . . lose interest. But it was months ago."

"So you've had no contact with Elena for months?"

"Exactly."

Kate unfolded a copy of Elena's phone records, slid it toward him. "According to this, she called you only days before she died."

Washington's dark eyes narrowed. "You know, this is beginning to sound like an interrogation. If the police want to question me about Ms. Solana, that's fine. But right now, I'm finished talking."

"I don't think so," said Kate, laying her temporary NYPD ID on the coffee table.

Darton was up from the couch as if he'd been stung, almost dancing backward across that bright red floor, putting distance between Kate and himself. "What the fuck is this? You call, say you're a friend of Willie's, and—"

"I *am* a friend of Willie's—but I'm assisting the NYPD." Kate stood. "And you *will* answer my questions, Mr. Washington—either here or at the station. Which will it be?"

Washington took a few steps toward her, jaw clenched, hands twitching at his sides. They were three feet apart, the air between them buzzing, electric. Kate's hand hovered close to her hidden Glock, but she maintained her cool. "Look, I'm not here to fuck you over. Simply to fill in some blanks about Elena's life."

"Nobody fucks me over. *Nobody*. Not me. Not the people I care about. You got that?"

"Nobody fucks *me* over either, Mr. Washington. You got *that*? Now, you want to tell me what you and Elena Solana talked about when she called, or you want me to have a patrol car pick you up and haul you over to the Sixth Precinct? It's up to you." Kate's eyes had not left his, but she remained alert for any sign of movement.

Washington sighed. "She was thinking about working again—on the CD."

"And?"

"And . . . I didn't want to."

"I thought it was great. Why wouldn't you?"

"It had been months. I'd lost interest. I had other projects going. I wasn't about to stop everything and just pick up where we left off."

"Pick up with . . . what, exactly?"

"With the CD. What else?"

"You tell me."

"I told you. I'd gone past it."

"Past it, or past *her*? You two were involved, weren't you?"

"Involved in making a CD—until Elena stopped being involved."

"And that made you mad."

"I was annoyed, yes. That she'd been so cavalier. That she just let the thing go. I'd invested in her. Thought we had a future together—in *business*." His sensuous lips tightened. "I'll admit it. My pride was hurt."

"So she hurt you."

"She hurt *herself*—and her career."

"And *your* career?"

"My career is just fine." Washington folded his arms across his chest. "And there was no way I was just going to dump everything and start up working with her again just because *she* felt like it."

"Can I hear them?"

"What?"

"The demo tapes."

Washington turned away, lit another cigar, puffed. "If I can locate them."

"It must have meant a loss of revenue not to finish Elena's CD."

"I made a decision," said Washington. "To cut my losses."

"Really?" said Kate. "Sounds like bad business, Mr. Washington."

Washington and Elena? Kate tried to picture them together as she headed down the cold white hallway. The man certainly fit Fat Wally's description—a black man who looked like a football player or prizefighter. Not that Fat Wally was what Kate would call a reliable witness.

Washington had admitted to a business relationship with Elena. But was it more than that? Kate wanted to push him further, but also wanted to get more information before she did.

There were just too many connections—Trip, Pruitt, the pornographic films, Washington owning an Ethan Stein painting. It was as if she'd stumbled into a seething nest.

Kate checked her watch. She was supposed to meet Richard for dinner, and it looked as if she was going to be late. Again.

25

A police car streaked past, amber lights flashing, the siren so loud, Willie's ears shivered with pain.

Harlem—125th Street and Martin Luther King Jr. Boulevard. Willie checked out the new street sign: AFRICAN SQUARE. It struck him as a white man's idea of what African Americans wanted.

Now it was a fire engine, blaring. Willie covered his ears as it tore past him. Was that the same direction as the cop car? He was still wondering when, seconds later, another one screamed down the street. Willie followed it with his eyes, wondered if some kid had fallen out of a tenement window that had no bars because the landlord knew he could get away with it up here; or if a family had been wiped out because there were no goddamn smoke alarms or usable fire escapes. The sirens faded into blasting rap music—a kid in low-slung baggy jeans, exposed boxer shorts, a handheld boom box to his ear. Oh, yeah, you're cool, thought Willie, real cool. Just don't be boppin' down these mean streets when you're forty.

Then a couple of white guys, hunched over, scoping out the street, looking to score. Looking for trouble, too, thought Willie—better wait till morning, boys, join the Sunday tour groups of white folks, cameras at the ready to snap the colorful coloreds up in Harlem.

Willie dug his hands into the pockets of his leather jacket, twice cleaned. Now it no longer smelled of death—nor leather—just chemicals. He sniffed at a sleeve: Chemicals or not, the action brought back that night, and Elena's shattered body.

"Shit."

At Lenox Avenue the crowd thickened: mostly men, mostly young, some duded up for the evening ahead. Others—for whom Saturday night was like any other night—shuffled farther east, where abandoned buildings hugged the periphery of the elevated subway like empty husks: rags on their heads, bottles wrapped in crumpled paper bags at their lips.

A pot of coffee crashed to the floor. Brown liquid splashed in slow motion. Shards of glass flashed silver, then morphed into a knife slashing through space. Elena's arms crisscrossed in front of her screaming face.

Then there was another face. But a kitchen light swinging on a chain dissolved it into a network of fractured shadows, an unrecognizable abstraction.

Willie strained to hold on to the vision—to see the face. But it was no use. It faded from blood red to the painted purple facade of the corner bar, the Lenox Lounge.

A place Willie knew, a memory.

Plush velvet booths. Bitter-tasting beer. Trying hard to look older than sixteen. Henry beside him. And the talk. A kind of talk Willie rarely heard, surely not around his South Bronx project. But in the Lenox Lounge it was different. Not angry talk. Not scared talk. Just men talking, laughing, too. Henry's arm around his shoulders, more father than brother. Just remembering that now, the hurt was too much.

Across the street, the Apollo's neon announced PIONEERS OF MOTOWN—the Four Tops, Smokey Robinson and the Miracles. Kate's favorite music. *Shit.* He did not want to think about her. Not now.

He kept his head down, walked with purpose. He knew where he was headed, hoped he was right. The wind kicked up with a slight mist. Willie shivered inside his ruined jacket. Would spring ever settle in?

Now he was with the lost men, beside the El, sidestepping the lean, mangy dogs who hunted for food the way the lost men prowled for drugs and drink—the way Willie, too, prowled the dark street where the sun was never invited, kept out by the rusted hulk of overhead metal tracks. His Doc Martens kicked at garbage and broken glass; he shoved an abandoned shopping cart, like some goddamn symbol— a horn of plenty that had run dry for his brothers up here in Harlem.

Was it 132nd? Maybe. He wasn't sure. The street looked as if it had been waiting for something to happen—not enough activity; men huddled in doorways, faces hidden by the dark. But no, it was the wrong street.

Across the avenue, once-white lettering, now yellow and chipped, on a cobalt blue background—the Greater Central Baptist Church. Stained-glass windows—slabs of colored glass flowers framed an awkward head of Jesus. Tomorrow, he knew, the churchgoing ladies would be here in their Sunday-morning finery and it would be a whole different world. Maybe he should have waited until tomorrow, too. But no. This could not wait.

On the corner of Fifth, across from the church, was a whitewashed brick building that could use a second go-around with the white paint, now pigeon gray, a rusting metal sign dangling off-kilter above the double doors: TRANSIENTS—WEEKLY. Worth checking.

"You kiddin' me, boy?" The flesh around the proprietor's eyes was light pink, like raw meat. It's that disease, thought Willie, the one Michael Jackson's got—supposedly. "I don't get nobody's *name* here. What you think—they be paying by check with their names printed out on 'em?" The man scratched his two-toned neck.

Willie peered up the staircase to the right. The wallpaper—pink flamingos against a faded-blue sky—though peeling badly, looked hand-painted, as if maybe, at one time, this hotel had really been something. But how long ago, Willie couldn't imagine. Not in his lifetime, that was for sure. He asked if he could check the rooms, but even as the words passed his lips he knew how absurd it sounded.

Mr. Two-tone didn't even look his way, just lit a bent cigarette, shook the match out in Willie's face.

The mist had turned to rain. Halos of yellow light from the streetlights spilled onto the wet sidewalks like pale honey.

On the next corner, P.S. 121. Was it only last fall that he and Elena had been here with that class of seventh graders— a new foundation group—the teacher shushing them while Elena performed a few astonishing riffs—poetry as abstract music.

Afterward, Willie had taken the kids outside, into the little courtyard, to collect the leaves shed by the few trees. Five minutes, and a couple of brawls later, the kids had stripped the concrete of any hint of fall. Then he had them glue the leaves onto colored construction paper, paint on and around them, or use them as stencils.

Now, when Willie looked up and saw the second-story windows still dotted with those same construction-paper leaves—so many months later—it made his heart ache.

Another block and there it was. The eight-foot-high fence of corrugated aluminum jammed up around the corner building. First, one man, jacket hiked up to hide his face, darted a look over his shoulder, slipped behind the aluminum. Then, a minute later, there was another.

The street lamp painted the brick building a sour-lemony hue, and through the blown-out upper windows and the caved-in roof irregular patches of blue-black sky formed themselves into a mean abstract painting.

Another man squeezed past the aluminum grating.

Willie paced halfway down the street and back, trying to rev up his nerve. He watched two more men disappear behind the aluminum.

Okay, man. It's time. Do it. He took a breath, then another, pumping up his courage; then fast, almost without thinking, he squeezed past the metal, his feet taking the crumbling gray stones that were once front stairs, then through the open archway that functioned as a front door onto the torn-up floorboards, which slowed him down.

He reached out in the dark for support, but there were no walls.

Whispers echoed in the open space.

Across the blackness, a glowing mass of red-orange, and figures.

It took a moment before he could figure it all out: the makeshift oven an upended garbage can, and how many men—four? five?—all huddled around it, their hands, glass syringes, metal spoons flickering white-hot.

Another deep breath, and Willie moved out of the dark.

"What d'fuck—?" A black cutout, a man with a red-orange outline, shimmered toward him, blurring into darkness.

Willie could feel the fire's heat on his face. Or was it fear? He caught sight of his hands, glowing like a jack-o'-lanterns, in front of him—and realized he was the only one illuminated.

But then another man spoke up—a scarecrow with a spoon, melting crack over flames. "Wil? That you?"

"Henry." Willie let out a breath. "You gotta come with me."

"What? You crazy, man? What the fuck you doing here?"

"You're in trouble, Henry. Big trouble." Willie couldn't see his eyes, but his brother's fingers tightened on his arm.

"Wait for me out front, little bro."

"This is *real* serious, Henry. You've got—"

"Wait out front." Henry shoved Willie back toward the door, his strength always a surprise to Willie, considering how frail he looked. Henry slid back into the dark until the fire painted him orange again and he got that spoon back over the flames.

Outside, Willie kicked at shards of glass, stared up at those sad school windows with their sad colored-paper leaves, rain sprinkling his face, his hair. He shifted his weight from one foot to the other. Ten minutes felt like hours.

When Henry strutted out, high, smiling and bold, Willie felt as if he could kill him. "You are in big fucking trouble," he said, producing the police-artist sketch, crumpled and damp, from his pocket.

Henry stared at the image, his hand shaking as he took hold of it, but his voice was cocky. "Goddamn it, man. This fucking thing. Hell, this could be anyone."

"You think so," said Willie, barely able to control his rage. "Then how come it took me about half a fucking second to recognize you? You think the cops won't?"

The street lamp provided enough light for Willie to see the desperate look that suddenly animated his brother's once handsome face, but it was enough to soften him—at least for a moment.

"Please, Henry, tell me. What were you doing at Elena's place?"

Henry sagged. "I—I just wanted to see her. Nothing serious, man. Like . . . maybe have a drink, you know? Be with her."

"Why?"

"I . . ." Henry stared down at the wet sidewalk. "I knew her since school, man. Since before I dropped out. You know that. I liked her. Is that so bad?"

"And that night—the night she was murdered? You were there."

"But I didn't *do* anything, Wil. You gotta believe that." He paced under the sickly yellow light, his hands shoved into his pockets. "When I got there, her bell was out, but the front door was wide open. So I went up and . . . I saw her, all cut up. I . . . I just got out of there, fast. You believe me, don't you?"

"I believe you—but there's a killer out there, and the cops think it's you."

"What? They think I'm the goddamn death artist?"

Henry's mouth fell open, then broke into a sickly grin. His cackling laugh cut through the mist.

"You think this is *funny*?" Willie grabbed him by the shoulders.

Henry's hands were around Willie's throat, fast.

Willie gasped, the muscles in his throat twitched for air. His big brother, no matter how wasted by drugs, could still overpower him. Willie pulled at Henry's hands, tried to speak, but couldn't. The yellow street lamp above was spiraling like a whirlpool, and he was falling into it, swooning.

A minute later—or was it an hour?—Willie was sitting on the damp sidewalk, stroking the sore tendons in his neck, Henry's face coming into focus only inches from his.

"Oh, man. Oh, man. Forgive me." Henry hugged Willie to him. "I didn't mean it. It was the crack, man. I love you, Wil. You know that, don't you?"

Willie eyed his brother gravely. Was it the drugs working that night at Elena's? He stared into Henry's face, the face of this junkie who was once the big brother he loved. "Yeah, Henry. I know that."

"And you believe me?"

"I believe you." Yes, he knew his brother. He wasn't capable of murder. He wasn't. Willie repeated the phrase—*he wasn't*—in his head, trying to convince himself, almost believing it, too. But would anyone else? "Why didn't you tell me this before, Henry?"

"I *tried*, man. Last time I saw you, but . . ."

Willie shoved the envelope of money into Henry's hands. "You've got to get out of town. Before the cops find you."

Henry licked his dry lips, fingered the bills.

"There's five hundred dollars there. Get on a train or a plane or a bus, but get away."

"I don't have to run," said Henry, some of that cockiness back. "I've got a place to hide out. No one can find me there."

"Then go." Willie sighed. "And don't blow the money on drugs."

"I'm almost clean," said Henry, his face going soft. "A little crack is all. I've been off junk for weeks. You believe me, right?"

Willie thought of what their mother, Iris, would say— *You're throwing good money away, son*—but he was doing it for her, too. The shame would kill her. Guilty or not, Henry was the perfect patsy. He took his brother's hand, the one that only moments ago had been choking the life out of him. Henry squeezed back, this time with tenderness. Then Willie turned away, hurried down the street.

Forgive me, Kate. He's my brother.

Richard was at the very last table in Joe Allen's, on the bar side of the dimly lit, passionately old-fashioned watering hole. Kate couldn't hear what he was saying, but he was giving the reporter his best smile, complete with that almost-wink thing he did.

Did he think he was cute? Oh, yeah. Leaning in toward the young blonde—Why did they always have to be blond?—Ms. Kathy Kraft of the *New York Fucking Times,* who was laughing, her bleached-blond head thrown back like Richard had just told her the fucking joke of the century.

This was definitely not what she'd had in mind.

But Kate would not let her mood get the better of her. No. She'd have a little fun.

She checked herself in the bar's antique mirror. Yes, she'd had better days, but it was not her worst. She pushed her hair into shape, strutted half the length of the bar, hesitated a second until she was sure Richard had spotted her. Then, a quick scan down the bar. A few steps and she laid one hand on a Calvin Klein suit, the other on a Mr. Armani, then leaned in between the two of them.

A toss of her hair, a bedroom smile, her best Lauren Bacall purr: "Oh, sorry to bother you, gentlemen, but I seem to have forgotten my cigarettes." The suits started a fumbling contest for cigarettes and lighters.

Mr. Armani practically vaulted off his barstool. "Hey, join us."

"Please," piped in Mr. Klein. "Bartender"—he gestured—"a drink for the lady."

Kate rewarded them with another warm flash of her hazel eyes, then a quick look in Richard's direction. "I'd love to, but—" She angled herself to the left so that Richard got a full view of the show, then added another dazzling smile. "Really, I would just love to, but—" One more smile. "Thank you, gentlemen." She felt their eyes follow her as she sauntered across the room.

Richard was already on his feet.

"Darling," she said, unable to hide a mischievous grin.

"Ah, finally," he said to the laughing reporter. "The *late* Mrs. Richard Rothstein. My wife, Kate."

Kate took the reporter's hand. "Am I terribly late? I'm so sorry."

"That's all right," the reporter said. "Your husband's been the most delightful company."

"He always is. Aren't you, darling?" Kate raised an eyebrow in his direction.

"But I've really got to be going." The reporter stood, took Richard's hand. "And don't you worry about the tone of my article, Rich."

Rich? Kate's other eyebrow arched.

"Thank you, Kathy." Richard smiled, did that almost-wink again.

"Something wrong with your eye, dear? Your conjunctivitis isn't coming back, is it?" Kate quick-turned to the young reporter. "Oh, it was just awful. Oozy and—ugh, never mind. It's too disgusting to even talk about."

Richard whisked the young reporter away, walking her to the front of the restaurant, holding her hand too long as they said good-bye.

No, she would not be angry. He was just paying her back for her performance. Still, she couldn't resist serving up an aperitif in her best Walter Cronkite voice: "No. *Really,* Your Honor. We're just good friends. And *honestly,* I had no idea she was *thirteen.*"

"And you're what—*sixteen*? Miss Flirting-at-the-Bar?"

"I was simply bumming a cigarette."

"Uh-huh. You left the poor bastards drooling all over their twelve-hundred-dollar suits."

Kate kissed him, pushed the curls off his forehead. "I'm sorry I'm late. Really. Anyway, it gave you time to slobber all over Ms. *New York Times*." She smiled. "Forgive me?"

"This time."

She signaled the waiter for a drink.

"How was your day? Any more bruises?"

"Just on my heart." Kate downed her martini as soon as it arrived.

Richard looked at her with concern. "You okay?"

Kate signaled for another drink, the flirty, giddy mood she had manufactured a moment ago deflating. "I don't like what I'm discovering about Elena—" Her mind played a string of images: Trip, Washington, Elena dancing nude. She gulped half of her second drink, tried to wash that last picture away.

"Like what?"

"It's like I didn't know her," she said.

"There are certain things that we never know about another person—no matter how close we are." Richard stared into his tumbler of Scotch. "Maybe we aren't meant to disclose every bit of ourselves."

"I don't like the sound of that, Counselor. Something you're not telling me?"

Richard did not look up from his drink. "Don't be silly."

"Did Elena ever talk to you about boyfriends?"

"That was your department, wasn't it?"

"Apparently not." For a moment, Kate felt tears burning behind her eyes. Who cared about the boyfriends Elena did, or did not, tell her about? She was dead. Gone. Never coming back. She took another hit of her martini.

"You all right, darling?" He touched her hand.

"I'll survive. I hope."

"I'm sort of counting on it."

"By the way, Bill Pruitt may have had a more interesting social life than anyone ever suspected."

"Meaning?"

"Possibly sadomasochistic sex."

"Nothing about that guy would surprise me." Richard scowled, reached for his Scotch. "Any news on his stolen artwork?"

"Nothing yet. Does that surprise you, I mean that he may have been involved with art theft?"

"Yes—and no. I never trusted that guy."

"Or liked him."

"You know anyone who did?"

No, she didn't. But at the moment, none of it was making much sense. Pruitt, Elena, Ethan Stein—why were the three of them killed? What was the connection? But there was just too much to think about at the moment. Her brain was overloaded. Tomorrow; like Scarlett O'Hara, she'd think about it tomorrow.

26

A decent night's sleep with the aid of a sleeping pill and Kate was ready to think it all through. She arranged her copies of the crime scene photos on her corkboard wall, beside them the corresponding art reproductions.

BILL PRUITT—*THE DEATH OF MARAT* by Jacques-Louis David

ETHAN STEIN—*THE FLAYING OF MARSYAS* by Titian

ELENA—Picasso *SELF-PORTRAIT*

Now she filled in more index cards with names and notes.

DAMIEN TRIP
  Suspect?
  Elena's boyfriend
  Filmmaker—probably pornographer
  Last saw victim?

DARTON WASHINGTON
  Suspect?
  Involved with Elena?
  Music producer/Art lover

Worked on Elena's CD
Last saw victim?

JANINE COOK
Friend of victim (Solana)
Prostitute?
Knew Damien Trip

Mrs. Prawsinsky
Witness (Solana)
Saw skinny black man in hallway night of murder

Winnie Pruitt
Mother of victim (Pruitt)
Says victim had painting, now missing

Kate pinned everything onto the wall, stood back, considered what was missing, and immediately started printing information onto more index cards, this time the particulars pertaining to each victim, which she pinned beneath their crime scene photos and art reproductions.

PRUITT
Museum president/Financier
Drowned

STEIN
Artist/Minimal painter
Skinned alive

SOLANA
Performance artist
Stabbed

Kate surveyed the wall. What was it she was missing?

*   *   *

Row after row of identical cubicles, all beige and blond wood, half-walls covered in corkboard, thick tan carpeting that swallowed the beat of Kate's heels. The only sounds: ringing phones, tapping keyboards, muffled voices. FBI Headquarters, Manhattan.

Kate found her friend in the middle of the second row—or was it the third? She'd lost track.

"It must be you," said Liz, squinting up at the name tag Kate had stuck to her cashmere sweater. "Behind those shades."

"This place gives me the creeps," said Kate.

"Shhh." Liz rolled her eyes, whispered, "This is the FBI, honey. We don't say things like that here."

"No?"

"*No.*"

A couple of ramrod-straight agents, both tall, with identical crew cuts, passed without so much as a nod or a blink.

Kate leaned down, stage-whispered, "Replicants?"

"Oh, Jesus. You're going to get me fired."

"Sorry." Kate bit her lip.

"So, about the checks you want me to run—who and what?" Liz whispered, then eyed the cubicles on either side of hers—one empty, in the other a guy with headphones over his ears.

"Ethan Stein—one of the vics. Also a guy named Damien Trip. Another named Darton Washington." Kate pulled up a chair beside Liz. "I went on-line, but couldn't find anything on either Trip or Washington. Stein had a website for his art, but nothing else."

"What exactly are you looking for?"

"Basically anything and everything you can dig up on them—all the way back to grade school. Is that possible?"

"I can go into the FBI website. You wouldn't believe what they've got in there." Another furtive peek at the guy with the earphones. He wasn't listening. "What were those names again?"

Kate supplied the info while Liz tapped one code after another into her computer.

Fifteen minutes later Kate was collecting a sheaf of papers the printer had spit out. "Have I learned this computer shit, or what?"

"Impressive," said Kate.

"Me, or the info I got you?"

"Both."

Kate read through them quickly. The more she read, the faster her adrenaline pumped.

Kate huddled around the conference table with Mead, Brown, and Slattery.

Brown tugged on a pair of plastic gloves, laid a small soft-covered book on the table. "Ethan Stein's appointment book." He opened to a flagged page. "Ten A.M., D. Washington. Studio visit."

"Let me see that," said Kate, pulling on gloves. "This is only two weeks before Ethan Stein was killed. Jesus, Brown, I wish you'd shown me this *before* I talked to Washington."

"The lab was going over it until now. And let's make absolutely certain it's your D. Washington."

"He owns one of Stein's paintings," said Kate. "I'd say it's a pretty safe bet. Any other significant names in Stein's diary I should know about?"

"Slattery's done the checking."

"Thirty-nine personal interviews with gallery owners and directors," said Slattery. "About a dozen had their names in Stein's date book. Lotta uptight people in your business, McKinnon."

"Please," said Kate. "I'm not in the *business*."

"Whatever." Slattery shrugged. "The only suspicious character so far is a guy who owns the"—she surveyed her list—"the Ward Wasserman Gallery, on Fifty-seventh. Snooty place, I'll tell you. Anyway, the owner, Wasserman, has his name in Stein's book six or seven times. He got very agitated when I asked about his whereabouts on the nights of the murders."

"I know Ward Wasserman," said Kate. "He's a lovely man. A tad high-strung, that's all."

"Well, he may be *lovely*," said Slattery, rolling her eyes, "but in case you didn't know, he now controls the Ethan Stein estate. And his gallery's not wasting any time. Wasserman is already planning a memorial show. And I asked about prices. Twenty to thirty grand for white paintings seems like a shitload of moola to me."

"Not really," Kate said, then modified her statement when she saw the three sets of incredulous eyes. "Well, yes, of course, thirty thousand is a lot of money. What I mean is that it's not a lot for an artist of reputation, who is now dead. Stein may have been in a slump recently, but he was an important part of the Post-Minimal art movement." Mead, Brown, and Slattery continued to stare at her, bewildered. "Post-Minimal," she said. "As in *after* the first wave of Minimal art. Stein's white paintings are paintings about painting—about painting *language*."

"You mind putting that into *our* language?" said Mead.

"Think of it like science—one discovery or invention leading to another. The same is true of art. Say one artist reduces painting to pure color. Then another, like Stein, reduces it to pure white brushstrokes. It's an *idea* of what painting can be at its most basic, in its most reductive state—just strokes on a canvas."

Mead yawned.

"If you say so," said Slattery, "but I'm still putting a tail on Wasserman. The guy had a lot to gain by Stein's death."

"Fine," said Kate. "But it's a waste of time. Ward Wasserman is a lamb."

"I think that's what they said about Ted Bundy," said Mead.

"By the way, I went over the copies of those calendars—Perez's and Mills's—that you sent over," said Slattery. "Perez re-created his Palm Pilot, but I'd say it's pretty loose.

Mills, on the other hand, has his life mapped out by the minute—when he ate lunch, with whom, practically tells you when he took a leak."

"Doesn't surprise me," said Kate. "He's a meticulous guy. Have you cross-checked their alibis for the nights of the murders?"

"Some," said Slattery. "A few still pending."

"Get on it," said Mead.

"Clearly Mills and Perez had opportunity," said Kate. "They were both there that night, at Elena's last performance."

"Yeah, but what about motive?" asked Mead.

Kate shook her head. "None that I can think of."

"I got the latest stolen-art printout from Interpol." Brown laid it on the table. "No altarpieces this month."

"Maybe not. But it was on an earlier report I saw at the Delano-Sharfstein Gallery." Kate laid the card of Ethan Stein's *White Light* on the table, explained where she got it. "Damien Trip had this reproduction of Stein's work right on his desk. Also, he lied when he said that he and Elena Solana had broken up *six* months ago. Her friend Janine Cook says she saw them together, Elena and Trip, about a week ago." Kate glanced up at Mead. "I want to search Trip's place."

Mead sucked his teeth. "You can bring him in for questioning, McKinnon. But for a search you need reasonable cause."

"Damien Trip was Elena's boyfriend. You know the statistics. A woman's murdered, you check the husband or boyfriend. Eight times out of ten, he's your man." Kate looked from Mead to Brown. "Okay. Look. Suppose Trip *did* kill her. Just suppose. And now I've talked to him. So now, he's a little spooked."

"But you didn't ID yourself as police," said Brown. "Why would a friend of the vic's spook him?"

"Must you have *all* the answers, Brown?"

"Only the right ones." He leaned back in his chair.

"Brown's just trying to watch out for you," said Mead.

"Everything's by the book nowadays. You screw up, Mc-Kinnon, your ass is on the line." He tugged at his pink-and-blue-striped bow tie. "Of course, with the chief of police as your friend, it'll be *my* ass that's fried, not yours."

"I can live with that." Kate offered a wry smile. "Okay, you want some reasonable cause?" She retrieved the large stack of printouts she got from Liz. "Lots of interesting info here."

"Where'd you get all this?" Mead plucked a paper from Kate's hands.

"FBI Manhattan. I've got a friend there."

"Seems like you've got friends everywhere, McKinnon."

"I'm a popular girl, what can I say?" She offered Mead an arched eyebrow. "Nothing terribly interesting about Darton Washington except that he has a juvey record, though it does not say what, exactly. I'll have to check further. But look at this on our boy Trip. First of all, he was arrested for transporting minors across state lines when he was twenty-five. And this—" She folded Trip's printout for Mead. "Art school, Pratt Institute, Brooklyn, New York. Fine arts major. Trip's got the art background for these crimes. Now look at this." She handed Mead a printout on Ethan Stein. "*His* Pratt Institute transcript. Also fine arts. And exactly the same years as Trip. They were classmates, for Christ's sake." Kate flipped another page. "Check out Trip's school record. Here: Suspended from high school three times for fighting; once for punching out a teacher. The boy has a violent temper. And if you look at the Pratt transcript, you'll see Trip failed painting. Failed advanced drawing, too. About the only thing he was good at, according to his painting teacher, was copying—which is particularly interesting, don't you think? He left school—or rather, was *asked* to leave—in the middle of his junior year. Now look at Stein's transcript: Top of the class. Graduated with honors."

"That doesn't prove Trip killed him," said Mead.

"No," said Kate. "But it confirms a connection between the two men. They knew each other." She shuffled through more papers. "Somewhere in here is Trip's NYU film school transcript. He only made it through one semester. Another failure. Oh, and there are a few foster-parent reports regarding Trip's early years. He was always in trouble." Kate shook her head. "Though the kid had it rough, I'll admit that."

"Oh, another poor little orphan, huh?" said Slattery.

"Get me copies of all this," said Mead, looking over the FBI printouts. "Plus anything else you have on Trip—the drugs—everything. I'll get you the warrant. But you're taking Brown along with you."

"I can handle a search," said Kate.

"I'm sure you can," said Mead. "But you're going with backup."

What to add to the reproduction? Maybe this, maybe that. The process almost as much fun as the act.

And now that he's documenting his work, even better.

In a long row along the pitted wall, he pins up the Polaroids of Ethan Stein: close-ups of the artist's leg, then chest, the skin being removed in ever-expanding inches of gore.

Lovely. So lovely it causes his cock to strain inside his shorts. He won't look at the pictures right now. It's too distracting.

He sits back, wonders if she's figured out that little piece of tape he sent her. If so, she must be going crazy. And a mind clouded with emotion, well . . .

He studies the reproduction in front of him, the chair, the coat, the figure with those glass rods shooting out of her belly. Ethan Stein's scene was relatively simple. This next one is going to be complicated.

And it's a birthday card.

Now all he has to do is find someone who's having a birthday.

27

The midday light played across the tenements and projects as Floyd Brown turned the car onto Avenue D. "So, McKinnon. Anything in particular we're looking for?"

"Anything incriminating," said Kate, trying to avoid the question.

"You wanna be more specific?"

"Just a routine search," she said, pushing the car door open, coming face-to-face with a youngish black man, his hair wild and matted. "Beautiful lady . . . how you doin' today?"

"I'm doing just fine," said Kate, peeling off a couple of dollar bills.

Brown took her arm roughly, steered her toward the building. "Why'd you give that man money? You John D. Rockefeller, giving handouts to the poor?"

"I just haven't been called beautiful in a while; is that okay with you?"

Brown shook his head. "People like you just don't get it."

"People like me?"

"That's right. Rich people. White people. Liberals. You think you're helping that man? You're helping him all right—helping him stay just the way he is. But as long as it made you feel good, that's all that matters, right?"

"You missed your calling, Brown. You should have been one of those Sunday-morning TV evangelists."

"The black man doesn't need *you* to do for him what he can't do for himself, McKinnon. Every time you give a handout to someone who should be doing for themselves, you're keeping him down."

"Okay, you've got me. I admit it. Guilty as charged. Third-degree white liberalism." Kate thrust her hands toward Brown, her wrists together. "Cuff me, Officer."

The super told them that Trip had just gone out, handed over the keys to his place. Kate and Brown made the four-flight climb.

The place was empty. Stale cigarette smoke hovered in the outer office. Kate got a look at some of those invoices Damien Trip had been trying to shield—all for videos or video equipment. Nothing incriminating. Still, she pocketed a few, then rummaged through Trip's art cards. No more Ethan Stein reproductions.

Behind that second steel door they found a huge white-washed space, windows boarded up, dead quiet. In the center, a professional-style video camera was trained on a king-size bed with rumpled lavender sheets, flanked by a couple of halogen lights on stands.

What Kate was looking for, hoping not to find.

Tucked into a corner was a beat-up wooden table stacked with cassettes and magazines; beside it, two televisions with VCRs beneath them.

"Looks like Mr. Trip's taste is not exactly literary," said Brown, plucking copies of porn magazines from the table— *Amateur Couples, Young Virgins, Swinging Times.*

Kate held her breath.

Brown handed her a pair of latex gloves, pulled on a pair himself before lifting a spoon from the table, which he dropped into a plastic bag. Next he bagged the contents of an ashtray. From under the bed, Kate retrieved a syringe. Without speaking she handed it to Brown.

They worked in silence, moving about the room taking samples like astronauts on the moon.

Down a hallway, a tiny bathroom. The blue-green water in the toilet might have been disinfectant, but more likely it was mold; the sink was slick with hair and grease. The medicine cabinet's mirror was cracked. Inside, Kate found a few promising vials, which she bagged.

Behind a half-wall, Kate and Brown discovered metal bookshelves crammed with cassettes. She plucked one out. On the cover a blonde displayed silicone-enhanced breasts. She tugged out a few others—*Thighs Wide Shut, The Bitches of Eastwick, The Return of the Pink Pussy*—all courtesy of Amateur Films. Students of film, all right. Another time, another place, she might have laughed. But not here, not now, knowing what she was looking for.

Brown, cradling an armful of cassettes, said, "Let's take a look, see what we find."

Kate sucked in air, wanted to stop him, but how could she?

Without speaking they hauled dozens of cassettes beside the TV sets. Brown loaded the VCRs.

The videos were a bit grainy, the color off. Familiar, thought Kate. Too familiar.

Both televisions were going. Five minutes on fast forward to view a sixty-minute film, Kate hardly breathing.

Fifteen minutes and several cassettes later, she saw Janine Cook, naked except for a pair of thigh-high black boots, whipping some middle-aged fat guy in a leather hooded mask. Kate slowed the film.

"That's Elena Solana's friend Janine Cook." Kate stared at the screen. "Wait a minute. That guy—" She hit fast forward, but nothing much changed, more whipping, red welts appearing on the guy's mushy chest.

"What is it?" asked Brown.

"I can't be sure," said Kate. "I mean, with the hood and all, but—*Jesus*—I think it could be Bill Pruitt!"

Brown came in for a closer look.

Kate hit reverse, watched as the guy pulled the hood off—a nanosecond of film time—just before the tape went blank.

"Was it him?" asked Brown.

They played that split second over and over. "I *think* so," said Kate.

"Well, that could definitely be the hood we found at his place."

"What about the watch and ring he's wearing? We can get the film enlarged." Kate thought a moment. "Pruitt wore a Yale ring. And we should have information on the watch somewhere—if he was wearing it when he died."

"Personal effects went to his mother."

"Right. Then we can check the ring and watch through her. That would confirm it." She peered at the film, now playing in slow motion, Janine's whip looping lazily through the air. "The guy's got an appendix scar. We can check Pruitt's medical history, see if he's had his appendix out—or ask the ME."

One more time, Kate watched those fractions of a second when the man pulled off the hood. "I'm pretty sure it's him," she said.

Brown removed the cassette, bagged it, wrote COOK, then PRUITT? across the top. "This could tie Trip to both the Solana and Pruitt murders," he said.

Kate's mind was racing. She had to talk to Janine Cook. But first she had to watch more of these damn films, and she knew it. She sat back, lit a Marlboro, said a silent prayer—maybe this is all she would discover.

But no. It took only five films and twenty minutes for her to see what she did not want to see. She jerked forward, slammed the stop button.

Brown looked at her, then at the blank screen. He knew the answer, but asked anyway, "Solana?"

Kate just barely nodded. Then, quietly: "Do you mind if . . ."

Brown got up, moved away.

Kate started the film again. Elena in front of the bed. *The one right there, halfway across the space.*

This time it was all too clear. Kate could almost imagine that Elena was here in the room with her, not just on that small screen with bad color, bad lighting. Elena smiling, maybe nervous. Not the usual porno queen come-on, but it was her all right. Kate had trouble locating her feelings. But when she did, she realized that what she felt was nothing.

And then Elena started undressing, swaying, almost a dance, peeling out of her skirt. *Jesus. The Mexican skirt.* A throbbing had started in Kate's head. Still, she forced herself to watch. Elena's movements seemed unbearably slow, as though time itself were drunk. Five excruciating minutes, an eternity until Elena was naked. Kate hit the fast-forward button. Now Elena was on the bed, and the shadowy figure of a man joined her. Kate slowed the film to normal speed. The man was Trip—who looked at the camera while Elena performed oral sex, and smiled that rotten choirboy smile.

Another hit to fast forward. Elena and Trip, fucking. The camera zoomed in on Elena's face, eyes closed, head back. Closer now. Perspiration on her brow. Lips parted. Kate stared at the image until it dissolved into an abstraction—a blur of dots.

"Was that Trip?" Brown helped her to her feet, started to bag the video.

"Yes." Kate reached for the video with a shaking hand. "Wait." For a moment she was sure she would hurl it against the concrete wall, watch it shatter to pieces. But she didn't. She'd caught sight of the title: *Lace Is More.* Mulled it over. "It's like the famous Bauhaus expression, '*Less* is more.' "

"Meaning?"

"We're looking for an artist, remember? Or someone pretending to be. Trip was an art student as well as a filmmaker." Kate thought it through. " 'Less is more' was not only the credo of the German Bauhaus movement, but it was picked up again here in the States by Minimal artists. It became their motto. Ethan Stein was a Minimal painter. Maybe this could hint at something with Stein, too."

Kate suddenly felt sick, managed to make it down the hall to the bathroom, splashed cold water on her face, avoided looking at the moldy sink, which would surely make her vomit. She wanted to scream, to punch someone, kick something. And she did. The wall, then the wooden vanity supporting the sink, which splintered. Small bags of white powder tumbled over her feet; disposable syringes clattered to the floor.

"Brown!"

Kate was actually smiling as she displayed the find. "A solid reason to pick up Trip."

Brown nodded, bagged the evidence. "You look like shit, McKinnon. Go home. I'll put out an APB on Trip."

"I'll go home," she said. "After I see Janine Cook."

He wasn't sure how much they knew, or exactly what they had found, but Damien Trip had a fairly good idea. *Cunt. Fucking cunt.*

He hovered across the street, inside the bodega, sneaking peeks through the window, waited until Kate and Brown had left, watched their car slip around the corner. No question they were cops. He'd had her scent the other day. Now he had to think, decide which loose ends to tie up first. He had a pretty good idea where Kate would go, whom she would talk to. But he could deal with that. No problem.

Kate gripped the videocassette hard. "Why didn't you tell me about this?"

Janine Cook shrugged, waved a hand at the cassette. "You don't like it, don't watch."

"Janine." She clutched the girl by the shoulders. The purple sequins on her skintight bodysuit felt like fish scales under Kate's fingers. She didn't have the patience to be subtle. "Do you know who this guy in the film is?"

"Which guy?" said Janine, bored. "Which film you talking about?"

Kate displayed the cover. "An S and M scene. You whipping a middle-aged man. He's wearing a leather hood."

"Oh, right." Janine faked a yawn.

Kate wanted to slap her, but controlled herself, stayed calm. "I think that man is William Pruitt. He was murdered, Janine. *Murdered*. By the same person who murdered Elena. And you could be next." Kate let that sink in for a minute. "You claim you were Elena's friend. Well, be her friend, for Christ's sake."

Janine chewed her lower lip like a little kid.

"Did you know the man?"

"No. But . . ." She reached for the arm of her velvet couch, seemed momentarily unsteady on her feet. "Damien filmed that scene personally. The guy gave him a wad of bills. Hundreds."

"Was it money for making the film, or—what?"

"I don't know. I never saw the guy before—or ever again."

Kate tried to think it through. Did Pruitt back Trip's little video business, or was it a onetime thing? Did Pruitt start withholding money, and Trip lost it? Or maybe Trip was blackmailing Pruitt with the film? Her head was spinning. "Janine, did you know Elena was making films for Trip?"

Janine nodded quietly. "She needed money."

That stopped Kate. Why would Elena need money? And if she did, why wouldn't Elena have come to her? "Was Trip blackmailing her with the films?"

"I don't know." Janine pulled away, knocked into the coffee table, sent a delicate glass vase crashing to the floor. Slowly she bent down, plucked up a longish shard of pale violet glass. "I know what you think." She tilted her face to look up at Kate, her features twisted, fighting back tears. "That I'm a whore and she was an angel. That I was jealous of her—that I wanted to hurt her because she had it better than me. But it's not true. I would never hurt her."

Kate reached out, but too late. The girl's hand closed around the glass.

"Oh, shit." Kate pulled Janine close, cradled the girl's arm. "Where's the sink?"

Janine nodded weakly toward a swinging door just off the entranceway to the fancy apartment.

Janine leaned over the sink, crying softly. She stared at the dish towel Kate had wrapped around her hand; watched small spots of blood rise to the surface like water lilies.

"How did Elena meet Trip? Through you?" Kate asked gently.

Janine just barely nodded, tears staining her cheeks now as she talked. "Yes." Janine winced. Those pink water lilies were starting to turn scarlet. "I tried to warn her, but—"

"Any idea why Damien would want Elena out of the way?"

"You think it's my fault, don't you?" Janine's eyes searched out Kate's. "I got Elena to Trip and now she's dead. My fault. That's what you think."

"I don't know about fault, Janine, and I'm not in the business of blame, but—" The dish towel looked like a crumpled rose, bright vermilion.

Kate found some gauze and wrapped it carefully around Janine's hand, keeping it above her head. "So, tell me. *Please*. What was Trip's hold over her—over Elena? Can you explain it to me?"

Janine shook her head. "All I know is that Elena wanted to cut him loose, and he wouldn't let her go. He had some sort of weird hold on her. I never understood it, exactly. But he just wouldn't let go."

"Why not?"

"Maybe because Elena was the best thing he'd ever had."

Kate finished bandaging Janine's hand; the whole time her mind just wouldn't stop: Trip and Elena making films; Trip and Ethan Stein going to art school together; Bill Pruitt starring in one of Trip's porno flicks. It was all starting to swim around in her brain. She looked up at Janine's hand. Blood was oozing through the layers of gauze.

"Jesus. We'd better get you to the emergency room."

*   *   *

Four hours at Lenox Hill Hospital for six lousy stitches. Four hours of rehashing the same information: Elena and Trip, his Svengali-like hold over her.

Kate helped Janine out of the car, mindful of the fresh white bandage on the young woman's hand.

"Is there anyone I can call?" Kate asked, as the two women traipsed toward Janine's high-rise building.

"Yeah, you can call— I was about to say you could call Elena. Funny, huh?"

"No," said Kate softly. "I start to call her a half dozen times a day."

"After my brother died, I did that for almost a year. Even now, sometimes I forget. It's like . . ." Tears were collecting in Janine's large brown eyes. ". . . everyone close to me . . . dies."

Kate wrapped her arms around Janine, who leaned into her, crying like a little girl.

Now what? Kate couldn't just go home. Not when she felt like this, her mind still racing with pictures of Elena and Trip that she never wanted to see and thought she always would. She had to *do* something, *see* something, anything to wipe away those images. She needed to get away from it, think clearly.

She got Richard on her cellular. "Would you consider taking a tired, middle-aged woman out for a movie and a burger?" She tried hard not to sound too needy, added a joke: "Who knows? You might even get lucky."

"Sure," he said. "Give me her number."

Now that he had followed her here, he wasn't quite sure what to do.

He slipped through the crowd easily. He'd keep an eye on her from a distance, that was all. Inside, he ordered up a caffè latte and a croissant that didn't look all that fresh, but he'd worked up an appetite, what with his extra-special delivery to Elena's pal, that big-mouthed whore, who would not have much to say for long. She didn't deserve such a generous gift, but hell, that's just who he was, a real generous guy. Dead or alive, they were all the same: goddamn motherfucking, cocksucking bitches!

He steadied himself with a swig of lukewarm latte. He had to stay cool.

The crowd along the sidewalk and clogging the wide staircase leading up to SoHo's Angelika Film Center was a Gallup poll fantasy: funky artists and fancy artists; Lower East Side grunges and Upper East Side media planners; Wall Street execs and Madison Avenue publicists; gay, straight, undetermined, black, white, yellow, and every shade in between. They were all here. Why? Because the Angelika was an *art* house, one of the last of its kind, and new all at once. It was where you went if you were hip, arty—or trying to be; smart, cool—or trying to be; and still into real movies.

Richard loosened his colorful silk tie as he finally made it to the tiny crowded box office at the top of the stairs. Kate waited on the side, desperately inhaling the last drags on her Marlboro.

"It's sold out," Richard yelled over to her. "But that Danish film starts at the same time."

"Anything," she said.

Inside, the spacious Angelika lobby looked more like a fifties coffeehouse than a movie theater. If only those Westphalian ham and Brie sandwiches weren't so pricey, and the espresso were more than mediocre. Still, the disparate New York crowd was chewing, drinking, laughing, and talking. The scene could have been an art film itself—one of those French existential numbers where there's lots of activity but no plot.

Kate leaned against Richard. He stroked the back of her neck. "God, your muscles feel like rock."

"I'm beyond tense. Hope I can sit through the movie. I already saw one today that I wish I hadn't." Images of Elena and Trip, on the king-size bed. She couldn't stop it from playing. The best she could do was switch it to Janine whipping the fat guy, Bill Pruitt. She was about to explain it to Richard when a tubby blue triangle, topped by a mass of tangled curls, pushed through the crowd.

"Kate! Richard!" Amy Schwartz, director of the Contemporary, in one of her oversized tent dresses—this one sky blue with tiny white polka dots—kissed Kate's cheek.

"Where did you get that dress?" asked Kate. "The blue matches your eyes perfectly."

"Broke into the mortuary the night Mama Cass died. Ripped it right off the bitch!"

Kate laughed. "God, I'm glad to see you. What are you here to see?"

"Who knows? Roberta got the tickets. I think it's one of those dark Scandinavian pieces. A kind of postmodern love triangle: man, woman, dog."

"Oh, great." Kate looked at Richard. "Is that what we're seeing?"

"Don't blame me. I don't read Danish."

Amy waved to a woman with short steel-gray hair. "Roberta, over here."

"I've got to pee. Maybe it's just raging PMS, but I feel ready to explode." Kate turned away, and somehow the crowd parted, creating a clear open channel. But then she stopped. Because there he was, right at the end of the pathway, nodding by the espresso bar, eating a croissant. And he'd seen her, too. For a moment it looked as if he might bolt, but no, he just stood there, smiling.

Kate wasn't sure what she'd do when she got there, but those were judgments, and at the moment, that part of her psyche had shut down. Right now, she was all instinct. All the noise—talking, laughing, loudspeaker announcements of movies beginning—surrounded her, but she just kept on moving, now only a few feet away from Damien Trip, who met her eyes, smiled his rotten-sweet smile, and rubbed his finger across the scar on his chin.

"Well well well . . . isn't this a surprise," he said, popping the last of the croissant into his mouth, then licking a long buttery index finger. His baby blues did a slow take up and down Kate's body. "Can't stay away from me, that it, Kate?"

"Oh, you are going to wish I stayed away—"

And then he was saying something else and she said something else, but the words sounded as if they were coming from far away, the blood was pumping so loud in her ears. All she could see was his pink tongue licking his bony finger, and his grin—the same one that he fixed on the camera—and that was it. Her arm stretched back and sprang forward, fast. But Trip was fast, too. He swiveled and ducked. Kate's fist connected with a framed poster—*La Mort aux Tousses*—the French version of Hitchcock's *North by Northwest*. Her blood streaked across the glass, staining Cary Grant's dimpled chin and Eva Marie Saint's perfect white teeth.

Trip howled. "Are you crazy?"

Kate did not feel the pain in her hand, or see the blood. She was blind. Here it was: that part of herself that was terrifying; what she discovered the very first time she ever strapped on a gun to right a wrong.

Trip saw it in her eyes. He used what he could, what he'd been relying on, for years: the smile, the dimples. "Calm down, Kate," he said, laying a hand on her shoulder, practically massaging it.

"Oh," she said, barely above a whisper. "You . . . are . . . a . . . dead . . . man."

Trip spun around, quickly merging into the crowd. But the glint of his blond hair reemerged for a second at the narrow hallway leading to the Angelika's tiny unisex bathrooms.

"Trip!" Kate was shouting over the crowd. "Stop right there!"

A scream—"She's got a gun!"—and the crowd scattered.

Kate did not remember retrieving her Glock, but there it was, clenched in her fist.

Richard broke through the crowd, saw his wife tearing

across the theater lobby, gun in hand, fury in her eyes. He called her name. But she couldn't hear him. She was charging toward that narrow hallway.

Her foot connected with the bathroom door. Hinges tore from plaster. Wood splintered.

"Jesus! *Help!*" Trip was bellowing. "This bitch is crazy!"

The force of her kick propelled Kate into the tiny bathroom where Trip was literally cowering between the toilet and the sink.

A voice was screaming Elena's name, harsh and unfamiliar. But it was not until Richard was there, pushing between them, that Kate realized it was her own voice, and that she had one hand around Trip's throat, the other holding the gun to his temple.

"Break it up!" Two cops, pistols in the air, charged down the narrow corridor. Two more followed.

An overweight cop, huffing as if he'd just run the marathon, shoved Richard out of the way. He planted his gun in Kate's face.

"I'm with NYPD," she said. "This creep resisted arrest."

"Holy shit!" Amy Schwartz pushed past the crowd, got a good look at the shattered bathroom door, the uniforms, Kate, breathing hard, still pumped up on adrenaline. "Wonder Woman *lives*! Forget the movie. Talk about getting your money's worth! Whoa, Mama! If you think I'm ever again going to relax in the can when *you're* around . . . !"

Kate touched her cheek, suddenly aware of an intense throbbing, looked at her hand, saw that her knuckles were bleeding, and when she took a step, she was off-balance. "Three-hundred-dollar shoes shot to shit," she grumbled, scanning the corridor floor. "Anyone see my heel anywhere?"

Richard gave Kate a look she couldn't quite grasp.

It was nearly midnight. Two uniforms were dragging a teen who was screaming about demons and devils past Kate's tiny cubicle.

Damien Trip was put in lockup after an intern checked

him over. The same intern who cleaned Kate's knuckles and bandaged her hand.

"Are you okay?" Richard asked.

"I'll live."

"Well, that's good. I'm going to find some coffee. You want any?"

"You'll be sorry," said Kate, shaking her head. "I mean, about the coffee. It's awful."

Now that the adrenaline had drained away, Kate felt like curling up on the floor.

Floyd Brown was wearing gray sweatpants on his legs, Nikes on his feet, and a none-to-happy look on his face. "Had yourself quite a night, didn't you, McKinnon?"

"I've had better," she said, touching her cheek with her bruised knuckles.

"I had an APB out on Trip. I would have appreciated a call."

"I know. I sort of lost it."

"*Sort of?* Do I need to go through the book with you? List all the things you did wrong? Like no backup, no 'reasonable nondeadly.' You want me to go on?" But Brown knew what had set her off. He sighed. "So we got Trip. Any witnesses to his *supposedly* resisting arrest?"

"Only if we can get the sink and toilet to testify—"

"This isn't a joke, McKinnon. We've got to build a case."

"I know that," said Kate. "We've got the drugs—"

"But no way to tie him to any of the murders without prints or DNA."

"What about a polygraph?"

"Only if his lawyer will agree to one."

"Grab one of these," said Richard, entering the room with a steaming styrofoam cup in each hand. "They're burning my fingers off." He looked up. "Oh—"

Kate took a cup. "Floyd Brown. My husband, Richard Rothstein."

The two men assessed each other for a moment before shaking hands.

"Detective Brown's been reading me the riot act."

"Not a bad idea," said Richard.

"You got quite a wife here," said Brown.

"No shit," said Richard.

Kate looked from one to the other.

"Okay," said Brown, looking uncomfortable. "Tomorrow, McKinnon. Early. We've got to work on Trip, fast." He shook his head. "Funny, I can't seem to find that quarter Trip needs to call his—" He stopped short, eyed Richard.

"Don't worry about me," said Richard. "*I'm* not going to represent him."

"You realize," said Brown, "that Trip could press charges against you, McKinnon."

"I don't think Kate will have to worry about that," said Richard. "The man was obviously resisting arrest. Kate was acting on information gleaned through a legitimate police investigation. It was a standard 101 arrest."

"You her lawyer?"

"If she needs one."

"Thanks for stepping in," said Kate, after Brown had gone. "I wasn't quite up to another fight."

"It was pure legalese bullshit, but what the hell." He tossed his coffee cup into the trash. "So what exactly is the deal with this Trip character?"

"He was Elena's boyfriend. A pornographer and drug dealer."

"Are you kidding me?"

"I wish I were."

"When did you find all this out?"

"Just."

"Maybe you *should* have killed him. I haven't had a murder case in a long time."

"I can just see it," said Kate. " 'Husband Defends Lunatic Wife.' "

"And I always will." He smiled.

Kate laced her fingers through his. It helped for a minute. But her adrenaline was totally gone. All she could think of was sleep.

28

The uniform deposited a thick stack of papers onto the table beside Kate and Brown. "Mead said you should look through these."

Kate flipped the first few pages. "William Pruitt's financials. His stock portfolio." She slid a sheet out, tried to skim it, though she was so tired her vision was blurring. She'd had less than four hours sleep. She ached all over. "Stocks, bank account receipts." She dropped the sheets back onto the stack. "I'm too tired to read it. I'm going to ask one of the detectives in General to check all these over, cross-reference with any of our vics and suspects, see what they come up with."

"Good idea," said Brown. "You feeling up to this, Mc-Kinnon? To interrogating Trip?"

Kate nailed Brown with a sober look. "Absolutely."

"Oh. And you should know, it *was* Pruitt in the video. The Yale ring, Rolex watch. Both confirmed."

Kate nodded.

"I went through it all with Mead. He's going to overlook your somewhat unorthodox arrest procedure. He's glad you got the guy." He offered Kate a warm smile. "Mead wanted me to do the interrogation, but I told him it was your kill. So don't screw this up, okay? Because you may only get one shot at him."

Kate nodded again. "According to Trip's rap sheet, he got off with a slap on the wrist for that interstate charge. I don't get it."

"Good lawyer, I guess," said Brown. "Fact is, if Trip is involved with both porn and drugs, he's probably got himself a *real* good lawyer—one who specializes." Brown tapped his fingers along the edge of his desk. "In fact, it's time. Overdue. I gotta let Trip make that call before you talk to him."

Janine Cook was feeling bad, and nothing seemed to help.

She'd already snorted a little coke, and yeah, it took the edge off, but not nearly enough. Now she tore through her dresser drawers, pushing lace panties, garter belts, and Wonderbras aside. From under her supply of tank tops she retrieved a Ziploc bag. It yielded a couple of reefers. She lit one, held the smoke in her lungs. The act helped calm her. But not enough. One look at the photo—two young girls in plaid skirts, white shirts, knee-high socks—and Janine was reeling.

Damn. It was just a snapshot. A little blurry, even, colors fading. Janine remembered the day it was taken by her brother, Germaine, who was dead now going on six years, shot to death in that very same playground.

Another long hit of marijuana.

Janine studied herself in the photo—the way her lips formed an innocent smile—and wondered where it had gone, all that innocence. Perhaps it had never really existed. Elena, beside her, was laughing, tugging at Janine's cornrows. Elena, who was always getting her out of one jam or another all the way through school.

She turned the picture over for the umpteenth time. There, in her neat, very particular handwriting, Elena had written "Me and Janine. 1984."

It was just getting light out, the city coming to life for another day. Thank God, Janine thought, the night was finally over.

*   *   *

Interrogation Room 4 was like all the others: a small gray cube with an eleven-by-sixteen-inch pane of one-way mirror in the door. Two fluorescent tubes were suspended from the ceiling like large glowworms. They washed the room with an unhealthy blue-white glare. The only furniture was a rectangular metal table and a few intentionally stiff wooden chairs. It had been a long time since Kate had been in a room like this, but not so long that she'd forgotten. She checked the two chairs—sure enough, one was slightly higher than the other—and moved them into position. She got a pack of Marlboros out of her bag—only three left—bought another pack from the cigarette machine in the hall.

In the ladies' room, she splashed her face with cold water. Not quite enough to revive her after the rough night, but enough to wash the Estée Lauder pancake makeup off her cheek and expose the bruise she had gotten when she slammed through the Angelika's bathroom. She shouldn't have looked in the mirror. It was reflecting a very tired forty-one-year-old woman who should very possibly consider listening to her husband and friends, or anyone else, for that matter, and go back to planning charity benefits or writing her next art book.

Too late for that now. Kate patted her face with a rough paper towel. Fuck the makeup. She was ready.

The living room was growing lighter, but Janine pulled the shades down, watched the tiny orange glow of the second reefer go pale yellow, then burn out.

Eight A.M. All over the city, people were getting up, getting dressed, going to their regular, normal jobs. She pulled herself off the velvet couch, bare feet on deep-pile rugs, wooden hallway floors, bedroom carpet. She turned on the television for company, flipped past that sickeningly chipper *Today* show with that annoying Miss White Bread, Katie Whatever-the-Fuck-Her-Name-Is. She settled on VH-1, stretched out on her king-size canopied bed, ran her hands along satin sheets, listened to Vanessa Williams croon a love song, hummed along, distracted, thinking Vanessa was one smart black bitch—though she was not too sure just how black the ex–Miss America, the ex–skin star, really was.

Her head throbbed.

She just wanted to sleep.

She beat the overstuffed pillows, pushed, pulled at them, finally flung them to the floor.

Trip was bruised, moving slowly. Kate could see she had hurt him a lot more than he had hurt her. She offered him the lower chair. He stared at it before sitting. He'd been through this before, knew the drill.

Kate circled the room once, twice, the action helping to pump her up. Trip watched her through swollen eyes. "I assume you've been read your rights?" she said.

"I've got nothing to hide." Trip played with a loose button on his cotton shirt.

"That's good." Kate folded herself into the higher chair. She towered over Trip. She took her time lighting a Marlboro, then slid a sheet of paper across the table. "List of what we took out of your place—particularly from under the sink in the bathroom." She exhaled a plume of smoke. "You might want to check the last items—the heroin and coke. From what they tell me, there's enough there to put your ass in the stir for quite a while. And *your* sweet little ass, Damien?" She tsked. "It'll be *real* popular."

"Go to hell," said Trip. "And don't think I'm not pressing charges against you."

"You do that. Meantime, let me tell you a story." Kate sat back, folded her arms across her chest. "Once upon a time there was a boy named Damien Trip who met a girl named Elena Solana—"

"Hey—you want a story?" Trip shook a cigarette out of her pack, stuck it between his lips, his hand shaking as he lit it. "Well, I got one you're not going to like."

"Go ahead. Entertain me."

Under the bad light Damien's skin looked sallow, the dimples more like cuts. "Okay. The story of Damien and Elena." He offered Kate a tight-lipped grin.

She wanted to hurt him all over again.

"Men in porn?" said Trip, his head cocked, the cigarette hanging from the corner of his mouth as if he were some French movie star. "A dime a dozen. Not that I wasn't good in my day. I was a timid kid, you know, Kate. But damn, get me in front of those cameras and . . . well, I don't want to brag, but—"

"So you were going to be a star."

"No, Kate. You've got it all wrong. I was pretty much finished with performing. Not that I can't still get the wood up on command."

"Oh, I'm very impressed. But it's a funny thing. I always think it's the braggarts who have a problem in that department." She shook her head slowly. "You couldn't perform. That what happened?"

"No way."

"There was no semen, Damien. No penetration." Kate leaned across the table. "You couldn't manage it, could you?" She stopped, tried for some compassion in her voice. "Look, I understand. It's a pride thing. Elena laughed. You cracked. It's embarrassing. You *had* to shut her up. You couldn't have her telling people. Not in *your* line of work."

"You got it *all* wrong, Kate. Elena was a performer, remember? Excuse me, performance *artist*." Trip laughed. "What a fucking crock. But I got her to perform, all right— and she was damn good." He paused, eyes on Kate's. "You saw her, didn't you? She had the stuff."

Kate's muscles were twitching. Trip had no idea how lucky he was to be in the safety of a police station.

"We were going to be big. *Really* big. And Elena, she was something different."

"Maybe a whole lot different than you thought, Damien."

"Maybe a whole lot different than *you* thought, Kate."

Kate narrowed her eyes, regarded him closely. "You don't like me very much, do you?"

"Why would I even give a shit about you?"

"Oh, the way Elena talked about me—the great mother. And then there's you, the sad, motherless boy. It didn't feel so good, did it? I saw those foster-home statistics. Seven homes in eight years. Not pretty."

"That's one way to put it." He rolled up his sleeve, displayed a variety of scars. "You ever have a cigarette put out on your flesh, Kate? How about scalding water poured over you because you asked for something to eat?"

"I know you had it rough, Damien."

"Do you?" His pale eyes were like two hard pieces of stone. *"You?"* He smirked. "Hey, you know Elena told me you couldn't have kids of your own. Faulty wiring, that it, Kate?"

Kate felt the sting, but she would not let him see it.

Why hadn't she thought of this before? 'Cause she was just a dumb bitch, that's why. Janine popped open the vial of Percocet the nice young doctor had given her in case the stitches in her hand gave her any trouble.

She got a bottle of vodka out of the freezer, toted it back to the bedroom, its icy neck wedged between her fingers. She rearranged the pillows, propped herself against them, popped a couple of the Percocets, chased them down with ice-cold vodka.

The cold television light shimmered into the room, dissolving edges of pearl-gray Formica furniture and white satin sheets. VH-1 was doing two-for-one and that damn Vanessa Williams was singing another moody ballad. Janine thought that if she'd been light-skinned, too, had Vanessa's green eyes and thin lips, well, maybe then her life would have been better. Maybe she, too, could have swapped porn for the big time, made millions, lived happily ever after. But it made her head pound to think about it. Another Percocet helped, and a gulp of vodka.

Why'd she have to go and introduce Elena to Trip? *Fuck.* Just thinking about her friend, the pain started up again. Not in her hand, or head, nowhere she could actually locate it, but it was real, eating her up inside, more than she could bear. Janine pushed herself off the bed. She needed something stronger.

She was going to save it, but why bother? The heroin Damien Trip delivered. Now that was a surprise. And without her even asking—or paying. Maybe because it's not the best stuff, weak is what he called it, and since he couldn't get away with selling it, he gave it to her. More likely dumping the shit. Whatever. But Janine was no fool. She knew that Trip was trying to buy her silence—figured if he was good to her she wouldn't tell that she saw him with Elena the very day she was killed. A little late for that. Though she swore to him that she hadn't said a word. Funny, though, that Trip hadn't threatened her. It wasn't like him. But with the Percocet and vodka kicking in, she couldn't quite figure it out; her brain had gone fuzzy.

In the kitchen, she cooked up some of the heroin, filled a syringe.

The Interrogation Room was airless.

"Lace Is More," said Kate. "Real funny title, Damien. Like 'Less Is More.' An art pun?"

"You tell me. You're the fucking art expert," said Trip. *"Artists' Lives.* What a piece of shit that was."

"I'm sorry you didn't like my book, Damien. But let's get back to your spectacular film, okay? Minimal artists always say that—*less is more*—don't they? You know any Minimal artists, Damien?"

"Who gives a flying fuck about Minimal art?"

"Well, Ethan Stein did," Kate said. "You know Ethan Stein, Damien?"

Trip seemed to twitch a second, said, "No."

Kate sorted through the stacks of FBI printouts she had on the table, came up with Trip's school records. "That's odd. Because you two were classmates, at Pratt."

Trip strained to see the printout. "Maybe."

"Not maybe. Definitely."

"I don't remember him."

"Really? You don't remember the top painting student in your class? The one who went on to have a career in art, while you . . . you accomplished . . ." Kate ran her finger along the Pratt transcript. "Let's see. You failed painting, failed drawing, in fact, you *flunked* out of art school. Then you *flunked* out of film school." She leaned in close, her smile mean. "In fact, you're kind of a *loser,* aren't you, Damien? A real frustrated artist."

Trip stared hard into her eyes.

"So now you're getting it all out of your system. Taking revenge, right?" Kate laid the Ethan Stein card, *White Light,* on the table. "And you hated Stein, resented his success. Just couldn't stand it, could you?"

"That guy was so fucking *over,* it wasn't funny."

"Oh. So you *did* know him?"

"I . . . followed his career—which was *over*." He regarded the reproduction of Stein's painting. "You call that shit art? I could do that with my eyes closed."

"You're so jealous of real artists it tears you apart, doesn't it, Damien? They're out there doing it, having success, making real art, while you—"

"Me?" Trip faltered a moment. "I'm not jealous of anyone."

"No?" Kate spread a group of crime scene photos onto the table—Bill Pruitt, dead in his tub. "How about these? They look familiar to you?"

"What? You trying to pin this on me?"

"Pruitt had a whole collection of Amateur Films."

"Hey, I love a fan."

"But he was more than a fan, wasn't he?" She slid the video onto the table. "Bill Pruitt and Janine Cook. A real sweet little film."

Trip had gone pale. "He paid me to make that film."

"How'd you meet him?"

"He came to me. He liked my films."

Kate leaned in close again. "So Pruitt pays you to film him. Then what? You make your own copy, start blackmailing him?"

"I want to see my lawyer."

Kate stayed right in his face. "Or was Pruitt financing your little porn operation, then decided he wanted out, and you got pissed?" She slid the printout of Trip's high school suspensions at him. "You've always had a little temper problem, haven't you?" Trip turned away, but Kate wouldn't let up. She pushed Elena's picture—the one with the bloody Picasso along her cheek—into his face. "So, what happened, Damien? Elena wanted out and you couldn't take the humiliation?"

Trip looked up, his pale eyes on Kate's, totally cold. "Who said she wanted out?"

"The way I hear it, she wanted out but you wouldn't let her go."

"Where'd you hear that? From her whore girlfriend, from Janine Cook? Well, she's a liar! Elena wasn't going anywhere."

"So *now* you're telling me that you and Elena did *not* break up, that it?" She was so close she could see the pores on his nose. "You can't have it both ways, Damien. Either you were together, or apart. Either you broke up, or you didn't. Together, or not? *Which is it?*" Trip pulled back, but Kate followed him. "The date on the film *Lace Is More,* with you and Elena, is only one month ago. *One month ago*. You get that? Or you need me to do the math?"

"Okay. So we *were* together. Big deal."

Brown leaned into the room. "Lawyer'll be here any minute."

Kate grabbed hold of Trip's wrist. "One more question, Damien. Why'd Elena do it? Make the films?"

That smirk was back on Trip's swollen lips. "For the *money,* Kate. The money."

* * *

Light streaked into the darkened bedroom. The photo of two smiling girls rested on the bedside table. Elena, thought Janine, staring at the photo, who I got killed.

Now it was some old Nina Simone concert video. Nina Simone: angry, sad—Janine's all-time number one favorite. Nina, at the piano, not playing yet, singing a cappella, one of her usual sadder-than-sad numbers.

Janine pulled the rubber tube as tight as she could, slapped the veins in her arm, though she didn't have much strength, just enough to slip the needle in and send the drug into her bloodstream. Nina Simone hit the piano keys. The tinkling ivory sounded like delicate raindrops on glass. Nina was singing about a bird, the breeze, something about the dawn and a new life.

Janine tried to echo the words. They dragged out as slow and thick as the vodka.

And then she felt it, the heroin speeding along her arteries, to her brain, her heart.

Was Nina Simone singing about a new life or was she just imagining it? The voice was so far away, the TV screen a blur of wild color, dissolving, melting in the corner. Then the drug was burning, setting off rockets. Janine's eyes flickered. Her breath caught in her throat. Then she saw them—those two little girls in matching plaid skirts, white shirts, knee-high socks, laughing—just before the drug stopped her heart.

The youngish woman brushed her way past Brown, laid her soft brown leather briefcase on the metal table, popped it open. "I want a copy of the arrest papers. All the charges," she said. Then to Trip: "They have no right to be questioning you." Then to Brown and Kate: "Nothing my client said here is admissible." She regarded his bruised face. "Harassment? Assault? Oh, this is going to be a very nice case."

"I've been here all night," Trip whined. "In the tank."

"And you've detained my client since last night?" She removed her tortoiseshell glasses. "Detective Brown, I'm surprised. I thought you knew better."

"Nice to see you, too, Susan," said Brown.

The lawyer shoved her hands into the pockets of her chalk-stripe suit jacket, eyed Kate. "And you are?"

Kate thought the suit made her look like a gangster. "Katherine McKinnon Rothstein."

"Oh." A look of recognition spread across the lawyer's face. "I know your husband." She half smiled. "I have a feeling you'll be needing his services." The lawyer's attention quickly returned to Trip. "Bail's been made. Come on."

"Lawyers," said Brown, disgusted, as the Interrogation Room door slammed shut. "Susan Chase. Name mean anything to you?"

"Drug lawyer to the stars, right?"

"Right. Trip must be tied into some heavy hitters."

"We still have Janine Cook. She can place Damien Trip with Elena Solana on the day of the murder."

"Better get her in here," said Brown. "Fast."

"I already sent a uniform to her place." Kate's head was starting to ache. "What if Trip decides to skip town?"

"With that lawyer?" said Brown. "He won't be going anywhere. I doubt he's even worried."

Twenty minutes later, Kate was slumped in a chair opposite Floyd Brown.

"Janine Cook is dead," he said.

Kate sat forward; her face had gone white. "What? When?"

"Sometime this morning. Heroin overdose." Brown sighed.

Kate shook her head slowly. "Damn it. Damien Trip could have supplied the stuff. He had the drugs."

"Yeah," said Brown, frowning. "But we gotta prove it."

The conference room seemed airless. Kate was feeling that mixture of adrenaline and exhaustion, the way she used to feel when she pulled an all-nighter for an art history exam, used a little speed to help, and it wore off.

Mead was sweating. "I just got a slew of papers from Chase, Shebairo, and Mason," he said. "Trip's lawyers are charging us with harassment, and—"

"I wouldn't worry about that," said Brown.

"No?" Mead tugged at his collar. "Well, maybe you'd better."

"Look," said Brown. "We've got enough on Trip to tie him to Pruitt and Stein—"

"Circumstantially," said Mead.

"We can place him with Solana the day of her murder," said Slattery.

"Yeah," said Mead, sucking his teeth with disgust, "by a dead witness." He sighed. "Okay. I can see that Trip is linked to the vics. But why *you,* McKinnon? Why would Trip pick you out?"

"He hated my guts. Elena built me up as some sort of angel, the perfect mom. I think it stuck in his craw. Then there's the art angle, the fact that I wrote a book about artists, that I made Elena and other artists famous. Plus the fact that he's a total failure, so sick with jealousy toward any real artist that it's fucking palpable."

Mead nodded, folded his hands tightly. "Okay, people. Trip's arraignment is set for next Thursday. Meanwhile, I want you to pull everything together on the guy and get it to the DA." He looked from Kate to Brown. "You two, go back and search every inch of Trip's place."

"Anything in particular we're looking for?" Brown asked.

"I want to see every video in that place—every letter, every invoice, every scrap of paper. I want to see his fucking underwear, for Christ's sake! I want this case tighter than a virgin's pussy." Mead wiped the sweat off his upper lip. "Anything I'm missing? I don't want us getting caught off-guard here."

"One thing," said Kate. "Darton Washington. There's Ethan Stein's diary entry, plus the phone records that prove he was in contact with Elena Solana just before she was murdered."

"Get on it," said Mead.

29

The large room was a buzz of activity: thirty, forty uniforms and detectives all working phones. It could have been a bookie joint, if it weren't General Investigation.

Kate found the detective behind a desk piled high with stacks of papers, four or five empty Fresca cans, what looked like a half-eaten tuna on rye with the lettuce picked out and wilting on some curling wax paper. The detective looked up, pulled a hand through his thick salt-and-pepper hair.

"You called. Said you had something for me?"

"Right." He started shifting everything around frantically, the Fresca cans, tuna sandwich, stacks of paper. "It's here somewhere, I swear."

"How do you find *anything*, Rizak?"

"I got a system." He dumped the empty cans into an already overflowing trash basket. "Here it is." He handed Kate a single sheet of paper with one short paragraph, typed. "We ran Pruitt's stock portfolio through the computer with all the names you gave me—Solana, Stein, Washington, Trip. Only one match." He tapped the paper in her hand. "Darton Washington. He worked for FirstRate Music. Pruitt was a major stockholder." Rizak shuffled more papers, found what he was looking for on a crumpled Post-It. "My notes," he said. "I called FirstRate, asked about Washington. He was fired three weeks ago. And according to the CEO, guy named Aaron Feldman, there was a lot of pressure to dump the rap music division. Considered too smutty, or something." Rizak made a who-cares? face. "But the one leading the battle against all that dirty-mouthed rap music was your very own William Pruitt."

Kate gave Rizak's shoulder a tap. "Great work. I'll let them know about you in homicide."

The detective grinned, scooped up his tuna on rye, took a big bite.

A schizophrenic library: one side dusty narrow corridors of shelves stacked with boxes; the other, a row of fancy new computers. Kate attempted to fill in forms as quickly as possible. *Darton Washington fired because of Bill Pruitt.* Now she wanted to check further, see what that juvey case was all about.

The clerk rapped her nails along the counter as if she were practicing "Chopsticks" on the piano. "I was supposed to go on break five minutes ago," she chirped in nasal Brooklynese. She glanced down at Kate's ID, then up, gave her the once-over. "You don't look familiar."

"Working with Mead" was all Kate offered.

"Lucky you." The clerk rolled her eyes, plucked Kate's request from her hand, disappeared behind her computer.

Kate filled the time staring at a wall of police notices: a party for the Benevolent Society, a recruitment poster for Big Brother, a couple of apartment-share requests from rookies.

The clerk's pale face came back to the window, framed, picking up a greenish glow from the computer. "We got about two hundred Washingtons on microfiche. Of that, sixty-three Ds."

"Oh. Sorry. His first name is Darton. D-A-R—"

"Yeah. Yeah. I can spell." She disappeared again, then was

back, sat, sighed, punched something into the computer. "Okay. Washington, Darton. Yeah. Here we go." She slapped another form onto the counter.

"What's this for?"

"You want the printout? You gotta sign for it."

"So you found it?"

"Washington, Darton. Two arrests. Assault and statutory rape."

Kate peered through the two-way mirror into the Interrogation Room, watched as Darton Washington twisted a chunky gold ring around his index finger, his powerful body squeezed into a wooden chair that looked as if it could shatter.

Her first thought had been to race all the way down to Washington Street, but she was just too tired and, truthfully, she liked having the security of the police station around her—she sensed more than a little rage behind Washington's polished veneer.

Kate mustered what remained of her vigor as she walked into the room.

"What's going on?" Washington's eyes sparked with anger.

"I need to ask you a few questions."

He shifted his muscular bulk; the chair creaked. "I'm not saying a word until I call my lawyer."

Kate handed him copies of his two old rap sheets.

"*This?* Are you kidding? I was *seventeen* when I had that fight. Assault, my ass. And this other one—did you even bother to read it all the way through? I was *cleared*. Get it? No conviction. That girl looked older than *me*! Fifteen? She looked thirty." His fists were opening and closing as if they were being mechanically pumped. "My lawyer had it dismissed." He rapped the table. "Why does it even exist? I want to see my lawyer."

Kate kept her voice level. "By all means, talk to your lawyer. If you were seventeen, this should have been expunged. As for the other one, I don't know. But it's still in the program, and nowhere does it say it was dismissed." She spread her hands on the table. "Look, Darton. I don't care about that."

"So then why am I here?"

"You owned an Ethan Stein painting—"

"And there's a law against that?"

"You went to the artist's studio a week before he was murdered."

"No. I did not."

"Your name is in Ethan Stein's date book."

Washington shifted his weight uncomfortably. "I canceled that appointment. I was tied up at work."

No way Kate could prove or dispute that—now that Stein was dead.

"I was thinking about buying another one of his paintings, particularly since his market was low. I liked his work. I already told you that."

"But you didn't tell me you had planned to see him only a week before he was murdered."

"I didn't think it was important."

"Really? A man is murdered—a man you were supposed to visit—and you don't find that important?"

Washington smoldered, said nothing.

"Did you know William Pruitt?"

"No."

Kate let a moment pass, continued to speak in a matter-of-fact manner. "You didn't exactly leave your job at FirstRate Music voluntarily, did you, Mr. Washington? You were fired."

"And your point?"

"My point is that William Pruitt owned a substantial amount of stock in FirstRate Music. And according to your boss, Aaron Feldman, it was Pruitt's fault you lost your job."

Washington's dark eyes flashed. "A bunch of lily-white assholes afraid of a little music. But you know what? Pruitt did me a favor. I'm a lot happier out on my own—I told you that last time."

"So you did. You just omitted the part about knowing Bill Pruitt."

"I didn't *know* him." Washington eyed her with contempt. "I knew who he was, knew he was the one leading the lynch mob against us crazy jive-talkin' niggers." Washington laid it on thick. "But I never met the man."

Kate looked into his eyes. "Knowing that Pruitt was the man who had you fired is enough of a motive."

"I told you. He did me a favor. I'm better solo."

"Maybe," said Kate. "Suppose I decide to believe you on that point. Will you level with me—about Elena?"

He folded his arms across his massive chest. "How so?"

"You *were* involved."

Washington stared at her, said nothing.

"Darton." Kate leaned toward him. "You fit the description of a man who Elena Solana's landlord says was more than an occasional visitor. You want me to get the landlord down here, put you in a lineup, or do you just want to tell me the truth?"

"Okay." Washington's huge shoulders sagged. "We were involved."

"So what happened?"

"It was going along fine—at least I thought so—and then, boom, she dumped me for another guy."

"You know who that was?"

Washington's eyes slid off Kate's toward the dull gray walls. "I saw her one time with the guy—she didn't see me—a blond guy, tall, slim, maybe thirty-five, he had his arm around her." Washington's hands curled into fists again. "She dumped me for a white guy. Way of the world, isn't it?" He laughed, ironic, no gaiety in it. "I followed them. Saw where he lived. Got his name, too." His eyes had gone black. "Damien Trip."

"But you and Elena spoke again. And Darton, please remember—we have the phone records to prove it."

"Yes. No. I hung up on her. She wanted my help, but . . ." He looked down at his hands.

Kate's voice took on an insistent tone. "Why did she want your help?"

"I think Trip was scaring her, but . . ." He shook his head. "I don't know. I wouldn't listen. I thought, oh, now you want my help, do you? She'd hurt me, you know, and—*Fuck!* Why didn't I listen?" His body stiffened again, but there were tears in his eyes. "Fuck," he said again, but this time only a whisper.

"We've talked to Trip."

Washington sat upright. "Thank God."

"Well, let's not thank him yet. Trip's got a very good lawyer."

"You let him *go*?"

"We had no choice." Kate sighed.

Darton Washington flexed his shoulders; the ropy muscles in his thick neck stood out in high relief. "You've *got* to get him."

"We're trying to."

"Don't just *try*." His mouth twitched with fury. "*Do it*."

Kate could feel his rage. But was he just trying to deflect suspicion from himself by putting it on Damien Trip? "You want Trip out of the way, that it, Darton?"

"Don't *you*?"

"That wasn't my question." Kate dragged a chair close, sat. "Let me recap, shall I?" She counted off on her fingers. "One: Elena Solana called you. Days later she's dead. Two: Ethan Stein has your name in his date book. Days later *he's* dead. Three: You get fired. A couple of weeks later the man behind your firing is dead. I'll tell you something, Darton. From where I sit, it doesn't look good."

"And from where I sit, it looks like coincidence. I was not in Elena Solana's apartment for weeks. I didn't make it to Ethan Stein's studio because I was cutting a demo. And I never met Pruitt. You've got nothing tangible to connect me to any of these crimes."

"Not yet," said Kate. "But I'll be working on it."

Washington stared down at his hands, just barely whispered, "I loved her. Elena."

Unrequited love? Hell, that was an even stronger motive. "So you loved her and she rejected you," said Kate.

"I didn't kill her." Washington looked up, his brown eyes moist. "I told you. I loved her."

Kate rapped on the half-wall of Maureen Slattery's cubicle. "You have a message for me?"

"Oh, McKinnon." Maureen looked up, fingers resting on her computer keyboard. "Yeah. Got a message from Brown. He's out in Brooklyn. Something about the Shooter case, from months ago. Said to tell you he'd meet you at Trip's, along with a tech team, at six P.M. Also, you should bring the warrant in case Trip is on the premises."

"Thanks."

Maureen tilted her head at the bulletin board above her desk, where she'd pinned a reproduction of *The Death of Marat*. "Hey, I was wondering, like, why'd this painter, what's his name, David, paint it in the first place?"

"He was Napoleon's court painter," said Kate. "He painted lots of historical scenes. This was just one of them. In those days, if you wanted something documented or re-created, you needed a painter to do it. Of course that all changed when photography was invented." She glanced over at the reproduction, thought of poor Bill Pruitt as a weak imitation of Marat. "I'll get you a book of David's paintings. Wait'll you see his *Coronation of Napoleon* painting. It's a knockout."

"This death artist might turn me into an art lover yet." Slattery laughed.

Kate laughed, too, then got serious, filled Slattery in on her talk with Darton Washington.

"You think we're jumping the gun on Trip—that Washington could be a suspect?"

"It's completely possible," said Kate, considering the question. "But I believed him when he said he loved Elena."

"Always a popular motive for murder."

"I agree," Kate said. "But we've got nothing to prove he

was at the Solana scene. No prints. Nothing to DNA. He says he was out of town when Elena died, home alone the night Pruitt was drowned, cutting a demo CD in a midtown studio from late afternoon till almost two in the morning the night Ethan Stein died. I'm having all the alibis checked out, but we had to let him go—for the moment."

"We should put a tail on him. Trip, too. I'll speak to Mead about it."

"Good idea." Kate's foot was tapping, her adrenaline starting to pump in anticipation of the search. She checked her watch. She had an hour to kill. "You want to get a cup of coffee?"

"Love to. But I can't. Mead wants the reports of the gallery and museum interrogations on his desk, ASAP." She gave Kate the once-over. "You look tired, McKinnon. Why don't you take a rest before the search?"

Kate could use a rest—like a month on a Caribbean island, for starters. She checked her bag to make sure the search warrant for Damien Trip's apartment was still there. "Maybe later," she said.

He glances across the room at the still life, the plate of rotting fruit, a few slices of deli turkey now sprouting green and blue mold, all drenched in rat poison, and the rats—in various stages of decomposition, here, there; one gagging, choking, its tiny red eyes ready to explode out of its skull.

Maybe he should send her one?

He sits back, pictures her opening the package, imagines the smell, the look on her face. That would serve her right.

But no, it's not part of the game, doesn't really prove anything.

He stares down at the reproduction. He's just about finished his latest piece, the birthday card, admires his additions—the clock, the totally confusing calendar, the clump of real hair he has glued onto it. He resists the urge to stroke it, knows what will happen if he does.

He paces. He's ready. More than ready.

He's got everything he needs. Six knives, a plastic fishbowl, the piece of old luggage he picked up at the flea market. He hoists the suitcase onto the table. It's not exactly like the one in the picture, but close enough. He places the knives carefully into it, noting the worn interior, trying to imagine the people who once owned it, the places they had traveled. Was it a family, a tortured, hideous family? His head begins to ache. But then seeing how perfectly the fishbowl and knives fit into the case soothes him.

He flips open *Who's Who in American Art* to the page he has marked, his eyes flitting over the biography he has chosen one more time. Particularly the birth date.

Could it possibly have worked out any better than this? He doesn't see how.

30

The one time Kate was not in a hurry and there was no traffic. She guided her car into a spot across the street from Damien Trip's building. She'd sit awhile, wait for Brown and the tech team, force herself to relax. She switched the car key to battery, hit the CD player, listened to Sade crooning about a "smooth operator," lit a cigarette, and leaned back against the headrest.

She was just watching the smoke snake out the window when she heard the three loud pops in succession. Gunshots. No mistaking it.

A second later she was pushing through the front door, charging up the stairs, her gun drawn.

On the second-floor landing, a woman with a baby in her arms poked her head out, saw Kate, and froze.

Kate screamed, "Back inside! *Now!*"

Kate took the next staircase slowly. The old wooden stairs creaked under her crepe soles. Was someone waiting for her? Trip?

But on the top floor it was quiet, Trip's door slightly ajar. Kate aimed the pistol out in front of her, pivoted through the door.

Damien Trip was on the floor beside that king-size bed and the lights on tripods, sitting up, hands gripping his belly.

Trip stared at her, his baby blues filled with panic. Blood was pumping, spilling between his fingers so fast that it looked fake.

Kate yanked the stained sheet from the bed, tore off a long strip, balled it up and pressed it against Trip's midsection. It soaked through in less than twenty seconds.

Trip opened his mouth to speak, but no words came out, only more blood, bubbling past his lips. He managed a nod toward an open window, his eyes blinking like a cartoon character.

Kate was on her feet fast; she peered out the window, spotted him—a jerking staccato figure, on the fire escape. A split-second look back at Trip, who had fallen to the floor, arms stretched out, blood spreading beneath his inert body like a satiny ocean of deep red. It was way too late to help him.

The fire escape groaned, even sagged a bit as Kate made the vertiginous descent. It was like a German Expressionist film set, all oblique angles and dingy gray.

Below her, the man leaped from the last bit of hanging ladder.

A minute later, Kate was doing the same. She came down hard on her heels, rocked backward, banged against the brick wall, then pitched forward into one of several steel Dumpsters.

Shit.

She'd have a bruise on her rib cage for sure.

She sprinted around the building, caught a glimpse of a shadow as the door to a BMW slammed shut, the engine revved, tires squealed.

But Kate was right on him, angling her car into the street, her foot bearing down on the accelerator.

Jesus fucking Christ. A car chase. A fucking car chase. Last time she did this she was what, twenty-eight? But her adrenaline was pumping again, as fast as the gas was pouring into the engine, thoughts ping-ponging in her brain: *Trip. Shot. But who? Why?*

The speedometer read sixty. The strip of project buildings flew by, blurring like scenes glimpsed through a train window. There were horns blaring, pedestrians racing back to the safety of curbs.

Ahead of her, the BMW ran six red lights in a row and Kate did the same. All around them drivers were hitting their brakes, cars were bouncing up on the sidewalks, slamming into each other.

It might have been over a decade since she had maneuvered a car at raceway speeds, but Kate McKinnon had been the drag-racing princess of Astoria, Queens. No one even came close; not Johnny Bertinelli in his souped-up Chevy II, nor Timmy O'Brien in his dad's eight-cylinder Grand Prix. Kate had left them all in the dust—little boys with their tails between their legs.

Kate managed to call in for backup with one hand on the wheel.

"Damien Trip is dead," she said, giving his address.

"Brown was just at the scene," said the desk cop. "He called it in."

"I'm in pursuit of the assailant. I've just passed Eighteenth Street on Park Avenue South, heading north. First three digits of the license plate are DJW. That's David John West." She clicked off.

The BMW charged all the way up to Twenty-third Street, hung a screeching left, which Kate echoed. They raced across to the West Side, darting between cars, trucks, cabs, and traffic cops gesturing like wind-up dolls gone berserk. Alongside him a moment ago, Kate tried to catch a nanosecond glimpse, but everything was a blur.

At the intersection of Ninth Avenue and Twenty-third, the BMW was trapped between a bus and a cab, but Kate was boxed in, too. From somewhere behind, sirens were getting louder.

First the BMW, then Kate zigzagged a way out. They were back up to hazardous speed in a minute, the two of them in their own fast-forward movie, out of sync with the normal rpm world. The BMW was a half a block ahead, not far from the piers and the new Chelsea sports complex, an intersection where the West Side Highway met normal city traffic, where four or five thoroughfares converged.

Kate eased off the gas. She had him. No way he could speed through this.

The sirens were behind her now, their lights flashing in her rearview mirror.

But he didn't slow down; he virtually flew through the intersection.

Jesus. Where's he going?

Framed through her windshield, Kate watched the BMW swerve to the left so sharply, its right side lifted off the ground before straightening out, and once again was racing west.

The screech and squeal of brakes and tires matched the shrill police sirens, with all vehicles coming to a dead stop.

All except the tourist bus, which, after depositing its visitors for a lazy riverside stroll, pulled out of the Chelsea Piers parking lot, somehow blind to the silver bullet hurtling toward it at breakneck speed.

Too late.

The BMW folded like an accordion, the entire front half disappearing as though the bus had opened its hungry jaws and chomped it off.

The noise was like a full-scale orchestra made up entirely of cymbals and drums with a strange chorus of altos, groaning.

Fire engines had clogged Twenty-third Street from Tenth Avenue to the Hudson River. Over a dozen cop cars looped around the scene, their beacons flashing; uniforms, out of their vehicles, formed a ring—rigid toy soldiers keeping thrill seekers and gawkers at bay. Two ambulances stood by, sirens deafening. A couple of local TV news vans had managed to slip in, angle-parked on the sidewalk. Firemen hosed down the smashed bus, steam rising off it like Old Faithful.

Another group of firemen were working a chainsaw on the BMW while Kate huddled with Floyd Brown.

"Trip's dead," he said, shaking his head. "But you obviously know that."

Kate nodded, but wasn't really listening. She had turned to see the firemen tear the crumpled door off the BMW, and the paramedics attempt to pry Darton Washington's huge body from the mass of steaming, mangled metal. They signaled her over.

Kate wrapped her hand around Washington's. The younger medic caught her eye, led her vision toward Washington's lower half, where the ragged edge of what might have been the dashboard had cut across the man's legs, severing them just below the knees.

Washington's pupils were dilated in shock. "I'm cold," he whispered.

"We can fix that," said Kate, laying her jacket over his chest. A medic shot morphine into Washington's arm, probably enough to kill him before the loss of blood did. Either way, it was only a matter of minutes.

The TV reporters were storming the uniforms, waving microphones like prehistoric men with bones.

Brown trotted back, made sure they were kept away.

"Someone said it's the death artist," said a young guy with an ABC press pass stuck to his corduroy blazer. "Is he dead?"

"No comment, fellas," said Brown, turning to look at Kate, who was cradling Washington's dying head in her arms. It made him think of Michelangelo's *Pietà*, the Blessed Virgin with Christ in her lap. He remembered seeing the statue at the New York World's Fair when he was a kid, and crying.

Kate tried to sip coffee from a styrofoam cup, but her hands were trembling too badly. Trip dead. Washington dead. Kate didn't know what to think. Both men had connections to each of the victims—Elena, Pruitt, Stein. Had all of the answers to her questions died with them?

"Lord works in mysterious ways," said Brown, watching them load the remains of Darton Washington into the back of an ambulance.

"Killing Trip was an act of passion," said Kate. "Washington loved her. He loved Elena."

"You loved her, too. But you didn't go and shoot Trip."

"No," said Kate. "But I wanted to."

31

Randy Mead rapped a Bic pen against the edge of the conference table. "Who do you think you are, McKinnon, fucking Superman?"

Almost any other time Kate would have given him a cocky yes, but not while she was thinking about Darton Washington; the image of the man dying in that mangled BMW would always be with her—just one more hideous image she could add to her gallery of grotesqueries.

"You didn't, by any chance, get a deathbed confession from Trip, did you, McKinnon?"

"By the time I found him, Trip wasn't talking at all," said Kate. "I hate to say it, but I think we should search Washington's place. See if there's anything definitive that might tie him to the murders."

"Isn't it a little late for that?" said Mead.

"Not if we want something conclusive," said Kate. "Both Trip and Washington had connections to the victims. The fact is, Washington could have killed Trip to silence him."

"All right," said Mead. "I'll send a team over to Washington's place."

"What about the press? They were all over the scene yesterday," said Brown. "What's the official word going to be?"

"I don't know." Mead pinched the bridge of his nose. "I

gotta talk to Tapell first. And you, McKinnon, you gotta meet with Mobile, Accident Investigation, *and* Crime Scene. Your little joy ride managed to hit every other division in the NYPD. And I need the papers from each of them on my desk ASAP—plus your personal account of the chain of events leading to Trip's and Washington's demise."

Six hours of interviews and paperwork. Kate was exhausted. Still, she made the trek over to Willie's studio, wanted him to hear it from her lips. How his collector and friend had died.

But she was too late—the news reports had beaten her to it. How was it they always got the goddamn story so fast?

Kate's eyes followed Willie as he darted about his studio, stepping over boxes of spilled nails, shreds of sandpaper, tubes of squeezed-out oil paint. "Darton told me you were on his case, hounding him."

"It wasn't like that."

"But now he's dead. So, like what would you call it?"

"An *accident*." Kate wove a lock of her hair between her fingers, nervously. "Look, Willie. Darton killed Damien Trip. Shot him in cold blood, and—"

"And what? I'm supposed to feel bad?" Willie looked away, pictured Darton Washington in his studio, the cool elegance of the man, a man not unlike himself, out of the ghetto, who had made something of his life, pattering away about music and art and how big Willie was going to be, that he was a "genius." He turned back to Kate, his green eyes like cool lasers. "Trip killed Elena. *Killed* her. I thought that's what you cared about. Why you were doing this."

"I—" Kate stammered a moment. "I'm as sorry about Darton as you are."

"I don't think so," said Willie. He turned away, head tucked in, shoulders hunched. "You should leave now." The words were whispered so softly Kate could only just hear them; so strong they bore right through her skin, into her heart.

DEATH ARTIST DEAD

The city, particularly the art world, is breathing a sigh of relief today after news that the serial killer dubbed the "death artist" died yesterday. His identity is temporarily being held by the authorities until all details surrounding his death are resolved.

At this time, rumor has it that he was killed by a relative or lover of one of the victims who died in a car crash escaping the scene.

Katherine McKinnon Rothstein, who has been advising the NYPD, was reportedly involved in the incident, but would not return calls. There is speculation that the police have . . .

How well this has worked out. Granted, he is a genius, but still, this was damn good luck, and he has to admit it. He knew she would read the video all wrong, but never in his wildest dreams did he imagine this amazing outcome—connections she made that he'd never anticipated.

But now what? It suddenly dawns on him that he could simply give it all up, go back to his normal life.

The words—*normal life*—cause him to smile. The fact is, it is getting harder and harder to control himself. Sometimes he just wants to say it, to whisper the words in someone's ear: *It's me, you know. I'm the one.* What is it that stops him? Perhaps the fact that he's not sure he is the one, not sure which is his real self.

But with that thought comes despair—that they will never know his work, that everything he has done has been in vain.

He shakes his head against the thoughts.

He holds up the finished birthday card. "My best goddamn piece of work." He stops a moment, thinks. "No. It *will* be my best work. Perfect."

Now all he has to do is wait.

But can he? His hands start to shake. And then he feels it—his need—like a hot coal burning through the walls of his stomach, bleeding into his organs; he can actually see his heart exploding, ribs cracking through flesh, blood splattering everywhere. He's got his hands pressed against his shirt, but they're useless to stop it. The pain is overwhelming. His liver is melting into a mass of purplish goo, his groin's on fire, the intensity so stunning that he tears his pants off, thinks he can see the flesh on his prick bubbling, searing off.

A moment later, he is standing in this abandoned building holding his limp dick under a faucet of cool, rusty water.

But the cold water isn't nearly enough to quell the fire inside him.

He slides the reproduction into an envelope with a trembling hand. Yes, it's time to send it. He just can't wait.

nother one of those nights. Awake. Asleep. Hot.
Cold. Crazy dreams. Nightmares.
Richard was already gone by the time Kate dragged
herself out of bed, a note scribbled on a Post-it adhered to
the bathroom mirror: "I love you."

Kate could barely remember their conversation, just that
she told him about her fight with Willie, her maddening day
of attempting to deal with four different NYPD divisions,
that she was tired. So tired.

She wanted to go back to bed, but couldn't.

There were still so many questions she needed answers
to—though she didn't know how or where to get them.

The station house seemed calmer this morning—or was
she projecting? There wasn't much on her desk—a memo
from Mead about another meeting, the usual plastic bag of
rerouted mail waiting for her to go through, a three-dollar
umbrella she'd picked up the other day.

Out of habit, Kate put on gloves and spilled the mail onto
her desk.

Was the case actually over? Could she simply pick up
where she'd left off—planning charity events, lunch with the
girls, the occasional lecture? Maybe it was time to start another book. She'd heard that there was a joke circulating in

the art world, that she should write a sequel—*Artists' Deaths*.
Typical.

Kate flipped through bills and brochures, gloom falling
over her like a frost, until she saw the plain manila envelope.
In an instant, she was alert.

Her gloved fingers trembled slightly on the envelope's
edge.

Another art reproduction. This one an installation piece—a
figure, or mannequin, cast in some sort of resin, lying on top
of an old gynecologist's table, six glass tubes shooting out of
her belly, a fishbowl stuck in her mouth; beside the figure, a
coat on a hat stand, a chair, an open suitcase on a floor of
checkerboard tiles, a clock and calendar on the wall with two
indecipherable paintings.

But it was the actual tuft of hair attached to the pictorial
woman's head that made Kate shiver.

Kienholz. That was it. Ed Kienholz. The sixties Pop artist.
Kate didn't know this particular piece, but his style was un-
mistakable. She'd written a paper on him in college.

She held the picture in her hand, stared at it. Could
Damien Trip or Darton Washington have made this before
they died? And why? It didn't appear to document anything.
Unless there was a body somewhere that they'd missed.
Kate felt the chill inching up her spine. There was, she
knew, another possibility—that the death artist was still out
there.

Kate could actually see her breath in the lab's frigid air. She
handed Hernandez the Kienholz reproduction.

"Sorry 'bout the cold," said Hernandez. "We got a couple
of day-old stiffs ready to ship to the ME. Didn't want them
to stink up the place."

Kate shivered. "Do you have any hair samples here from
previous victims, specifically Elena Solana's or Ethan
Stein's? It can't be Pruitt. The man was practically bald."

"You'd have to check with the ME," said Hernandez. "No,
wait. I got the contents of Solana's Dustbuster. They're sep-

arated and bagged. One of the samples—the main one—was Solana's hair. I can see if they're a match."

Minutes later, Hernandez was looking through a microscope. "It's Solana's hair, all right."

Kate swiped the reproduction with her gloved fingers. "I have to show it to the squad right away. I'll bring this back."

"Gloves," Hernandez called after her. "Everyone. Gloves."

Kate laid the Kienholz picture on the conference table between Floyd Brown and Maureen Slattery. "It's no copycat or crank. Not with Solana's hair attached to it."

Slattery leaned her elbows onto the table. "But it's different from the others. I mean, we haven't found any vic like this."

"I have a feeling he's changing the rules," said Kate.

Slattery frowned. "Why would he change now?"

"From what I've seen," said Brown, "these guys change the rules as fast as we can figure them out. All they care about is their goddamn ritual."

"And his ritual is making art," said Kate. "*That* hasn't changed."

Slattery studied the picture. "Those fucking things jutting out of her belly. Nasty."

"Or *into* it," said Brown. "What do you make of the fishbowl wedged against her open mouth?"

"A silent scream? Suffocation? Kienholz is symbolic," said Kate. "It's some kind of an abortion piece—or sexual violation—or both."

Randy Mead cut into the room. His smile shut down the minute he saw the three of them huddled over the reproduction. "What the fuck is this?"

Kate filled him in.

Mead tugged at his bow tie, his features screwed up. "Maybe it was something Trip was planning. But never got to."

"I thought that, too," said Kate. "But check out the postmark. It was express-mailed from the Main Post Office on Thirty-fourth Street and Eighth yesterday at four twenty-five P.M."

"And I'm still waitin' for the check that my ex *supposedly* mailed a week ago." Slattery shook her head.

"It was around five when I found Trip," Kate continued. "He'd just been shot. That doesn't leave a lot of time to get from midtown to the Lower East Side."

"But enough," said Mead. "Leave the post office at four twenty-five. Back downtown by five. Could do it by cab if the traffic was good."

"At that hour?" Kate tapped her gloved fingers along the conference table.

"Subway," said Slattery. "But there's no direct line. He'd have to transfer."

"And walk several blocks," Brown added.

"And get into his place and have the altercation with Washington," said Kate.

"It doesn't take long to shoot someone," said Mead. "Or it could be Washington's work. We can't rule that out yet." He sagged into one of the metal chairs. "But I hear you." His face had gone pale. "But it still *could* be Trip—or Washington. I mean, maybe there's a body out there we haven't found." His voice cracked, the desperation having an effect. "I'm gonna send out the troops, contact all the districts, see if anything like this has turned up."

Brown rubbed a hand over his skull. "We have to consider that our unsub is still out there, Randy. That Trip was *not* the man we were looking for—and neither was Washington."

"You think I'm not considering that?" Randy Mead looked as if he could cry. "You realize the FBI boys were ready to step in? They backed off since our two main suspects, Trip and Washington, died. Now . . ." He sighed.

"I'll talk to my friend in the Bureau," said Kate. "In the meantime, let's concentrate on what we know."

"So, if the rules are different . . ." Brown went back to the altered Kienholz picture. "What's this tell us?"

"I'm not sure," said Kate. "But these have been drawn on." She indicated the clock and calendar. "So they have to mean something. Could be he's giving us the day and time. He's drawn the hands on the clock to eleven. On the calendar, he's crossed out half the days of the month up till today."

"So it could go down today? *Shit*." Mead sucked his teeth.

"Maybe," said Kate. "And we don't know if it's A.M. or P.M."

"I'd vote for P.M.," said Brown. "All the others were killed at night."

"Maybe the guy has a day job," said Kate, considering it.

"What about the circled two dates on the calendar?" asked Slattery. "The tenth and the thirteenth?"

"Both those dates are already past. Could be next month," said Mead.

"I don't think so." Kate shook her head. "He's clearly labeled it May."

"And that's too long for one of these guys to go," said Brown. "They're like pressure cookers. The more they kill, the more they want to. The intervals in between will be getting shorter, not longer."

"Unless we missed it," said Mead. "And the body is waiting for us, that it *was* Trip's—or Washington's—work."

Kate could see Mead was praying to be right. But her gut was telling her he was wrong. "There's one more thing. See here?" She aimed a gloved finger at a tiny playing card, a joker, glued over a tile in the checkerboard floor.

"Maybe it's a symbol for him," said Brown. "You know, that he's a joker, playing with us."

"Could be." Kate tried to think it through. "But it could be something totally different."

"Like what?" asked Mead.

Kate shrugged. "I don't know yet."

Mead pushed himself away from the table. "If this is from him and he's still alive, we have a tiny window if he's not striking until eleven tonight. In the meantime, let's do everything. Contact every precinct, see if there's any abortion-related killings, anything at all like this that we haven't heard about. Brown, Slattery, get a crew together, start calling." He turned to Kate. "And you, art lady. I want you studying that reproduction like your mother's life depended on it."

33

Not exactly the kind of party Amanda Lowe had in mind. One more disappointment. But then, most things were.

Why was that?

Here she was, one of the hottest art dealers in the hottest art city in the hottest art market representing a dozen of the hottest young artists—well, eight out of twelve (and those other four wouldn't be around much longer), and still, she felt . . . what? Unfulfilled? Depressed? Lonely? Maybe all three.

How could that be? She was taking that damn Zoloft religiously. But still, there was that low-level malaise, a kind of ennui that seemed to ruin everything.

Everything except a good sale. Now *that* got her going. Could even make her happy. For a while. Like the other day, selling two WLK Hand paintings to that German couple, sight unseen, by telling them there was a waiting list for the work, when there wasn't. If there was one thing Amanda Lowe knew, it was how to create a market. She thought she could sell just about anything.

So, why, tonight, after a totally hip party, a private room, no less, in the grooviest Meat Market watering hole, with all her little art stars and art collectors surrounding her, and a

few wanna-bes to kiss her ass, did Amanda Lowe feel so
bad?

It was not just that it was her forty-seventh birthday and
she was going home alone. Hell, if she'd wanted to get laid
she could always find some hungry young artist-on-the-
make more than willing to come home with her. No, that
wasn't it. *So what was it?*

Thirteenth Street was fairly deserted, just a few twenty-
somethings at the far end of the street, laughing. Amanda
Lowe instantly detested them—for their youth, the beauty she
supposed they possessed, their lives stretching ahead of them
filled with so much promise. She wanted to call out: *You'll see.
It will all turn to shit!* But she just looked away, hurried down
the dark street, the whole time holding her breath. When, she
wondered, will those awful butchers and wholesale meat pur-
veyors be pushed out of the neighborhood by the high rents—
and take their stink with them? Not soon enough for her.

Though it was hardly cold, a shiver coiled its way through
Amanda Lowe's emaciated body, as though, for a moment,
something had passed through her. A spirit, or . . . ? She
pulled her black leather Prada car coat tighter, hugged her
thin arms around her bony torso, quickened her step.

The metal gate, which guarded the huge green-tinted
glass fronting her gallery, was down for the night. It made
her sad. As though the only thing she cared about—her art
business—was in jail, caged.

Inside, she wrestled with the old freight elevator—one of
the minuses to owning an entire building by herself—finally
getting it almost level with her new, wide-paneled oak floor.

She stepped in. Flicked a switch. Cool halogen lights illuminated the stark four-thousand-square-foot space she
shared only with one Siamese cat that bore an uncanny resemblance to its mistress. She checked her Piaget watch.
Ten-fifteen. At least she was home early.

Back in her tiny office, Kate was following Mead's order—
concentrating as though her mother were alive, and the

woman's life depended on it. The invention warmed her, actually propelled her.

So far, Slattery and Brown had turned up a half dozen unidentified bodies. But only one with a connection to the Kienholz picture—an apparently illegal abortion gone wrong, the girl dumped at a landfill on Staten Island. But there was no ritual there. None of the others had anything at all that might suggest the work of the death artist.

Kate had had the Kienholz picture enlarged two hundred percent, could now read the clock and calendar added to the artwork clearly, could see every strand of that lock of hair. But even two-dimensionally—knowing that it was actually Elena's hair—it was enough to make Kate cringe.

She stared at the image. How should she think about this one? There was no crime scene photo to compare it with.

She had had the large coffee-table book on the work of Ed Kienholz delivered to the station house, and now flipped pages until she found the piece she was looking for.

The Birthday, 1964. Tableau. 84 x 120 x 60 inches.
Mannequin, Lucite, gynecologist's examination table,
    suitcase, clothing, paper, fiberglass, paint, polyester
    resin.

She gazed at the picture in the book, then back at the enlargement.

Could those crossed-out dates—or the circled ones—be someone's birthday? Maybe. But whose? And what about the card, the joker, which was practically hidden in the pattern of the black and white floor tiles?

Kate just didn't know.

Had Damien Trip left this to drive her crazy? If so, it was working. But would Trip have sent her a teaser when he had just been interrogated, when he was clearly under suspicion?

Kate stared at the joker. Maybe Brown was right, that it was a symbol for the killer himself, that he saw himself as a joker, playing with her, with the cops.

But what else?

Checkerboard floors? Kate thought a moment. Flemish paintings almost always had checkerboard floors. What else did they have? Symbols. Everything in a Flemish painting was standing in for something else. So what could a joker be?

A jester? A comedian?

No. Something to do with art.

A joker? A card?

Neither of those made any sense. What else?

A deck of cards? Fifty-two. Numbers. Pictures. Suits. Betting. Dealing.

She thought about the victims: Elena. Pruitt. Ethan Stein. Performance artist. Museum president. Minimal painter.

Was the guy breaking down the art world? Picking off representatives? *Painter. Performer . . .* Kate stared at the reproductions. *A card. Dealing. A dealer. An art dealer!*

Of course. It had to be. Kate's adrenaline was pumping about as fast as her frustration was mounting. Which art dealer? And how to find out?

Back to the enlargement. It was here. Somewhere. Kate knew it. Felt it. The guy was more than playing with her. He was testing her. The clock. The calendar. Something in there.

But what?

Her mind was clicking away, but she just couldn't get at it.

She slammed the Kienholz book shut.

There was not much time left—and someone was in for a very unpleasant birthday present.

"The piece is called *The Birthday*." Kate paced, her low heels click-clacking on the conference room's hard cement floor. "He's got to be indicating someone's birthday."

"Like whose?" Mead sucked his teeth.

"An art dealer's. He's not just making art. He's choosing his victims as representatives of the art world: Elena

Solana's the performance artist, Pruitt's the museum man, Stein's the traditional-type painter."

"You call white paintings traditional?" said Slattery.

"Nowadays, if you paint, you're traditional," said Kate.

Mead sighed heavily. "But how can we possibly get the birthdays of hundreds of art dealers in New York?"

"It'd be in their bios." Kate thought a second. "We could check *Who's Who in American Art*. Of course, that would be thousands to go through, and not everyone includes their birthdays—especially the women."

"Come on, people." Mead tugged at his bow tie. "I don't want to lose another vic to this guy."

"It's all in here." Kate tapped the reproduction. "In the picture. Everything's a visual clue."

"Okay," said Slattery. "So what do the circled dates mean?"

"I've been trying to figure that out. If it's not the date of the crime—and I don't think it is, since both of those dates have passed—then what else?"

"A statistic?" said Brown.

"Or numerology?" Slattery offered.

"I don't think so," said Kate. "The guy seems to be more specific than that. What numbers are specific?"

"Phone numbers," said Brown.

"Not enough for a phone number." Kate's foot was tapping out a nervous tune on the concrete floor. "The tenth and the thirteenth?"

"Ten-thirteen," said Slattery. "The *time* of the murder."

"I'd stick with eleven," said Kate, checking her watch.

So did Mead. "Shit. It's ten-fifty, people."

"Wait a second. What about an address?" Kate's foot stopped tapping. "Tenth Street. Thirteenth Street? No. Wait. Thirteenth Street and Tenth *Avenue*. The Meat Market. Chelsea. Of course. A gallery. That makes sense if he's going to do an art dealer." She quick-turned to Mead. "Randy. You've got to get cars out to Thirteenth and Tenth Avenue—to every gallery along the street. ASAP." Then to Slattery. "Maureen, you still have that *Gallery Guide*?"

Maureen had already gotten it out, ran her finger along the Chelsea street map. "There are four—no, five—galleries along Thirteenth."

"Any on Tenth Avenue at Thirteenth?"

"Uh . . . Just a restaurant."

"Go back to Thirteenth Street. The Kienholz piece is about a woman's violation. So we're most likely looking for a woman gallery dealer."

Slattery read through the listing. "Gallery 505—could be either sex. Valerie Kennedy Gallery—that's one. Art Resource International—maybe. Amanda Lowe Gallery—for sure."

Mead already had the cellular to his ear, barking instructions. "Six cars already on the way," he said, clicking off. "Ambulance, too."

"Get someone to contact those dealers ASAP," said Kate. "The galleries are probably closed, so get home numbers and addresses."

"Get someone to go on-line," Brown barked at a uniform. "Of those galleries, see who might be having a birthday, and call us en route."

"I'm coming with you," said Kate.

"All right," said Mead. "Go with Slattery—and let *her* drive."

Amanda Lowe has barely gotten her Prada jacket off when he grabs her, whispers, "Happy birthday," one hand around her throat, the other pressing a rag soaked with some awful-smelling chemical into her nose and mouth.

The ambulance had shut off its siren, but the cop cars' beacons were still streaking blips of stark light across Thirteenth Street.

The young uniformed cop looked shaken, his face gray-green, as if he was going to be sick. "She's in there. Second floor. Above the gallery."

"You found her?" asked Brown.

"Me and Diaz." He nodded to another uniform, sitting on the stairs in front of the Amanda Lowe Gallery. "A couple of detectives are up there now." He bit his lip, seemed close to tears. Brown patted the guy's shoulder as he headed into the building.

The scene was so surreal Kate could barely take it in.

Amanda Lowe was strapped onto her sleek dining room table. Six long knives in her belly. Handles jutting out exactly like the Lucite cylinders of the Kienholz piece. Blood on the table, dripping onto the rug—unctuous, oily waterfalls. Her coat had been hung on the wall beside the table, just as in the reproduction. There was even a suitcase on the floor.

A detective was crouched beside the scene. He turned, nodded acknowledgment at Mead, said, "Look at this."

Mead took a step closer. Kate peered over his shoulder.

Just beside the suitcase, on the pale rug, ragged, shaky lettering.

Kate looked more closely. It was writing, in blood:

DEATH ARTIST

"Jesus," said Brown. "He likes the name."

"Yes," said Kate. "And now he's signing his work."

34

F irst you have him, then you don't," said Clare Tapell. "The press is having a field day with this, Randy! The mayor is getting twenty calls a day from art world mucky-mucks screaming about their safety and the police department's ineptitude—and then he calls *me*." Tapell took a long breath.

It was bad enough knowing that the chief of police didn't like him, but to be chewed out in front of his squad and a half dozen other homicide detectives was just too much for Randy Mead. "I can't help it if some reporter on the scene goes blabbing . . ." He shook his head, sucked his teeth. "If McKinnon hadn't screwed up—"

Kate didn't even flinch. She continued to stare down at the newspaper in her lap, would not bother to acknowledge, or shoot, a drowning man. She flipped a page, loudly.

Brown said, "McKinnon was in pursuit of a suspect."

Tapell bore down on Mead again. "You should have contacted Operations, Randy. Had a SWAT team called in."

"There wasn't time," Mead whined.

"There's *always* time." Tapell looked at him with disgust. She folded her hands onto the conference table, let loose with a big sigh. "Okay. First. Damage control. I've already held a press conference, so there's no need for anyone in this room—anyone in the police department—to say a single word to the press." She eyed the detectives. "You all got that? Second. If the death artist makes a move—a hiccup— I want to know about it. Understood?"

"As soon as he contacts me," said Kate. "But Randy is right. There wasn't enough time."

Mead's head jerked in Kate's direction, bow tie practically strangling him, mouth open in surprise at her defense of him.

"The ME says Amanda Lowe was dead less than a hour when the body was discovered," said Brown. "We were damn close."

"Close doesn't really count, does it, Detective Brown?" Tapell checked her watch. "Mitch Freeman from the FBI will join us any minute. He's a criminal psych. He's been going over the reports and crime scene pictures and he'll tell us what he thinks."

"We already know about our guy's kinks," said Mead.

"Well, you don't have a choice, Randy. So you'll hear it all again."

"They taking over the case?" asked Slattery.

"We have to send all evidence, old and new, to Quantico, keep the Bureau informed on a daily basis, and we have to listen to them," said Tapell. "That's all I know right now."

"I've been hearing a lot about you," said Mitch Freeman, offering his hand to Kate.

"I can only imagine," said Kate. Freeman was maybe forty-five, dirty-blond hair, rugged features. Not at all what Kate had expected. No crew cut. No suit. No attitude either.

Freeman took a seat between Kate and Brown and spread his papers on the table. "I'll tell you how I've been profiling him," he said, getting his wireless reading glasses in place. "Organized, obviously. Intelligent. Also obvious. He doesn't appear to lose control—or hasn't yet. But he might, as the intervals between crimes decrease, or if he thinks you're getting closer to him."

"But he seems to want us close," said Brown. "Why else would he be in contact with McKinnon?"

"Some of these guys get off on the contact, like to flirt with getting caught because the publicity is so damn exciting to them." Freeman took his glasses off, rubbed his eyes. "Thinking criminals like your boy tend to be not only articulate and extroverted, but highly narcissistic. They like attention."

"Could he be living a double life?" asked Kate.

"Absolutely. I'd guess he's got a safe house where he can act out." Freeman rubbed his hand over his chin. "Eventually these guys start to break down. The organized eventually become disorganized. That's when they start to mess up and get caught."

"How long will that be?" asked Tapell.

"No way to know." Freeman put his glasses back on, regarded the most recent crime scene photos of Amanda Lowe. "Unfortunately, these don't indicate that he's losing it. In fact, he seems to be getting more complicated."

"Excuse me, Dr. Freeman." Kate laid a hand on his arm. "I think you may be confusing something here."

"Let the man speak, McKinnon." This from Mead, who hadn't uttered a single sound, other than sucking his teeth, since the Quantico psychiatrist had showed up.

"No. Please," said Freeman.

"Well, I think the complexity has to do with the art the killer is trying to create, or copying. His next one might be totally simple. I think it depends entirely on the art he's referencing."

"I see. Of course." Freeman nodded.

Kate pushed her hair behind her ears. "I certainly agree that he's intelligent and organized. But rather than profile him as an ordinary psychotic, how about looking at him as an artistic personality?"

"Go on," said Freeman.

"Artists," said Kate, "they're vain, but insecure. They want attention, like you said, but hide behind their work.

They like to be alone, but want their work in the public eye. Artists are all about the work," she says. "Maybe we can figure out certain things about this guy from his work, his— forgive me—his *art*."

"How so?" said Freeman, studying her intently.

"Well, I'd say he's got a fairly classical eye. *The Death of Marat* and the Titian painting are both very classical paintings. Even the Kienholz, which looks bizarre, is a very structured, classical piece. Plus, he's choosing real art. No crap. So, I think he's serious and intelligent. Though that doesn't necessarily mean he's been schooled. He could be self-taught. If so, he's got access to an art library—or art books, at the very least. I don't think he could keep all those art details in his head."

Freeman folded his arms across his chest, leaned back in the chair. "Interesting."

"You mentioned before about the intervals between the crimes decreasing," said Kate. "Is that always the case?"

"Pretty much," said Freeman. "The only thing that slows these guys down, or stops them, is death. *Theirs*."

"Why does he keep contacting McKinnon?" asked Tapell.

"Obsession," said Freeman. "A very strong emotion." He turned to Kate. "Can you think of any reason why this guy has focused on you?"

"I've been thinking and thinking about it," said Kate. "My book? My TV show? Maybe, to him, I'm the big expert. Maybe he wants my approval, or—"

"You'd better be careful," said Freeman. "These guys have a way of changing their minds about who and what they like. He's obviously obsessed with you, but . . ." He shook his head.

"What?"

"Well, I don't want to scare you, but these guys almost always confuse love and hate. Ultimately, they want to . . . kill their love object."

"Exactly what my friend at the FBI said."

"Liz Jacobs?"

"You know her?"

"No. But I know she's in town, and that the two of you used to work together."

"You guys don't miss much, do you?" said Kate. She added a smile.

"We try not to," said Freeman, who returned the smile, but it faded fast. "Look, I'm sorry to confirm what your friend said."

"We got a man stationed at McKinnon's house," said Mead.

"Good idea," said Freeman. "But you've really got to be on your guard, McKinnon. And I mean every minute."

"I'm kind of hoping that he's enjoying the game too much—manipulating me, playing with me—to want to go and ruin it by killing me."

"Could be so," said Freeman. "But eventually he'll tire of the game."

"He's changed the rules," said Kate. "Now he's feeding us the art clues *before* he strikes. So he needs me around to figure them out."

"That's good," said Freeman. "But no guarantee."

"What about a bodyguard for Kate?" Tapell asked.

"Could scare him off," said Freeman.

"And we need him close," said Kate.

"We'll keep an eye on her," said Mead. "Meanwhile, Crime Search is poring over every inch of the last crime scene." He handed Freeman the report. "These are brand-new, prelims. You might not have seen them."

"Have you got Mobile on standby, Randy?" Tapell asked.

"Yeah." Mead nodded. "And I've pulled in another dozen suits from General."

Freeman pushed himself up from the chair. "I'll give my report to the Bureau, Chief Tapell. They'll be in touch." He turned back to Kate. "Be careful," he said. "I mean it."

That last time was close. Too close. A half hour earlier and the cops would have walked in on him, ruined everything.

But you did it.

Truthfully, it's hard to believe no one heard her screaming, the drug having worn off quicker than expected. He'd have thought a woman like that—supposedly interested in art—would let him do his work in peace. But no. One lousy stab into her gut and she's squealing like a fucking banshee. Good thing she lived alone in that place, and that he'd brought that fishbowl to Krazy Glue over her mouth. That shut her up.

"But I managed it," he says aloud. "Didn't I? I mean, it was . . . beautiful."

He thrusts metal pushpins through the recent photographs, stabs them into the damp, porous wall in a crooked row.

"Look at that, will you. I did a great job. Look. *Look.*" He yanks the earphones out. "Will you look, man. At the way her eyes are wide open, the way I draped her dress, removed her shoes. Exactly like that fucking Kienholz. No. Better. My piece is more . . ." He searches for the right word. "Alive."

But now the only response is the coo of pigeons above, the lapping waves of the river. Did he give her too much information? Hell, that's what made it fun. Of course he knew she'd figure it out. Just not so fast.

Caution.

"Don't worry. I hear you. I'm adding something to slow her down next time."

Like what?

"Like moving the location."

Not bad.

Jesus. Was that a compliment? He can hardly believe it. He feels, for the moment, the most exquisite sensation of—can it be?—approval.

He's put a lot of thought into the next piece, wants it to be really subtle, challenging—for both of them. And this time he's going for something really fantastic. He's bored with solos. This one's going to be a duet.

Now, his biggest problem is waiting. He needs to disappear for a while, even if it's only a few days, make them wonder where he's gone.

But how to satisfy his needs? Already there is that longing, the deep, almost crushing need. Will it work if there's no audience? It used to, in the old days. Of course that was so long ago. He was a different person entirely. Now, things are expected of him. After all, he's the death artist. And he can't—he won't—disappoint them.

t's been three days, Liz. Not a word, nothing," said
Kate.

The front parlor of Payard Patisserie was packed. Skinny
women nibbled on salads. Housekeepers picked up boxed cakes.
Nannies tried to control their young wards after sugar shock.
Kate and Liz were huddled at a small table in this Upper East
Side version of the famous French bakery. "I think he's playing
with me, disappearing like this. But still, I keep looking over my
shoulder. I can't sleep." She pushed her salad aside. "Can't eat."

"If only that would happen to me." Liz glanced at her
half-eaten three-layer pastry concoction. "Sorry. I didn't
mean to make light of it. Look, my guess would be he's just
protecting himself, gone into retreat." She noted the neigh-
boring tables before speaking again, careful to keep her
voice down. "Serial killers are smart, Kate. You got too
close. He's backed away. But . . . he'll be back."

"I know that. Believe me, I won't let my guard down. I
couldn't even if I wanted to."

"Good. Just remember, his crimes are manifestations of
his fantasies—which he's acting out—and those fantasies
won't just go away."

"No, but I'm pretty sure I can now figure out his fantasies
based on the way he stages his crimes."

"Serial killers are particularly cunning, Kate. They honestly believe what they are doing is normal and acceptable, which makes them very hard to catch. A significant percentage of them are never apprehended."

"Oh, that cheers me up."

"Look, I know you're smart." Liz peered at Kate gravely. "But every killing makes him stronger, more confident, more convinced that he's smarter than you, Kate. And mentally sparring with a killer is a dangerous game."

"I know. But it's a little late for me to back off now." Kate flagged the waiter. "Coffee, please. Black." She sighed. "Hey, you know a guy from the Bureau, a shrink named Freeman?"

Liz shook her head.

"Well, he knows who you are and that we're friends."

"The Bureau never sleeps."

"He seemed smart, plus he listened. I liked him. Didn't hurt that he was good-looking." Kate smiled. "At least this little vacation gave me time to have my hair done and get a manicure, though I thought I'd just about explode sitting in that chair. Which reminds me. The gala is tomorrow night. Did you get the dresses I had sent over from Bergdorf's?"

"Yeah," said Liz. "But I decided I'd be more comfortable in my plaid polyester jumpsuit."

Kate didn't even blink. "Which one did you choose—the black or the red?"

"I'm going with the red number. I've never had a Valentino—Rudolph or otherwise."

"You'll be stunning."

"How'd you know my size?"

"I just asked for the biggest one they had." Kate laughed.

"Bitch." Liz slapped Kate's hand, laughed, too.

Kate suddenly deflated. "Truthfully, Liz, I don't know how I'm going to get through the event. All I can think about is the case, that this maniac is still out there, waiting, and that we can't do a damn thing about it until he makes his move." She sighed deeply. "I don't know how I read those signals so wrong."

"Obviously you weren't alone. The squad agreed with you, didn't they?"

"Unfortunately, yes."

Liz patted her mouth with a napkin. "So, what other avenues are there?"

Kate took a sip of coffee, thought a moment. "Well . . . There's the stolen art—the altarpiece that was snatched from Bill Pruitt's apartment that never turned up."

"I'd go back and rethink everything. That's what you'd have done in the old days, right?"

Kate and Slattery were poring over the Bill Pruitt file for what seemed like the hundredth time.

"Usually they have two doormen working Pruitt's Park Avenue building." Maureen Slattery picked a piece of lint off her cotton sweater. "But that night, the night he died, one of the doormen had the Hong Kong flu or something. Let's see . . ." She plucked the Pruitt folder from a mass of papers on her desk. "The one who *was* working said no one came up to Pruitt's that night except for a well-dressed man in his forties. But he thinks that was a lot earlier than we pegged the time of death. And Pruitt must have okayed the guy because everyone is announced in that building."

"Did the doorman see the guy leave?"

Slattery consulted her papers, shrugged. "Doesn't say."

"You mean no one ever did a follow-up on this guy?"

"I was the one who talked to the doorman. He didn't remember the guy's name. All he said was he was white, tall, in his forties, well dressed. Nothing suspicious about him."

"Damien Trip was tall, dressed neatly. Maybe a little young for that description." Kate tapped her finger against her lip. "Was the doorman ever shown Trip's picture?"

"Uh . . . no." Slattery looked down. "I would have done it, should have, but things snowballed kinda fast, you know."

Kate caught Slattery's guilty look. "Forget it, Maureen. It wouldn't have made any difference." She lifted Trip's arrest photo from Slattery's file. "But I think I'll show his picture around just for the hell of it."

"The doorman admitted to a couple of breaks that night—three minutes for a pee and five minutes for a cup a coffee."

"That means at least ten to empty his bladder, fifteen or twenty to refill it."

"Probably."

"So someone else could easily have slipped through." Kate lifted the toxicology sheet on Pruitt from Slattery's desk. "Marijuana. Cocaine. Amyl nitrite. A two-point alcohol level. Jesus. Wasn't that enough to kill the guy?"

"According to the lab, no. Pruitt was stoned, but it was all just traces—not enough to kill him."

Kate looked again at one of the crime scene photos. "The coroner said that the bruise on Pruitt's jaw was fresh, that it happened either during the assault, or sometime just before." Kate thought a minute. "Were there any prints on the scene that were never typed?"

Slattery rustled through the papers. "There were two sets of unidentified prints, which didn't link up with anyone on file. I guess until we catch our unsub we got nothing to compare them with."

Grecian urns in glass cases. Black-and-white marble floors. The lobby at 870 Park Avenue could have passed for an antiquities gallery—if only the men in uniform were guards and not doormen.

Kate found the one who was on duty the night Pruitt died.

"I already talked to the *police*," he said, regarding Kate suspiciously. She looked too much like the well-dressed women who passed through these doors every day to be a cop. "I gave them my statement—many times."

Kate displayed her temporary ID, along with a photo of Damien Trip.

The doorman's frosty mien melted. He took the photo-

graph into his gray-gloved hand, leaned back against the inlaid marble wall. "No." He shook his head. "I never saw this
man. Sorry."

"Are you sure? Never?"

"I'm certain."

"According to your statement, Bill Pruitt received a visitor that night."

"Yes. But it's not the man in your photo. He was older.
And not blond."

"Can you describe him? Any distinguishing features that
you might remember?"

"Well, he was tall. And wearing a raincoat." He closed his
eyes, sucked on his lower lip. "But his face is a blur."

"You remember his *coat* but not his *face*?"

The doorman looked slightly abashed. "A lot of people
pass through this lobby."

"You must have announced him to Mr. Pruitt. Do you recall a name?"

The doorman looked down at his perfectly polished
shoes, frowned. "It was a crazy night. I was working the
door alone. Patrick had the flu, and no one else was on, and
so . . ."

"That's okay." Kate patted his arm.

Could there be something in Pruitt's apartment that might
link him to Trip? They already had the Amateur Films porno
tapes—what else could there be? She couldn't remember
seeing Pruitt's diary. And what about that damn altarpiece?
She was here, she might as well have a look.

Bill Pruitt's apartment could have been a set for *Masterpiece
Theatre,* all dark wood and leather. Kate scanned the artwork—mostly French Impressionist, a few John Marin wa-
tercolor seascapes, a smattering of Early American prints, a
couple of Steichen black-and-white photographs from the
thirties, but not a sign of any rare Italian art—at least not on
view. The furniture appeared to be in place, though the
carved doors of a huge armoire were open, the contents—

photo albums, rare books, a couple of antique vases—obviously rearranged, pushed into corners, or stacked on the floor in front.

In the library, Kate went right for Pruitt's large oak desk. But the crime scene boys had obviously beaten her to it; every drawer was open, papers in disarray. The only things left were bills and canceled checks.

Had the killer gone through these papers, too?

Once more, Kate got that eerie feeling she had had at Elena's apartment—that the killer had been here, that she was doing exactly what he had done. She could sense him like a shadow, hovering. She wheeled around. But there was nothing there. She took a deep breath.

At the scene of the crime—Pruitt's bathroom—Kate found little: medicine cabinet empty, nothing on the tub's edge. The only indication that a human being had ever lived here was a digital scale. Kate pictured Bill Pruitt in high black socks and starched white boxers weighing in, worrying about heart attacks, hardening arteries, strokes. *Poor Bill.* Those were, as it turned out, the least of his worries.

So what happened, exactly? Had the killer come in, interrupted Bill's bath? Pruitt would have put on a robe to answer the door. Then what? They fought. Struggled. The man dragged Bill into the tub, held him under until he died? Or did he punch Bill, then fill the tub and drop him into it? Pruitt was stoned. He would not have put up much of a fight.

Kate tried to imagine the night. Pruitt dead, his body arranged like the painting *The Death of Marat.* Then the killer must have moved around the apartment in search of his memento. Was the altarpiece in plain sight? No, probably hidden. It was, after all, a stolen artwork. So the guy took his time going through Pruitt's things.

Kate tried to retrace the killer's steps. She moved from the bathroom into the bedroom.

It had been torn apart by the cops: the naked mattress sad, sagging slightly in the center; closet open, business suits and blazers shoved around, a pair of charcoal pants on the floor rumpled over several pairs of shoes—wing tips, tasseled loafers, Top-Siders; dresser drawers like small open tombs, their contents—perfectly laundered white and blue shirts with *WMP* monogrammed on the pockets, along with nine or ten pairs of black socks and at least a dozen starched white boxer shorts—scattered on the floor.

Nothing like dying to have your life laid bare, your personal artifacts treated with contempt, thought Kate. She checked the bedside tables, pulled open drawers. Nothing of value left, only a pack of unused lubricated Trojans, a half-eaten pack of Spearmint Life Savers, nail clippers.

Kate moved from the bedroom back to the bath, once again into the library. But it was no use.

The living room was the only room that had not been ransacked by the cops. Kate stopped a moment to admire a painting. She might as well; there was nothing more to do. A Monet landscape, his garden at Giverny. But the dark room swallowed most of the details. Kate threw back the heavy drapes for a better look. Light poured into the room.

She lingered a minute, her eyes playing over Monet's impasto paint and lush color; and when she turned to go, she noticed, too, how the light picked out the fleur-de-lis flocking in the wallpaper, the grain in the dark wood wainscoting, the detail in the Oriental rugs, and something else peeking from the edge of the rug, almost but not quite hidden by the leg of a small end table—a tiny object, glittering in the shaft of light.

A cuff link.

Kate gripped it between her thumb and forefinger: a perfect oval of eighteen-karat gold outlined in black onyx, elegant without being fussy. She stiffened. It *must* be one of Pruitt's. And why not? It was a common enough style. Still, Kate held her breath as she rotated the cuff link and raised it for closer inspection.

The inscription was as clear as the day she'd had it engraved: "To R. Love K."

Oh my God. The tall, well-dressed stranger.

36

Twenty minutes to get to Richard's office. Twenty minutes of pure hell.

Richard's cuff link at the scene of Bill Pruitt's murder. How was it possible?

Kate stared out the cab's windows at office buildings, people, signs, lights—everything a blur.

In the outer office, Richard's secretary, Anne-Marie, smiled, put her hand out, but Kate sprinted past her.

"Kate!" Richard's blue eyes widened.

Kate stopped short, half in, half out of his office.

Richard made awkward introductions. "Mr. Krauser. My wife."

"Oh." Kate inhaled, sharply. "Sorry, I—"

"That's all right." The man was either very gracious or scared by the look on Kate's face. "Your husband and I were just finished."

Richard was eyeing Kate suspiciously as he closed the door behind his client. "Do you know who that was, Kate? The German investment banker, who—"

Kate rolled the cuff link onto his desk.

"Oh." The anger drained out of Richard's voice. "I've been looking for this."

"I'll bet you have." Kate stood still, holding her breath.

"Where did you find it?"

"At Bill Pruitt's apartment."

For a moment neither one of them spoke. Then Kate exploded: "Jesus Christ, Richard! What does this mean? Explain it to me. *Please.*"

Richard paced to the end of his office, adjusted a framed Warhol *Marilyn,* which had been perfectly straight in the first place. He turned, regarded her gravely. "Pruitt was embezzling money from Let There Be a Future. I'd found some discrepancies in the financials Pruitt kept for the foundation. I went to see him that night, and—" Richard spoke calmly, though he continued to adjust frames, pick imaginary lint from his pin-striped jacket, shuffle papers on his desk, pace. "Well, it's not the way it looks, damn it. I simply went there to have him explain it to me. The bastard laughed in my face. He was drunk. I just sort of lost it. I punched him." Richard's lanky frame collapsed onto the leather love seat below a series of David Hockney prints—all swimming pools and palm trees and California-blue sky. He looked up at Kate. "You don't think I killed him, do you?"

Kate stood looking down at Richard. "I don't know what I think." She felt like collapsing, too.

"Oh, come on, Kate. It's *me.* Richard. Your husband."

Yes. The husband who had lied to her. Deceived her. Kate's hazel eyes flashed. "Why didn't you tell me?"

"I wanted to, but . . ."

"But *what?*" Kate shook her head back and forth, trying to make sense of it, but images were flashing in her mind: Richard punching Bill Pruitt, that cuff link on the floor, the bruise on Pruitt's chin. Kate pressed her fingertips to her forehead as though trying to turn off the switch to this awful movie. "After ten years of marriage, how could you *not* tell me?"

"I had every intention of telling you, but Elena had just been murdered, and it didn't seem important." Richard rubbed at his temples. "I figured I'd just tell you later."

"*Later?*" Kate laced her fingers together, her knuckles

turning white, but she was listening. She would hear this. "So what happened later?"

"Later, Pruitt was dead. I still intended to tell you. But Arlen James didn't want anyone to know about Pruitt's embezzling from Let There Be a Future. Arlen and I intended to confront Pruitt together the next day. But when Bill was found dead, Arlen was in a panic, worried about the foundation's reputation. He didn't want the embezzlement story made public. It was bad enough the foundation was dealing with Elena's death, then Bill's. But who's going to support a charity that can't hold on to its money?"

True. Still, Kate could not help all of the doubt that had been stirred up in her. She felt shaky, confused.

"I was freaked. I mean, Bill was dead, and I'd been there, in his apartment, and we fought—"

Richard suddenly looked like a little boy, and a lost one. Kate had the urge to hold him, hug him toward her, pat his curls, tell him it was all right. But at the same time everything he'd ever said to her was suddenly suspect, tainted. Was he really working late all those nights? What about the trips out of town? And if he really hit Pruitt, why not take it a step further—that he killed the man? Though she fought it, the image of Pruitt in the bath, Richard holding the man under, took shape in her mind. And what about the way Richard had always looked at Elena—was it more than paternal? *Jesus*. She did not want to think these thoughts, but just couldn't stop them.

"I thought we were a team," she said.

"We are."

"Were," said Kate. "If you'd told me, I might have been able to help."

"*How*, Kate?" Richard shook his head. "After Bill's death it just made better sense for you *not* to know—knowing could have put you in a very awkward position—you working the cases, and your husband having had a fight with one of the victims. How would that look? It just got too late." He opened his hands, palms up. "I figured, hell, let it go. Tell her when it's all over." Richard lifted a glass paperweight off his desk, rolled it from one hand to the other. "Bill Pruitt was perfectly fine when I left him. Come on, Kate. You know me. I could never kill anyone."

"I didn't think you could punch anyone either," said Kate. She eased herself onto Richard's leather couch. "Suppose Bill's embezzling was the reason he was killed?"

"Impossible." He rolled the paperweight back and forth, back and forth. "Arlen and I were the only ones who knew about it."

"Did you and Arlen actually think I would go blabbing that information around indiscriminately?" Kate took a deep breath. "You should know me better than that, Richard."

"If you knew it, you might not have had a choice but to divulge it—and there was no need—it obviously had nothing to do with Bill's murder—or with the death artist." Richard's eyes widened. "God. Do you realize I was there, at Pruitt's, just before that maniac killed him?"

"Yes, I certainly do realize that." A chill rippled the muscles of her back. "Jesus, they have your prints, Richard."

"So what? My prints aren't on record. I'm not a felon." He looked toward the large picture window framing an impressive piece of the Hudson River, a couple of brand-new buildings, a few deserted piers dotting the river's edge.

"God, Richard. If this comes out . . ." Kate flattened her fingers over her eyes. She wanted it all to go away—Elena's death, Richard at Pruitt's apartment, this conversation. Spots floated in the darkness behind her lids.

"Why would it come out?" Richard stopped playing with the paperweight, dropped it onto his desk with a thud. "You're the only one who knows."

"For now." Kate opened her eyes. It took a moment for Richard's face to come into focus.

"Well, you're not going to tell anyone, are you?" He pushed away from his desk and stood up.

"Of course not." Kate twisted her wedding band around her finger, pictured the two of them dancing at a party, the soft touch of Richard's hand at the base of her spine, her cheek against his, the smell of his aftershave. Was that only a few weeks ago?

Richard took hold of her hand.

The action calmed her a bit, helped her concentrate. "Richard, when you were there, at Bill Pruitt's, did you notice a small altarpiece, a Madonna and Child?"

"No. Why?"

"Because Bill Pruitt had one that's missing, remember?"

Richard dropped her hand. "You're not accusing me of stealing it, are you?"

Kate stiffened. "I only asked if you *saw* it. Don't go turning this around—making *me* the bad guy."

"No. I didn't see one. If I had, I might have taken it—as payment for his embezzling." He reached out again, touched her arm. "I'm sorry. Really I am. Forgive me?"

Kate wanted to forgive him, to believe him, to have all of this behind them, but those images and feelings continued to nag at her. "I'm not sure."

"Oh, come on, Kate." His fingers skittered lightly over her flesh, producing goose bumps.

She laid her hand over his. "I'm trying."

Richard attempted a kiss, but Kate pushed him away.

"I'm sorry, but it's going to take me more than a minute to get over this."

"I was trying to protect the foundation, Kate. I'd have thought you'd agree with that."

"I might have." Kate couldn't keep the disappointment out of her voice. "If you'd given me the chance."

"I made a mistake, Kate. I'm sorry. I should have told you."

"Yes, you should have." Kate swallowed, fought the tears that had gathered behind her eyes.

"How about a hug?"

Kate let her body sag against his. "Please, Richard. Don't ever keep anything from me. I don't care how bad it is."

Richard wrapped his arms around her. "Okay, I admit it.

Bookies are threatening my life, I fucked Elizabeth Hurley, and I shot the sheriff."

"Very funny," said Kate.

"Hey, what happened to your sense of humor?"

Kate looked into his eyes. "It sort of disappeared when I found your cuff link at a murder scene."

Kate sat on the edge of her all-white bed. She didn't have the nerve to go back to the station. What if Slattery or Brown asked her if she'd found anything at Pruitt's? *Oh, just my husband's cuff link, that's all.*

It was as if everything was collapsing at the same time. Her husband lying to her, the foundation's finances a wreck, the case at a standstill, Willie barely talking to her. It felt as if it was all unraveling; that *she* was unraveling. Kate could practically see pieces of herself being torn off, disappearing.

She flopped back onto her bed, closed her eyes, saw that shaft of light, Richard's cuff link edging out from the corner of the rug. Could he be lying to her? What was it he'd said just the other day? That you never really know anyone, that everyone had secrets. *Does he?* Damn it, she didn't want to think like that. Richard was no murderer. Nor was she one of those naive wives who never suspect a thing while their husbands are out raping cheerleaders.

The phone rang, but Kate let the machine get it. It was her friend Blair going on about the foundation benefit, then something about Kate's dwindling social status.

Oh, great. Just one more loss Kate could add to her list.

The young boy won't be found for weeks. The bricks tied to his feet before he was dropped into the river make that pretty much a certainty.

But it feels . . . incomplete. Oh, sure, it was nice while it lasted. But now what? How to make something of it?

Try.

He shuts his eyes, imagines the dead teen floating under-water. For color, he adds a kaleidoscopic school of fish swimming around the body. Then some Hudson River detritus—an old tire, a bent metal chair covered with soft green moss, a headless baby doll—found objects to turn it into a surreal still life. That's it! One of those big aquarium pieces like that British artist Damien Hirst makes. Oh, wouldn't Mr. Hirst be jealous to have a real body to play with.

Still, he must admit it did not feel as good without his audience. He needs to get close again.

He paces in the room. Maybe it's too soon. But there's no stopping it now.

He finds the electronic device he's bought on-line. It feels light in his hands, the metal cold. He's tested and retested it, and it works, makes his voice hollow, unidentifiable. He speaks into it: "Testing, testing, testing." The word echoes into the room, again and again, his voice strange, completely altered.

"Hello," he says. "Good evening. Are you surprised to hear from me?" His voice so alien, for a moment he's thrown—it's one too many voices, one too many psyches to deal with. But he speaks again, concentrates on the fact that it is *his* voice distorted through the metal device. "It's me," he says, listening to the echo: *Me me me me me me* . . .

He laughs. Won't she be surprised. But can he really go through with it?

Do it.

"I'm not sure."

Do it! You're smarter. Invisible.

He thinks about that a moment. It's true. Just look at the way he slips in and out of places, no one noticing. He really can be invisible—when he wants to be.

The receiver's in his hand.

Really, it's for her own good. He doesn't want her getting complacent.

In her dream, she is running through a field. It's night. She's naked.

She comes to the edge of a forest, the trees so dense she

has to squeeze through them; spindly, leafless limbs nick her flesh.

But now he's here, too, the man, calling her name. Why is she so scared—the voice is familiar, not threatening. "Please. I need that back."

The forest has thinned out.

She sprints, can feel him behind her. Hear him panting.

She chances a quick peek over her shoulder, trips over a jagged rock, drops the small object she's been clutching in her hand, which skitters along the ground and comes to rest beside a sodden mound of leaves.

She bends forward, stretches out her arm to retrieve it—a small gold-and-onyx cuff link. The man's shadow falls across her back. He's got a knife.

She hears herself scream, a reverberating chime, over and over and over.

The sound ripped her from the nightmare.

Kate realized it was the phone ringing beside her bed. She reached for the receiver, her heart pounding. "Hello."

"Hel . . . lo," he said.

Still half in the dream, she asked, "Who is this?"

"You . . . know." The voice was distorted, metallic, hollow-sounding, dead slow.

That was all it took. Kate was wide awake. *My God. Is it him?*

She remembered the wire tap Mead had put on her phone. *Keep him talking.*

"Where have you been?"

"Resting."

"Why?"

"Miss . . . me?"

Kate considered what she should say for a moment. Which answer was he looking for? "Yes," she said. "I have missed you."

She could practically hear him smile.

"I'll . . . be . . . back."

"When?"

"Look . . . for . . . me . . . tomorrow."

"Where?"

"At . . . the . . . party."

"How will I—"

But he'd hung up.

Kate listened to the dial tone, then quickly tapped in the code, got another voice, this one tired.

"Did you get that?" she asked.

"Yeah," he said. "I got it."

"Can you trace it?"

"I'll try."

Kate waited. Realized for the first time that she had fallen asleep in her clothes. She looked at the bedside clock. It was just after 5:00 A.M. No way she would get back to sleep now.

The cop came back on the line. "He wasn't on long enough for a trace," he said. "But it's all on tape."

"Get in touch with Randy Mead," she said. "Right away. Tell him that the guy's called me. And make sure that's relayed to Chief Tapell, as well."

Kate dragged herself out of bed. She wished Richard were here instead of on a plane to Chicago to take early-morning depositions. *Damn.* She could really use a hug.

Then she remembered the dream, the cuff link, and shivered.

She grabbed up the phone again, tried to keep her hand from shaking. Hell, it didn't matter what time it was. She was calling Mead and Tapell herself.

37

You heard the phone tapes," said Kate, eyeing each of the squad members seated around the conference table. "He said he'd be at the gala for Let There Be a Future— at the Plaza. Tonight."

Brown drummed his nails on the table. "Exactly how many guests are we talking here?"

Kate drew a deep breath. "About five hundred."

"I've been on it since I got your call." Mead sucked his teeth. "We got twenty cops for inside the Plaza, and two at every exit. Of course the FBI is supplying their own men." He sighed. "And the FBI shrink, Freeman, is on his way over now."

"McKinnon should wear a wire," said Brown. "And I want to be there, too."

"You'll need a tux," said Kate, working hard to keep her voice calm. "I can have one sent over for you. You're what— about a forty-two long?"

"Forty," said Brown, sucking in his gut involuntarily.

Mitch Freeman cut into the room a bit breathless. He smoothed back his sandy hair and slid into a chair. "So exactly what have we got here?"

"The fucking psycho called McKinnon," said Mead.

"Says he's going to show up at this charity gala tonight," Slattery added.

"I know that. Tapell filled me in." Freeman nodded at Kate. "What else?"

"Well, he hasn't given me any art clue to interpret," said Kate. "It's a departure from his ritual."

"These guys absolutely *must* have their ritual," said Freeman. "But that doesn't mean he won't show up." He offered Kate a prudent look. "He might tend to his ritual *after* the fact—if you get my drift."

Kate fought a chill, hugged her arms close to her body. "I can't imagine him trying something in front of five hundred people."

Freeman thought a minute, then his eyes met Kate's. "Unless he's become totally delusional."

There were four men in the room. Three of them staring at the walls.

The guy taping the mike to Kate's diaphragm looked about seventeen—no beard, slight acne on his forehead—and seemed to be taking an awfully long time. She had goose bumps on her arms; God knew where else.

"You finished?" She could feel the smooth edges of his fingers pressing tape to her rib cage. "How am I supposed to breathe?"

"Carefully," he said.

Mitch Freeman stood beside Floyd Brown, rocking back and forth on his heels. Brown talked to the wall. "Make sure that mike's in good working order," he said. "Where's the van going to be?"

Another detective, angled away from Kate's half-stripped body, said, "Just behind the Plaza. Don't worry. That mike is good for several miles."

"Look," said Freeman. "If he *does* show up, you have to keep your wits about you."

"What should I do? Ask him to dance?" Kate joked, though her body shuddered.

"Truthfully," said Freeman, "that wouldn't be a bad idea. This guy wants to be close to you."

"I was *kidding*," said Kate, swallowing hard.

"I know you were. Look, we have no idea if he'll show or what he might do. My best guess would be that he simply wants to observe you. He'll use the crowd as his shield. On the other hand, these guys tend to think of themselves as superhuman, so you never know."

"Would he actually *talk* to me?" Kate fought another shiver.

"Maybe." Freeman turned, caught a glimpse of Kate in her black lace bra, quickly looked away. "All I'm saying is that you have to stay alert to any weird people or actions, anyone who might want to touch you."

"Jesus, Freeman." Kate expelled a deep sigh. "There'll be hundreds of people kissing me or shaking my hand."

"We'll be right next to you," said Brown. "You have a place to keep your gun?"

"Not my Glock." Kate could feel anxiety rising like heartburn.

"I'll get you a small thirty-eight. You can strap it to your leg, under your skirt."

"Look, chances are he won't do anything even if he shows," said Freeman.

"You just saying that to make me feel better?" Kate glanced down at the kid taping the mike. His cool fingers were making her tremble. "You finished?"

"One second. There," he said. "You're all taped up." He spoke into the mike. It was as if he were whispering into Kate's navel. "Testing, testing . . ." The words echoed from the listening device across the room.

"Just take it slow and easy," said Freeman.

"Oh, sure," said Kate, trying to button her blouse with shaking fingers. "Only fox-trots."

With the mike taped across her ribs, the sleek, body-clinging Armani Kate had purchased for this event just wouldn't work. She looked as if she'd sprouted a third breast.

She combed through her closet, pushed dresses aside until

she found a John Galliano number she'd bought on impulse in Paris the year before, and had never worn—a bodice covered with ruffle upon ruffle. What had she been thinking? Ruffles were never her thing. Well, tonight they were. She could hide a machine gun in all that froufrou.

Kate laid the dress on the bed.

It was too late to call Richard. His plane would be touching down at LaGuardia any minute.

If only he'd told her about the fight with Pruitt before. Too late to think about that now.

In the bathroom, she tried to apply her makeup, but her fingers were trembling. She had to calm down. Be on her toes tonight, as Freeman had said. She had all those guests to assuage—and the threat of a maniac, lurking.

The thought did not help her relax.

She sat on the edge of the bed, took long deep breaths, grateful for that weekly yoga class she hadn't had time for in weeks.

Ten minutes later, Kate was calm enough to apply mascara without blinding herself.

She twisted her hair up into a French knot. It was not salon-perfect but it would have to do. She slipped on a pair of black panty hose, and then her dress. The ruffles worked. Her chest was an ocean of wavy black chiffon. No unsightly bulges.

She checked herself in the mirror. Not bad.

Beneath all those ruffles, the tape on the mike was pulling at her skin. She shimmied her hand down below her bra, tried to pick at the edge of the tape, but it didn't help. She'd just have to live with it. It suddenly brought back another memory. That last case. Ruby Pringle. She was wearing a mike that day, too; thought maybe she'd come face-to-face with that guy instead of the body of that poor kid.

I know where she is because I know where I put her.

The note. Red Magic Marker like dried blood.

Jesus.

Kate tore down the hall to her office, her satin party dress

billowing. There it was on the corkboard wall: the image the
death artist had sent—Kate with wings and halo, outlined
with red marker, and the word HELLO.

The writing was similar.

Kate closed her eyes: Ruby Pringle, spread out on a sea of
wavy plastic, aluminum foil surrounding her head, jeans
pulled down.

An angel. A naked angel. *Could it be?* Plastic wings. A
foil halo.

The death artist? So many years ago? Kate's mind raced
with the names and faces of people from her past. Who
could have followed her—and why?

She stared at her wall of crime scene photos—all those
art-posed deaths.

Was Ruby Pringle an early attempt at art? The scene was
not as specific as what he was creating now. But why not?

She placed a call to her old Astoria station, got a desk cop.
There was no one there she knew. No one she could talk to
about the Ruby Pringle case. The desk cop didn't even know
what she was referring to.

Kate clipped the small .38 into a holster, then hiked up her
dress and strapped the contraption to her thigh.

Ruby Pringle's old murder case would have to wait until
tomorrow.

Unless he struck tonight.

Men in tuxedos, women in party dresses, were filing into the
Plaza for their thousand-dollar-a-plate meal.

As patrons and co-hosts, Kate and Richard had purchased
two tables, at which they had seated their friends strategi-
cally among potential foundation donors. Tonight, their
friends were expected to chatter and charm the donors; tomorrow, the donors were expected to write their tax-
deductible checks to Let There Be a Future. Everyone knew
the rules. Those who didn't wouldn't be invited back.

Kate had gotten through to Richard's cell phone. He was
on the way.

Floyd Brown was already there, at the entrance to the Plaza's Grand Ballroom leaning against the wall, looking equally handsome and uncomfortable in his snazzy rental tux. Kate had to smile.

"You wearing the mike?" he whispered into her chest.

"You think I'd be dressed like Bo Peep if I wasn't?"

"Dugan," Brown said, listing toward Kate's bosom. "I hope you're picking this up."

"Floyd. Could you please stop talking to my breasts?"

Brown straightened abruptly, flustered, rammed his hands into his tuxedo pockets.

Kate's co-host, Blair, angled by, giving them a curious look. Kate made hasty introductions, looped her arm through Brown's, dragged him away. She was feeling anxious, but kept taking deep breaths, which helped her maintain an air of calm. A month ago, this event had been the most important thing in her life. Now, all she hoped to do was live through it.

After twenty-five minutes of introductions—the mayor, Henry Kissinger, a steady flow of assorted socialites and moneymen—Brown was close to speechless. It was just too many people shoving and talking and shaking hands and kissing, all opportunities to do McKinnon real harm. Both she and Brown had been scrutinizing every person who came within an inch of Kate. It was making Brown incredibly nervous. Kate continued to remain cool, but it was an act. Brown noticed how her eyes swept the room, checking the guests' hands, trying to spot the nearest tuxedo-clad cop, all the while maintaining her smile, even an air of nonchalance.

A photographer, one of Patrick McMullan's crew, had been snapping them everywhere they turned, Kate and Brown trying hard not to lose control in the few seconds when the flashbulbs left them temporarily blind.

Everywhere Kate looked another face loomed close to hers. Every hand in a pocket posed a potential threat. She held her breath, smiled on automatic. But inside, her panic was just barely contained.

"I want to check with the door guards," said Brown. "See if they've noticed anything suspicious." He leaned in close, whispered, "The guy over there who looks worse in his rental tux than I do is a cop—and he's only two feet away from you."

"I'll be okay." She patted her thigh, indicating the gun to Brown, but her hand was trembling.

Willie made an appearance with Charlie Kent on his arm. As an artist, he was not expected to wear the requisite tux. He had a black silk turtleneck on under a sleek leather sports jacket. Kate kissed his cheeks. He didn't kiss back.

It added a layer of sadness over Kate's anxiety. She eyed a man just behind Charlie, reaching into his breast pocket. She didn't know him, saw him listing toward her. She signaled the nearby cop with her eyes. He shoved guests aside, got a grip on the man's arm, slowly eased the guy's hand out of his tux—there was a handkerchief in the man's fingers.

"Excuse me?" The man threw him a look of derision and incredulity.

"Sorry," said the cop. "I thought you were someone else."

Kate took a breath, scanned the room. *Was he here?*

And with that thought, for the briefest moment, the entire crowd blurred. Even the music grew distant, hushed. It was as though everyone and everything were leaving the stage, and only two actors remained.

So this is why he called me, thought Kate—to make me feel his presence.

And it was working. Kate could not shake it—that feeling that he was here, beside her, watching her every move, pulling the strings.

And then it started all over again, the room coming to life, the clamor and bustle, every other second someone bumping into her or shaking her hand or kissing her cheek. Kate was trying to keep that smile in place, but her nerves were starting to fray.

If he's here, why the hell doesn't he show himself?

But of course, he might already have said hello, shaken

her hand, kissed her cheek. The thought chilled her. Is he someone she knew? Or a complete stranger? And if he was here, what would he do? Shoot her? No. There wouldn't be any art in that. Plus, the guests had to walk through a goddamn metal detector. Jesus, what were the society columnists going to say about that?

Kate glanced around the room, paintings flashing in her mind—Renoir's sweeping party scenes, Manet's crowded cafés, Goya's royal-family portraits. The death artist could go for any one of those. A dozen others. But what part would she play in them? And why her? *Why?*

A man was to her right, bussing her cheek; a woman to the left, whispering something. Then two more in front of her. Features were blurring, replaced by the faces of the death artist's victim's—Stein, Pruitt, Amanda Lowe, Elena. Always Elena.

Kate was starting to tremble. Was she still smiling, shaking hands? She had no idea. She heard his voice on the telephone, hollow and metallic, echoing in her ears; the image of herself with wings and halo, and that one written word— HELLO—shimmering in her brain.

A tap on her shoulder. Kate whirled around so fast she almost tumbled. Richard caught her.

"Steady there, tiger." He kissed her cheek.

Kate sagged against him.

"Are you okay?" His blue eyes looked intently into hers, his brow furrowed.

"Where've you been?" she asked, coming back to the moment, feeling the crowd surrounding her, humming, electric. She took a long, deep breath.

"Traffic," said Richard, stroking the back of her neck. "What's the matter?"

"I'm okay. Just nervous," said Kate, painting on a smile.

Around them, people were nibbling canapés, swilling cocktails, chatting.

"Come on." Richard took her by the arm. "You look like you need to sit down."

*   *   *

The florists had not disappointed. The centerpieces were huge, but low, all white—roses, freesia, tulips. White table-cloths and china to match.

Somehow Kate was managing to make small talk, though she hadn't a clue how she was doing it—the words seemed to come out of her mouth on their own.

"You look beautiful," she said to Liz, whom she'd seated beside her. "And I'm glad you're here."

"You holding up?"

"Just."

Liz eyed her with concern, was about to speak when Arlen James took the podium and launched into his speech about education and its importance, what the foundation achieved, how many kids it put through college each year, how to become a supporter, all with the charm and ease of a man to the manor born—which he was not. Kate admired his stamina, considering that he had just written a two-million-dollar check to cover the embezzling of the late William Mason Pruitt, whose name was never once mentioned.

But Kate could not relax, her eyes moved from one table to the next, searching the corners of the room, the shadows. *Where is he?* She played with her napkin, twisting it in her lap. Had the death artist set her up just to torment her? It was possible. She glanced across the table at Richard, who smiled. The cuff link on Pruitt's living room floor flashed in her mind. Arlen James was still talking, but Kate couldn't concentrate. She was up fast, whispering excuses to the people at her table, hurrying out of the room.

The cops and FBI agents at the door were right on her heels, spinning as Kate moved through the Grand Ballroom's entrance, following her into the hallway.

"I'm just going to the ladies' room." She needed to be alone.

A cop scanned the ladies' room first, checked the stalls before giving her the all-clear sign.

Inside, Kate leaned against the sink, took a few deep breaths, a sip of water, dotted her brow with more. She was pale. Her hands were shaking.

Damn him. He was playing with her, and she knew it.

And that damn wire on her torso was itching like crazy. Kate tried to get at it, but couldn't. She ducked into a stall, had the top of her dress half unzipped when she heard footsteps on the tiles. She looked down. Black shoes. *Men's.*

She went for her gun, but a second later a herd of storm troopers had charged into the ladies' room, all shouting: "Freeze! Hands in the air! Don't make a move!"

Kate gripped the .38, kicked the stall door open.

A guy in a tuxedo was on the floor, sixty, possibly older, the look on his face pure terror. The cops and agents had him pinned down. Three pistols were aimed at his head. Two at his heart. One cop had a hand around his throat.

"Jesus," said Kate. "You're going to kill him."

The guy was practically in tears. "I din' know I was in the ladeesh room." His words slurred. He was drunk.

"He didn't do anything," said Kate, offering the man her hand. No way this man was a threat. "Are you okay?" she said, truly concerned, holding on to his hand.

The guy could barely speak. His face was ashen, his hands shaking uncontrollably.

At the Plaza's front entrance, Kate and Richard, with Floyd Brown not far behind, were hit with a barrage of flashbulbs. A band of TV and news reporters had descended, cameras and microphones ready. Apparently news of the police storming the Grand Ballroom's ladies' room had traveled fast.

On automatic, Kate pulled back, retreated into the lobby, clutching Richard's arm.

Brown suggested the side entrance, and Kate was about to agree when a thought stopped her: *Now it's my turn.*

She huddled with Brown, the two of them whispering, then sent him off to deal with the media while she checked herself in one of the Plaza's huge gilded mirrors.

"What's going on?" asked Richard, impatient.

"C'mon," said Kate. "Watch the show."

"One at a time," said Brown to the crowd assembled on the Plaza's front steps. He signaled an attractive TV reporter to begin.

"So it was *not* the death artist who attacked you tonight?"

"No," said Kate. "I wasn't attacked at all."

The reporters all started talking at once. Brown silenced them, pointed at a local TV anchor, who stepped forward. "As one of the country's leading art experts, what do you make of the death artist?"

Kate gave the reporter a subtle nod—he'd asked the exact question she had requested. She stared directly into the large camcorder. "You must remember that most art today is *idea*-based—and has been since Conceptual art came on the scene in the late sixties."

A few of the reporters exchanged confused looks, but Kate was speaking to *him* now. Not to camera crews. Not to reporters. Only him. "In Conceptual art, it's the *idea* that drives the work. The finished work of art is, or should be, a perfect illustration of the artist's idea and intent. Now, if you view the death artist's *work* in those terms, well . . . it comes up short." She paused, her eyes focused on the camera, imagining him there, at the other end of it, watching, listening. "The fact is that his work isn't all that clear. I don't get what he's trying to do. I'd like to, but . . ." She continued to stare at the camera. "I just *don't*."

A reporter shouted: "What about the case? Can you comment on its progress?"

"No," said Kate. "I can only discuss the art."

Now all the reporters were shouting questions, but she turned away, her mission accomplished.

38

Kate tapped a copy of the newspaper photo—the one where the death artist had given her halo and wings, now pinned to the conference room's bulletin board. "The writing is what made me think of it," she said. "It's very similar to a note I got on my last case, in Astoria."

"Astoria was a long time ago," said Mead.

"Not so long," said Kate. "And the case was never solved. I called the station last night, and again this morning. I wanted them to send me what they have on it, particularly a fingerprint that was never matched."

"You think it might actually have been the death artist's?" asked Slattery.

"We've got prints from each of the crime scenes that we can't match to anything. If one of them matches the print I had from the scene ten years ago—"

"So what does Astoria say?" asked Brown.

"That all their unsolved homicides over eight years old were put on microfiche, and then transferred to discs and sent to Quantico a year ago."

"We do that, too," said Mead. "It's automatic now."

"I tried to get the information through the FBI's website but was denied access," said Kate.

"I'm sure those boys would be happy to get you the info." Mead scowled.

"Yes, but I'd rather ask my friend. No need to overtax the Bureau."

Mead almost smiled. "So." He leaned his elbows on the conference table. "You mind explaining your little late-night TV performance to me?"

"I was just giving our murderous unsub what he wants," said Kate. "To be treated like an artist. It was serious art talk, and whether or not the death artist understands it, I'm pretty sure it will intrigue him, make him want to play ball with me even more."

"This isn't a game," said Mead.

"That's where you're wrong, Randy. It *is* a game." Kate's eyes narrowed. "I think it will please him—that I tried to engage him as I would any artist. And my words were calculated. I said I wasn't quite *getting* his work because I want him to spell it out for me—for *us*. I did that whole Conceptual art rap because I want him to hone his ideas, make them perfectly clear." She folded her arms across her chest. "Get it?"

Slattery shook her head. "Not completely."

"Look. If his ideas are clear, his clues will be, too. The clearer his clues, the faster I can figure them out. The faster I figure them out, the quicker we go on the hunt. And hopefully beat him. I want to get it right next time." Kate looked from Slattery to Brown to Mead. "Don't you?"

"Suppose he doesn't send you any more clues?" Mead tugged at his bow tie.

"Are you kidding? I gave the guy a mixed review—on national TV. I said his work was good, but not good enough. My guess is the death artist just can't wait to show me how fucking good—and clear—he can be."

Damn her.

His anger bubbles up, thoughts of destroying her run through his brain, wild, uncontrolled. But then he sees it—

she is toying with him, playing the game. Of course she knows his work is brilliant. How could she not?

She's making a request. And he should listen. Take up her challenge. If it's clarity she wants, it's clarity she will get.

But how can he possibly be more clear. Is she kidding? Has she ever tried to work with living subjects? The way they fight, resist, try to thwart his creativity at every turn.

He paces. Rats skitter into corners, disappear into cracked floorboards.

He's got to come up with something really special, something exceptional, worthy of them both.

You must do it.

The voices.

Just today, he got so scared, convinced that others could hear them. How could they not? They are so fucking loud. Piercing. But no, they only smiled, his stupid secretary, his co-workers.

He stares at his wall—the Polaroids of Amanda Lowe— his current one-man exhibition.

How can she not see his brilliance? But of course she does. She must.

He thinks about his phone call, how well it worked. All those cops, just waiting. So stupid. Did they really think he was dumb enough to risk it all for such a cheap trick? What art is there in that?

He drums his fingers on his worktable.

Artists' Lives. The book practically telegraphs itself from the far end of the table. He lifts it into his lap, cradles it like a baby, flips the pages, slowly, studies the illustrations, pictures of Willie, Elena, all the other artists. Why isn't *he* in here?

But he will be written about. He knows that. One day they will write entire books about his work.

On the last page of Kate's book, just under the author's photo, he reads about her schooling, the impressive degrees, even the title of her Ph.D. thesis: *Abstract Expressionism— Painting with the Body.*

That's when it comes to him. The perfect idea.

Now all he has to do is apply it to the duet he's been planning.

He drags the carton of well-worn cards and pictures closer. This time, he goes through them methodically, meticulously, one at a time. And it doesn't take long to find what he needs. The perfect images. The perfect idea.

His gloved fingers tremble with excitement as he places the images side by side.

Clear?

Oh, man, if it were any clearer . . .

Floyd Brown was not smiling—neither in the photo nor in real life.

There they were, he and McKinnon, she in her ball gown, he in a tux. And Henry Kissinger. The picture, carefully cut from the society party page of the *New York Times,* was tacked up on the police-events bulletin board.

Katherine McKinnon Rothstein, Floyd Brown Jr., and Henry Kissinger, at the Let There Be a Future Benefit Ball at the Plaza.

He'd been getting cracks and jokes and snide innuendos about it all day long.

"How's Henry?"

"Give my best to Hank."

"Nice tux."

"You and McKinnon, heh, heh, heh."

The next person to say a single word was going to get decked. Brown tore the photo off, was about to crumble it in his hand, but couldn't quite do it. After all, there he was, standing next to Henry Fucking Kissinger. Brown actually smiled, then quickly stashed the picture into his pocket. At least Vonette would get a kick out of it.

"Brown!" The uniform who called his name was all the way down a long dark hall, just outside Mead's office, heading toward him at breakneck speed. Brown thought, *If this kid says one word—one fucking word about that picture—he's a dead man.*

"Brown." The kid stopped short, breathless. "Mead wants you in the third-floor conference room. ASAP."

The plastic bag of Kate's mail sat heavily in the center of the long conference table. Slattery was handing the uniform a large manila envelope as Floyd Brown came into the room. "The lab," said Slattery. "Tell Hernandez it's priority. Prints and fibers. Inside and out."

Kate was leaning over the image they had just received, reading glasses on, her brow furrowed.

Mead was beside her, magnifier in hand. "What do you make of it? Do you think—"

"Please," said Kate, a hand up to silence him. "Give me a minute."

There were two images. One tall, vertical; the other, almost a square. Both contained vague but wildly painted figures in swirling visceral pinks and hemoglobin reds, slashes of crimson and magenta.

"Looks like a bloodbath," said Slattery.

"Shhh!" Kate tucked her hair behind her ears. "Okay. First off, it's two paintings pasted side by side. They're both by Willem de Kooning, the great American Abstract Expressionist painter."

"They don't look so great," said Slattery.

"They are," said Kate. "Take my word for it."

"Doesn't sound American," said Brown.

"He's Dutch," said Kate, trying to be patient. "But he lived, and worked, in this country."

Mead whined, anxious. "But what do they *mean*?"

"If you guys don't shut up for two minutes—so I can think," said Kate, nailing them each with a murderous look.

Mead backed up.

Slattery said, "Sorry."

In the near distance, there were footsteps, phones ringing, sirens. But the conference room had gone dead quiet.

A minute passed. Kate remained hunched over the pictures. The squad seemed to be holding its collective breath.

"Maybe it'll help if I free-associate a minute," Kate finally said. "De Kooning. Abstract Expressionism. Two pictures. Two paintings." She stopped a moment, stared at the wall of crime scene photos. "Two paintings. Two *victims*! He must be going after two people this time. Jesus!"

"Are you sure?" asked Mead, his hand twitching on his cellular.

"No. But I'd say it's a good bet. I dared him to be *clear*, remember? This is the first time he's given us two pictures— side by side. And they're both figures. That's two people. I'm guessing everything he does now has to be taken literally."

"Shit," Mead muttered under his breath.

"I'm going to need my art books," said Kate. "I want to see the titles of these two—all the pertinent info."

"We can try the Internet," said Slattery.

"Maybe," said Kate. "Though I'm not sure these paintings would be there. They're not particularly well known pictures by de Kooning."

Mead already had a patrol car on the line. "I got a car on Central Park West and Eightieth," he announced. "They can be in your apartment in minutes." He handed the phone to Kate.

"Okay," she said. "Don't scare the doormen—or my housekeeper. Once you're inside, I can direct you to the books." A minute later, Kate led them into her library, specified the two books she needed. "They'll be here soon," she said, handing the phone back to Mead. "Depends on the traffic." She went back to the two paintings. "It's all got to be in here. Clear. Obvious. That was my challenge."

"Suppose he didn't take you up on it?" asked Slattery.

"Then we're sunk," said Kate. "But I'd bet my life that he did." She looked from one painting to the other, took a deep breath. "Damn it. I'm stuck. *Now* you can start asking me questions—anything to jog my brain."

"Well, I can sort of see the two figures," said Slattery. "But I don't really get it. I mean, they're a mess, all over the place. What's the deal?"

"Okay," said Kate. "Let's see if I can sum it up. The artist, de Kooning, wants you to feel as though the painting is coming into existence, like he's painting it right in front of your eyes."

"Oh. Yeah. I sort of get that," said Slattery. "The way the paint is all swirling around and drippy, right?"

"Right," said Kate. "The figures are emerging during the act of painting—right out of the artist's subconscious, right out of the paint. They're coming into being." Kate paced. "What else? What *else*?" She tapped her lip, ran her hand through her hair. "De Kooning was part of Abstract Expressionism. Jackson Pollock. Franz Kline. Those artists are all about the process. The moment of creation. The painting as an extension of their body." She stopped short. "Wait a minute. Wait a fucking minute! That's what my Ph.D. thesis was about—painting as an extension of the body."

"How could he know that?" asked Brown.

"It says so right in the back of my book—and you can be sure that he owns a copy." An idea took hold in Kate's mind; a look of shock spread over her face. "Jesus. I just had a horrible thought—that he's going to prove to me how fucking clear he can be—that he's going to *illustrate* my goddamn thesis."

"What do you mean?" asked Brown.

"Painting as an extension of the *body*. He's going to use a body—a victim—to actually paint a painting." The thought came into her mind so clearly, it shocked her. It was like that feeling she kept having, that he was right behind her, directing her, whispering in her ear. As if she could hear him thinking.

"How's he going to do that?" asked Slattery.

Kate shook her head. "I don't know."

"Who?" asked Mead.

Kate returned to the de Kooning prints. "It's got to be in here." She reached for the magnifier, ran it slowly over the reproductions. "Wait. Look. He's drawn on the paintings. Just like he did on the Kienholz reproduction. It's very faint, but . . ." Kate pointed at the pictures, handed Mead the magnifying glass. "Right there. On the left painting he's drawn a tiny butterfly and a tiny postage stamp. See?"

Mead eyed the paintings through the glass, nodded. "What the fuck does *that* mean?"

"I don't know," said Kate. "Help me out here, people."

"Insects?" said Slattery.

"Mailmen," said Mead.

"But what connects them?" Kate shook her head, turned to Mead. "I know this is a smoke-free building, Randy, but if I don't have a cigarette I'm going to explode."

"Smoke away," he said.

Kate lit up, inhaled. "So what connects stamps and butterflies?"

"They're both small," said Mead.

"Not all of them," said Brown. "I got an uncle who collects butterflies. He's got a couple of big mothers."

"Collects . . ." Kate blew smoke toward the ceiling. "People collect stamps and butterflies. *Shit! That's it!* Last time it was a dealer. This time, it's a collector! *Two* collectors. He's completing the art pie. Painter, museum president, dealer, now it's collectors. *Shit.*"

"But who?" asked Mead, sucking his teeth as if he were on speed. *"Who?"*

A couple of uniforms burst into the room with Kate's books—two large coffee-table volumes on Willem de Kooning. "There was a fucking tie-up in midtown," said one.

Kate grabbed one book, shoved the other at Brown. "Here. Look for either of the paintings he's sent us."

The two of them started flipping pages furiously.

Mead barked into his cellular, calling for an emergency squad to stand by.

"Got one," said Brown.

"Me, too," said Kate. They laid their open books side by side. Kate went from one page to the other, ran her finger under titles. On the left: *The Visit.* 1966–1967. On the right: *Woman, Sag Harbor.* 1964.

Kate flipped to the back of the books. "*The Visit* is in the Tate Gallery, in London. So that's no good." She scanned the page, her finger sliding along other titles. "Here. Here it is. The other one. *Woman, Sag Harbor.* Collection of Nathan and Bea Sachs, New York."

"Get the phone book," said Mead to one of the uniforms.

"I know them," said Kate. "They live on Park Avenue, around Sixty-seventh."

Mead had the cellular to his ear, already disseminating the information.

"No, wait," said Kate. "They have a place out in the Hamptons. Of course. Sag Harbor." She looked at Brown and Slattery, then Mead. "I asked him to be clear, didn't I?"

Now everyone was moving fast.

Slattery got hold of the emergency squad at Patrol.

Mead dispatched cars to the Park Avenue apartment, just to be sure, then spelled it out for the Suffolk County Police, giving them the particulars, telling them to get out to the Sag Harbor residence, ASAP. "I gotta call Tapell. And she'll have to notify the Bureau."

Kate stared at the de Kooning paintings. What was it Slattery had said? "Like a bloodbath." She hoped to God they would get there fast enough to prevent it from becoming one.

Bea Sachs was disappointed. First, because her husband, Nathan, had not come with her to the artist's studio, and second, that the artist, now unrolling a large abstract drawing in the corner of the small East Hampton studio, was old. Well, not old exactly, but not young either. Forty-plus, for sure, and not a household name yet, and on top of that, a woman. Three strikes. *Forget it.* Did this middle-aged artist really think that collectors on the level of Bea and Nathan Sachs could possibly be interested?

Bea managed a tight smile. She smoothed her short tennis skirt, crossed her legs, which she had been told—by many of her closest friends—were as good as any thirty-year-old's. Not bad for a woman who admitted to sixty-five. Particularly since next week she would turn seventy-three.

The artist was saying something about form and function, but Bea wasn't really listening. What she was thinking was that she would absolutely kill her friend Babs for setting up this dreadful studio visit. After all, she and Nathan had spent years building up their art collection, starting out with second-rate Impressionists, which they sold, of course, after realizing, to their horror, that no one, absolutely no one, gave a hoot for second-rate anything. They made a damn good profit, too, selling it all at auction. And then, with the help of that savvy private art dealer, they started buying up the Abstract Expressionists—Franz Kline, Willem de Kooning, Robert Motherwell—in the late sixties, when the market for that kind of art was way down, everyone dumping it for the new Pop art.

The "Ab Ex" paintings now hung in their Sag Harbor home, along with a few Warhols and Lichtensteins—naturally, they did have to buy a few of those Pop icons.

Oh, yes, she and Nathan were very hip collectors. One look at the art that covered the walls of their Park Avenue duplex—the latest, hottest artists to hit the scene in the past five years, and not an unknown name in the group—and anyone could see that.

Now Bea was trying to think of what to say to cut this visit short, to get home to Nathan, who was coming down with a cold.

But the artist kept displaying one painting after another. "This one is the progenitor of so much of my work," she said.

Oh, brother. Bea thought of a question, just to be polite. "Do you show in New York?"

The woman artist shook her head. "I would, only my astrologer doesn't think I'm ready."

Oy vey. Bea smiled weakly. "But isn't it hard selling your work without New York representation?"

The artist looked distressed by the question.

Bea was so bored she could cry. And this middle-aged, unknown woman artist just would not take the hint. Every time Bea started to get up, the artist hauled out another boring little abstraction. *Abstraction? Come on. Where's the edge? The cool.* Something brand-new that would spark conversation at Bea's weekly dinner parties.

Oh, no. The woman was making her tea. Some horrible-smelling whole-earth sort of brew. Bea sighed. She could see there was no way she'd be getting out of here anytime soon. And with poor Nathan waiting for her at home—waiting for the NyQuil and nose drops she'd promised to pick up at the local pharmacy.

39

Damn. Who'd have expected a tiny, shriveled old man to be so heavy?

He's got his hands under the old man's armpits, dragging him back and forth, up and down along the wall. Good thing he is wearing the plasticized coverall, or he'd be a fucking mess.

Nathan Sachs moans, half conscious.

"You're making history, Natie boy. *History!*"

The once-white wall is a mass of splatters and streaks, looping, swirling red blood, the barely discernible image of a figure emerging.

"We're getting there, Natie. Hang on." He's breathing heavy, the weight of the old man getting to him. "Just a little bit more. It's not quite there yet."

He strains to lift Nathan Sachs higher, to get the old guy's stumps up into a clean white area of wall. "That's it. Just there. We've got to concentrate now, Nate. We've gotta make it perfectly clear." The blood, spurting out of the man's wrists a minute ago, is starting to slow down. He hauls the old man back and forth, back and forth. There's a puddle of blood on the floor. The old man's canvas deck shoes drag through it, whipping it up, creating bubbles of bloody foam.

"It's looking good," he says, then almost stumbles over

one of Nathan Sachs's hands. He kicks the amputated appendage away in disgust. "Who needs that," he says. "I'm painting with the body. The *body*!"

He stands back for a view of his painting, the weight of the old man growing heavy in his arms. He drops Nathan Sachs into the crimson river at their feet. The old man curls into a fetal position, his bloody stumps tight against his body. He shudders once. Then lies stock-still.

Where is she? He checks his watch. He can't wait much longer. He'll have to move fast.

He looks over at the other white wall, the inferior-quality painting he's taken down to make room for the masterpiece he is going to create with Bea Sachs. *Damn her.* Leave it to a woman to screw up his perfect plan, his duet. He plucks Nathan Sachs's other hand off the floor, dips the index finger in blood, then prints his initials—a large *D*, then an *A*—in the lower right corner of the wall. But a moment later, he reconsiders. It's not quite right. He rubs them out with the back of the hand, dips Nathan's finger in some fresh blood, replaces the letters with a small *d* and large *K*.

Yes, that's it.

He stares at Nathan's severed limb—an interesting prolongation of his own hand—one more way to make a painting as an extension of the body. He should have thought of it sooner. It would have been a lot easier than lugging the old man around.

But he wanted to be clear. Literal. And a body is a body, no getting around it. This way he is certain he will not disappoint Kate.

He's feeling so close to her, as though she were here, in this room, watching him work, viewing the finished painting with him, making aesthetic judgments. What would she say?

A bit too red?

Perhaps.

He scans the room for something, anything he might be able to use, finds it in the fireplace, a few shards of burned wood, homemade charcoal.

Now, with a few bold strokes, he suggests the outline of a female form, nothing too specific, then draws a pair of large circular breasts, the hardwood charcoal biting into the still-wet blood on the wall.

He moves back, takes it in, absentmindedly using Nathan Sachs's hand to scratch his itchy nose.

My God, the painting is even better than he expected. She will be so impressed.

He tucks the hand into the pocket of his coverall. He's decided to keep it.

He checks his watch. Should he wait another minute for the wife? No, he'd better not. If Kate has figured it out as he imagines, they will be here soon.

He doesn't bother taking the portable electric jigsaw lying on the floor beside Sachs's body. There's no need. He's left no prints on it.

Once outside, he pulls the plastic bags off his shoes, strips out of the jumpsuit, stuffs them all into the easy-to-carry gym bag he's left by the Sachs's back door.

A minute later he is running past the swimming pool, scaling the picket fence, disappearing into the arbor of trees. There are sirens shrieking in the distance, but he's almost at the car now.

Bea Sachs trembled. Kate laid her sweater over the woman's thin shoulders.

Mead was huddled with the chief of the Sag Harbor Police Department and three of his local detectives. They'd arrived at the scene just as Bea Sachs was putting her key in the front door. Crime scene cops were now crawling all over the Sachs's home like pigs sniffing out truffles.

Kate, Brown, Slattery, and Mead had been in the same car for over two hours, Mead driving ninety miles an hour, the siren blaring the whole way out on the Long Island Expressway. Kate's head was aching, her nerves on edge.

Bea Sachs had been over the events of the day five or six times. Her hands were shaking. Her lips trembled as she spoke. She'd left the house around noon to play tennis at the club. She had called Nathan just after to see how he was feeling. He said he was feeling a bit worse, that he was going to take a nap, that she should make the studio visit without him. Bea had promised to pick up the cold remedies he'd requested. Their last communication. Then she drove to East Hampton, to the artist's studio. After that, to the Sag Harbor Pharmacy.

The Suffolk detectives were making the usual inquiries—any enemies, anyone who was seeking retribution?—but Kate and the squad knew those were worthless questions. The death artist had chosen the couple—his symbol for art collectors—purely out of convenience. They fit the bill, and their house was isolated.

"At least we saved the wife," said Mead, after they got Bea Sachs sedated and off to the hospital. He nodded at Kate, mumbled, "Good work."

Kate just barely nodded back.

"The alarm was still on," said one of the Suffolk County detectives. "The vic obviously let the unsub in."

"So Sachs knew his assailant," said Brown. "Or the guy just didn't seem like a threat."

One of the Suffolk tech team photographed the wall several times, came in for a close-up on the initials in the lower right-hand corner.

"I get the *d* for death," said Brown. "But what about the *K*?"

"He's not using his initials this time," said Kate. "He's signing for the artist whose work he is emulating—for de Kooning—small *d,* capital *K.* He's being clear, remember." She shook her head. *Damn it, what good is figuring it out if I'm always too late?* She watched a cop bag the severed hand.

"You find the other one?" he shouted to a crime scene cop across the room.

"You won't find it," said Kate, totally flat. "He took it with him."

Mead turned away from the Suffolk chief of police. "How do you know that, McKinnon?"

"I just know." She closed her eyes, could see the death artist using Nathan Sachs's hand to add the initials, then not wanting to give it up, his newly discovered, perverse paint-brush. *Jesus.* She was so fucking plugged into this guy, it sickened her.

"Too bad he didn't hang around a few minutes more," said one of the Suffolk detectives.

"He knew how much time he had," said Kate.

The guy looked at her, his face screwed up. "How?"

"Never mind," said Brown, answering for Kate, who had already turned out of the room, was lighting a cigarette on the back porch. Brown saw the match, then the tip of her cigarette, glowing. He hoped to God she didn't crack. He knew what it was like to be inside one of these psychos' heads. He'd been there. Couldn't wait to get out.

40

I t's coming up now," said Liz.

Kate pulled up a chair in Liz's small FBI Manhattan cubicle, watched as a file number, then a name, PRINGLE, RUBY, appeared on Liz's computer screen. Her eyes felt itchy, irritated from lack of sleep.

It had taken almost three hours to get back from Sag Harbor last night with Kate, Mead, Brown, and Slattery, going over and over Nathan Sachs's murder—if only they had figured out the clues faster, if only they had gotten there an hour earlier, if only . . .

Then the FBI needed to hear every single detail. The only reason they hadn't taken over the case was because Mitch Freeman had convinced them that Kate and her team were close. Kate wasn't sure if that was a blessing or a curse.

By the time she got home, all Kate was capable of doing was kicking off her shoes and falling into bed. She was glad Richard had been called back to Chicago for more depositions. No way she'd have been able to answer any questions.

"I'd like any crime scene photos, any lab reports," said Kate, focusing on Liz's screen. "And there should be something about a fingerprint we were trying to type way back when, but couldn't."

"Did you try AFIS?"

"Yes. But the fingerprint didn't appear. It may have been before the system was put into effect."

"Hold on." Liz scrolled through the document.

A series of black-and-white images took turns filling the screen: The Dumpster. Garbage. That poor dead kid. All of it so vivid in Kate's mind, she could even feel the heat of that summer day.

"I can make the resolution better." Liz hit a few keys. The picture's details sharpened so that Kate could make out the chips in Ruby Pringle's powder-pink fingernail polish, a similar color on the girl's lips, smudged across her cheek. Ruby Pringle's eyes were wide open, staring back at Kate now as they did then. On the screen they looked dark, but Kate remembered they were blue.

A moment later, Liz was lifting images out of the laser printer, handing them to Kate.

"Jesus." Kate took a deep breath. "I never wanted to see any of this again." But she took in the details—the halolike aluminum foil crumpled over the girl's head, the wavy plastic wings. "She really does look like an angel. It *could* be the death artist's work." Kate glanced back at the screen, thought a minute. "Would you see if there's a note in the file? A sort of ransom note? I'm pretty sure it was documented."

Liz scrolled through the case file. There it was:

I know where she is because I know where I put her.

"That's it," said Kate. She stared at the writing on the screen, then pictured the actual note on the seat of her car, directing her, drawing her to that hideous scene so many years before.

Kate's fingers trembled as she unfolded the newspaper photo of herself with wings and halo, and the word HELLO written across it. "Obviously, the FBI has a handwriting department."

"Sure. But not here," said Liz. "I can fax them to Quantico's handwriting analysis."

"How long would that take?"

"Depends. If my pal Marie is working today, you could have an answer back in no time." Liz fed both writing samples into her fax machine, then turned back to the Ruby Pringle file on her computer. "Here's the lab stuff. And your fingerprint, large as life. I'll print it on Mylar so it can be overlaid with any of the recent prints you've got in your lab, to see if they match."

Kate watched the fingerprint spit out of the printer. Would it lead her to him—or to another body? Kate practiced a few of those deep-cleansing yoga breaths.

"You have gotten good at this, Liz."

"Thanks." Liz handed over the Mylar fingerprint. "I'll let you know as soon as I hear anything from Quantico on the handwriting."

All the way back to the station house Kate couldn't stop thinking about it. Had he written HELLO as a clue, to let her know how long he had been a part of her life, or was it simply a mistake? No. The death artist was too clever, too meticulous for that. He wanted her to know.

Okay, so he was leading her. But this time she knew she was being led.

"Dead-on match," said Hernandez.

Now Kate was staring at another computer screen, one into which had been fed the Mylar print supplied by Liz. It had been flipping fingerprints over and under each other for about ninety seconds until the two had wed, and the screen flashed MATCH.

"What's the match?" asked Kate. "Which case?"

"It's from the Stein scene," said Hernandez, checking her records. "Let's see. According to this, the print was pulled off a painting—one that had that little violin picture stuck onto it."

Thank God she had sent them back for it, that she recognized the violin was a prop, part of the death artist's staging of Titian's *The Flaying of Marsyas*.

"Your unsub must have taken off his gloves to stick the violin picture onto the painting and accidentally leaned his finger into the painting while he was doing it. He wiped the little violin print clean, but not the painting."

"Even if he'd wiped the painting," said Kate, "the tacky oil-paint surface would be very sensitive to fingerprints, wouldn't it?"

"Right."

"So this is the only match to any of the prints we have from *all* the death artist's crime scenes?" asked Kate.

"So far," said Hernandez. She handed Kate the Mylar fingerprint along with another set of Quantico faxes. "These came for you."

Minutes later, Kate had the Ruby Pringle crime scene photocopies spread out on the conference table in front of the squad, along with the results of the lab's fingerprint search, Quantico's handwriting analysis, and two large art books—*Renaissance Painting* and *Early Christian Art*.

Behind her, pinned up on the wall, were technicolor pictures of the Nathan Sachs crime scene—lurid and bloody. Beside them were the de Kooning paintings from Kate's books.

The entire squad looked exhausted, including Mitch Freeman—dark circles under their eyes, lines around their mouths from constant frowning.

"With the fingerprint match and Quantico's handwriting people saying the notes are a seventy-percent match, it makes it pretty damn conclusive that it's the death artist's work," said Kate.

"Who supplied the info?" Freeman squinted at the FBI documents.

"The Bureau," said Kate with an offhand "Who else?" sort of shrug.

Freeman didn't push, just nodded.

"Jesus," said Chief of Police Tapell. "This guy's been on your tail since Astoria."

"But he disappeared for years," said Mead.

"He disappeared on McKinnon," said Freeman. "But he could have been working all along, undetected."

"And then I wrote the art book, made the TV series, and came back onto his radar screen," said Kate. She flipped a few pages in the art books. "There are angels in practically every one of these paintings. They're called putto." She showed a few examples to the group. "I can't find anything specific, but you can see what he must have been going for with Ruby Pringle. This was an early attempt. He hadn't perfected his ritual yet."

"It might be a good idea to check and see what other unsolved cases could be the death artist's work," said Tapell.

"No offense," said Kate. "But looking at old cases isn't going to do much but prove he's been active all these years. The fact is that for the past ten years no one knew the guy's ritual because it kept changing, kept *looking* different. But now we know his ritual is based on art. Nobody had that information before. It's a totally different ball game now. We can get him. All we have to do is wait for him to send me another clue."

"What if he decides not to?" asked Tapell.

"Oh, he will," said Kate. "He *wants* me there. I know it."

"I agree," said Freeman. "And this time we have to work fast, be ready for him."

"We will," said Tapell. She regarded Kate with a frown. "I heard a rumor that you were thinking about leaving town. Going to Venice?"

Kate shook her head. "Forget it." She shivered, though the room was warm. Is this what the death artist wanted, to control her life, manipulate her, keep her here, bring her there? "I'm not going anywhere."

It's true. That last time was awfully close. But he figured it out, didn't he? Had the timing down perfectly. It was that stupid woman's fault for not showing up. *Damn*. He wishes he could have stayed to finish the job.

He feels a slight stab of regret. But no, he will not permit it. That's history. The past. It's over. Not everything can be a masterpiece.

After all, even he is human. He's allowed the occasional imperfection, isn't he? And it wasn't bad, nothing to be ashamed of. Okay, the color wasn't perfect—the old man's blood a little thin, anemic, but the spirit of the painting was there, and that's enough. She got it.

She got it too fast.

"Not really," he says, staring at the wall of shiny tin. "But all right. I'll slow it down."

No. Keep going. Do it.

The tin wall distorts his face, reflects someone totally un-recognizable. He moves in closer, runs his hand over the metal as if caressing his misshapen features. "Who are you?"

You are me. I am you.

He shakes his head, watches the face in the tin twist and turn. He pulls back. It dissolves.

He shoves Nathan Sachs's hand out of the way—the thing looks like a shriveled claw, purple-brown flesh, fingers curled up—and dips into his carton of art cards and repro-ductions. He needs something to ground him. Make him feel safe. Yes. He should do it now. While he is at the peak of his powers. And really, why not? He has thought about it for so long, knows just the kind of image he wants to use—something wonderfully grand and mythic—something that will suit her perfectly.

He sets to work. Replaces the blade in his X-Acto knife, checks his glue. Not even the voices can distract him. An hour passes. His table is a mess, covered with scraps of paper. But the finished product is simplicity itself. Clear. Bold. Iconic.

Still, when he holds it up, a swell of sadness overtakes him. This isn't like giving up one of those inane photographs or a tuft of hair. This is major. This is it. Her. She. The one.

Are those tears on his cheeks? He's not surprised to see his gloved hand is wet when he wipes his eyes.

Be strong. Remember, you are superhuman.

He straightens his shoulders. Yes, he can do this.

But what about later—when she's gone? God, he's going to miss her.

You can always find another muse.

Charlie Kent placed her passport and airline tickets together with her schedule of Venice Biennale events, slid them all into her burnished leather Filofax. Now she opened her closet—an act that never failed to soothe her, this feat of absolute space maximization, and the one true luxury in her modest apartment.

Twenty floor-to-ceiling shelves. Eight pairs of shoes per shelf. Suede, alligator, snakeskin, patent leather. Pumps, flats, heels. Dressy, casual, sporty, elegant. Buckles, bows, clasps, ties. Two shelves, made taller, just for boots. All arranged by color: white to beige, beige to tan, tan to brown, brown to rust, rust to orange, orange to red. Three shelves devoted entirely to black.

Charlie sighed, an expression of pure contentment. She selected nine pairs for her two and a half days in Venice, then spent the next twenty minutes putting each pair into its own chamois string bag, and then, only then, carefully nestled them between the layers of clothes in her suitcase. She threw in a sexy pink nightgown.

There had been virtually no opposition from the small board at Otherness to covering the cost of Willie's accompanying her to Venice—not after she had acquired that major WLK Hand directly from the artist. Charlie thought Morty Bernstein, chairman of the board and avid collector of Willie's work, was going to bend over and kiss her ass.

Charlie smiled, glanced over at the drawing Willie had given her, already framed, hanging right above her bed with all the other artwork she had received, over the years, as gifts from so many aspiring artists.

Oh, this was going to work out just fine.

And she had bigger plans than the Museum for Otherness.

She'd already met with a few select members of the Contemporary board, let them know that she, and she alone, had the vision to bring their museum into the twenty-first century. Not that creep, Raphael Perez, whom Charlie had made it her business to besmirch whenever possible, or Schuyler Mills, that was for sure. No, the job would be hers.

She glanced back at her open closet. Perhaps one more pair of shoes, just to be on the safe side; the blue-and-white Chanel spectators, which she hardly ever wore in New York, but which were just perfect for Venice.

Raphael Perez tossed four pairs of Perry Ellis bikini briefs into a small leather Coach bag opened on the couch just below a spotlit poster of his very first exhibition for the Museum of Contemporary Art—"The Body Beautiful: Eating Disorders as Art." Images of women ramming fingers down their throats, inserting enemas, vomiting, brought a smile to Raphael's lips.

Venice, he knew, would be a lot of work. So much to do: attend the best parties; schmooze the right people; deal with that bitch Charlie Kent; ignore his co-curator, Schuyler Mills—all of which would be very easy with so many collectors and museum people he needed to suck up to.

He opened the top drawer of his perfectly distressed armoire, selected two handkerchiefs, a favorite blue silk and a paisley print of olive green, which he tucked beside the briefs. Director of the Museum of Contemporary Art. Yes, the title suited him perfectly. And with Amy Schwartz retiring, and Bill Pruitt dead, who was going to stop him?

Willie wished he knew what the weather was going to be like in Venice. Should he bring his new leather jacket? Why not? If it got hot, he could always take it off.

He folded two white shirts, the plain black tie Elena had bought him for his very first gallery opening—his good-luck charm—into his backpack along with his Discman, six or seven CDs, underwear, his standard toiletries.

He considered packing the bottle of expensive-looking English cologne Kate had given him months ago, unscrewed the pewter cap, splashed a little into his palms, patted his cheeks. The slightest smell of lime, a hint of orange, refreshing, clean. He liked it. Leave it to Kate to find the perfect scent.

Willie glanced up at a half-finished painting, one Darton Washington had admired, even expressed interest in buying only a few weeks ago.

He'd been trying to get past it, Darton's death, and all the anger he felt. But it was not just anger. That would be simple. Willie balled up a pair of socks, squashed them into the backpack.

It was also the guilt. The fact that he'd deceived Kate. That he'd given his brother, Henry, money to lie low. If he was really honest with himself, he knew that was why he'd let Darton Washington's death drive a wedge between him and Kate.

Willie reached for the phone. He should call her. She'd been through a lot of shit. Maybe even more than him. But he just couldn't do it.

Fuck. He wondered if she missed him as much as he missed her.

Thank God he was getting out of town for a few days.

He tucked a black leather belt into his backpack.

An image flashed before his eyes so fast, it sent him careening backward. It was like the last one, the one he had had in the car—*Kate, struggling, in water.* Except this time he was in it, too. But he wasn't struggling. He wasn't moving at all.

Willie opened his eyes, but could not see. Another blinding moment of darkness. There it was again: *Murky water. He and Kate.* Then it was gone.

Brown drummed his nails on the edge of the conference table. Mead sucked his teeth. Mitch Freeman, usually cool, was cracking his knuckles in between loud sighs. Slattery chewed gum, popping it loud.

That did it. Kate looked up. "Maureen. *Please.* Stop making that obnoxious noise."

"Me?" Slattery spit the gum into a trash can. "What about them?" She looked from one man to the other.

"What'd I do?" asked Mead.

"Everyone," said Brown, "just cool it."

They were all huddled over the death artist's latest creation.

He had kept them waiting. But not for long.

"Okay, let's just get through this, shall we?" Once more, Kate regarded the work in front of her—a painting of a man tethered to an ancient pillar, his body pierced with a dozen or more arrows, Kate's face pasted right over the man's.

"It's *Saint Sebastian*," said Kate. "By Andrea Mantegna. He's a fifteenth-century Italian painter."

"With your face," said Slattery.

"It's the photo of you from the *New York Times*," said Brown. "From the gala."

Kate took one of her yoga breaths. She'd been waiting for the death artist to get around to her. It was inevitable. She'd felt him getting closer and closer. And here it was. Finally. Just the two of them. "I complete the pie," she said. "I'm the art writer."

"Oh, you're a lot more than that," said Freeman. "You're his prize."

His prize. The words reverberated. Kate moved the magnifying glass over the image of the saint, trying to keep her hand from shaking. "No hidden drawings this time. Just my picture over the saint's face, and the saint pasted over the other reproduction, which is Canaletto's *View of the Grand Canal*." She took another deep breath. "No mistaking the message. He's telling us who and where: Me. In Venice."

The death artist had sent her an invitation. Should she let him pull the strings again, let him lure her to Venice? She could picture him, thinking about it, about her. Planning. Yes, she had to do it. "I'll go," she said. "I have to."

"Hold on," said Mead. "It's way too dangerous."

"Mead is right," said Freeman.

Kate thrust her shaking hands into her pockets. "He's expecting me. I can't disappoint him." Her gut was twisting into a knot. But she wouldn't show it.

"How am I supposed to protect you over there?" asked Mead.

"I didn't know you cared, Randy." Kate managed a wry smile. "But I have to go."

Mead's lips were tight, brow furrowed. "Let me talk to Tapell. See if she can set something up with Interpol and the Italian police."

"The Bureau can handle that," said Freeman. "We can deal directly with Interpol."

"Let me go with McKinnon," said Slattery.

Mead considered it a moment. "Maybe. I don't know. Let me think."

"Might not be a bad idea," said Freeman.

"I could go, too," said Brown.

"No way," said Mead. "I can't have all of you there. Someone's got to stay here in case this is just a ruse to get McKinnon out of town."

"No," said Kate. "He doesn't work that way."

"His call to you, before the gala, was a ruse." Mead sucked his teeth. "You forget that?"

"His call was just to yank my chain, to toy with me," said Kate. "There was no art in it. No plan. Nothing he had to follow through on." She tapped the image of the martyred saint. "But this is *specific*. Clear. He'll see it through—or try to." She ran her hands through her hair, then clasped them in her lap to keep them from shaking.

Freeman sat forward. "I think she's right. She should go. I'm sure the Bureau could supply a team to protect her."

Kate shook her head. "If I'm surrounded by a bunch of crew-cut American robots, it'll be obvious they're FBI. It'll just scare him off."

"I see your point," said Freeman. "I'll try to keep the *robots* at bay a while longer."

"Thanks." Kate glanced at the death artist's collage—her face pasted over the martyred Saint Sebastian. She took a breath. "The opening events of the Venice Biennale are tomorrow. He'll have to strike this weekend—and we have to be ready for him."

Not her usual neat job of packing—tissue paper layered between blouses, each cosmetic and toiletry in its own plastic bag. Instead, Kate had her one evening outfit in a garment bag and everything else jumbled into a small carry-on.

"I would have been going with you if you hadn't canceled the trip," said Richard. "Now I'm totally overbooked with meetings and depositions."

"I'm sorry," said Kate. "I didn't think I could possibly go, but then, well, I decided I really needed the break."

"Well, I'm glad you're going." Richard sat on the edge of their bed, clipping his nails.

"Richard, please. I'll be stepping on fingernail shards for days."

"No, you won't." He stopped clipping, looked up. "You'll be in Venice. And Lucille vacuums every day."

He was right. Who cared where Richard cut his nails? She was tense, that's all. And he'd made an effort, left work early to see her off.

"Willie will appreciate it. You being there, representing us both." He went back to his nails. *Clip. Clip.*

"I hope so," said Kate. She grabbed her smallest bottle of Bal à Versailles, shoved it into her bag. The absurdity of it struck her. *Perfume? For a murderer?*

"A few days away will do you good."

"Uh-huh." She hadn't told him why she was now going. If he knew about the Saint Sebastian collage—that her life was clearly in danger—he'd never let her go. And maybe he'd be right. But she had to go. She was determined to beat the death artist at his game.

Richard was using the metal file now, dragging it across his thumbnail, squaring it off. A picture winked in her mind:

Holding Elena's hand at the coroner's office, the girl's nails, blunt-cut. Kate shook her head, tried to dislodge the image, but it wouldn't let go. "Richard. *Please*. Stop doing that."

"What?"

"Your *nails*. It's . . . bothering me."

Richard dropped the nail clipper onto the bed, frowned.

"I'm just a little tense." She balled up a pair of panty hose, shoved them into her bag.

Richard got his arm around her shoulders. "You've got to relax, sweetheart."

"I'm trying to."

He massaged her neck with his fingers. "You sure you don't want me to try and cancel everything, come with you?"

Kate touched his cheek. "No. You'd better not." Would she like him to come? More than anything. But not since the death artist had contacted her. "I'll bring back a stack of art catalogs for you to drool over."

"Great." He kissed her cheek. "And hurry back. I'll miss you."

Historically, Venice had been sinking at the rate of about three to five inches per century. That number had increased to ten inches in the twentieth century and continued to climb. Sidewalks and canal walls were being raised, telephone and power lines elevated, people were moving from first to second floors of their homes. At that rate, Venetians would soon be crowded into attics, and tourists would be viewing the fabled Jewel of the Adriatic from helicopters.

Still, to Maureen Slattery, the jewel glowed bright. As the vaporetto glided down the Grand Canal, she couldn't get enough of the cerulean blue sky, the dark emerald waters, the gilded palazzos. If only the Italian *polizia* weren't hovering over them.

Marcarini and Passatta. After much discussion between the various law enforcement agencies, it was decided that the two cops would be assigned to guard Kate on a twenty-four-hour basis, with bihourly check-ins to both the Italian police and Interpol. In Slattery's mind, they were Macaroni and Pasta. Marcarini was in his late twenties, dark, cute; Passatta was maybe forty, handsome, unsmiling, chain-smoking, nervous. Both spoke English, occasionally haltingly.

The day was warm, moist, a slightly sweet-rotten smell in the air.

"Fucking beautiful," said Slattery.

"Uh-huh," said Kate, staring out at the palazzos that lined the canal.

"Something bothering you, McKinnon? You haven't said more than two words since we landed."

"Yes. There's plenty to bother me, Maureen." Kate gave her a look.

"Oh, right. Sorry. I got overwhelmed by the place."

"Forgiven," said Kate, staring into the dark Venetian waters. She could feel the death artist's presence everywhere she turned. Was she imagining it? She didn't think so.

The vaporetto deposited them at San Marco.

Slattery took in the Basilica, the Doges' Palace, the amazing square. "How the hell does this place stay afloat?"

"It has been here for centuries, signorina," said Passatta, a scowl on his lips. "I think it will remain standing—at least until you are to leave."

"Thanks, pal." Slattery smiled.

Marcarini and Passatta escorted them to the Gritti Palace—one of the oldest, most luxurious hotels in Venice, and the site of Kate and Richard's honeymoon—then set up camp just outside their door.

The porter laid Kate's and Maureen's bags onto waiting stands. Kate handed him a twenty-thousand-lire note.

Slattery surveyed the sumptuous room, the picture-perfect view through the open window: the Grand Canal, gondolas, churches. "Oh my God. I've fucking died and gone to heaven. It'd be like a dream, except for those meatball cops on our heels. Although they're both good-looking, especially Macaroni."

"Macaroni?" said Kate, smiling for the first time.

"Yeah," said Slattery. "And the sourpuss is Pasta."

Kate laughed, happy that Slattery was along, that she was not alone. "All Italian cops are handsome. It's part of the job description." She moved into the other rooms. "Maureen. Come in here."

"Jesus fucking Christ," said Slattery, standing at the entrance to the marble-and-gilt bathroom. "It's bigger than my entire apartment."

"We have to check in with Mead." Kate lifted the hotel phone. "Oh. Typical. The lines are out."

"In a fancy place like this?"

"The phones in Italy work about half the time. In Venice, less." She tried her cell phone. "Shit, I forgot to charge it."

"Call him later," said Slattery. "Hey, who gets the big bed?"

"All yours," said Kate.

The facade of the Venice Police Headquarters was all sculpture and gilt, although more than half the gilding had worn off, with mold climbing up the bottom third of the building.

Inside, Kate and Slattery were treated to an endurance test called Italian time. Almost an hour's wait. Then another hour with some sort of higher-up, though they couldn't figure out who or what he was supposed to do, and he never told them, the three of them sitting around sipping espressos while he recounted a memorable visit to the Big Apple, years ago. Then another hour-long tour of the station.

Outside, finally, Marcarini and Passatta still glued to their sides, Kate attempted to shed some of her gloom as she and Slattery crossed over the Rialto Bridge, passing through an assortment of colorful markets and shops. But everywhere she looked, shadows won over light, alleys were ominous rather than charming.

Slattery didn't seem to notice. She took it all in like a kid at Disneyland. "What's this church?"

Kate looked up. "Oh. Saint Zachary's. It's a little Renaissance church. God. It feels like centuries ago that I came here to look at the Bellini."

"The *who*?"

"Giovanni Bellini. One of the greatest Venetian painters ever, and one of my personal favorites."

"Can we go in?"

Kate sighed. "We don't have much time, Slattery. We've got to get over to the Biennale, and—"

"Come on, McKinnon. This may be my one and only trip to Venice." She gave Kate a pleading look.

"All right," said Kate. They were, after all, in one of the great art cities of the world.

"You call this little?" said Slattery, stepping through the doors, taking in the high vaulted ceiling, decorated pillars, patterned marble floors, carved pews, paintings everywhere.

"For Italy it is." Kate shivered. Though ornate, the church was dark and damp.

Slattery kneeled, crossed herself. "Habit."

Marcarini and Passatta lingered beside the front door as Kate led Slattery down the north aisle to the second altar.

"This is it? The Bellini?"

"Yes. But hold on." Kate signaled the sacristan, who ambled slowly toward them, his robed form casting a long shadow.

Kate felt another chill. Was it only the dampness?

She folded several thousand lire into the sacristan's hand. A moment later, he threw a switch. Giovanni Bellini's masterpiece burst out of the dreary shadows, illuminated in all its splendor.

"Wow," said Slattery. "It's amazing. The way he's painted his own pillars beside the real ones and the dome in there looks just like a miniversion of a real one, and all the figures sitting inside like that."

"Hey, you have the makings of a real art historian, Maureen."

"No shit?" Slattery slapped her hand over her mouth. "Oops."

"Don't worry. God's not listening." Kate wondered if he ever did.

Maureen moved closer to Bellini's fictive church-within-a-church painting. "I don't know how these guys did it. I mean, I can't even draw a straight line."

"Well, they were trained from a very young age, in workshops, apprenticed to great artists where they learned everything from mixing the master's colors for him to washing his brushes to painting minor parts of the background."

"Art slaves, huh?"

"You got it. But in Giovanni Bellini's case, his father, Jacopo, who was also a great painter, taught both him and his brother, Gentile."

Passatta and Marcarini, straining to listen, had moved into the aisle beside Kate and Slattery.

"You teach the art, signorina?" asked Marcarini.

"Sort of," said Kate.

"Not *sort of,*" said Slattery. "She's famous."

Passatta raised an eyebrow.

Slattery leaned on the rail, staring up at the Virgin. "She's so beautiful, and it all looks so real. Like you could just walk right into it, and sit down on the Madonna's lap."

"That's what Renaissance painting was all about," said Kate. "Rounded form and deep, deep space. Inviting the viewer into rooms and through windows. Perspective had only recently been rediscovered."

"Who lost it?"

"A lot of things were lost in the Dark Ages," said Kate, peering into the shadows and recesses of Bellini's painting. *The Dark Ages.* Exactly what it had felt like this past couple of weeks.

Marcarini and Passatta lagged behind as Kate led them back to St. Mark's Square.

The Doges' Palace was glittering gold in the afternoon light.

"I think jet lag is starting to set in," said Slattery. "Can we sit a minute?"

Kate and Slattery settled onto a bench with a view of the square. Slattery ordered a cappuccino. Kate, a double espresso. Marcarini leaned against a pillar, a few feet away; Passatta was in the arcade, puffing on a cigarette; neither man took his eyes off of Kate. But Kate didn't get a chance to relax. One after another, people were stopping by, New

Yorkers mostly, here for the Biennale. Each time someone approached, she flinched. So did Marcarini and Passatta.

"Jeez, do you know everyone in the *world,* McKinnon?"

"Only in Venice. And only this week. They're all collectors or artists or art writers." She paid the check. "Come on. Before your jet lag totally gets hold of you. I've got to see the exhibition and Willie's paintings."

But that wasn't all. Kate knew the death artist expected her to be there—and she did not want to disappoint him.

The International Venice Biennale was like a world's fair, without the rides, without the kids, without the fun, held every other year in the Giardini—a large park away from the main tourist attractions of the city. A number of old buildings were turned into national pavilions, crammed with each country's artists of the moment. Hordes of sophisticated Europeans and Americans could be seen racing around with shopping bags sagging under the weight of giveaway art catalogs as they scurried from one pavilion to the next, afraid they might be missing something or someone, worried they had not been invited to the right parties. The exhibition remained on view for months. But only the opening days counted. After that, well, *anyone* could go see the art.

Kate and Slattery had been moving with the crowd, Marcarini and Passatta glued to their sides, the odd quartet going from one pavilion to the next, attempting to take in the scope of this helter-skelter exhibition, most of it dark and depressing—large-scale photographs of genitalia and corpses, dismembered animals in formaldehyde, cluttered installations of indecipherable political content—all of it in direct contrast with the flat-out beauty of Venice. The creepiness of the show had added to Kate's paranoia—everyone was a potential threat; friendly faces were filled with menace.

The American Pavilion, formally an Italian bank, was large but unimpressive, and so crammed with installations—artworks made up of found and created objects that scattered across floors and walls without much visible coherence—

that it was almost impossible to figure out where one work ended and another began. Willie's pieces stood out not only because they were good, but because they hung, like traditional paintings, on a wall. At the moment there were several people standing in front of them. Raphael Perez was holding court.

"WLK Hand is one of our most gifted young artists."

Kate noticed Willie practically hiding behind a pillar, but Perez waved him over insistently.

Willie took a shy bow, mumbled, "Thanks."

"That's Willie Handley," said Kate.

"He's cute," said Slattery.

"You never met him?"

"No. Wasn't me who questioned him in relation to the Solana murder."

For a split second it was all there in front of Kate's eyes: Elena, dead on the floor, the bloody Picasso painting on her cheek, and the thought that the death artist was here, somewhere, waiting. She peered down the center aisle at people ducking in and out of booths like animals in search of prey, imagined him grabbing her from behind, slitting her throat. A breath; an inchoate, reflexive cry.

"*What?* What is it?" Slattery stiffened, was immediately scoping the area. Marcarini and Passatta did the same.

Kate forced the images away. "Nothing. I'm fine." She took Slattery by the arm. "Come. I'll introduce you to Willie."

They caught up to him as he was making his escape from Perez.

Kate kissed Willie's cheek. "You have the best paintings in the show."

"I'll take that as a compliment, even though they're, like, the *only* paintings in the show." Willie looked at the floor. "I didn't think you'd be here."

"I wasn't sure either. But I'm glad I am. I'm proud of you. Your paintings are really beautiful."

"Yeah. Very cool," Slattery added.

Willie regarded her oddly. This was not one of Kate's typical friends.

Perez sidled over. Kate started, jumpy.

"Proud of our boy?" Perez asked.

Kate eyed the young curator. *Could he be the one?*

Slattery noticed, her cop instinct clicking in, her hand idling over her pocket, the gun inside.

Kate threw her a look, the slightest nod to indicate it was okay—she thought.

Perez slid his arm around Willie's shoulders. Willie shrugged it off. "I can't stand around in front of my own paintings all day." He headed quickly into another stall, this one plastered—walls, floors, ceiling—with pornographic images of women cut from magazines, scrawled over with contradictory anti-women, antipornography statements.

"Hey, McKinnon," said Slattery, scanning the walls. "Where's *your* picture?"

Kate laughed. But not for long. A shadow flickered at the corner of her eye. Her body went rigid as someone put a hand on her shoulder. She spun around, lunged at the man. He stumbled backward, fell.

Slattery went for her gun. Marcarini and Passatta reached for theirs.

"No—" Kate stopped them, offered her hand to the guy on the floor. "Jesus. Sorry, Judd." She helped the startled art writer to his feet.

"Wow," he said. "I thought I reviewed your book rather well, Kate." He managed a nervous smile.

"Forgive me. I—"

"No, no," he said, brushing himself off. "I'm fine."

A small crowd had gathered. Marcarini and Passatta were checking everyone out.

"Everything's okay," said Kate. "It was an accident."

"You okay, McKinnon?" Slattery asked, once they were away from all the fuss.

"I'm just so fucking jumpy," said Kate.

"What'd that guy do to you?" asked Willie.

"He didn't do anything."

"So you're okay?"

"Yes." Kate suddenly grabbed him, hugged him to her.

"You'll be there tonight?" he asked, when she finally released him.

"Wouldn't miss it for the world."

Beautiful.

The old concrete staircases descending into black water. Rotting doorways. Garbage in the back-alley canals.

He should have thought of this before selecting the Canaletto painting as a backdrop for Saint Sebastian. Perhaps it's too pretty. No matter. Work is work. And there is so much to do and not a lot of time.

He has seen her once, watched her sip a cappuccino. She didn't look nervous. But then, she rarely does. It's one of the things that he so admires about her—that cool air of elegance she wears even under the most dire circumstance.

Will she be able to maintain it when he plunges the arrows into her flesh?

Saint Kate.

It will be a truly spectacular icon. He pictures it frozen, a color plate in an art history book, his name below it, the date, and, finally, the materials: arrows, robe, human body.

Does she feel his presence here? Is she waiting for him to come to her, like a lover?

The thought excites him.

He closes his eyes, drifts a moment, imaging the moment.

Patience, Kate. I'm coming.

Back in their suite, Kate slipped on a pair of white tuxedo pants.

It was time. And she was ready.

Slattery yawned, sprawled out on the big bed.

"You don't have to go tonight, Maureen. Really."

"Tell you the truth," said Slattery, stifling another yawn. "I've been dreaming about that tub all day."

"Have a nice soak." Kate whipped her tuxedo jacket on over her white lace bra. "I'll be back before you know it."

"No," said Slattery. "I should go with you."

"I'll have Macaroni and Pasta glued to my sides. I'll be fine. Don't worry."

"You talked me into it," said Slattery, sinking back into the pillows.

Kate buttoned her jacket.

"Hey," Slattery called after her. "Aren't you forgetting something?"

"Nope." Kate patted her side. "I've got my little thirty-eight strapped into a shoulder holster under my jacket."

"I meant a *blouse*," said Slattery.

The minute Kate stepped through the door, Marcarini and Passatta attached themselves to her sides. Marcarini had a little trouble keeping his eyes off the white lace peeking out of the top of her jacket.

The room looked as if it were right out of an eighteenth-century party scene by Antoine Watteau, one of his *fêtes galantes* paintings, elegant and decadent, packed with consorts and courtiers, all of them working, working, working.

"You realize, if you dropped a bomb on this place, there would be no more art world," Schuyler Mills whispered to Willie.

They stood in the middle of the Peggy Guggenheim Collection, surrounded by the art world two hundred—every notable mover and shaker, moving and shaking even more than usual. A confluence of myriad languages hovered above the crowd like a cloud of buzzing locusts while waiters weaved their way through, dispensing that most peculiar Venetian drink of champagne and peach juice, the bellini.

Massimo Santasiero, the organizer of this year's Biennale, greeted Schuyler Mills while still shaking hands with someone else. Santasiero was wearing one of those suits only Italian men can get away with—heathery blue-gray, and so slouchy it looked as if it had been balled up on the floor of his closet for weeks. In comparison, Schuyler's starchy Brooks Brothers number looked as if it were still on the hanger. Willie had on a new white shirt, the good-luck tie, his usual black jeans, and the new leather jacket.

"The American Pavilion is—how do you say?—so gritty this year," said Massimo.

"It was not an easy show to curate," said Schuyler. "But I think I've succeeded. And *you* have done the impossible—coordinating such a complex exhibition."

Willie watched the pros at work: toiling in the fields of ass-kissing.

"I admire your work," Massimo said to Willie. "It is so . . . personal."

"Well, it is *my* work."

The Italian looked at him quizzically, not quite getting the smart-ass retort.

"Young artists," Schuyler said, throwing Willie a look, "they enjoy shooting themselves in the foot. Don't you, Willie?"

Santasiero didn't get that either, but Willie did. "I hope you'll come see my show at the Contemporary this summer," he said, this time garnering an approving nod from Schuyler.

Charlie Kent, in a black Lycra-spandex number hugging her body from midbust to midthigh, broke away from a European collecting couple. Trotting over to Willie on her eye-shattering lime-green pumps, she looked from Schuyler to Santasiero, her radar sharply tuned. "Massimo." She extended her hand.

The Italian took her in. "Ah, Signora Kent. I was just making plans to see the WLK Hand show at Signor Mills's Contemporary Museum in New York."

Charlie had to bite her tongue at his calling it Mills's museum. "And you must see the new piece we'll have at *my* museum. We can all have lunch—you, me, Willie." She winked at Willie.

More than half the heads in the room turned as Kate made

an entrance in her white tux and spectator stilettos. Every step she took, the jacket's satin lapels slithered and shimmered, exposing a hint of white lace brassiere.

Willie pulled free of Schuyler Mills, joined several other men and three or four waiters, who all converged on Kate at once. Marcarini and Passatta didn't know where to look first.

"Signora Rothstein. So very good to see you." Massimo kissed Kate's cheeks while his eyes did a slow dance up and down her body. "And looking so *bellissima.*"

"Grazie," said Kate, lifting a bellini off a tray, struggling to keep her trembling hand from spilling the drink all over herself. She peered at the Italian curator from behind her raised glass. *Has he been in New York lately? Did he know Pruitt from the museum? Could he have ever met Elena?* She sipped her bellini. She was getting carried away, and she knew it.

Willie moved in for a quick kiss. "How are you holding up?" she whispered.

"Trying," he said.

Massimo intervened, took Kate by the hand, and began introducing her to anyone he thought she should know. But Kate couldn't concentrate; everywhere she looked there were signs flashing danger. Massimo was speaking, smiling at her, but Kate wasn't listening.

He's here. In Venice. Kate could feel it like an electric current buzzing through her. She scanned the room.

Could he be here, now, at the party? No, she didn't think so. The setting wasn't right. He'd need to get her alone to turn her into a saint. It was not going to happen here. She was sure of that. The death artist was a stickler for detail.

An hour later, her tension showed no sign of abatement, and when the director of a well-known New York museum backed into her, she spun around and grabbed the man's arm so hard he yelped. She spent the next ten minutes apologizing.

"Kate! You look absolutely fabulous!" This from a

woman with the taut, shiny skin of one too many face-lifts. "Where is that handsome husband of yours tonight?"

"Richard couldn't make it to Venice, I'm afraid. Too much work at home."

"Stop kidding, Kate. I saw him this afternoon."

"That's impossible."

The woman screwed up her face—a true feat, her skin was so tight. "Well, I could have sworn it was him."

"No, it couldn't be." *Richard, in Venice?* "He's home, working." Then, suddenly, Kate's mind was all over the place—*Could he be here?* Images—the cuff link glittering on the floor, Pruitt dead in his bath—flashed in her mind.

Kate drew her hand across her forehead. It was hot. She shouldn't have had that drink. Her imagination was running wild. *No way Richard is here. It's absurd.* "It just can't be," she said, trying to sound calm.

The woman shrugged. "Well, it *was* all the way across a piazza. I guess my eyes are going."

Kate tried to smile, but couldn't.

Willie brushed into her, whispered: "I've had enough. I need a walk. Want to join me?"

Kate started to follow, but Massimo stopped her, his hand on her wrist. He held fast, speaking to her in his halting English, something about art and Italy—or was it art and Italian cooking?

Kate couldn't concentrate. Willie was already halfway out the door, and she wanted to talk to him. A good five minutes passed before she could break away. Finally, she pulled out of the Italian curator's grasp, uttered a lame *"Scusami,"* hurried toward the door.

Marcarini and Passatta fell into step just behind her.

Maureen Slattery just couldn't believe it. The bubble-bath cubes supplied by the hotel smelled like heaven. She lay back, let the warm soapy water soothe her tired body while her eyes took in the bathroom's elegant details: variegated marble walls and floor, brass plumbing fixtures, frolicking cherubs painted on the ceiling. If it were not for her gun, resting beside her on the huge marble sink, she wouldn't have believed that any of this was real. She would not even remember that she was a cop.

She laughed, closed her eyes, let herself sink down into the water until the bubbles tickled her chin.

In her next life, thought Slattery, lifting a handful of aromatic suds, she was coming back as Kate McKinnon.

There was no sign of Willie. *Damn it.*

Another reason to make Kate sad. Well, at least he'd wanted to take a walk with her. He must have forgiven her. She checked her watch. It was getting late. She should be getting back to Slattery.

"Let's head back to the hotel," she said to her two Italian bodyguards.

Passatta nodded. Marcarini lit up one of his unfiltered cigarettes as they headed down the small street directly in front of the Peggy Guggenheim Museum, then took the large Ponte dell'Accademia Bridge to cross the Grand Canal.

The night had turned cool, humid, a blanket of eerie mist draped over everything. The moon darted in and around clouds like a flirty young girl, peeking out just long enough to illuminate the edge of a cathedral, a piece of Byzantine architecture, then retreating, shy and coy, waiting for a change of costume before making its next appearance.

Kate's head felt about as soggy as the night. She hugged the jacket to her nearly naked chest.

The moon's reflection did a slow silvery waltz along an alleylike canal. They crossed another tiny bridge. Kate listened to the sound of small waves lapping against foundations, felt the slimy moss under her hand as she ran it along an old iron railing. It gave her a chill. She stopped. Stared into the fog. The image of herself as a martyred Saint Sebastian oozed into her mind.

"Did you guys hear anything?" That electric buzz she'd felt earlier was sending a shiver up and down her spine.

"Like what, signora?" asked Marcarini.

Kate shrugged. Maybe she was inventing it. "Never mind." She quickened her step. Not so easy in stiletto heels.

The trio turned into a tiny piazza, one Kate had never seen before, shops and cafés closed up, no tourists, everything about the place still. In the center of the square, there were four different ways out.

"Which way?" she asked.

"The alley," said Passatta. "It will bring us to Calle del Campanile, then into San Marco."

The alleyway was dark, with only a few ancient street lamps attached to the front of closed-up buildings. They offered about as much light as a handful of fireflies.

The three of them were halfway down the alley when the footsteps started, faint at first, from behind.

The cops stopped short, drew their pistols.

Kate got her .38 out, peered over her shoulder, saw nothing but mist.

There were no footsteps now, just the sound of their collective breathing, and pigeons batting their wings.

"Please to stay here, signora," said Passatta.

The cops split up. Marcarini to the right. Passatta to the left. Kate watched as their forms dissolved into the fog.

That buzzing sensation was even stronger now. *Damn.* She heard Passatta call out to Marcarini, his voice cutting through the mist, echoing slightly.

Kate couldn't just stand there, waiting. *For what?* A sudden panic gripped her. She hurried toward the end of the alley, found herself right at the edge of a canal, no railing at all, dark, murky water lapping up onto her shoes, impossible to tell where the land actually ended and the water began. Another couple of feet and she would have landed right in the canal. Goose bumps had broken out on her arms.

Marcarini grabbed hold of her arm. Kate whirled around, her .38 right in his face. "Oh! Jesus. You scared the shit out of me."

"Scusami, scusami," he said. "Please to stay near us, sig-nora."

They cut out of the small piazza, moving faster now, turned into another dim alleyway, Kate's nerves jangled.

Halfway through, a man's shadow rolled toward them like a figure in a de Chirico painting. A tiny overhead light caught the sheen of something metallic in his hand.

Marcarini and Passatta shoved Kate behind them, pistols trained on the man's dark contour.

But the man had seen them, too, flattened himself against the alley wall, that same tiny light illuminating his face.

The cops sprinted.

"No!" Kate called out. "Stop! It's okay."

Seconds later, after the cops had backed off, Willie took a deep breath. "Fuck, man."

"You guys have got to cool it," Kate said to the cops, though she was equally edgy. "What's that in your hand, Willie?"

"Oh. This?" He displayed a six-inch strip of oxidized bronze, a bit of baroque filigree along the edge. "It's a piece of old metal railing, I think. I picked it up off the street. Beautiful, isn't it?"

"Do me a favor," said Kate. "Don't play with metal ob-jects, okay?"

They turned into St. Mark's Square.

"Ah, Florian's." She looped her arm around Willie. "Come on. I'm sure you could use a drink."

Kate and Willie settled into one of the plush booths in the old café, just inside. Marcarini and Passatta took up their posts in the square, each leaning against a pillar, both smok-ing their unfiltered cigarettes.

"Bodyguards?" asked Willie.

"Stuck like glue," said Kate, trying to smile. "I'm sorry about that."

"Hey, so I like lost twenty years off my life. It's no big thing."

Kate smiled, ordered brandies for all of them, had the

waiter bring glasses out to Marcarini and Passatta, who offered up a silent toast.

"I'm really glad to see you." Kate squeezed his hand.

"Me, too," said Willie.

The gilded cathedral's facade illuminated in the dark piazza twinkled soft and blurry.

"Man, what a beautiful place."

"Did you ever see this movie—it takes place in Venice, with Julie Christie and Donald Sutherland? It's even an oldie to me. You probably weren't born yet."

"Don't Look Now," said Willie.

"How do you know that?"

"Me? Is there a movie I *don't* know? They're in Venice, and their kid has died, and everywhere they look they see the kid's ghost."

"Exactly," said Kate. "Well, that's the way Venice felt to me tonight. Creepy."

"Really? To me, Venice is like a dream."

Kate looked into the square, at the fog settling in. *Is he out there?* She shivered.

"You cold?"

"No." Kate laid her hand over Willie's. "I'm sorry," she said. "For what happened with Darton Washington, and . . . everything."

"It's not your fault." For a moment, he considered telling her about Henry, but he just couldn't.

Kate stared across the piazza, at the bell tower, an evanescent spire in the fog. She finished the brandy, checked her watch. "I should be getting back to the hotel."

At the front entrance to the Gritti Palace, Kate bid Marcarini and Passatta *"Buona notte,"* but they wouldn't have any of it.

Marcarini shook his handsome head. Passatta scowled. "We are to walk you into your room, signorina, and then we are to stay the night."

"In my room?"

"In the hall," said Marcarini, a smile tugging at his lips.

The brandy on top of the bellini had really hit. Kate was feeling woozy, the keys unsteady in her hand.

"You need for me to help?" asked Marcarini.

"I think I can manage it," said Kate. "See you in the morning." Bed. Pillows. Thick, soft duvet covers. That's what she was thinking about.

But the cops insisted on checking the room first.

Just in front of her, Marcarini and Passatta had gone rigid.

Kate felt the chill—this one real, from the wide-open window—before the scene came into sharp focus—horrifying and surreal, her brain hardly able to process it.

The two cops were shouting, but Kate couldn't hear them, that electric buzz she'd been feeling all night was now so loud, it was deafening. *Oh, God. Jesus. No.*

In minutes, the room was crowded. Or had it been hours? Kate wasn't sure. A horde of carabinieri and *polizia* were arguing, waving their hands about; someone snapped pictures of the gruesome scene, while that higher-up from the Venice police station asked Kate questions.

She stared past him.

A flashbulb lit up the night view of Venice through the open window—and Maureen Slattery, as if she were levitating, in front of it.

She was nude, strung up with the curtains, one of them coiled around her neck, the other pulled through her thighs and wrapped like a loincloth. Her body was pierced in a dozen places with arrowlike spears, jutting out like deadly porcupine quills. Streams of blood striped her body, ran over her bound feet, collected in an amoeba-shaped puddle, and soaked into the carpet.

42

So many uniforms. So much blue.

But not the sky, which was appropriately gray with heavy clouds, the threat of rain.

First the mayor. Then Chief of Police Tapell. Short speeches. Official, but heartfelt.

A cop's funeral.

Maureen Slattery's funeral.

Kate stared at row after row of tombstones disappearing into perfect one-point perspective. It took her back to Giovanni Bellini's illusionistic church-within-a-church painting, and how much Maureen had loved it. One more artist, one more memory, destroyed by the death artist.

Was that only two days ago?

The plane ride home had been a nightmare, Kate's attempt to fortify herself with Scotch a total failure. Nothing helped. How could it? With Slattery's body in the airplane's hull.

She glanced at Maureen's parents beside the gravesite, tears streaking both of their faces.

She gripped Richard's arm.

Kate pushed her sandwich aside. No chance she could eat. "I still can't believe it." She stared through the glass front of the coffee shop at passersby, cars blurring.

Liz offered a sympathetic look, but her words were tough. "Look, Kate. Slattery was a cop. On an assignment. She knew the danger. It could just as easily have been you."

"It was *supposed* to be me."

"A lot of good that would have done." She stared into Kate's eyes. "You can't let it get to you. It'll destroy you—and you know it. You were—*are*—a cop. You know the rules. So did Slattery."

"I just keep playing it back, Liz. Thinking if only the Italian cops had split up, one with me, the other with her. If only—"

"You can play the 'if only' game forever, Kate. But it won't do any good. Maureen's loss is a tragedy. No question. But right now you have to focus. The death artist is still out there."

Kate took a deep breath, nodded agreement. Liz was right. There was only one way to survive this.

She had to get this guy. She had to make him pay.

There were cops in every chair, leaning against walls, crowding into doorways. The squad room vibrated with rage.

Kate was sitting beside Brown, in the front row, staring at cracks in the old plaster ceiling until they reminded her of Venice, of aging and decay, of bodies on slabs, of Elena in the morgue, and now Slattery, too, hanging in front of that open window. She shut her eyes, took a breath.

Tapell flicked her finger against the microphone. "Everybody. Everybody."

Kate thought the chief looked old today, anxious, not so *unflappable*.

"We're going to deal with this," said Tapell. "But we have to keep our heads."

"When?" someone shouted from the back of the room. Others joined in: "Yeah, *when*? How *long*? Come on already!" The voices commingled into a single garbled cry.

"We almost had him," said the chief. She sighed, obviously feeling the inadequacy of the words as she said them.

One more time the cops started shouting at once.

"That's not going to get us anywhere," said Tapell. "I know you're frustrated. We're *all* frustrated." She stopped, let her dark eyes sweep the room. "Just *listen* for a minute. Randy Mead is going to update every one of you."

Mead sucked his teeth, then explained the rescue of Bea Sachs—how close they'd come to capturing the death artist. Old news, but it was enough to garner the crowd's attention. Then he laid out plans for activating all departments. Also old news. But it sounded good; words like "full-scale mobilization" and "manhunt" seemed to calm them. "We will catch this motherfucking cop killer," he said.

That produced cheers, detectives and uniforms shouting, punching one another, the old camaraderie of blood lust. Kate could see it in their eyes.

Mitch Freeman stood to the side with two crew-cut FBI men who were whispering, their otherwise immobile faces with expressions that betrayed nothing but the slightest trace of disdain.

Kate looked over at them, two of the *robots* she'd spent half a day with, explaining over and over every detail of what had happened in Venice. The Bureau had now set up a small campsite in the Sixth Precinct, and they were strutting up and down the aisles, faxing Quantico every five minutes, producing reams of paper and whispering to one another, always whispering.

Mrs. Prawsinsky's tight bleached curls were crimped against her scalp. She patted her hair. "I had it done," she said to Kate. "Cost me an arm and a leg, dahlink. You shouldn't know from it."

"You look lovely." Kate forced a smile, tried to get Elena's downstairs neighbor to focus.

The police artist's rendering was on the table. So far, it had produced nothing.

Kate had lugged out a dozen bound books of mug shots— everything from misdemeanors to murder, all committed within the past five years.

Mrs. Prawsinsky turned the pages slowly. "Oh, this one has a very nasty face."

Kate practically tore the book out of the old woman's hands. "Is it him?"

"Oh, no. No." She turned another page. "Just that his face, you know, it's such a mean one."

Kate sighed. She could be here for days. But they were trying everything, and this was something they should have done before—and would have, if they had not been chasing after the wrong man.

Mrs. Prawsinsky stopped. "Ooh," she said. "Look at him." She pointed with an arthritic finger.

"What? What!"

"He looks just like Merv Griffin, doesn't he, dahlink?"

Oh, brother. Kate needed a break, coffee, anything. "I'll be back." She managed to smile at Mrs. Prawsinsky, whose nose was an inch from a page of mug shots. "But you keep looking."

They are streaming down the street, hordes of people, threatening, terrifying, advancing upon him.

But he is not afraid.

One at a time he picks them off. Arms, legs, torn from sockets. A head lobbed off. A throat slit. The street is littered with broken bodies. Sidewalks, gutters, running red.

He is all-powerful. A warrior.

But why is that stupid man smiling at him? Doesn't he see that the warrior, the death artist, has just reached into his rib cage and ripped his heart out, that he is dying?

Oh, now he gets it. He acts so normal, they don't even know it's he who does them harm.

By the time he reaches his refuge by the river, he knows for sure that he is invincible as well as invisible.

But the sight of his messy table, the remnants of hours spent conceiving of Kate as Saint Sebastian, dampens his spirit.

It should have been over in Venice. She, her, should have been over. It was time. That was the plan. And it would have been if it hadn't been for that stupid cop.

He smashes his hand down onto the table. Scissors, glue, pencils hop, skip across the surface in a sort of cockeyed marathon.

How was he to know that someone else would be there, in the hotel room—in the tub, of all places? He wishes he could have come up with another bath scene. But on such short notice? Not possible. He's not a machine. He's an artist.

And now, worst of all, he has no pictures, no documentation at all.

Whose fault is that?

"I forgot the goddamn camera. I had too much to carry. I'm human, you know."

I thought you were superhuman.

"Fuck you!"

You didn't forget. You were lazy. Now I have no proof. Maybe you never even did it.

"You want proof?" He snatches the newspaper off the table, holds it up. "Read all about it!"

FUNERAL FOR HERO COP

Oh, I see. She's the hero. Not you.

"Are you kidding? She cried like a little girl." He mashes the newspaper into a ball, pitches it to the floor. "What a waste. To use up Saint Sebastian on the likes of her."

And you call yourself an artist?

"It looked great! Anyone could see that!" He slumps into his chair. It's quiet now. The voices have subsided, taking his anger, as well as his strength, with them. He feels so tired. So . . . depleted. The thought of continuing, of taking one more breath is agony.

The sound of pigeons. He raises his eyes toward the high broken ceiling. If only he could join them, fly above all the filth and rot and disgust of this world—of his life. Flashes: flayed skin, hacked-off hands, screams, tears, so much pain.

How many times has he wished he could stop? Promised himself that he would?

I'll be good. I promise, Daddy. I promise.

He twitches in his chair. Who was that talking? He's so confused.

He seeks refuge in the small altarpiece he took from Bill Pruitt. He's come to think it has special powers—the Madonna, with her beatific smile, watching over him, the innocent Christ Child, a symbol of himself. If only he could curl into the sanctity of her lap, have her protect him.

Of course. Why hadn't he thought of it before? It's so much better than Saint Sebastian. She the Madonna. He the Child. The two of them. Together.

Immediately he's up, collecting what he needs, his little arsenal—a pistol, the hypodermics, even the stun gun, the kind they use on animals. Amazing what one could buy online these days, what they will send to absolutely anyone.

Oh, he feels so much better. Venice was just not meant to be. And this will be even better.

Now he must bring her to him.

But how?

He spreads more cards and reproductions across the table, studies each one of them, all the images, the colors, moods. But nothing strikes him. Not until he finds the black-and-white self-portrait, and with it, the idea finally takes shape: *Go for him. Get her.*

Of course. Perfect symmetry. First he takes one child. Now, he will take the other.

But can he possibly do it? Despite everything, he must admit that he loves the boy.

If you love him, you will make the sacrifice.

"I don't know . . . I'm not sure . . ."

Think of Abraham and his son. And remember, he is simply a pawn. A way to bring her to you.

"But then—must I kill him?"

Yes.

He studies the painting he has chosen, lets it distract him from the thought of loss, all the years he has invested. He can do this.

Now, using his X-Acto knife, he oh-so-carefully cuts around the figure of a young black man with dreadlocks. Then he scrambles through his box of cards looking for something to complete the vision, trying one, then another, laying the cutout figure on top, testing, testing, testing. Should the background have more color, or less? No. That's not what matters. What matters is that it be clear.

Then he finds it. A scene.

He rests the cutout black man with dreadlocks onto it gently. The two meld flawlessly.

He takes a moment, revels in his genius, then glues the figure down.

Now, really to show off his talent, he dips his tiniest brush, a double-zero pointed sable, into some black acrylic paint, adds a touch of titanium white, mixes a gray almost identical to the one in the reproduction, then paints three tiny water towers onto the roof of a small cabin in the painting. He blows on the surface to help dry the paint. It only takes a minute. And it's perfect.

A building by the river with three water towers, his little additions, so small, so flawlessly rendered, they look like part of the original.

He sits back.

One child gone. One to go. Yes. He is up to the sacrifice.

He looks again at his creation. It's perfectly clear. She will understand it. And it will terrify her.

Floyd Brown looked solemn as Kate came into the room. He slid the book of mug shots toward her, stabbed his finger below a slightly blurry photo.

HENRY DARNELL HANDLEY

#0090122-M
Burglary/Breaking & Entering/Possession

Last-known address: 508 East 129th Street

"This is who the neighbor, Prawsinsky, picked out. I sent out an APB thirty minutes ago. Turns out the address on One Hundred Twenty-ninth Street is a burned-out apartment building. But the cars are out canvassing Harlem. Couple of the Bureau robots went along. They'll find him. And we'll deal with your boy, the brother, later."

Kate tried to digest all of this information at once. "Willie is not his brother's keeper," she said, not sure what that meant, just something to say. *Willie's brother the death artist?* She'd never known him, met him once, at Willie's high school graduation. She stared at the mug shot. The guy looked nothing like Willie, but pretty close to the police sketch.

Brown's beeper went off. "Hold on." He grabbed his cellular.

Kate paced.

Willie's brother? How is it possible? Did Willie have any idea?

Kate's mind was racing. She'd given Willie the police sketch. He *knew* who the police were looking for. How could he have continued to shield his brother?

His brother.

Of course. Kate got it. Willie was doing exactly what she'd done—protecting a loved one.

"They found him in Spanish Harlem," said Brown, clicking off. "Henry Handley. He's holed up somewhere over near the East River. They're bringing him in."

Willie hung up the phone with a deep sigh.

He didn't much feel like making a studio visit, traipsing over to some artist's place, looking at the guy's work, dredging up things to say—*Oh, like, nice color, and I sure do like the way you painted that what-the-fuck*—but how could he say no?

He had to do it. He owed the guy. If all he wanted was for Willie to visit some artist—as a "personal favor to me"— well, Willie could hardly refuse, could he? He recognized a command performance when he heard one.

He set his paintbrushes aside.

Maybe the break would do him good.

Willie glanced up at the deep cobalt sky, the sun making a last stab at drama and succeeding, gilding the edges of SoHo's cast-iron structures bronze.

The air was warm, slightly humid, a hint of summer.

He cut across Hudson Street, noted the address he'd jotted down—not really an address, more a vague description: West on Jane Street, cross over the highway, then a right, continue north along the river. You can't miss it.

A studio by the river.

Well, at least it sounded exotic.

Willie quickened his step.

43

Not a tree in sight. Only a couple of high-rise project-type buildings on either side of a lot filled with old tires and broken bottles fighting for space with garbage and weeds. The rest of the street was desolate, leveled, one lone building left standing.

"It don't look habitable, does it?" The young cop played nervously with the ends of his mustache, stared through the car's windshield at the one-story cinder-block structure, most of the windows gone, the river a dark blue-gray strip of ribbon just behind it.

His partner, pasty-faced, also young, just shrugged, bored, or trying hard to fake it.

The building did look deserted, but Henry's mug shot as well as the police sketch had been identified by the two shopkeepers just across the street.

The cops had been instructed to wait for backup. They didn't know who this clown was they were going after, but Mead and Brown had both told them repeatedly to "proceed with caution."

Moments later, a second NYPD vehicle cruised down the street, no beacons, no sirens, as it sidled alongside the first car. The window rolled down and a uniform leaned out, said, "Detectives just behind us in an unmarked vehicle."

Now it was a blue Ford sedan, early nineties variety, sliding in behind the other cars. Doors creaked open, two detectives signaled the others out of their cars. The six of them huddled together.

One of the homicide detectives, a guy about forty in shirt-sleeves, a nervous tic in his right eye, asked, "You sure he's in there?"

The mustachioed uniform tipped his head toward the bodega and liquor store. "According to the store owners. They say he's been holed up in the warehouse for over a week. Comes into the stores once or twice a day. Has money for baloney sandwiches and rotgut Thunderbird."

"Okay." The detective swatted at his flicking eye. "You two guys see if there's egress from the back. We'll wait for your signal, then head in the front." He nodded at his partner, who already had his pistol out.

The two uniforms fell into that half-crouch walk made familiar by TV cop shows and movies, made their way across the sad-looking street, disappeared behind the warehouse.

"You know who the perp is?" asked one of the waiting uniforms.

"No," said the homicide detective with the eye problem. But that was a lie. He'd spoken to Brown, had a pretty good idea who it was, but no way he was saying anything. If it was who he thought, it would be his job to stay cool, not let the other cops know. If they did, they'd shoot the mother-fucker on sight.

The air was thick, tension palpable.

"Gettin' hot," said his partner, rocking back and forth on his heels.

Eye-tic nodded.

The uniform's voice crackled over the transceiver. "No egress in back," he whispered. "The door's boarded up. Windows, too."

The detective rubbed at his eye, signaled the other uniforms to get ready. "You guys come around front," he said into his handheld radio. "We're right behind you. And take it easy. Real slow. We don't need no fuckin' heroes."

They scrambled toward the warehouse entrance, met up with the other two uniforms, took turns pivoting through the door, pistols out in front of them.

The broken windows and cracked ceiling allowed in just enough of the dying daylight to illuminate the scene: four or five guys huddled around a garbage can, smoking crack.

All the cops shouted at once: "Hands in the air, mother-fuckers!" "Don't fuckin' move!" "Don't fucking breathe!"

The junkies scattered like mice.

But the cops were faster, grabbing one guy, then another, slamming bodies against brick walls, guns hard into backs.

When they marched them into the street, handcuffed, shuffling, the junkies looked like a bunch of sad, lost children.

The detectives separated Henry from the group just as the police van arrived.

"What do you want?" Henry's lip was trembling, though he was trying for tough.

The two detectives slammed him against the cold metal of the police van, spread his legs, patted him down, came up with a knife he had in one pocket, a handful of photos of a young Latina in the other.

Eye-tic looked them over, recognized Elena. "You're under arrest." He attempted to push Henry into the cop car, but Henry turned, bumped his chest up against the guy as if he were some NFL champion.

The cop double-punched him in the gut.

Henry buckled, fell to his knees, dry-heaved.

The detectives got him under the arms, threw his sad ass into the back of the car. Two uniforms got in on either side of him.

Back at the station, Kate could see that the cops had had their way with Henry—one of his eyes was half-closed, turning purple; his lip split. He was still handcuffed, his arms stretched over the back of a metal chair, fluorescent lights of the Interrogation Room giving his skin a grayish cast.

Mead was doing the interrogating. For the past half hour he'd been badgering Henry, but not really getting anywhere.

Mitch Freeman was beside Mead, taking notes, a couple of Bureau robots on either side of Henry, ready to spring into action, as if somehow Henry could burst out of the steel cuffs, kill everyone in the room.

Kate and Brown stared through the one-way mirror.

Mead spread the photos found on Henry across the table. "You wanna tell me where you got these pictures of Solana?" he asked, for what Kate guessed was the tenth time.

Henry's eyes were glazed; he was thinking: *How did I get them?* He wasn't sure. It all seemed so long ago. So far away.

"You had a thing for the Solana girl," said Mead. "Hey, I get that." He sucked his teeth. "What's the matter? She brush you off? You couldn't take it, a girl like that. Who's she think she is, right? Women." He added a wink of camaraderie. "Fuckin' kill you. The lot of them."

Henry just stared at him, eyes blank.

Kate wondered when they were going to get the poor bastard a lawyer. Something she had not worried about when she was interrogating Damien Trip. But could they possibly think Henry, this pathetic junkie, was their man? "I don't believe this," Kate said to Brown. "They're wasting their time."

"I don't know," said Brown. "I've seen stranger things. Librarian-type guys, real Milquetoasts, who gunned down families, kids. Fall apart when you catch them."

Mead lifted a paper from the table. "Says here you worked for Manhattan Messenger Service. Damn good way to get in and out of places, to deliver packages, envelopes, right, Henry?"

Freeman suggested they undo the cuffs, offered Henry a cigarette and a warm smile. He winked, too, but not at Henry; at Mead, who gave a slight nod.

Henry sucked on the weed as if it were oxygen.

"The way you arranged that girl, Elena Solana," said Freeman. "That was beautiful, man. I mean, I was impressed."

Henry's eyelids were half-closed; his brain playing it back, Elena's bloodied body. But he was confused. He didn't actually remember the killing part. Was it the junk? The crack? Maybe. All he remembered was the blood on his fingers, and the photos he took off her dresser. Right, that's how he got them. "I took them," he said. "The pictures. I took them."

Mead's face lit up.

"So it *was* you who did that beautiful work," said Freeman. "God, you're good."

Henry blinked uncertainly.

"They're setting him up," said Kate. "It's absurd."

"So you took Solana's pictures," Mead enunciated into a recording device on the table between them. "You were there."

"Well, of course he was there," said Freeman. "How else would Henry have done such great work if he wasn't there." He beamed at Henry, elbowed him as if they were good pals. "Isn't that right, Henry?"

Henry almost smiled.

"Say it," said Freeman: "You were there."

"I was there," Henry repeated.

Kate couldn't take it anymore. She would not stand by and watch them railroad Henry just because they needed a scapegoat. She turned to Brown. "I'll be right back."

Minutes later, photos in hand, Kate pushed through the Interrogation Room door.

"Not now, McKinnon," said Mead.

"Henry. I'm Kate McKinnon. We met a long time ago."

Henry squinted up at her.

"McKinnon—" Mead sucked his teeth, gave her a threatening look.

So did the two robots.

"Just one minute, Randy." She laid one of the photos of Elena's crime scene on the table. "Tell me, Henry. Where'd you get the idea for this? What was your . . . inspiration?"

Henry regarded her with a flat stare.

"What about this one?" She held an Ethan Stein crime scene photo under Henry's nose. "What's this based on?"

Henry pulled back from the picture. "What do you mean . . . based on?"

Mead sighed heavily.

Kate said, "I'm just looking for a couple of names, Henry. *Painting* names."

Henry repeated the words as though they had no meaning: "Painting names?"

"He's stoned, McKinnon," said Mead.

"Clearly," said Kate. "And he doesn't know what I'm talking about either." She patted Henry's shoulder. "Do you, Henry?"

Henry smiled at her.

"Sorry, fellas." Kate shook her head. "No matter how much you'd like it to be him, it's just *not*."

"So then how'd he get the pictures of Solana?" Mead asked.

Kate thought a minute. "Mrs. Prawsinsky said she saw a black man at Solana's the night of the murder, and I believe she was right. It was probably Henry. He had a thing for the girl, for Christ's sake. But that doesn't make him our killer." She leveled a look at Mitch Freeman, unable to hide her disappointment. "Come on, Mitch. You know this isn't our man."

Freeman sighed.

Kate was tired, about to go home, when Brown slapped the collage onto her desk. "No postage. Nothing. According to the desk cop, some street kid dropped it by. It was given to him by another street kid—who we can't locate."

"Jesus." Kate stared at it. "Another one."

"What's it mean?"

"It means the death artist is still out there." Kate studied the image, thought a minute. "Okay. You've basically got two images put together here. One of a black man. The other, a landscape. The figure is easy. It's a Basquiat."

"A what?"

"Jean-Michel Basquiat. An eighties hotshot artist. Overdosed on heroin before he hit thirty. I'm pretty sure what you're looking at is one of his self-portraits."

"And the landscape?"

"That's easy. Frederic Church. He was part of the Hudson River school. A nineteenth-century group of landscape painters. I'd say this is a view of the Hudson."

"Wait a minute," said Brown. "You've got a self-portrait of a black guy, and a river scene. It *does* sound like Henry Handley."

"But it's not," said Kate. She was sure of it.

Willie had actually started to enjoy his walk. He picked up his pace, weaved in between bikers and Rollerbladers that filled the narrow path between the highway and river, everyone taking advantage of the warm night.

At the Christopher Street Pier, a scene out of *The Rite of Spring*—an orgy of men, displaying muscled physiques, strolling back and forth on the groaning planks of the old jetty. Willie took it in, thought maybe he should spend a bit more time at the gym. But by the next pier, or what remained of it—a cross-hatching of planks, a few upright posts over murky green water—there were no more beautiful men, just homeless ones passing a bottle, and the thought of pumping iron, of washboard abs, just seemed absurd.

Willie leaned against the fence, stared at a bunch of moss-covered wooden pilings jutting out of the river. They reminded him of Venice—minus the glamour or decadent beauty—and of his time spent with Charlie Kent, who had stood him up only yesterday and was not returning his calls. Apparently, she had gotten what she wanted from him—his painting.

He looked across at the New Jersey coastline, the high-rise apartment buildings on the Palisades, a series of stark monoliths against a darkening sky.

Ahead, a few construction sites had shut down for the day; just beyond them, what appeared to be an old docking building built out over the river.

Willie checked his bearings. He had just passed Jane Street.

That must be the place.

Mead had his head cupped in his hands, elbows on the conference table. "Henry Handley's in lockup," he said, without much enthusiasm. "Just until we know for sure."

Mitch Freeman sat across from him, the two robots still on either side of him.

Clare Tapell's arms were folded tight across her chest. "Okay," she said. "So, I understand it's *not* Henry Handley. Who, then?"

Kate handed Tapell, Mead, and Freeman copies she'd had made of the death artist's latest message—the cutout black man pasted on top of a river view, while she and Brown leaned over the original.

"Spell it out for me, Kate. *Please*." Tapell's dark eyes regarded Kate's with a hint of desperation. "I just came from the mayor's office." She expelled a breath, shook her head. "Don't ask."

"I've looked up the paintings to be absolutely certain," said Kate. "The painted scene is definitely Frederic Church. It's a view from Olana, the artist's home near Hudson, New York, painted around 1879, just before the artist's arthritis made it nearly impossible for him to paint at all."

"What's that tell us?" Freeman asked.

"I'd say, *location*," said Kate. "Hudson being the clue—as in Hudson River. I think that's mainly what it's about. Maybe there's more, but if so, I'm not getting it. Not yet." She tapped the figure, which was almost totally black—big hands, spiky hair, white ovals for eyes, a checkerboard mouth. The death artist had added a big red knife, crayoned on top of the black figure, stabbed into its chest. "This is a Basquiat painting, for sure. From 1982. It's a self-portrait, but not a likeness," said Kate. "I've seen plenty of photos of Jean-Michel Basquiat, and this looks nothing like him." She thought for a minute. "I guess it's a symbol of generic black youth. It could be any kid with dreadlocks." It only took a moment for the words to sink in: *Any kid with dreadlocks.*

"Oh my God!" She got her cellular to her ear.

"What is it?" asked Tapell. *"What?"*

"Wait a minute." Kate put one hand up to quiet her, the other pressed the phone to her ear. She hit her autodial. "Damn. A machine. *Damn.*" She clicked off.

They were all waiting—Mead, Tapell, Brown, Freeman, even the robots—hanging on her words.

"Willie," said Kate. "Willie Handley." She put her hand up again, hit that autodial again, this time left a message: "Willie. This is Kate. If you get this message, I want you to call me ASAP. You hear me, *right* away? Do *not* go anywhere, Willie." She snapped her phone shut, drew a breath. "I think the death artist has targeted Willie Handley."

"Why?" asked Brown.

Kate pushed her hair behind her ears. "To get to me," she said. "Look, the guy's been on my tail from the beginning. Getting closer and closer. He wants to get to me, and now he's figured out a sure way to do it—through someone I love." The words rippled through her. She shuddered. "But Willie's just the bait. It's *me* he wants." Kate snatched up the death artist's collage. "It's all here. Simple. Clear. Just what I asked for. The Hudson River. A young black man. That's got to be his next victim." Kate took a breath. "It was supposed to be me in Venice, remember? *My* face on the dead saint. But Slattery got in the way. Now he's calling me, beckoning me to him. This is a fucking invitation. It *has* to be." Kate stared at the picture. She had a sense of him imagining this very scene—her figuring out his little preparatory sketch, the terror she would feel at losing Willie. Oh yes, he knew her, all right. But she knew him, too. "He must have a place by the river."

"His safe house," said Freeman.

Kate tried calling Willie one more time. Still no answer. She turned to Mead. "Get a car out to Willie's place—in case he comes back. Don't let him leave." She looked back at the collage. "There's no indication of time on this picture. We've got to get moving."

"Are you sure?" asked Tapell. "About the safe house on the Hudson, I mean?"

Kate looked again. "I can't swear to it, Clare. But I *feel* it. In my gut. This is where he is. Where he plans his work."

Freeman nodded.

Kate regarded the image again. "And he's waiting for me."

Tapell eyed her gravely. "Well, you've been right so far." She got the phone to her ear.

"Suppose he hasn't even got Willie Handley?" said Mead.

"Well, then, it's time I met him, no matter what." Kate got her Glock, checked her ammo. "It's an opportunity, Randy, to get him—whether he's got Willie, or—"

"I want you alive, McKinnon."

"Me, too," said Kate, shoving the Glock into her jacket pocket. She got her .38, too, hiked up her pant leg, strapped it to her ankle.

"I've got to let the Bureau know what's going on," said Freeman.

Tapell nodded as he cut out of the room, the two robots on his heels.

Tapell worked two phones. Mead snapped orders at a couple of uniforms.

Ten minutes later, they laid it out.

"The SWAT team is being assembled," said Tapell. "But they need about forty-five minutes to mobilize."

"Patrol is putting two dozen cars at our disposal," said Mead. "Half the cars will start at Battery Park and work up. The others will be starting north and meet up with them."

Freeman called in to say that the Bureau wanted agents in every car.

"Let's get a helicopter," said Brown. "To light up the riverfront, move up and down with the cars."

Tapell made the call.

"I can't wait," Kate said to Brown. "I'm going."

"You don't know where to start," said Mead.

"Let me call Ortega, in Housing," said Brown.

Kate checked her watch. "It's too late. It's long closed." She was getting impatient. She couldn't wait much longer.

"I can call him at home," said Brown, the phone already to his ear.

"The chopper will be taking off from the Thirty-fourth Street heliport in twenty-five minutes," said Tapell.

Kate paced to one end of the room and back.

Tapell was back on the phone, mobilizing the troops.

"Ortega says there's a computer map of the entire riverfront," said Brown, his phone in hand. "It can tell us which buildings are new, which are old, anything under construction." He grabbed hold of a rookie who had just walked into the conference room. "You must be able to work this thing." He maneuvered the rookie into a chair in front of a computer, handed him the phone. "Talk to Ortega."

A few minutes later, the rookie printed out a map.

"It's not much," said Kate.

"It's something. At least we know that such and such"— Brown stabbed a finger at the map—"is a sewage dump. He wouldn't be there."

"Come on," said Kate. "We'll take your Pinto."

"The cars from Patrol will be taking off any minute," said Mead. He shouted after them: "You find anything—*any-thing*—you call for backup. You hear me?"

44

Across the river, the reflected lights of Hoboken rippled over the Hudson's surface like silvery eels. Willie stopped a moment to watch a tugboat push lazily through the water.

Just ahead, that great hulking warehouse, the old docking building, hovered, a black cube against a pewter sky. He checked his watch. Eight P.M. He was exactly on time.

Could this possibly be the place? The door, thick wood and steel-edged, was slightly ajar. Willie leaned into it with his shoulder. It groaned open.

Inside, it was damp and cold; enormous, like a gymnasium. Thirty-foot-high ceilings with a few patches of sky streaking through cracks; four or five metal spotlights clipped onto thick wooden beams provided a minimum of light. Across the room, drawings and photos were pinned to the wall; in the center was a large metal worktable strewn with cut-up images, scissors, X-Acto knives, glue.

"How do you like it?" The words came from behind him, echoed in every direction.

Willie spun around. "Oh, you're here. Good. I was beginning to wonder what this place was."

"A great studio, no? During the day the light is pure gold."

Willie took a few steps forward. "But it's fucking cold, man. What does he do for heat?"

"Artists have worked under poor conditions for centuries. It's only recently—your generation—that's so spoiled."

"*Me?* Like the projects where I grew up had swimming pools and tennis courts?" Willie laughed.

"Boo-hoo. Everyone's always whining about their sad childhood." He can feel the separation beginning, the fugue state that comes over him when he makes his work. But he's excited, too. He's never had a living artist in his studio.

A clamoring from above. Willie looked up. A small flock of pigeons, batting their wings.

"A bunch of them have made a nest up there. Sweet, isn't it?"

"Reminds me of Venice," said Willie. He took a few steps in. The drawings on the wall were still fuzzy, indistinct. But when he moved in for a closer look, he stopped short. "What the—" Willie's eyes scanned the pitted wall, the hideous photographs—Ethan Stein, Amanda Lowe, snapshots of Elena.

He gasped.

Brown moved the Pinto so slowly that traffic was backing up behind them, horns blaring. They could put the beacon on the roof, but didn't want to announce themselves in the event that they actually found the place.

Kate had both the housing map of the riverfront and the death artist's collage in her lap. She had tried calling Willie four or five times, but without luck. *Please, God. Just let him be out somewhere—anywhere but here.* But she had that queasy feeling in the pit of her stomach—the one she got when she knew something had gone wrong.

The radio crackled to life. "Brown. McKinnon."

Kate snatched up the receiver. It was Mead.

"Where are you?"

"We just started," she said. "Down around South Ferry. I can't talk now, Randy. We've got to start looking."

"Patrol cars will be cruising into action any minute," he said. "And the Bureau has decided to add a few cars of their own."

"Fine," said Kate. She clicked off, her frustration mounting even before they'd actually started their search. "Jesus, we could be doing this all night, Floyd. What do we look for?"

"Check the map," said Brown.

"Right." Kate took a breath, tried to calm herself, dragged the map closer. "According to this, there are a few old buildings just below the Holland Tunnel that could be habitable—slightly. Then, some warehouses, and a couple of old docking houses slated for demolition from the West Village up to where the Chelsea Piers start. A few more in the West Thirties." She stared out the window, at the waterfront going dark, a thought taking shape. "Lights," she said. "We should be looking for lights. If the buildings are supposed to be abandoned, they'd be dark."

"Right," said Brown.

Even the Statue of Liberty looked ominous to Kate, as if the old gal were hiding a secret, her arm up to halt visitors rather than welcome them. Kate peered across the river at the venerable icon, torch glowing in the dusky sky, then spotted a building on the side of the highway that looked suspicious. But when they pulled off they could see it was a construction site—a string of naked bulbs hanging on wires illuminated what wasn't much more than a large brick shell.

Brown inched the Pinto along the highway that traced the river, as near to the shoulder as possible.

He was out here. Somewhere. Waiting for her. Kate could feel it.

She checked the map again, then looked at the collage—the cutout black man against the Hudson River scene.

The next group of buildings were totally boarded up.

Kate and Brown made it to up to Greenwich Village without much else to distract them, neither one of them speaking, the tension in the car thick.

In front of Westbeth, the artists' residence building, the Pinto was forced to a full stop. Fire trucks completely blocked the highway, sirens blared, beacons painted red-orange shafts of light onto the building. About a hundred car horns were competing with the fire sirens, blasting out a symphony of frustration. Brown tried to back up, but was completely wedged in. For a minute, he joined the horn blowers, but it was no use. Kate was out of the car fast.

"Probably a false alarm, but we gotta keep checking," said a beefy fireman. "Give us ten minutes."

"We don't have *one* minute. We're NYPD," said Kate. "And it's an emergency."

Minutes later, the fireman was directing traffic, getting one driver to pull this way, another that, until the Pinto was free, Brown backing up the wrong way on a one-way street, then screeching around a corner, until they found their way back onto the highway.

"According to the map, there should be a couple of old warehouses coming up," said Kate.

"There they are, just ahead," said Brown.

"Is that light inside one of the buildings?" said Kate.

Brown steered the Pinto onto the dirt shoulder, the two of them out of the car fast.

The building was big, dilapidated. Kate hesitated a minute, heard something—*voices*?—from inside. Glock in hand, she dropped back, then leveled a solid kick against the old wooden door. It splintered, fell away like a bunch of Pick Up sticks.

Six or seven homeless men were huddled together around a small fire, toasting hot dogs on sticks. They looked up, unimpressed. There was garbage everywhere. The smell— awful. Kate and Brown backed up. Smallish black creatures—mice, rats—scurried for shelter.

"Great art. It's always a shock. At first. Until you get used to it."

Willie was inching backward. Should he make a dash for it? He wasn't sure. His mind was all over the place. *How can this be? Schuyler Mills?* The man who had nurtured his work?

But the curator had read Willie's thoughts, took a quick step forward, his fingers tightening around Willie's arm, a small revolver now pointed at Willie's temple. "Come," he urged gently. "I need to show you something."

Willie's heart was beating about as fast as his mind was racing. *No way. Sky the death artist?* He just couldn't believe it. Should he attack? Should he risk getting shot?

"In here." Schuyler led Willie through another doorway into a connecting room.

The room was smaller, long and narrow, like a bowling alley. The only light, streaks of neon from advertising signs across the Hudson, peeked through holes in the walls. Willie couldn't see much, but felt water bubbling up through the rotting floor, soaking his shoes.

"Wait." Mills relaxed his grip on Willie's arm to reach for a spotlight clipped to a pillar.

Willie thought, *This is it*—his time to break away; but then the barrel of the cold metal revolver grazed his ear.

"Steady," said Mills. He squeezed a switch. A beam of light shot out, illuminating the scene in high contrast. "Don't judge it too harshly. Please. It's only a work in progress."

It took Willie a moment to figure it out. He could see it was a figure leaning against a wall, or what was left of it, and—*Jesus Christ!*—was that a head, in a dish, on the floor?

"Artemisia Gentileschi," said Mills. "The one truly great woman painter of the Italian Renaissance. I was certain Ms. Kent would be happy to star in it."

Willie saw it now. Too clearly. The head. Charlie's head. On the plate. Floating in an inch of congealed blood, like aspic. Her headless body was propped against the wall. It was just like the vision he'd had. He felt he would be sick. But then his mind produced another flash—himself in waist-high water—and with it, the full realization that he was surely about to die.

"It's Judith beheading the Assyrian general. But what makes it truly great is that Ms. Kent plays *both* parts—Judith and the general. It's a very conceptual piece. Maybe not as clear as your friend Kate would like, but . . ." He seemed to go off for a moment, and Willie sensed it. He pivoted, fast, whacked Mills in the throat, hard. The gun flew, skidded across the floor. Willie made a dive for it. But just as his fingers were reaching for the handle, he felt the needle prick his thigh. Toxins coursed through muscle, speeding into his bloodstream, the burning almost intolerable. Willie groaned. By the time he had the revolver in his hand, he could no longer grasp it.

Shit. He had been saving that hypodermic for Kate. He rubbed at his tender throat. "You didn't have to go and hit me. That hurt, you know."

Willie could barely feel his legs or arms. He tried dragging himself to safety—*but where*? His body scraped against the concrete floor; a rusty nail slashed his hand, then through his pant leg. Blood gushed from his palm, up through his pants. But Willie felt nothing.

"Relax. It won't kill you. Temporary paralysis, that's all." Mills lowered himself so that their eyes were only inches apart. "I'd never intentionally harm you. You know that, don't you?" He stroked Willie's forehead. "You're like a son to me."

Willie tried to speak, but could not.

"All of your muscles will be paralyzed, throat included." He got Willie around the ankles, dragged him to a corner of the room. Willie's head bumped across the hard, damp floor. But the pain was nothing compared with the fear.

"I didn't have a lot of time to make this. You must forgive me."

Willie stared at him, helpless, his arms a deadweight, legs totally numb.

Drawn across the wall was a crude sketch—a river scene.

"Hudson River school. Frederic Church," said Mills. "But it's just an impression." He pushed Willie against it, arranged his body just so. "Do you think you can stand?" he asked. "No, of course not." He had one of those thick oil sticks that artists use in his fist. He clutched Willie's jaw. "Hold still," he said. "I've got to make you look like the Basquiat *Self-portrait*." He outlined Willie's eyes with the white oil stick, then made crisscrossing marks around Willie's mouth.

He stood back.

"Not bad. But I've really got to get you to stand up." He sidled back, ferreted around on his worktable. "I know I've got a hammer and nails here somewhere."

Kate was having that feeling, the one she'd had when she was on her way to save Ruby Pringle: that it was too late. *Please, God, no.* She referred to the riverfront map. "This isn't helping, Floyd. We're going to be too late!"

"Hang on, McKinnon."

Kate looked back at the map. There was sweat beading up on her forehead.

Brown lifted the receiver, called in to the station. "Any of the cars find anything?"

"No. Nothing yet." Mead's voice crackled over the radio. "You?"

"Still looking." Brown clicked off, swerved the Pinto around a slow-moving car. The map and collage slid onto the floor.

Kate lifted the map, then the death artist's collage, her fingers sliding over the surface. "What's this?" She pulled the collage closer, rubbed her finger lightly over the image again. "There's something painted on this that I missed before."

"What?"

"I don't know. I can't make it out." She held the collage beside the dashboard's light, drew her fingers over it again, felt something she could not feel when she'd had the plastic gloves on her fingers. Now she saw it, too—three tiny water towers hand-painted over Frederic Church's little cabin beside the Hudson. She hadn't noticed it before, the larger, more obvious clues had taken up her attention.

"Water towers," she said. "We're looking for three large water towers."

"Jesus."

"What?"

"I think we just passed them."

Brown waited for a break in the traffic, swerved the Pinto into a U-turn, bumped over the divider. They were heading south again.

"It's an old docking station," said Kate, referring to the map. Her mouth had gone dry; adrenaline was coursing through her veins.

"There it is." The dark monolith slid into view, taking the moon with it. "Three water towers." Kate drew a breath.

Brown bumped the Pinto up onto the gravel path.

They were out of the car fast, doors left open—no way they'd announce their arrival by slamming one.

"I think there are lights on inside," said Kate, barely whispering.

Brown's tone was equally hushed. "We gotta call for backup."

"Not yet. Not until we're absolutely sure. I don't want to pull those patrol cars off the search if we're wrong." She had her Glock in hand.

The big wooden door was half-open. Kate peered into the dark. She heard something—a scraping sound? She couldn't be sure with the hum of highway traffic just behind her. She and Brown took a few steps in, both dropped to a crouch, guns straight out in front of them. They hovered there a minute, waiting for their eyes to adjust to the dim light. Slowly now, practically creeping, they edged forward. Kate's nerve endings were tingling.

A rat zipped across her path. She stifled a gasp. A fluttering above. She spun the Glock overhead. Pigeons. She let out a small breath.

Then those pictures on the wall zoomed into focus before Kate's eyes. *Oh my God. This is the place.* She elbowed Brown, nodded at the images.

They both stood stock-still, almost not breathing, scanning the room for any sign of life. Kate saw nothing, but could sense it—movement, a vibration of life, somewhere close by.

"I'm calling for backup," Brown whispered, pulling his radio from his pocket.

Schuyler Mills had the nail poised above Willie's wrist, the hammer about to strike a blow—but his hands were twitching. "I just can't do it," he said. "Not to you. My son." Then he thought of Abraham. *"What?"* He spun away from Willie as though acknowledging someone in the room. Willie's eyes, the only part of him able to move, searched the room. But there was no one, nothing there. He stared at Charlie Kent's head, the small bullet hole in her temple almost black, crusted over with dried blood.

Mills's eyes were half-closed.

"I can't. Don't you see? I love him."

Do it.

"What?" he said. "No."

Were those tears in the curator's eyes? Willie could not be sure, but he thought so.

"Leave me alone!" Mills swung the hammer wildly at some unseen phantom. That seemed to do it. A moment later, he was calm. "Sorry. Where was I?" He focused on Willie. "Oh. Right. I want to show you something." He plucked the small altarpiece from the floor. "Exquisite, isn't it?"

Willie stared at the tiny Madonna and Child.

"Here. Take a closer look. As they say, it's all in the details." But then he looked away, toward the outer room, cocked his head, listening. "Oh." He smiled. "I believe our guests are here." He moved swiftly now, grabbed a large dart gun off a small table where he'd laid out another two hypodermics. He held a finger to his lips, nodded at Willie. "Shhh . . ." Then he handed him Pruitt's small altarpiece. It crashed to the floor with a loud thunk. "Oh, right," he said. "You can't hold anything, can you?"

Kate and Brown pivoted toward the sound, saw the other doorway, the thin shaft of light.

They were both moving in slow motion. To Kate, it felt like an eternity before she crossed the room.

Brown was a couple of feet in front of her. He had both hands on his gun. He spun through the doorway.

There was the slightest sound—a sort of zipping whoosh, then a soft thump.

Floyd Brown reeled back, dropped his gun, clutched his shoulder. But there was no blood. He's okay, thought Kate. But then he stumbled backward, fell to the floor, right at her feet, eyes open, mouth, too, but no words, only a grunt.

Kate tightened her grasp on the Glock, laid her other hand on Brown's chest. Yes, his heart was beating. He was alive. *Thank God.*

She aimed her gun straight out in front of her, dared a peek through the open doorway and saw Willie slumped against a wall.

Willie's eyes shifted and blinked, desperate to telegraph a warning to Kate. But she already knew the death artist was there, waiting for her. She could practically taste him. She inched forward, the Glock ready, but sensed the shadow too late. The arm came down, hard, on her wrist. The Glock vaulted from her hand, skittered across the wet floor.

And he had it.

"Finally," he said, aiming the weapon directly at Kate's chest. "I have been waiting for you—for so long."

Schuyler Mills came into focus. Kate gasped.

"I knew you wouldn't come alone. But don't worry, your friend will live." He nodded at Floyd Brown's immobile body. "For a while. He's paralyzed, that's all. But later, well, I'm afraid his condition will worsen."

Kate took in the scene: Charlie Kent's decapitated body and the young woman's head, on a plate.

"Beautiful, isn't it?" said Mills. "Oh. I have an idea. One more game." He smiled. "Quick now, Kate. Artist and painting." He pointed the Glock away from her, at Willie's head.

"You've got three guesses. Then İ kill him. That's fair, isn't it? I mean, you are, after all, the great art historian." He smiled again. "I know, I know. According to my own drawing, I'm supposed to kill the boy with a knife. But let's not quibble. We're all professionals here." He cocked the trigger. "Okay. Come on. Start guessing."

Kate's mind had gone absolutely blank. All she could think of was the man standing in front of her, how she had known him—and never known him—for all those years. Schuyler Mills, senior curator at the Contemporary Museum. *My God. The man's had dinner in my house!*

"Come on," he said.

"Okay. Okay. Give me a minute."

"That's reasonable." He looked at his watch. "One minute. *Go*."

Kate's mind started clicking. "It's a Renaissance painting, right?"

"Very good. But not what I asked for. I want the artist's *name* and the painting *title*." He regarded his watch again. "Forty seconds."

"Caravaggio."

"Wrong. Thirty-three seconds."

Oh, God. Think. Think. "Titian."

"Wrong again. Twenty-eight seconds."

Oh my God. "Wait. Please."

"One hint. But I don't know why I should help you. It's a woman painter."

"Artemisia Gentileschi!"

"Damn, you're good. Okay now. Title?"

"David Slaying Goliath."

"Oh, come, now, Ms. Kent can't be playing those *boys*."

"Right. Right." Kate's blood was pumping in her ears. *"Judith Beheading the Assyrian!"*

"Bingo!" He smiled broadly. "I knew you were worth the trouble." He swung the Glock back toward her, training it on her heart. "You really do play the game well, Kate."

"Thank you," she said, trying to keep her voice steady.

"So do you, Sky." She was still half in shock. Schuyler Mills, all these years.

"It's a shame it has to end."

"Couldn't we just . . . go on playing?"

"Don't patronize me, Kate. I'm not a stupid man."

Kate took another step closer.

"Stay there," he said, the Glock trained on her heart again. "Now, what were we talking about?"

"Our game."

"Right. You missed one."

"I did. Really? What was that?"

"A long time ago. The teenager. A hitchhiker. Back in Queens."

"No, I didn't," said Kate, inching toward him in slow motion. "It was an early work. I didn't think you'd want me to make much of it, that's all. An angel, right? A sort of putto figure."

A huge smile broke across his face. "I can't believe it. You *knew*?"

"Well, to be perfectly honest . . ." She took another small step closer. "I only figured it out recently."

He nodded. "It showed promise, don't you think?"

"Oh, yes. Absolutely."

His face turned steely. "So why'd you fuck with it? Pull her pants up like that?" He swiveled the gun back toward Willie's head. Willie blinked.

"I, well, at the time, I—I didn't know it was *your* work. As I said, I only recently . . ." Kate was trying to remain calm, to think, but it was almost impossible.

"It's uncanny, isn't it? I mean, the way our lives have paralleled, Kate. There you were, the young cop, so tough, so beautiful, at the beginning of the birth. My birth. As an artist. Oh, sure, there were others, but they hardly mattered. And then, years pass—and there you are again. Your art book, and the TV series. And then you showed up at the museum. I could not believe it. *My* museum. On the board, no less. I took it as an omen."

Kate was watching him closely, as his eyes glazed slightly, his concentration not what it should be. *Soon. Soon.*

"And then, that night, as I watched her, your protégée, it came to me, a way to finally get your attention, for us to be together. I wasn't sure; I mean, it was still just an idea, something inchoate, not quite a *concept*." His lids fluttered.

Should she chance it? *Not yet. But soon.*

"But then, when I was in her apartment, I thought better of it. You see, it had been years. I thought I was over it. And then . . . she laughed at me." He frowned, then checked his watch. "The others will be coming soon, won't they?"

"Who?"

"Oh, please, Kate. You figured it out and told them. They'll be here. I know we haven't got much time left."

Behind him, Kate saw the small revolver on the floor, only inches from Willie's hand.

"I guess we were destined to be together, Kate. Me, the artist. You, the woman who would canonize my work."

"But how will I do that if I'm dead?"

"I have a plan." He looked down at Bill Pruitt's altarpiece. "You and me, Kate, Madonna and Child. What do you think?"

"Really? Who's playing who?"

His shrill laugh echoed into the space. The pigeons batted their wings overhead. "Very funny. I can always depend on you for irony, Kate." He aimed the Glock. "But I'm afraid I will have to kill you."

"Wait a minute." *Keep him talking.* "I don't quite get it. The Madonna and Child? You and me? Explain it to me. Be clear. I want to picture it perfectly."

"It's very simple. First, I kill you. Then, I arrange your body, just like the Madonna in the painting. Then I strip off my clothes, and curl in your arms. I'll be taking pills." He sighed, seemed to smile at the thought. "By the time they find us, I'll be dead, too."

"What about Willie?" Kate asked, her mind racing. "He's not part of this. Why not let him go? He can tell the world how you designed it, how beautifully it was conceived. Otherwise, they might not get it."

"Oh, Kate. They'll get it—with the actual altarpiece right beside us. Anyway, Willie has to star in his own piece, the Basquiat." He rotated the Glock toward Willie.

"Wait!" Kate had to stop him. "I want to ask you something."

"Yes?"

"Uh . . ." Kate searched her mind for something, anything, to stall. "Tell me about your work. Why you chose Bill Pruitt, for example?"

He sighed again. "Okay. But then we really must get down to work, okay?"

Kate nodded, watching him, waiting.

"Well, first of all, it was a matter of convenience. Pruitt wasn't going to choose me as director of the museum. I couldn't stand for that. Believe me, I did not enjoy working with him, touching his flaccid, fleshy body. But I made him a lot better in death than he ever was in life."

"That's true." Kate's eyes flickered at Willie, then at the revolver on the floor beside his hand. Willie blinked. His fingertips twitched slightly.

"I did the same for that boring painter, Ethan Stein."

Kate took a step. She was close enough to grab the gun.

"Stop!" He rammed the Glock into her gut.

Kate stared into his eyes. Were those tears?

"How odd life is, don't you think? I mean, I hadn't meant to start up again. Really, I had it under control. But I had to prove it to him."

"To *who*?"

"Him!" His eyes darted left, then right.

Kate was about to grab the gun, but he pushed it, hard, against her ribs.

"You can see that, can't you?"

She nodded, but had no idea what he was talking about. What she saw was madness, but she saw the pain, too, even identified with it. How strange. When all she'd thought about, dreamed of, was killing him—this man who had stolen lives from her, torn her heart beyond repair. "Let me help you," she said. "I can deliver your message, your work, to the world."

Mills smiled at her tenderly. "I wanted to stop, really I did."

Then the voices: *No, you didn't! You're a liar!*

"I'm not!" He jammed his free hand against his temple. His eyelids fluttered.

Willie managed to stretch out his fingers, to touch the revolver's barrel, but he only knocked it farther away.

Mills spun toward Willie.

This was it, her opportunity. Kate lunged, knocked the Glock from Schuyler's hands.

But he was fast, going for it, Kate right behind him, but off-balance. She tripped, landed on her back, looking up at him, and the Glock's barrel pointed directly at her forehead.

He cocked the trigger.

Kate kicked out at him.

He stumbled back.

She faked to the left just as he fired and missed. He was off-balance, but the Glock was still in his hands, shaking.

Kate rolled to her right, reached out, grabbed hold of his leg.

The Glock exploded again. This time, bullets sprayed the ceiling.

The pigeons scattered, beat their wings wildly.

It took all of three seconds for Kate to tear the .38 from her ankle and empty all six chambers.

Schuyler Mills clutched his chest. Beneath his fingers, his white shirt was a clean canvas for the dark red fanning out like a piece of cheap spin art. He looked surprised, then down at all the blood, at the assortment of holes in his shirt, then up at the black ceiling where the pigeons swooped and dived frantically. For a moment, he imagined himself with them, flying above all the pain. Then he slumped forward and crashed to the floor.

The gun was still smoking in Kate's hand.

She quick-turned to Brown. "You okay?"

He could just barely move his head, managed to croak, "Fine."

Kate tested for a pulse in the curator's wrist. "He's gone," she said, then turned back to Brown.

There were sirens in the distance.

"Here." Kate thrust the .38 into Brown's limp hands. "Take it before the cavalry gets here."

Brown's words came out a hoarse, cracked whisper. "They . . . won't believe . . . it. I'm . . . paralyzed."

"Sure they will," said Kate, wrapping his fingers around the barrel. "He shot that tranquilizer into you just as you fired at him, right?"

Brown's eyes searched Kate's. "But . . . why?"

"Because I'm just a civilian, remember, Floyd? But *you* might as well go down as the cop who killed the death artist."

Patrol cars crowded the street.

Flashing lights streaked amber across the old docking house.

Sirens filled the night air with electricity.

"It was Brown who shot him," Kate said to Mead and Tapell.

Brown was just able to wiggle his fingers. Kate watched a couple of medics hooking him up to an IV.

Willie was being loaded into the back of an ambulance. Kate touched his cheek lightly, stroked his forehead, fought back tears. "Take it easy, okay?"

A medic tore open Willie's pant leg, swabbed yellow disinfectant onto his slashed thigh, then started wrapping it tightly with gauze. A second medic was wrapping Willie's cut hand.

"You'll be fine," Kate whispered.

"Sure I will," Willie croaked. "It's only my . . . left hand. I paint . . . with my right."

45

News of the death artist's demise filled every newspaper for days; the tabloids for weeks. Psychological profiles of Schuyler Mills were cover stories on both *Time* and *Newsweek*; Mitch Freeman, FBI shrink, was generously quoted. Schuyler's co-workers, Amy Schwartz and Raphael Perez, were instant media stars. It was even rumored that the handsome Latino curator was to play himself in the USA movie—*The Death Artist*—in preproduction only days after the man's final curtain. Mead, too, had plenty to say, was often seen pontificating and sucking his teeth, on TV tabloid shows like *Geraldo*. Only Floyd Brown, considered the hero of the day (the mayor wanted to give him a medal, which he declined), avoided the spotlight.

The death artist had indeed achieved fame.

ArtNews ran a six-page story deconstructing the man's murders, matching crime scene photos with the art upon which they were based. No one at the police department seemed to know how the magazine had gotten their hands on the photographs. Ethan Stein's family was suing *ArtNews* and the NYPD. They were also suing the Ward Wasserman Gallery, where Stein's memorial exhibition had completely sold out, without the family's receiving a single penny.

The estate of Amanda Lowe was demanding both printed

and financial credit for the use of her death photos or mention of her name under the new licensing franchise they had established. It was rumored that they were already owed approximately half a million dollars, but were having trouble collecting.

Willie's cuts and bruises were mending. He was back in the studio, working. A necessity. Virtually every painting he had made had been spoken for or sold. Collectors were jockeying for positions on the waiting list for future pieces. He joked to Kate that if he had died, the demand would have been even higher. Kate did not laugh. She thanked God every day that she was able to save him.

For Kate, there remained a nagging lack of completion, coupled with melancholy. She was filling her time with charitable works—putting new seventh-grade classes together with the right people of means to adopt them through Let There Be a Future, establishing a scholarship in Maureen Slattery's name at the foundation, even donating a hefty sum to the NYPD, also in the young policewoman's name.

And she and Richard were drawing closer, managing to get past the anger, suspicions, and resentment built up over the past couple of weeks, and were working hard—if a bit too self-consciously—at considering each other's needs and feelings. Kate bought Richard a new pair of cuff links engraved with one word: SORRY. Richard had taken to leaving little gifts—a thin gold bracelet, a hand-painted scarf—on her pillow each morning before taking off for work, always with the same note: *I love you.*

But questions about Elena continued to nag her. Why had the girl taken up with the likes of Damien Trip? Kate still couldn't figure it out—and now there was no way she would ever know. Perhaps Richard was right, that you never really, fully knew anyone. But that thought only filled her with grief. The bigger question—why Elena had made those movies, why did she need money?—was something Kate needed to find out.

*   *   *

Did she really want to see Mrs. Solana? Kate was fairly certain the woman did not want to see her. But she was there now, knocking on the tenement door.

At first, when he saw Kate, Mendoza's features hardened, but only for a second. He didn't appear to have the strength to stay angry.

"May I come in?" Kate asked.

Mendoza hesitated, then opened the door. He looked thin, weary, so much older than Kate remembered. "I've come to see Mrs. Solana."

Mendoza nodded, as if they had been expecting her.

Kate followed him down the long narrow corridor of the railroad flat. It smelled of bodily functions and disinfectant. At the end of the hall, Mendoza pushed open the door to the bedroom.

The woman in the bed was Margarita Solana, but she was hardly recognizable. The once beautiful woman was ravaged, her lustrous black hair now a filigreed spiderweb spreading across the pillow. Her cheeks were sunken, with deep grooves at the corners of her mouth. Dark eyes, so much like Elena's, were hollow.

"The only thing to do for her now is the drugs," said Mendoza. "So many drugs."

Kate's eyes played over the bedside table—enough vials of pills to stock a small pharmacy.

"She is a proud woman," said Mendoza. "She did not want anyone to know." He rubbed at a purplish swelling on the back of his hand, closed his eyes a moment, trembled as if a chill had overtaken him. But the room was stifling.

"Luis!" Margarita Solana called out.

Mendoza went to her, stroked her forehead. "Shhh . . . *querida,* shhh . . ." He kissed her trembling lips, whispered, "There is someone here to see you, *querida.*"

Kate took a step forward.

Mrs. Solana's eyes focused on her. She managed to raise a bony hand.

Kate grasped it gently. "I'm sorry," she said.

The woman shook her head slowly, played with a silver crucifix hanging from a thick chain around her neck. "I have asked Jesus many times why all these things have happened," she said. "But he does not give me an answer."

"I've asked the same question," said Kate.

"Elena was a good girl." Mrs. Solana gazed up at Kate. "A good girl."

"Yes," said Kate softly. "She was."

Margarita Solana nodded. "My daughter loved you very much, and . . . I am a jealous woman." She let go of the crucifix, laid her other hand over Kate's. "But Jesus has forced me to look into my heart. I want to forgive, and I ask that you will forgive me, too."

Kate felt tears on her cheeks. "Of course." She saw it all too clearly now. Elena's mother and Mendoza, both former drug addicts, now terminally ill; Elena buying them the drugs they so desperately needed.

"We are paying for all those years," Margarita said, tears staining her cheeks. She looked up at Kate, a wry smile twisting her mouth. "But it is okay now. Only a matter of time. I am ready." She looked away from Kate, at Mendoza, across the dimly lit room, his thin frame leaning against the door.

"No," said Kate. "There are all sorts of new drugs. Some of them very effective. They can—"

"I have no money for that," the woman said, turning away again. "Not anymore. And the shame . . ."

"There is no shame in sickness," said Kate. "Please. Let me help you."

The woman shook her head no.

"Please," said Kate. "You must let me."

ONE WEEK LATER

The recording studio was state of the art, six people flitting around the large room, another two inside a smaller soundproof chamber.

The team Kate had hired to complete the work on Elena's unfinished CD.

One guy was manning a huge console as if he were an air traffic controller, adjusting levels and levers, pushing buttons, his brow knit, lips compressed. He signaled another guy; this one at a computer, hunched over, glasses so thick his eyes looked like golf balls. "Hey, Danny, loop this into the 103 sequence."

"Gotcha," said Danny.

A youngish woman yelled over, "This is the last one for the dat tape."

The guy at the console said, "Great," pulled off his headset, nodded at Kate. "We're putting several tracks together right now—all of it according to Elena's notes, which, thank God, are really detailed. Danny, over there, he's working on this amazing new computer program that allows you to insert any bit of music anywhere, anytime. It's called Protools. Really cool."

"What's a dat tape?" asked Kate.

"The master recording. We'll pull the CDs and tapes off it

when it's finished." He replaced his earphones, checked his big board, adjusted a lever, then pulled the earphones off again. "Wanna listen?"

Kate got the speakers to her ears. Elena's crystalline voice was moving up and down the scales, sliding, swooping, incredibly alive. Behind it, over it, they'd overlaid Elena speaking, reciting words, almost telling a story, but totally abstract—the two forms melding into the odd kind of visual music Elena had become known for in the performance world. All that was missing was the young woman herself. Kate closed her eyes, pictured Elena on a pure-white stage.

"That's the last piece in the CD," the technician said. "How's it sound to you?"

Kate was listening to Elena, but could read the guy's lips. "Beautiful," she said. "Really beautiful."

He smiled, gave the other techies a high sign.

Elena's words and music were playing somewhere far inside Kate's head. "Does it have a name?" she asked.

The technician motioned to the guy at the computer. "Danny, this last piece, does it have a name?"

Kate lifted one of the earphones away from her head, waited, still listening to Elena's amazing music being piped into her other ear.

Danny looked down at a sheet of Elena's notes. "Yes," he said. "It's called 'Kate's Song.'"

ACKNOWLEDGMENTS

This first novel was aided and abetted by the following people:

My daughter, Doria, a reader, a writer, and a beautiful listener.

My sister, Roberta, who was my first editor.

My mother, Edith, who taught me, among other things, the art of embellishing a story.

My sister-in-law, Kathy Rolland, for her generosity of spirit.

Jane O'Keefe for inspiration and true-blue friendship.

Jan Heller Levi, who taught me too many things about writing to list.

Janice Deaner for helping to make the book a reality.

Thanks to the following friends who not only helped but listened to me whine, and have for years: Susan Crile, Ward Mintz and Floyd Lattin, Marcia Tucker, Graham Leader, Jane Kent and David Storey, Judd Tully, Lynn Freed, Elaina Richardson, Jon Giswold, Jane and Jack Rivkin, Caren and Dave Cross, Richard Shebairo, Jim Kempner, Valerie McKenzie, Elizabeth Frank, and Reiner Leist and the rest of my tenth-floor studio buddies, David, Lisa, Sally, and Regina . . .

More thanks to:

Suzanne Gluck, a great agent.

Trish Grader for her excellent and compassionate editing, and Sarah Durand, as well.

Richard Abate for his tough guidance.

To the Corporation of Yaddo, which has nurtured my painting, given birth to my writing, and saved my sanity (more than once).

And to my wife, Joy, for everything else.